HIS WAYS

Love, service, and redemption are both timeless
and relevant in this book

*At its core and best, this is truely a love story.
The character of Billy is both sympathectic and complex
which makes the audience want to root for him.*

T R E S S A   O L D E N

Library of Congress Control Number: 2013902125
ISBN: 979-8-89465-024-1 (sc)
ISBN: 979-8-89465-025-8 (e)

Printed in the United States of America.

Integrity Publishing
39343 Harbor Hills Blvd Lady Lake,
FL 32159

www.integrity-publishing.com

Also by Tressa Olden

Kindergarten Friend
Inquiry Minds
Kachifo (Good-Bye)

To the men and women who have served and are still serving in
all branches of the United States military.

*In whom we had also obtained an inheritance, being predestinated
according to the purpose of him who worketh all things after
the counsel of his own will.*

—Ephesians 11:1

I am so grateful to the hundreds of thousands of men and
women who, while in uniform, sacrificed to serve our country
and those who are still putting their lives on the line making a
difference. I thank God for shaping my life and getting me to the
truths. And to you, the reader, thank you for letting me share.

PREFACE

WHY? DOES GOD ALLOW SUCH things to happen to us? Does He already know what we are going to go through? Can we help ourselves? All these questions are asked by the characters of *His Ways*. Each one finds themselves in situations when, living life from day to day, is so mind-boggling to figure out sometimes. We as humans fall short of pleasing God when faced with temptations of the heart. We say we love Him and are willing to go all the way, but life throws us a curve and we began to ponder our next move. We assume, like in baseball, that after three times, we are out and we may give up altogether. If we reason too long, we find ourselves compromising the matter. We know what's right and right to do, but the other thing seems better and we yield to it. Though often we are left confused, finding the grass is not always greener on the other side!

The Bible clearly states in Isaiah 55:8-11 "that His thoughts are not your thoughts neither your ways my ways, saith the Lord. For as the heavens are higher than the earth, so are my ways higher than your ways, and my thoughts than your thoughts. For as the rain cometh down, and the snow from heaven, and returneth not thither, but watereth the earth, and maketh it bring forth bud, that it make give seed to the sower, and bread to the eater: So shall my word be that goeth forth out of my mouth: it shall not return unto me void, but it shall accomplish that which I please, and it shall prosper wherein the thing I sent."

Did Erene find healing when he was able to forgive? Was Nora's life displaced when she chose not to forgive? Our walk with God is personal to each of us. What it takes for you to get through a matter may be different than it takes me. So, we must be very careful when handing out advice when it involves another individual or matters of the heart. Erene sought out God for everything good, while Nora chose wine. Not covering his sin, making him right, but he knew he needed something higher to pull him up from the pit he had fallen into.

William had been called by God, and he struggled with being good enough, waiting to get right, and being haunted by past sins. God uses anyone He chooses, the question is, are you willing to go? God uses everyday folk, intellectual folk, young, old, and most of all, willing folk to advance His kingdom. He used Joseph, a slave, to interpret dreams, who also spent time in prison before being placed as the right-hand man to the pharaoh of Egypt, and saved Egypt and his people from a famine. Most of us know about Moses and his inability to articulate words, and God chose him to lead the people to the Promised Land. Jephthah was only known as the son of a prostitute, and God used him to deliver Israel from the Ammorites. David was just a young boy when he brought down the mighty Goliath and later became king and called a man after God's own heart. The list is endless of everyday people who God chooses to further the Gospel. He used a peasant girl named Mary, she wasn't a big celebrity, not a great actress, famous politician, or well-known athlete, but her call was the greatest of all—she was the mother of Jesus. So, what I'm saying is never count yourself out, for greater is He that is in you than he that is in the world, and I can do all things through Christ Jesus who strengthens me. Obediently I—a common woman, wife, mother, grandmother, and yes, great-grandmother—wrote this book.

Tressa Olden

CHAPTER 1

NADA PARKER WAS PACKING HER husband's luggage for a men's retreat with his fellow brothers from the seminary. She smiled as she tossed in a love note with kisses and a handful of shiny red paper hearts. Putting in his study Bible as he had asked her to do, she closed the top and clicked the locks shut. As she turned around, she saw Millicent coming in with the baby.

"Hi, sweetheart," she said, reaching for her with opened hands. "She ate very well today, she was hungry, I guess."

"Good, thank you, she is growing so fast soon I won't have a baby," Nada said, smiling at her sweet little girl.

Peyton Holly Parker was born in December, so Holly was chosen for her middle name by her parents. Nada and William were so happy their little girl was healthy and happy as could be.

"Thank you, Mil, I'll take her and give her a bath before her dad gets home."

"You're sure? I'd love to do it!"

"Yes, but thanks."

Millicent reached and kissed Peyton's cheek and headed out of the room, waving bye-bye.

"My, my, look at your face, did you enjoy your breakfast?" she asked, smiling at her adorable two-year-old daughter. Nada enjoyed her child and was a perfect mother in every way. She read to her and talked to her as she splashed in her small tub sitting in the larger tub in the nursery.

All dressed in a pink outfit with a tiny little flowered pattern, she was ready for the first part of her day. Peyton and Nada headed out on the grounds for a sightseeing walk.

"Hello."

"Oh, look, Peyton, it's Daddy!" Nada said, seeing Billy coming up the walkway. "You said you were leaving early, I'm glad I got things all packed for you. Millicent fed Peyton today and she ate well, I was told," Nada added.

"She's really growing, isn't she?" Billy responded, picking her up and kissing her. Peyton squirmed, wanting to get down. She was exploring the grounds with her newfound independence of walking and did not want to be held. Her dad put her back down and off she went along the designed path looking and touching most things passed.

"She takes after you," Nada said smiling.

"That she does, that she does."

The Parkers spent an hour together ending with an early brunch before Billy had to leave on his retreat.

"Hello, Nada."

"Hello, Mother Parker, how are you?"

"Oh, I'm fine, how's my granddaughter?"

"Busy playing in the nursery right now, she loves the new toys you bought her."

"Oh, good, I know David says I buy too much for her, but of course, I don't agree," she said, laughing across the telephone line.

"Mother, hold on, I'm going to Skype so you can see how much she has grown in two months."

"Peyton, Peyton, look it's Grandma," Nada said, getting her attention to the screen on the laptop computer.

"Hi, Peyton," Tetra said, smiling, viewing the toddler walking around the nursery with her toys. Peyton held up a soft pink fluffy stuffed animal and babbled something. "Oh, she's talking. I must see her again soon, she's growing so fast."

"Yes, Mother Parker, Billy has me videoing every day while he's away."

"Well, do keep a good eye on her for him, children tend to grow so fast and that's precious time you can't get back," she commented.

"I know, Mother Parker. Is Dad working today?"

"He was here for breakfast but went out with Priscilla for lunch he said."

"They seem to see a lot of each other," Nada voiced.

"They do?" Tetra asked.

"Well, I mean every time I've asked him where he is or was, her name's come up."

"Is that a problem, they seem to complement one another."

"No, not really, but I do worry about him sometimes," Nada replied.

"That's your father and I understand, but I think he can take care of himself. Oh, look, here he comes now. Hello, Alfredo, your daughter's on the line. No, I was just watching our granddaughter, she's grown so much." She moved over, allowing Alfredo to see the computer screen she had been viewing.

"Kisses, Nada," Tetra shared, leaving the room.

"Hello, sweetheart, how are my two favorite girls doing while Billy's gone?"

"Oh, Daddy, we're fine. How are you and Priscilla?" she bravely asked.

"Now I see, you were worrying about me again."

"Well, maybe a little."

"Priscilla and I are doing just fine and that's all I'm going to say." He smiled.

"You look good, Daddy, are you happy?" she asked.

"Nada Lillian, I am blessed and I have my girls, what more could a man want? Sweetheart, I need to start dinner, I love you," Alfredo shared and stood watching as Nada helped Peyton throw him a kiss.

"Bye, Daddy."

"Bye, sweetheart." And the computer's screen returned to a Windows logo.

The guys had arrived at the retreat camp in Bangor, Maine. They were very excited about the week they were spending there and looked for a blessed time in the Lord.

"Bill, did you get settled into your cabin?" Don asked, seeing Billy heading to the dinner hall to eat.

"I did, there are four guys in our cabin and there is still plenty of room if you are looking for a space."

"No, I'm good," he explained, "I got here early."

"Oh, okay, so you headed up to eat?"

"That would be a yes," he said, joining him on the side walking along.

Maine Community had partnered with Calvary Chapel for this men's event retreat. Billy had met a lot of friends there because he attended the Bible college there. Despite his trying to deny it, he felt God had called him to the ministry and he was in his first full year there. He and Dan had now joined their fellow brothers for dinner.

"Hello, Rev.," they teased him as he looked around for an empty table to sit.

Nada had just walked into her daughter Peyton's dance class. She was picking up her daughter as well as Annie's daughter who was older but went there also but in a different class. She'd soon turn five. Annie was the legal secretary at her husband's law firm, and the Parkers were their daughter Riley's godparents.

The toddlers were still moving around to the beat of the music being played. Peyton, seeing Nada come in, ran over to her. "Mommy," she called, holding up her hands to be picked up. Nada smiled and lifted her daughter, kissing her cheek, and put her back down. Peyton ran back to play with her fellow classmates on the drums, bells, and small instruments the instructor had for the class.

"Hello, Mrs. Parker," Belle, the dance instructor, said.

"Hello," Nada replied. "How did she do today?"

"Very well, I think she really likes this type of music. She gets along well with everyone," she added.

"Good. She needs to get out now that she's older, I think it's good for her," she said as they watched her dance around with one of her classmates to "Ring Around the Roses."

After gathering both girls and heading to the law office, Nada decided she'd go shopping for Riley's birthday gift. Riley was Annie and Keith's little girl. He was also a lawyer of her husband's law firm. Riley was two years older than Peyton and had been going to the dance class and loved it. Annie had shared this with Nada and she decided to enroll Peyton there also. Riley was in a different class due to age though it was the same building, instructors, and curriculum for both throughout the day. Peyton came later in the day and was only there for a few hours, and Nada would pick the girls up and take Riley to the law office to meet her parents at the end of the day.

As Nada was taking the girls from the car, an elderly lady walked by admiring the girls. "My, your daughters are beautiful, both of them. You're lucky, I've always wanted two daughters," she said, continuing to walk down the sidewalk. Nada smiled with a thank-you, holding the girls' hand, leading them into the building.

"Hi," Jenin said, seeing Nada approaching with the girls to the elevator.

"Hi." Both waved, wanting to get away from Nada's hands and run.

"Let me help you," she said, seeing the purse and small book making its way from under Nada's arm.

This was a common occurrence Monday through Friday. Jenin helped Nada get the girls in the elevator and waved them bye as the doors closed. Up, up, up they went. When the doors opened, both girls ran out and into the law office. Riley went into the hands of a client standing by the desk waiting to be seen, and Annie wasn't at her desk.

"Well, howdy," he said, smiling, "is your daddy here?" Riley just shook her head as she now pushed away from the strange gentleman leaning forward to talk with her as he held her in his arms.

"Oh, hello, Mr. Baker," Nada said, walking up soon behind Riley.

"Hi there, I was just talking to your daughter." He smiled, letting her down because she was squirming to do so. "Oh my, you have two beautiful little daughters," he added.

"No, this is our daughter Peyton, Riley is Annie our secretary's daughter," she explained.

"Oh, I'm sorry. I was here to see your husband, just in the area."

"Oh I see, well, Mr. Parker, my husband, is out of the office this week."

"No problem. I'll stop in again," he stated, leaving as Annie came from the back.

"Are you sure? Annie's coming out," Nada said, seeing the gentleman prepare to leave.

"No, just a friendly stop, I'll stop again." And both ladies waved him bye as he left.

"Hi, Mommy," Riley voiced loudly, running to Annie.

"I see you all made it up safe. Jenin said you all were on your way up."

"Yes, the girls had a very good day. Billy called and shared you're having Riley's birthday party in two weeks. Peyton and I are going shopping since we have some girl time," she explained, standing at Annie's desk.

"Sorry it was such a short notice. Keith's parents are coming in from Colorado and we had to fit in the date."

"No problem. I understand, no time to mail it," Nada replied.

"Now where did those girls go?" Annie said, looking around the office space. Both were sitting in Billy's office at a small table he had for Peyton with paper and coloring pencils. Riley had light brown hair despite Keith and Annie were both blond. Though her blue eyes were definitely like Annie's. Riley looked up smiling, showing Annie a picture she had drawn or scribbled on the paper. Peyton, with dark wavy hair and hazel eyes, looked up smiling as well. Both girls were beautiful, but they looked nothing alike, Nada thought, as she took Peyton leaving the office. "Bye, bye," both said, leaving and waving at Annie and Riley.

"Hi, honey, how are things going?"

"Very well, dear, how's my best girls doing?" Billy asked, taking a time out to call. "I'm really enjoying this time with the guys and being enriched in the word."

"I'm glad," Nada replied. "But I miss you and so does your daughter," she added.

"Ohhh, I miss you both, but I'm glad I came."

"Oh, was there a doubt about going, dear?" Nada asked.

"Well, a little hesitant, I'm still getting used to being called by God to do His work," Billy shared. "Oh! Just me and my life, could I really be the one He's calling for."

"Do you say that because you think you're not perfect enough?" Nada questioned.

"Not really, I guess I just think about me and the past things I've done."

"Honey, that just allows you to be a more effective witness," Nada expressed.

"Thank you, dear, for your prayers, encouragement, and support, always."

"Yes, dear," she smiled.

"Where's my Peyton?" Billy asked.

"Okay, go ahead. I have the phone to her ear."

"Hi, Peyton, how are you? DA-Da, and the words sound like babbling but I'm sure she knew what she was saying," he said, laughing.

"Okay, dear, I love you, kisses. Oh yes, I almost forgot. I saw Mr. Baker today at your office."

"Mr. Baker. Oh yes, I helped him with some legal business and he stops by every now and then to say hello. So, what did he want?"

"Didn't say, but said he'd stop in again. He gave us another daughter?"

"Another daughter?" Billy asked. "As if Peyton wasn't a handful already," Billy replied.

"You're right, but he was thinking Riley was our daughter also."

"Oh I see, that's not the first time," Billy confessed.

"What do you mean?" Nada asked.

"When I picked up the girls last week, the new assistant at the day care brought Riley to me. I had to ask for my daughter." He laughed. "Belle apologized. I'm sure it was an honest mistake."

"I'm sure," Nada said quietly.

"Okay, sweetheart, you have a great day. I'm headed to prayer this morning."

"Love you, honey."

"Love you, bye," disconnecting the phone.

Dillard Patterson hurried from his downtown Los Angeles law office with his briefcase and mail-order box in his hand. Moving quickly along taking small quick steps to the back stairs, he entered the entrance of the garage parking underground.

"Dillard!" someone shouted. He turned to see a fellow attorney getting into his car. It was a bit dark, but this time of day, one couldn't easily be seen. Besides, everyone knew Dillard's silhouette. He always wore a small tight brimmed hat on his head. His hair was balding in the center back of his head so he'd joke about the grass not growing on a busy street. The outdated big rimmed glasses, cuffed slacks, and wing-tipped shoes aged him tremendously, but you'd never convince him of that.

"Why hello, Milburn," he said, pausing a minute as the gentleman walked toward him.

"I was wondering who this belonged to," he said, looking at Dillard now standing by his car. "Wow, pretty snazzy wheels you got there," he joked.

"Yes, thanks, now you know where my money goes. No wife, wheels," he replied back.

"Oh, so this is one of the perks for not having a wife. I think I'll trade mine in," he said, looking along the side of the Maybach Benz automobile.

Dillard laughed. "I have to go, don't want to be late seeing a client," he shared, trying to hurry Milburn along. He had become interested in looking at the inside and the workings of this fine car. "Some other time, okay?" he added, quickly opening the trunk putting the box in and opening his car door.

"Sure, I understand," Milburn replied but stood watching as Dillard shut the door and drove slowly from the garage.

Dillard hurried along to the busy LA freeway. Traffic went along smooth for a while, then came to an abrupt halt. The thick traffic was slowed to a crawl. Dillard gazed at his watch several times as if that would make a difference. After about thirty minutes, he was moving again and down the freeway he sped knowing now he'd be late. Dillard drove into an underground garage and closed the door behind him. Getting out, he wiped the fingerprints Milburn had left on the car with his jacket sleeve as he opened his trunk to retrieve the box. The traffic had caused him to be late, so he hurried up the stairs and knocked on the door.

"Delivery!" he yelled. After a few minutes, the door opened and Dillard quickly went in. Maybe five or ten minutes went by and Dillard was back in his Maybach and heading back onto the freeway.

It had been three years and a few months, Doris Woods thought as she sat in her office thinking about her sister Dana Demato-Williams who had fell victim to the chilly Atlantic River. Things with her estate had been settled a year after her death just as her sister had requested of her lawyer Dillard Patterson.

"I wonder if David Michael, her son, got everything he wanted from her condo," she sat thinking out loud to herself at this time.

After ringing his cell, she heard, "Hi, Aunt Doris, how are you?" He knew it was the anniversary of the tragic event and that was why he was getting this phone call, he reasoned.

"I'm fine, and how are studies going for you?" she asked. David Michael was in his last year of college at UCLA.

"Things are going well. Kara and I are flying out to see Daddy and Nada and, of course, my little sister Peyton this weekend."

"Oh good, it sounds like a wonderful trip," she replied, but David Michael could tell there was more.

"Aunt Doris, you were thinking about Dana, weren't you?" he asked.

"I'm sorry to bother you with that," she said.

"No, I understand. Sonjee and I were looking at photographs from your wedding last evening and it got a bit emotional, I must admit," he replied.

"David, do you know who got the painted photograph Dana had of our mother she had hanging on the wall?"

"I don't. I thought you had got it and just chose not to hang it," he said.

"I know most of her things went to some auction house Dana had requested, but it's puzzling to think she would have let that go," Doris shared.

"You're right. I guess you will have to give Mr. Patterson, her attorney, a call, maybe he knows where most of her things went," David Michael replied.

"I'll put a call in to him, you have a wonderful trip, love you."

"I love you too, Aunt Doris."

Adele walked into the Parker and Associates law firm. Entering, she remembered her visit there years ago when she was still in high school. William Parker had helped her and her three brothers to have and make a better life for themselves. The receptionist at the desk, seeing her standing there looking around, asked, "May I help you?"

"Yes, I'd like to go up and see William Parker, please?" she replied, standing now in a business suit and all grown up.

"Mr. Parker is on vacation. Was he expecting you?" she asked, tapping the keys of her computer.

"No, I work near here now and just stopped by, but while I'm here, may I please make an appointment?" she then requested.

"Sure," the clerk replied, "no problem, your name, please?"

"Adele Hodges," the young lady replied. The receptionist handed her a small card with her appointment on it and Adele walked out smiling.

Dillard drove a ways down the busy freeway of Los Angeles. He was focused and kept a close watch on the time. After driving to the eastern edge of the city and to the main business district, Dillard parked safely and got out going into a commercial-style building with his briefcase in hand. Walking into the restaurant and then to the reservation desk, he asked for Mark Massir, the realtor for a property he was interested in. Dillard was meeting him to talk about purchasing the property. This particular property was in Central Los Angeles known as Brentwood.

"Hello," Mark greeted Dillard with a business handshake. "So have you had time to think about any of the properties we saw last week?" Mark asked.

"Yes, I have," Dillard replied, sitting down to position his briefcase on his lap as Massir took his seat on the other side of the table.

"And?" Mark asked, looking at Dillard removing papers from his briefcase.

"I'm aware everyone has a price point," Dillard stated, now writing numbers on a piece of paper.

"You're aware I don't just sell houses, I sell a lifestyle," Massir said, sitting confidently across the table, awaiting Dillard's decision. "What property were you interested in?"

"I'd like to talk about the Brentwood property."

"Nice, very nice," Mark replied, getting out his laptop and pulling up his computer screen to the property.

"That's a lot of property, 36,828 square feet of lot you're asking about."

"Yes, I'm aware of the property and I was very impressed last week when we did the private walk through after the open house. Lots of garage space for my cars, 1,267 square feet, and plenty of square feet for living space. I've been looking for a while so I feel this is the closest I'm going to get to the location I want," Dillard replied.

"So now we need to talk about price."

"Yes, and I'm willing to pay a fair price with of course some negotiations if necessary," Dillard replied, smiling.

"Yes, yes, Dillard, I know. We have been over this before," Mark said.

Dillard wrote a figure on a piece of paper and handed it to Massir. "Very close to the asking price and I don't wish to doodle over petty dollars, so impress me!" Dillard added, gathering his things.

"Good start, I'll make the call to my client and let you know where we are tomorrow, sir, is that okay with you?" Massir asked, smiling at the figure on paper.

"Yes, but remember, I need to know a soon as possible. I want to get closed soon," Dillard shared, securing his briefcase, handshake and he was gone.

CHAPTER 2

NADA WAS UP AND MOVING after talking to Billy who was still at the men's retreat in Bangor.

"Dante, I'm headed out for my run. I'll be back soon," she said, waving as she exited the kitchen door. Nada ran along thinking about her life since coming to live in this beautiful home with her husband, William Parker. She had become a mommy to a beautiful little girl and she was very happy. She had decided to wait until Peyton, her daughter, was in kindergarten before she entered back into the workforce of teaching at the university. Nada was an instructor at the university before her marriage *to the man of her dreams*, she'd say. Nada ran along down the designed trail she and Billy ran almost every day. She always carried her cell phone with her because the five-mile trail wind and turned way out on the property line.

Ring. Ring. Nada touched the button on her earpiece.

"Hi, girl!"

"Hello, Madison, it's so good to hear from you," Nada replied. Madison was her bridesmaid and best friend from Washington State. "I'm out running trying to get my shape back even after two years," she teased.

"Oh really, you have left that beautiful daughter alone?"

"Absolutely not, Millicent would spoil her rotten if I did that," Nada smiled.

"So who's been shopping with you since I'm not around?" Madison asked.

"Annie sometimes, but mostly me and my daughter, she can't force her opinion on me yet," Nada said, sitting down on a bench to rest and talk to her friend laughing.

"I'm surprised you and Annie still get along so well," Madison said.

"Why she's very happily married and loves her husband and her child."

"I know, but she was once in love with Billy. Do you think she's gotten over him?"

"Honestly I had so much drama with Dana that very little thought was given to Annie. As a matter of fact, she married Keith before Billy and I started dating."

"I hear ya, but I would really keep an eye on that one!" Madison added.

"Madison, dear Madison, how are you and Charlie these days?"

"We are good, just got back from D.C. with all the women cooing over him in uniform."

"What's different?" Nada asked.

"Well, since Obama is there, there are more blacks in the White House and in high positions."

"And what does that have to do with anything, you're white, what makes you think your competition can't be either?" Nada teased. "Now that's funny! A white girl worrying about a black woman taking her man. YOU OUGHTA QUIT!" she said, laughing loudly.

"Why do you think I keep him in Washington State?" Madison said, laughing to agree.

"I love you, Madison, and I know Charlie does as well," Nada confessed.

"So, when are we getting together?"

"Soon, let me head back in. I'll call you soon."

"Love to Billy, Nada. Bye."

Nada smiled running along, thinking of her dear friend and their interesting conversation. Maybe there are some questions she needed to ask Annie.

Nada was busy most of the day after taking Peyton to her day care. She had an hour before she would pick both girls up and take Riley to meet Annie at the office. Nada was still learning her way around in Maine but GPS was God-sent, she admitted. She rushed into her nail salon and was soon sitting in a massage chair for her pedicure. She had shopped earlier for new sandals and a trip she could see in her view.

"This is ridiculous, why am I thinking about this woman? Madison, girl, you are a trip! Devil, you are a liar!" she found herself saying loudly in her thoughts. "If Billy had loved Annie, he would have married her. WHEN WERE THEY TOGETHER ANYWAY? Why did they break up? Oh, Madison, you're wrong for this, and I'm not going to let it come in, not today, not at all!" she said, leaving the salon heading to get the girls from day care.

Nada, unlike Billy, heads into her daughter's class not waiting for anyone to bring her child to the foyer to be picked up. They found it causes less confusion of some younger ones crying, wanting to go as well. But it's what Nada did, so they just looked over it.

"Hello, Mrs. Parker, the girls are ready," Belle said, seeing her come in.

"Oh!" Nada said, seeing the girls by the front and ready to go.

"I saved you a trip to Riley's classroom," Belle informed her, smiling.

"Her parents may be picking her up sometimes as well," Nada found herself saying selfishly.

Belle lifted her brows. "I understand, Mrs. Parker. Bye, girls," she said, walking back to her class that had started to be busy instead of napping.

Nada caught the girls' hands and walked them to the car, putting them in their car seats, and off she went to the law office.

"Annie?" Nada asked as she was leaving after dropping Riley with her. "Do you want to go shopping sometime? I mean you and Riley. We can take the girls to that new indoor play area at the Galleria Mall."

"Sounds fun," Annie replied, "thanks for asking me."

Nada just smiled. She didn't really want to think of what Madison had put into her thoughts, but it was there and she unfortunately had bought into it.

The week seemed very long as Nada woke up Friday morning. Billy was calling to say he'd be leaving the retreat in Bangor at noon.

"Oh, honey, you're up early," Nada said, still a bit sleepy from being awaken up by his phone call.

"I know, I'm sorry we had a change in schedule. We decided, the men here, to have an early prayer together in the chapel, then breakfast, and head out. That should put us home around noon," he said.

"Oh, honey, I can't wait to see you," she voiced.

"All right, dear, love you. I'll see you then," he said, hanging up the line. Nada lay in bed thinking about Billy. How much she loved him and how much she wanted a good marriage with him. God had blessed them with a beautiful little daughter and all was well! She again smiled lying there with her thoughts going a mile a minute. She was not about to let a misleading thought ruin her marriage relationship with her husband!

"I can't believe Madison is that insecure about Charlie," she confessed, still lying quietly on her pillow. "Thought, be gone!" As she turned in bed to get up, she heard babbling from the monitor on the nightstand. Smiling, she knew her day had begun, moving down the hall to the nursery finding Millicent heading in also.

"Good morning, Mrs. Parker."

"Good morning, Millicent. Thanks, but I'll get Peyton this morning, thank you though," Nada said, reaching into the crib.

"You sure?" Millicent asked.

"Yes, I'm sure," she said, smiling, putting Peyton on her lap in the big rocking chair and singing to her.

Millicent smiled and walked out to get breakfast started.

Dillard raced down the Santa Monica Freeway, heading into the heart of downtown where his law office is located in the area of the civic center. He slowed and pulled safely into his underground parking space and hurried up the three flights of stairs to his office. The elevator, he says, is too slow. He could build a case by the time he waited to get to his office riding it. Just has he had poured his coffee and sat behind his desk, his phone rang.

"Hello, Dillard Patterson," he answered.

"Good morning, Mr. Patterson," Doris replied.

"Yes, how may I help you?" he said, not really making a connection.

"Dillard, this is Doris Woods, Dana Williams's sister," she said.

"Oh, hold on, please," Dillard said and put the call on hold. He took a deep breath and took off his coat and sat at his desk. "I apologize, I just got in, my secretary's not in the office yet, what can I do for you, Mrs. Wri—I mean, Woods."

"I was calling about Dana's estate."

"Yes," Dillard replied. "That was all settled a year after her disappearance. Dana left specific details as to what she wanted with every cent of her money. What's the problem?"

"No, no problem with money," Doris replied.

Dillard let out a big sigh.

"I was asking about the property in her home she left behind."

"Oh?" he questioned. "I can't recall off the top of my head. I'll have to check my records, though I'm sure it went to some auction house and the proceeds are still going to David, her son," Dillard shared.

"Oh I see, well, if it's not any trouble, if I could get that name, I would surely appreciate it," Doris replied.

"Is there something I can help you find?" Dillard asked, now relieved there were no money issues.

"There was a piece of art, a large hand-painted photograph of our mother, and it meant so much to Dana I'd hate to have it leave our family," Doris confessed.

"I'll look and see what I can find, but that's been a while ago, it could be anywhere now," he thought.

"You're right, but please get back to me if you find something out about it. Thanks." And Doris hung up the line.

Dillard sat back in his chair. Soon his phone rang again. "Hello?"

"Hello, did you make the deal with the house?" the caller asked.

"Yes, I'm waiting for the realtor to call me back."

"I know, I know I shared time was of the essence!"

"There is plenty of room."

"Okay, okay."

"I have to deal with some painting."

"What?"

"A hand-painted portrait of a client's mother from the estate sale."

"OKAY!"

"Don't worry, I'll figure something out, see you later."

Ring!

"Dillard Patterson," he answered, a bit squeamish thinking it could be Doris again.

"Dillard, the house is yours!" Massir, the realtor, voiced loudly.

"Thanks, good news, very good news. I'll be by later today and we can get all the paperwork in order and thanks again. Wanda, hold all my calls," he yelled to his secretary after getting off the line from the realtor.

Mark Massir hung up smiling, thinking about his biggest commission to date!

Billy hurried to his car waving so long to the guys at church. He shared he was planning to meet and surprise his wife at their daughter's day care. He looked at his watch and drove swiftly down the freeway; with time to spare, he was there. He looked around a bit for Nada's SUV. Not seeing it, he decided to go in, meeting Belle at the front corridor.

"Hello, Mr. Parker, you're very relaxed today," she said, looking at his pullover shirt and jeans.

"Oh yes, pardon my attire, I'm coming from a camp retreat, thought I'd surprise Nada and pick the girls up," he replied. Billy usually came in from the law office and a suit and tie was the fashion of the day.

"Oh, I'm sorry, your wife already picked up your daughter."

"Oh really, did I just miss her?" he asked.

"No, sir, she came early, she also said Annie was picking up Riley, though she hasn't come yet," Belle shared, looking at her watch. The room was very quiet.

"So where are the children?" he asked.

"Riley and I are the only ones left today. I'm waiting for Annie. She said she would be late, but I didn't expect this late."

"Look, I'll give Riley a ride to the office and you can make your appointment on time," he replied, seeing her looking at her watch.

"No, it's my neighbor. I have to give him his insulin shot, that's all."

"Okay, I understand, please call Annie for me, let her know I'll bring Riley."

"Thank you, thank you, sir. I really appreciate what you are doing," she replied, gathering Riley's backpack and coat, handing the things to Billy.

Billy was in the car and on his way when a call came in his ear.

"Hello, William?"

"Yes, Annie. I have Riley. We should be there in about twenty minutes."

"William, thank you. I'm sorry, I got stuck here with a client regarding the case next week and Keith's in court. No problem I'm just glad she recognized me without a suit!" he teased. Billy then called Nada.

"Hello, honey, I thought you'd be home by now," she stated.

"I too, but I guess my surprise backfired."

"What do you mean?"

"I left the church hoping to meet up and Peyton at the day care but Belle said you came early and Annie—"

"Annie?" Nada interrupted.

"Yes, Annie got stuck with a client and now I'm headed to my office to take Riley."

"Where is Keith?"

"Keith is in court, so that's the problem, but I will be there in about an hour now. How's my Peyton?" he asked.

"She will probably be sleep by the time you get through running all over town!" she said, obviously upset.

"Sweetheart, are you tired?"

"Maybe a bit, it's been a long week," Nada confessed.

"Well I missed you too," he shared.

"See you soon." Nada hung up the phone and called the office.

"Parker and Associates," Annie answered.

"Oh, Annie, is Billy there yet?"

"Nada, no, he called about ten minutes ago, he should be here with Riley soon. Thank you for letting him bring her to me," Annie said. "I got stuck with a client."

"Sure, no problem, please have Billy call me when he gets there. Thanks, Annie." And Nada hung up the phone and sat watching the clock tick off each minute. Half hour had went by, *ring!*

"Nada, you asked me to call? Is something wrong?"

"Yes, honey, Peyton's getting pretty sleepy. I'll try to keep her awake, but you know how cranky she gets."

"I do and I'm sorry, look, let her go to sleep, I'll be heading that way soon," he added.

"Okay! William, I want to see you soon, you have been gone for a week."

"All right, dear, see you soon."

Annie left after getting Riley, going home to meet her husband. Billy was still there talking with McGuire, one of the attorneys on the big case coming up next week. Nada had fallen asleep in the nursery and was not happy and her face showed she had been crying when Billy came home at 6:30 p.m. That was three hours after his return from the retreat.

"Sweetheart, are you all right?" he asked, walking in with his bag in hand. "Did something happen?" he asked, putting his bag down and kneeling in front of the ottoman by the chair.

"No, I thought you would be home by now," she said.

"Honey, I called you, I'm sorry, I got into a discussion with McGuire at the office about a case he's working on. I'm sorry," he said, reaching to hold her hand and a bit confused at her mood.

"Was Annie still there too? No one answered the office phones."

"Why didn't you call my cell? You know the office closes at five thirty," Billy replied. "Annie left as soon as I arrived with Riley. Nada, what is this about?" he then asked, looking at her with tears still running down her face.

"You have been gone for a week and I thought you would rush home to be with us, me and Peyton, but you were at the office with Annie and Riley!"

"What? Are you serious? I'm so sorry for the mix-up and the way things turned out. I should have headed straight home but I was trying to help Belle out with her neighbor. I didn't realize you would be that bothered, I'm sorry, I'm learning and I promise to do better," he replied, hugging her and apologizing for the oversight.

"What's wrong with Belle's neighbor?" Nada asked, concerned.

"She needed to leave so that she could give him his insulin shot and Annie was running late, that's all."

"Oh, honey, I'm sorry. I should have never listened to Madison," Nada confessed.

"To Madison? What does Madison have to do with this?" Billy asked, getting up and sitting on the handle of the chair.

"Madison called me earlier this week, and I guess she was feeling a bit insecure about Charlie and started asking me questions about you and Annie working so closely together," Nada admitted. "She brought up a lot of things I had not even thought about regarding Annie, and even though I prayed about it and tried hard to forget about it, I couldn't. I guess I had been so frustrated with Dana I really hadn't given Annie any thought!"

Standing up, Billy said, "It's probably because there was not a reason to, sweetheart. Annie and I dated for a while but I never thought of marrying her. I just didn't love her like that."

"Why, she seems to be making Keith a good wife," Nada shared.

"Yes, they are happy from what I can see and I'm happy for the both of them. He was for her and it works. You see! I'm for you and I love you! Please I like Madison a lot but you can't allow those thoughts to cloud our relationship," he said.

"You're right, honey, you have not given me any reason to think or suggest there is anything still between you and Annie. Please forgive me," Nada said, standing up to kiss him passionately.

Agghh! The sound came from the crib.

"Oh, my how's my little darling?" Billy smiled, reaching in the crib getting her out and holding her tightly in his arms as Nada looked on.

"Fletcher, did you get the tickets I asked you to order from the Internet?" Adele asked, walking in from work.

It was now just the two of them at home. Hanson had graduated high school two years ago and had joined the military. Adele, Fletcher, and Riggins were going to San Diego to see his graduation and she was so excited. She had been, for the most part, raising all three brothers by herself for the past ten years. Two older siblings, Malcolm and Ariel, had left home and the responsibility fell to her. Of course their mother, Rhea, was there sometimes but not the past three years. Before that, she would come by once in a while or one of the children would run into her on the streets but she had sold out to the streets and was strung out on drugs. Adele worked hard to make a better life for her brothers and God had shown favor! Malcolm was the first victim to the system when their father left home after Adele was born. Rhea blamed herself for her husband leaving and disconnected herself from everything good. Since Adele graduated after two years of a city college and was now working in social services, she had helped her older brother after he was released after six months in jail for stealing. She worked with him finding an adult program for him to attend and, after getting his GED, was enrolled in an auto mechanics college to become a licensed mechanic with hopes he had learned his lesson.

"Ariel, I'm picking Malcolm up, he is riding in with us," she said, calling her sister who was also coming along. It was the family's first trip together and everyone was looking forward to seeing their brother graduate boot camp.

"Okay, no problem. I'll be there, so everyone has a way to the airport?" Ariel asked.

"Yes, and I'm so excited I can't way until the weekend," Adele said, laughing.

Riggins was right behind Adele in age, and by Adele nudging him, he enrolled in the junior college near home as well. He had fallen for a young lady he met at the church and working part-time for a telecommunications company in town. Adele had enrolled and had a planned day of graduation from the university in Maine to continue her education and had secured a job with social services on R Street not far from Parker and Associates law firm. She had been looking for her mother for the past two months. She wanted her to share in her son's big day by his request, but Adele couldn't find her anywhere she looked. That is why Adele had again gone to see Attorney Parker. He had helped her with her brothers so many years ago it seemed now. She hadn't been back since graduating high school. Billy shared he'd help her get into college and now she had successfully graduated from city college and found a career job in social work. Somehow I don't think that would surprise him. Fletcher, the youngest, was a junior, and he and Adele lived together. Not in the house that brought them so much joy and kept the mother home more often, but Adele had purchased a townhouse in the same school district so that Fletcher wouldn't have to change school in his last years. She loved it because it had three bedrooms and a large dining room. Every Sunday, they would get together and eat. Malcolm had a small place near his job downtown. Riggins had a much-nicer apartment in the suburbs not far from Adele and Fletcher's home. Ariel, the oldest sister, was married and had a young baby boy, Gabriel, and they lived quite a ways by car but committed every Sunday to being there with her family.

When Adele was asked to move from the former house, the family was devastated. Their mother stayed around more and was doing better. She didn't go out every night and things looked to be turning for her. But the owner, Reverend Morris, died, his family sold the property, and the new owners wanted to sell also. Adele had to move and the mother left too. For a while, she was seen around from time to time. Adele took food over to a friend's home where she said she was living. That lasted for a few months, but one day a few weeks later when Adele went back, the place was vacant and boarded up. She had been looking close to a year without results. Then one day, maybe a month ago after the first of the New Year, Fletcher saw his mother, Rhea, and brought her home. When Adele came home from work, she helped her find clothes to put on after taking a nice hot bath. She stayed around three days, and when Fletcher left for school, she took off taking his gaming system with her and had not been heard from since. As much as Adele loved her mother, she could see what it was doing to not only Fletcher but Riggins and Hanson too. So maybe she would just let her go; it's for the better. But Hanson had asked for her, so Adele tried again finding her but without success, so she decided to ask Attorney Parker for his help.

CHAPTER 3

BILLY AND NADA WERE GROWING mightily in the Lord. Billy had also started giving short sermons to the congregation and continuing his studies at the seminary. He was secure now that this is what God had for him to do.

"Honey, I would like to go see Daddy next week. Do you have the time in your schedule?" she asked, sitting across the breakfast table.

"Next week? I'll have to check my calendar, dear, and call you from my office. It should be fine, but I don't want to say something and then have to change," he added.

"Okay, I understand, sweetheart," she said, getting up to leave.

"Going somewhere this morning?" Billy asked, seeing her leave as he sat still finishing his breakfast roll.

"I need to get Peyton ready. I'm seeing if she can handle longer hours now. And before I forget, Annie and I are going shopping after work," Nada replied.

"Oh, I have an exam in my theology class Friday, and if it's anything like the bar exam, four hours and two hundred questions, I'm sure I will be late for dinner," Billy teased.

"Okay," Nada acknowledged.

"So I guess that's all right. You have gotten past whatever upset you."

Nada kissed Billy's forehead and walked out. "Have a good day, sweetheart," she said, leaving the room.

Billy had not even given thought to Annie and the working relationship. Annie had been working for the law firm as long as he had. They did date a lot! Now Nada had him questioning himself not about marriage, he could have married Annie long ago. "Now

I'll have to be more careful when we are in the office together or working too close on a case, because I really don't want to borrow trouble. And I truly love my wife!" he said, going up to his office from the covered garage.

"Good morning, William," Annie said, sitting at the desk to start her day. "I just made fresh coffee about to pour a cup for Keith. Can I bring you a cup?" she asked, getting up from the desk. The usual answer would be "Sure, thanks."

"No, no, Annie, that's all right. I'm headed to Keith's office. I'll take in his cup if you don't mind."

"Umm, okay," she said, sitting back at her computer screen.

Billy had been busy most of the morning when his next appointment walked in.

"Mr. Parker, please."

"Yes, Miss Hodges." Annie walked into Billy's office. "There is a Miss Hodges here to see you, and yes, she has an appointment," Annie teased.

"Good timing, just put down the Westingreen case. Annie, you can use your intercom, you know, you don't have to walk in for appointments," he suggested.

"Why is there a problem?"

"No, please send her in, thanks."

Annie stopped teasing and turned around to leave, thinking he's not in a playful mood today. "You may go in his office, it's the first on your left."

Billy had his head down looking at a brief.

"Hello, Mr. Parker."

"I'm sorry. Hello there, Miss Hodges?" he said, shaking her hand and inviting her to sit down. "My secretary didn't say why you needed to see me, how may I help you?" he continued, smiling, looking at the beautiful young lady.

"Well, Mr. Parker, what I need is some advice," she said.

"Advice. And you came to me?"

"Yes," she smiled, teasing him, not letting him know he knew her.

"I'm a lawyer and I'll do my best, but why would you come to me?"

"Because, Mr. Parker, I know you won't steer me wrong," she snickered.

"Well, thank you for the vote of confidence. What kind of advice can I help you with?" he said, writing now on a tablet.

"Well, sir, I'd like you to help me find my mother?"

"Your mother." *That's investigative work*, Billy quietly thought.

"Yes," the young lady answered.

"Her name?" Billy asked, looking up.

"Rhea, Rhea Hodges?"

"Umm, I've heard that name before. Rhea, Rhea? Adele Hodges? ADELE!" He looked into a big smile. "Oh my goodness! Look at you, you've grown up," he was talking so loud Annie and two fellow attorneys were now standing at his door.

"What's going on, Parker?"

Billy smiled. "This is Adele Hodges, wow, I haven't seen her since she was in high school, what, four or five years ago. My!" He smiled, hugging the young lady.

"Hi," Annie said, remembering her from that earlier visit as well.

"No problem, sit, let's talk. How are the boys?"

Two weeks had gone by and Dillard still had not returned a call to Doris Wright-Woods regarding her sister Dana's estate. He was so busy getting his things packed up for the movers to pick up and delivered to his new place.

"Dillard, you're moving quickly these days," a fellow attorney, Milburn, said, seeing him leaving from the building.

"Yes, pretty busy these days, you know how that can be sometimes," he replied.

"How's the new wheels?" he added.

"Just fine," Dillard again shared.

"So is there a new woman in your life? Our annual dance is coming up soon." He smiled, still kidding the balding lawyer.

"That's not a problem, Sally still works at the courthouse." He laughed.

"Yes, but last I heard, she had gotten married," Milburn replied.

"You're kidding, right?" Dillard said, surprise at the news. Sally was always available for a date. She worked at the courthouse in the records department. She was very friendly and outspoken on any subject, so most knew her and like her outgoing personality. Not that attractive but she'd work for a date, most thought. Dillard had asked her out to the last two dances and they seemed to have a good time.

"I will make a point of going by and see her, Milburn, because you're always up to your games," Dillard shared, laughing at the fellow attorney.

"Okay, she's married!" he said, laughing and walking away.

Dillard got in his car with the phone ringing. "Hello," he said, hitting his ear to answer.

"Hello, Mr. Patterson," Doris's voice said.

"Yes, sorry, I haven't gotten back to you, did you find that portrait?" he asked.

"No, I haven't, I have spoken with her son and he said something about you handled the estate sale."

"Yes, yes, that's correct, but things were flying out of there like no one's business. I didn't see who exactly purchased the photographs. I apologize for the delay. I'm in the middle of moving. Give me some time to get settled and I will see what I can come up with," he asked.

"Sure, please get back to me," was Doris's request and she hung up.

Adele sat talking and catching Billy up on things in her life. She shared about the trip her family was getting together to take of which she was so excited. "You know Justin Parker became Fletcher's big brother and he's truly been a blessing to us," she shared.

"Oh yes, that's great." She still had not made the connection that Justin was his younger brother.

"My older brother Malcolm is back with us and we enjoy dinners on Sundays as a family," Adele added.

"Adele, I am truly happy for you, you have done a great job with the responsibility you had to take on," Billy replied. "Well, I have married and we have a beautiful little girl named Peyton," he added, picking up the photo from his shelf for Adele to see.

"Ah, she's a doll," Adele said, smiling at the photograph. "And is that your wife?" she asked, pointing to another photo sitting on his desk.

"It is. Her name is Nada," he replied, handing the framed picture to her.

"I'm glad you seem happy."

"I am, I really am," Billy replied, smiling. "God has truly been good to me," he acknowledged. "So, what happened to your mother?" he asked. "She seemed to be doing better the last time we spoke."

"She was, but then she took off again and each time it seems to get worse," Adele confessed. "I couldn't hold her hand every hour though I wanted to," she said, very heartbroken.

"I understand, but you have so much on your plate, you have done way beyond what anyone should do at your age and now this," he said, feeling her sorrow.

"Hanson wanted to see her. He wanted to let her know she could make it if he did." Billy gave her a Kleenex to wipe her eyes of tears. "I didn't realize what she had gone through," Adele started. "I was angry at Rhea for what she had become. We had some good days when we laughed and talked about her past. You would never know this but she graduated from college, had a good job, and a marriage, she thought."

"So what happened?" Billy asked.

"After I was born, our daddy left for good. He was a committed husband for ten years. Then she said he started going away a lot mostly on weekends alone but he always came back. She didn't know Jude Hodges was fighting something himself." Billy just sat and listened. "The house was a mess all the time. I remember the electricity was off a lot as well after he left. That's when Mother started drinking. We were all pretty young and no one came to help her. I thought, do we have any other family? It wasn't until Ariel, my older sister, was eighteen and old enough to help us that we started to eat a regular meal again. The house was still in shambles, and Mom was torn up from life by then, but we hung in there. CPS almost got us more than once but we never opened the door and made sure we went to school every day. That was the key to them not getting us. What little we had we made it work. Ariel and Justin helped us a lot. And as you know, Justin helped us and then sent us to you," she said sadly. "When Rhea finally confronted Daddy about it, he told her he was gay."

"What!" Billy sat with his mouth wide open.

"He said he tried to be like everyone wanted him to be, but it finally got the best of him. She said she asked him why and cried for a long time. She ended up blaming herself and turned to the streets for comfort. That's when Riggins, Hanson, and Fletcher came along. She told me she felt bad for making us pay for not putting herself back together after that shock. The last time I spoke with her, begging her to come back home and get help, she said she didn't want us to pay anymore for her mistake." Then Adele broke down crying.

Billy stood up and held her tight. "Oh, Adele, I'm so sorry." Billy held on to her and let her continue to cry. He thought his childhood was bad. After a while, he asked, "Where is your father now?"

"Don't know," she said. "He moved out of town but we have never seen him again," Adele confessed.

Billy let out a sigh. "I'll see what I can do to help you find your mother and hopefully get her some help!"

"Thank you, Mr. Parker," she said, shaking his hand into a hug and leaving.

Billy heard Nada speaking with Annie as he sat in his office reading briefs.

"Hello, honey," he said, coming out and kissing her. "How's my best girl doing today?" he asked, picking up Peyton from the floor. Riley had run to her dad's office.

"Hi, sweetheart, excuse me, Annie," she said, walking her husband and daughter into his office.

"I'm headed out. I'll take Peyton home with me unless you just want to take her," he suggested.

"That sounds great, we can get pedicures if Riley doesn't come, so we will see."

Annie came back with purse in hand as Nada and Billy came from his office. "Riley's tired, she's going home with Keith," she shared.

"Good!" Annie looked puzzled. "No, William is taking Peyton home so now we can get our pedis," she said smiling, kissing Billy and leaving from the office with Annie.

Billy had gotten Peyton all packed up to go when Keith came out of his office with Riley. "Hello, I thought you had left already," he said, seeing Keith head his way.

"No, I had a documented fax to get out tonight before I left," Keith replied.

"Oh, can I help with something?"

"No, Riley was asleep, so it worked out well, just headed home now."

Keith and Billy stood talking for a while by the elevator with Riley sleeping across her daddy's shoulder and Peyton holding tight to her daddy's hand.

"Keith, you and Annie seemed to be very happy," he shared.

"We are, and Riley was the best thing that has happened to us."

"Are you all planning for another one? They grow so fast," Billy stated.

"Riley was a God-sent," Keith confessed. "Doctors had said I couldn't have children, but look, we have Riley. We want more, so we've been trying for a while now." He laughed.

"Nada and I want another as well, but we want Peyton to be at least two years older," he shared.

"Yes, that was our plan, so it's been fun trying but nothing yet." He again smiled. "Our Riley will be in kindergarten next year, so if she's it for me, I'm fine with it. The doctors said it was rare, but it could happen again, though I'm just thankful for her," Keith said.

"I hear you." Billy said, "Take care," as he pushed the elevator button.

Both rode down together and walked out getting in their cars.

"See you tomorrow, Poulton," Billy said.

Dillard had received a call as he drove the freeway to pick up a few things from his old apartment.

"Yes," he answered. "Good! Whew, I'll be right over to pick it up, take it to my office and have her pick it up there," he said, turning off the next exit and heading out to Brentwood.

Nada and Annie had spent an hour getting their nails and pedicures done and was now headed to the Pavilion's for some shopping.

"Annie, thank you for coming today, I really miss my shopping buddies in Washington," Nada shared.

"I enjoy shopping, and Keith, well, you know men," she joked.

"Oh yes!" She laughed back going into the store.

"Riley's party is Saturday and all the little ones will be running around all over."

"I can't believe she's going to be five," Annie said, looking at a beautiful dress she was thinking of buying.

"I know. Billy and I have been married for four years, it seems time just flew."

"That's right, you all were in Florida when Riley was born."

"Yes, I do recall that," Nada thought.

"So, are you and Keith having another, or is Riley going to be an only child?" Nada asked as she and Annie headed to the dressing room with an armload to try on.

"We've been trying since Riley was two and a half, but nothing yet," she said across the stalled wall.

"Billy and I want another as well, so when Peyton gets two, we'll start on another."

"Boy or girl?" Annie asked.

"Doesn't matter, we have David Michael and he loves his little sister," Nada bragged.

"That's nice, I do want a sibling for Riley, but the doctors said we were just blessed to have Riley. Some childhood problem Keith had," she admitted.

"REALLY!" Nada exclaimed, walking out to show Annie an outfit.

"Yes, the doctor said if we have another, it will be a while, so we're content for now," Annie smiled.

"I'm taking these." And both ladies left the dressing room heading to the counter to pay for their purchases.

"Thanks, Annie, we will have to do this more often," Nada suggested as they walked out to their cars.

"That sounds wonderful," Annie replied.

"See you tomorrow."

Nada drove home thinking of the conversation she had with Annie.

"She's nice," she thought to herself. "I haven't really allowed myself to get to know her. All this time, I have been treating her like an acquaintance, not a longtime friend. She appears to be very happy with Keith, and I admit I blew things out of whack after my conversation with Madison. God, forgive me," Nada confessed loudly with tears flowing down her face still driving home in her car. After her long trip home, Nada was now smiling as she pulled into her driveway and went inside to her husband and little girl sitting having reading time on the chaise before bedtime.

Dillard knocked gently on the door before using a key to enter.

"Hello," greeting someone at the foyer entrance.

"Everything seems to be coming along just fine," he acknowledged, looking around the beautiful spacious home.

"So, when are you moving all your things in?" the voiced asked. "Now, we must be very careful, I work with this very nosy Attorney Milburn in the office next to me who watches my every move, sometimes I think he knows what I ate for lunch," he added, laughing.

"Well there's nothing for you to fear, a man of your caliber and prominence could have whatever he wants," the voice said, tapping his shoulder and walking into an office space off the formal living area.

"Wow, this office is as big as my downtown one."

"Do you like it?"

"I do like it a lot," he replied, touching all the wood finishes and custom shelving.

"Good," the voice said, walking over to the closet and pulling out a large portrait wrapped in shipping paper.

"Thank you, I will see that Doris Wright gets this right away. I don't want to cause alarm on any level," he said nervously, removing his hat and then putting it back on his head. "Where should I tell her I found it?"

"Look, Patterson, you can't lose your cool. Things are fine, you just need to just chill."

"Milburn has always been the same way. He was always asking questions when I met him leaving your office."

"Don't trip because I need you, and if I can't count on you to do this, let me know now before I go out on a limb," she said.

"Okay, okay, I'm just getting used to this. I've been a loner for so many years, but I can do it!"

"Okay, I'm counting on you."

Dillard picked up the large package and headed for the door. "I will see you tomorrow," and out the door he went, putting the package in the backseat carefully as not to tear the seats in his Maybach Benz.

Dillard hurried along the freeway heading to his office downtown. He wanted to leave the large package there for Doris to pick up next week. "Umm, I have got to think of something to tell her about how or where I located this package for her," he thought out loud as he drove along. He was in all the way now in helping a friend and couldn't back out. New home, new automobile, and a new life he had to start embracing to pull this off for his client. "I certainly don't want her to think I know what happened to all of Dana William's estate from her townhouse, she will be calling me again for something. I have to be careful, she is still a client, thanks to her sister and son, so tact diplomacy for me is definitely in order he surmised pulling into the underground parking space. Slowly and carefully he took the package from his backseat."

"Need help with that?" Milburn yelled, standing over in a corner stall near his car.

"No thank you, just taking something to my office for a client," Dillard replied.

"No problem, I'll give you a hand," he said, taking hold of the large frame glancing quickly at the uncovered portion of the portrait while walking up the stairs with Dillard.

"I went to see Sally the other day," Dillard stated. "For once, you were right. I congratulated her on her marriage."

"Yes," Milburn replied, awfully quick though. "Don't you think?" he asked.

"Doesn't matter what I think at this point, but thanks for the hand," he said, shaking Milburn's hand and showing him out.

"Tomorrow, Patterson," Milburn said, heading back to the garage to leave.

CHAPTER 4

BILLY WAS SO BUSY WITH his law practice and the seminary. Nada and Peyton went to Washington State alone to visit his parents and her dad who work for the Parkers.

"Hello," Nada said after renting a car and heading to the family home. No one answered at the bungalow, so Nada went to the main house.

Tetra was out in her flower garden and saw them coming. "Oh my, my, my, it's my girls," she said, taking her garden gloves from her hands and running to meet them through the gate.

"Hello, Mother Parker," Nada said, embracing her. She had Peyton in a stroller and Peyton was ready to get out after the long ride from the airport.

"Come this way, I was just about to work with my flowers over there but I'm so glad to see you all. Where's Billy?," she then asked, looking around.

"Mother, you know Billy, he was too busy and I needed to see Daddy. How's he doing?" Nada confessed.

"Let me have my Peyton," she said, taking her out of the stroller and holding her tight in her arms, kissing her cheeks. "Your dad seems fine, well-adjusted, and happy. Why? Did he indicate a problem?"

"Not really," she replied, sitting down with Tetra and Peyton on the patio chairs. Peyton wanted down to run around, so Tetra put her down.

"Why are you really here, dear?"

Nada started to cry. "I'm not sure, I've been praying a lot and I want to be a good wife for William."

"What happened?" Tetra asked.

"Nothing," Nada replied.

"Nothing and you are down here talking to me. Come on, Nada, this is your mother-in-law." She smiled.

"Really nothing happened, it's just a series of happenings."

"No! No," Tetra said, getting up to run at Peyton going near the pool. It was covered but dirty and Tetra caught her before she fell. She picked her up and turned Peyton in another direction and she toddled off smiling to be free again. With Peyton safely sitting down playing with her pail in the sandbox David had built in the backyard, Tetra went back to Nada. "Now, Nada, be honest, what has Billy done?"

"Nothing, really he hasn't. My friend Madison was feeling insecure about her husband, I guess, so she started asking me questions about the relationship between Annie and William."

"That was over before you came along, even I know that," Tetra stated.

"I know, Mother Parker, but she got me thinking about them working so closely together and our children attending the same day care, we are always around each other. When William came back from his retreat, he saw them first."

"Them?" Tetra asked.

"Yes, Annie and Riley. He was coming to meet me at the day care and surprise me by picking up Peyton, but I had taken her home earlier so we would be there when he got home. But instead, Annie was late picking up Riley, and William took her to meet Annie at his office, so I wasn't too happy about that," Nada confessed.

"Oh, Nada, I see how that could be misconstrued, though I seriously don't think you have to worry about Annie. She's a beautiful girl, but not Billy's type," Tetra shared. "It is going to be very important that you and your husband trust one another. You and he talked a lot about him being called to the ministry and the responsibilities that go with it. All things about Annie were before you, let them go," she said, walking now to play with her granddaughter in the sandbox.

Nada walked over and handed Tetra a photograph. "Ah, so cute, it's a man carrying his daughter asleep on his shoulder," Tetra replied, giving the photo back to Nada.

"It's William and Riley," Nada said. Tetra stood from kneeling and took the photo from Nada. "The guy across the street from William's office is out there on the corner taking photographs of everyone who walks by," Nada informed her. "Then he paints beautiful portraits from them. This one was entitled 'Daddy's Little Girl,'" Nada said.

"Nada, what are you saying?" Tetra asked, now looking at her.

"I'm not saying anything, but I am suspicious and I've prayed so hard about this I had to get away," Nada explained. "Does William know you are thinking this way?"

"No, not about Riley, but Annie, we have discussed in detail."

"My God, my God, I can't believe this and won't believe this is happening again," Tetra said, going into the house.

After a few minutes, Alfredo and Priscilla came out the door to meet Nada.

"Hi, Daddy, hello, Miss Priscilla," she said, greeting the both of them warmly before heading over to get Peyton, picking her up. Nada headed into the house to continue the talk with Tetra, her mother-in-law.

Adele and her family had a wonderful time visiting Hanson in San Diego. He looked so handsome in his uniform as he marched around on the grounds to the podium.

"He did it," Riggins said, trying not to tear like a girl. But Adele and Ariel had their own Kleenex boxes to use.

"So where do you go from here?" Fletcher asked, seeing Hanson coming to hug them for being there.

"Now I will train how to take those big planes apart and put them back together." He smiled.

"Hanson, we are so proud," everyone said, hugging him over and over.

"Malcolm, brother, glad to see you," Hanson stated.

"Likewise, likewise," Malcolm replied. "Let's get something to eat."

"Sounds good, how about pizza?" Hanson replied, holding Fletcher around the shoulders.

"So, I guess you didn't find Mama?" Hanson asked as everyone sat around laughing and having pizza.

"No," Adele replied, "but I'm getting some help from Attorney Parker. You remember him, right?"

"Yes, I will never forget that guy, as a matter of fact, when I come home after training, I'm going to pay him a visit," Hanson smiled.

"He's gone into ministry now, I've heard," said Riggins.

"Yes, he has been called to the ministry," Adele said, taking a bite of her pizza slice.

"He is a really gifted man," Ariel shared. He has been a God-sent to this family, he and his brother Justin."

"Justin! You mean my big brother Justin Parker?"

"Yes," Ariel confessed. "I've known for some time but I was so angry with him. Justin was always willing to help me, I blew it and I was not about to make you all suffer for my mistakes," Ariel shared, smiling around the table at each one.

"So you knew?"

"I knew," Ariel said, holding Adele's hand with a gentle smile.

Nada went in the house while Alfredo and Priscilla played with Peyton outside as they talked.

"Mrs. Parker," Nada yelled, coming into the house. "Mrs. Parker," she said again, walking through the house. Soon she noticed Tetra coming down the stairs. "Mrs. Parker, I'm very sorry to upset you. I really am, but when I saw that photograph of William, I almost lost it. That was the day he picked her up after the retreat. So I knew about it. I don't think he's her daddy, but the picture leads everyone to think he is. I'm really sorry, I didn't mean to upset you. Annie and I get along fine. William had every chance to marry her if he wanted to, I know he loves me," she said, hugging her mother-in-law tightly. "Peyton and I are staying for a couple of days. I'm going to visit Ms. Manuel and Hazel tomorrow. Let's go back outside and start this visit all over," Nada said, heading out back with Tetra walking out by her side thinking silently to herself.

The next day, while Nada and Peyton were out visiting, Tetra called her son at his office.

"Hello, Mom, are you spoiling your granddaughter before she returns to me?" Billy asked, laughing softly across the airways.

"I'm enjoying their visit tremendously so far," Tetra responded.

"Good. So how are you doing today?"

"I'm well," Tetra again responded.

"Mother, I'm sensing a problem, what's going on?" he asked, now concerned.

"Where is Nada?"

"Nada and Peyton are fine. They're visiting friends while they are here," she stated.

"Okay," he replied, relieved after his mother's answer.

"How are you and Nada doing?" she then asked.

"We are fine, Mom, what's this call about?" he asked, knowing certain something's bothering her. "Mom, not sure what this is about, but I have an idea since you are calling and Peyton's visiting you."

"Yes," Tetra said.

"The conversation Nada and I had two weeks ago about Annie."

"What about Annie?" Tetra asked.

"Her friend Madison put thoughts into her head and she let them get to her. I had hoped we'd worked them out," he replied. "At Riley's birthday party, a lady thought I was Riley's dad and it hit a nerve with Nada. I understand how that might make her feel, but honestly, Annie and I split before I met Nada."

"Did you see the photograph?"

"What photograph, Mom? What are you talking about? This is all new to me." Billy was so confused right now and Tetra knew it.

"Look, when your wife returns home, my suggestion is that you and she get some alone time to yourselves. Talk, be open and honest about everything. You're taking on a tremendous work for the Lord, and Satan will get busy. I'm not sure what's going on, but it needs to stop now before it's too late."

"Thanks, Mom, for the call, and please continue to pray for me and my family because I love my wife," Billy said, hanging up the line, closing his office door, and praying.

Billy anxiously awaited the arrival of his wife and daughter.

"So how was your visit with our Washington family?" Billy asked, sitting across the table at dinner with Nada the following week.

"Peyton and I had a wonderful time," Nada replied, "and Ms. Manuel is still a cut-up you know. I was sad to hear that Hazel had fallen in her home trying to put some preserves on a shelf, Ms. Manuel said."

"Oh my, is she all right?"

"Ms. Manuel says her daughter is thinking of putting her in a convalescent hospital because she can't take care of her and she needs to work."

"How many children does Hazel have?"

"She had two children, a son killed in Vietnam, so it's just a daughter and she's in her early fifties," Nada explained.

"My, that's too bad, she loves her independence, and what will she do without Virginia Manuel?" Billy commented with a smile.

"I know Ms. Manuel has her ways, but she is really bothered by it. I'm praying for a good outcome," Nada shared.

"So, how's your dad and—"

Before he could finish, Nada said, "Priscilla, my new mother?" Then she laughed. "They're so cute together and he is happier than I have seen him in a very long time," Nada voiced with a smile. "I wish them the best."

"Good, I know he really likes her company," Billy added. "Mom told me she spoiled Peyton every chance she got, so there's no need to ask if she did," he shared, putting a bite from his entrée into his mouth.

Nada sat eating waiting for her husband's next question. "Nada, Mom said you had a photograph that was upsetting you? Does this have something to do with Riley and Annie?"

"Why would you think that?" she asked sarcastically, looking at him from across the table.

"Mom said you had a photo of Riley and I."

"Yes, the guy across from your building downtown had it."

"Okay, so why did his picture upset you?"

"Because again, it was one of those misconstrued moments with you carrying your little girl that in this case was Riley."

"What?" Billy couldn't believe these things just kept happening to upset his wife. He and Annie were long over, he thought to himself.

"It was the day you picked Riley up when you got back from the retreat," Nada said. "He took a photo of you carrying Riley in on your shoulder into the office. She appears to be sleeping," Nada added. "The guy titled it 'Daddy's Little Girl.'" Nada wiped a tear from her eyes and tried to continue eating her meal.

"Honey, I'm so sorry these things keep hurting you, but there is nothing between Annie and I. We broke it off before I even met you."

"I'm really trying hard to put this behind us, but Satan is fighting me tooth and nail. Honestly these coincidences are not my fault, but I do understand why you're upset and I'm sorry," Billy said, holding Nada's hand across the table.

"Okay," Nada said, "all is forgiven, new start again."

Adele just shook her head sitting now back at work after a wonderful family weekend and celebration. She still couldn't believe her sister had let her go on for years thinking she was fooling her regarding Justin. But like Adele, Ariel was looking out for her family too.

"Hello, Social Services," Adele said, answering her telephone at work.

"Ms. Hodges, this is Erene James, an investigator William Parker hired to help you find your mother, Rhea Hodges."

"Yes, sir," Adele replied, having never met the man she was speaking with.

"Okay, that sounds good. I'll meet you at one thirty in front of Montello's."

"No, no, that's fine, it's not far from here at all. See you then."

Adele had been waiting for his call since she spoke with him about finding her mom. She had armed herself with photographs and other information he would need as she waited for the meeting at 1:30 p.m.

"Back to work," she quietly voiced to herself, heading to a coworker's office cube for questions.

Dillard was more light-footed around his office these days. His personality was becoming that of a man of the world so different from his reclusive life of a boring attorney. He was even envied by Milburn when he showed up at a yearly gala affair with a beautiful blonde on his arm.

"Wow, new car and all," Milburn said, standing at the open bar ordering drinks. Dillard only smiled and walked away.

"Hello, Mrs. Wright, did you receive your package I sent you?" he asked, calling Doris regarding a portrait of her mother she had asked about.

"Yes, Dillard, thank you, and I apologize for not calling. I've been so busy, and thanks again."

"Whew, okay, book closed. That was close."

And after another busy day, Dillard left his office whistling with a box of roses under his arm. This was driving the nosy Milburn crazy. He wanted to know what was new in Dillard's life besides his Benz.

"Hey, Patterson," he yelled, seeing him coming down the steps to the garage.

"Good evening, sir, in a hurry, take care," he said and proceeded to his car and left. Dillard was a man on the move these days. He had a perfect new smile from his recent visit to his cosmetic dentist. His teeth were even and sparkling white. He was also sporting around without those huge glasses covering his face after Lasik surgery. Dillard was remaking himself to be the ultimate bachelor for the Hollywood scene.

"Good morning, Patterson," Milburn stated, walking into his office early the next day. "Just stopped in to see if you wanted to do lunch sometime soon?" he asked. He wanted to know what was going on with Dillard but couldn't get him still or alone long enough to ask.

"Sure, I don't have a problem with that when I get back," he replied.

"Oh, you're taking off somewhere?" Milburn asked, looking around Dillard's office.

"Yes, for about a week or two," Dillard replied.

"Where are you going, pleasure or business?" the nosy Milburn had to ask.

"Going to New York for a week of business and maybe take in a show or two while I'm there," he replied, trying to finish up some documents he was working on.

"Going alone?"

"Milburn, if I knew then I'd be stalked by you someday, I wouldn't have ever become your friend." Dillard laughed. "Look, I will put on my calendar a lunch date for when I return. And now I must finish this document before my client gets here," he said, showing his friend to the door.

"Is that beautiful lady going with you, what's her name anyway?"

Dillard shut the door and Milburn walked off. Dillard shook his head and sat down at his desk and continued on his document. With everything in place, he had made a date with Clinton and Stacy, the fashion divas, for a new wardrobe in New York and things were coming together nicely, he thought sitting at his desk awaiting his client.

CHAPTER 5

TETRA HAD PUT OUT OF her mind the visit that was three months ago now and hope things had smooth themselves over with the children she shared with David, her husband.

"I'm sure things are fine. Billy seems to be really digging deep into the Word," he stated.

"Yes, I'm very happy about that, but I know how busy Satan gets. We will continue to pray for this family as always."

"I know, dear. Tet, did Alfredo tell you the good news?"

"Yes, he did," Tetra replied.

"How do you think Nada will take it?"

"Oh, she's fine with it. As a matter of fact, we discussed Priscilla when she was here visiting."

"Well, good, he seems to be very happy and asked if he could still keep his job as chef."

"Really?" Tetra asked, surprised a bit by her husband's statement.

"Yes, he and Priscilla are buying a house together, so he will be moving," David shared.

"Well, that's good, did they set a date when?" Tetra asked, moving into the kitchen returning the breakfast tray.

"They are discussing it tonight and we will be the first to know," David replied, kissing Tetra and heading out to his office.

"Good morning," her voice said across the phone lines, calling her son at his office.

"Well, good morning, Mother, how are you?"

"I'm wonderful and I hear wonderful in your hello as well," Tetra replied to Billy.

"Mom, things are great and your two girls are doing just fine," he shared, laughing.

"You don't know how glad I am to hear that," Tetra said.

"Now don't you worry about that. I'm allowing God to take care of that matter and that's that!" he shared lovingly with his mom. "So why the call?" he asked.

"Shh, I'm sure he will tell her if he hasn't already, Alfredo has asked Priscilla to marry him."

"Why, that's wonderful, we were talking about them last night. Nada thinks they are cute together."

"Good, my prayers are with them."

"Ours as well," Billy explained.

"And how is the office doing?"

"Mom, things are fine here and that's all I'm going to say. I love you," he said, "just starting my day."

"Love you too, son," she replied, and he disconnected the line.

Billy had now started thinking again about Annie and when he last slept with her. Not that he wanted to think about this, but so many coincidences were coming up and he felt like Denzel in the movie *Out of Time* trying to keep things quiet.

Billy knew they were together after his grandparents' funerals and that was long before Nada. The bowling tournament, but by then, Dana had run her away with her constant visits to his office. That was in September. "So, it was either August or September, I'm thinking," Billy said, sitting at his desk lost in the moment.

"William! Can I get you coffee?" Annie asked, now standing in his office trying to get his attention.

"I'm sorry, just trying to go over some facts of this case," he replied back to her.

"Can I help? Which case is it?" she asked, coming over to lean across his arm by his desk as Nada walked into his office.

"Good morning," she voiced loudly, clearing her throat.

Annie stood up. "Oh, good morning, Nada, how are you?" she said, walking over to embrace a friend. Nada responded back callously, and Annie walked out the door. Billy had stood already as well.

"Good morning, sweetheart, nice to see you," he said.

"Oh, I bet you are!" was Nada's response.

Billy heard it but chose to ignore it. She had been praying constantly, praying to fight that jealous demon. Nada felt so bad after she realized what she had said, she rushed out to the office restroom to cry. Billy composed himself and sat waiting on her return to his office. After about five minutes, Nada stopped by Annie's desk and talked a short time before returning to her husband's office feeling much better, it seemed.

"Honey, I'm sorry, please forgive me, I'm really trying."

Billy stood up and hugged his wife so tight. "What God has joined together." He smiled. Nada felt better and shared with Billy why she had come by. "Nada, that's wonderful, I'm sure your dad will be a happier man in his later years," he replied after being told the news of her dad's pending wedded bliss to Priscilla.

"Annie and I are having lunch today," Nada then replied, waving bye as she left her husband's office.

After Nada had left the building, Billy asked over his intercom system, "Annie, could you please come to my office."

"Just a moment," she said and arranged things on her computer, then went into her boss's office with pen and tablet for notes.

"No, Annie, this is personal, no need for notes." He smiled. "Are you and Keith happy?"

"We are. Why would you ask that?" Annie asked defensively.

"He shared how happy he was to have a child and wanted another, but as of yet, nothing."

"Yes, he was so shocked when I shared with him about Riley. She's the apple of his eye!" she explained with her feelings glowing of joy.

"Shocked?" Billy replied. "Why?"

"Keith was very ill as a child. He had meningitis and it left him infertile. Doctors still left the door open for possibility. So when I conceived, the doctors said it could happen after all those years of him trying to have children and taking all the medicines. Why are you asking all these questions? Is Keith saying something about me?"

"No! You seem very happy and I just want to make sure things with you and he are fine, that's it," he concluded. Billy didn't want to set off a big confusion in any marriage.

"Thanks, William, we are fine and our family is well. What I am having problems with right now is Riley's hair, it's so coarse and wavy unlike mine or Keith's. Keith says she took her hair after his mother's side of the family, they are Greek with heads full of coarse hair, so that will probably be Nada's and my topic of conversation at lunch today." She smiled.

"Thanks, Annie. I'm glad things are well with you," he said, allowing her to leave. Billy returned to his desk not feeling any better after the talk with Annie. If anything, he felt worse and again he locked his door and prayed.

Adele quickly walked down the street and around the corner to the restaurant where she was meeting the investigator Erene James. "Montello's," she said, walking up to the establishment. "Very nice," Adele thought, slowing down as she approached.

"Ms. Hodges?" a young gentleman asked, seeing her approach.

"Yes," Adele replied.

"I'm Erene James, pleased to meet you."

"You as well," Adele shared, a bit surprised he sound so much older on the phone.

He beckoned her to the entrance and they were shown to a table. Erene pulled the chair out to allow Adele to sit down.

"Thank you," Adele said and sat down and started talking, taking pictures and papers from the case she carried.

"Slow down, I have an hour, how about you?" he asked, smiling at her.

"I'm sorry, I really did not want to waste your time and you can get on with your lunch," Adele shared.

"Well, the idea was we would eat and you can answer my questions along with our conversation, very relaxed and not hurried, an hour, I promise you we'll have plenty of time," Erene explained, giving Adele one of his business cards.

She looked a little confused. "You said your name was Aaron, right?"

"Yes, oh, the spelling. I get that all the time, kind of different, I know. But it's pronounced Aaron and spelled E-r-e-n-e." He smiled.

"I like it, it's very unique!" Adele said and relaxed into the moment.

"If you're sure"—putting some of the photographs back in her carrier—"let's order, shall we, and then we can get to business," the young man said, smiling.

Adele looked at the menu that she held up over her face. Erene reached over and slowly pushed it down smiling.

"See anything good?" he asked.

"Yes, this is my favorite restaurant. I eat here often," Adele replied.

"Oh, so why are you covering your face, shy?"

"Sorry, not really," Adele answered, putting the menu down on the table and smiled looking directly at the young man, giving him her undivided attention.

Billy had thought so hard now about Annie and would she keep something like that from him. If she was pregnant, why would she marry Keith? Surely, she would have told him about it despite Dana and her drama. "No, these thoughts are ridiculous, and I rebuke it in the name of Jesus. Nada has been so emotional lately. She cries at the drop of a hat. I have got to resolve this problem before it destroys our marriage and Keith and Annie's too. Lord, help me please," he cried out alone in his office after another long morning.

Nada and Annie had decided to have lunch at Olive Ridge. The salad was very crisp and fresh and endless.

"Let's sit by the window, do you mind?" Nada asked, taking the lead as the waiter gave them a choice of tables.

"That's fine," Annie replied, taking her sit in the chair at the other side of the table. "Nada, how are you and Billy doing?" Annie asked as soon as she sat down.

"We are fine? But why are you asking?"

"Oh, you seemed a bit emotional earlier when you were at the office."

"Oh no, that was about my dad, he has decided to remarry."

"Aren't you glad for him?"

"I am, but it brings a bit of sadness thinking about my mom, that's all."

"I understand, sorry I asked about it," Annie concluded.

"No, but Billy and I are wonderful, and thanks for asking really," Nada replied, looking at the menu.

After both had ordered, Annie asked about suggestions for Riley's hair, making mom talked. Both always shared about their cute little girls—Riley, five years old, and Peyton, two.

"Her hair is so thick and coarse unlike mine, I'm not sure what to do with it most days. I put hair lotion on it, and a few minutes later, it looks like I haven't done anything to it," Annie explained. "My hairdresser wanted to give her a perm. She explained that's what she does to some of her clients when they want to remove some of the curl from their hair."

"Oh really, I know that's true for me, but I never knew it to be true for you." Nada smiled. "But speaking of appointments, I have been a bit under the weather lately, so I've made an appointment with my doctor," Nada shared before taking a bite of her salad.

"Is everything okay?" Annie asked, looking directly at her.

"Yes, I'm sure, but just to keep my husband from worrying, I'm going in."

"I know how that can be, I was late last month, and Keith was telling me the next day to go in and be checked. He really wants another baby before Riley gets older, and she will be in kindergarten when school starts," Annie confessed. "I guess we have something in common after all," Annie said, smiling.

"What, wanting another child? I guess," Nada said.

Both enjoyed lunch and conversation, and Annie headed back to the office while Nada headed to her doctor's appointment.

Dillard was off on his vacation, but that did not stop Milburn from snooping around and asking question of the maids who clean the office space in the building.

"Hello, Helga," Milburn said, seeing her going into Dillard's office.

"Why, hello, Mr. Milburn, how are you?" she asked with a friendly greeting.

"Is Dillard in?" he asked, coming into his office looking around.

"No," she said, slowly looking at Milburn touching things in the office. "I don't think you should be in here," she said, pointing for him to leave.

"Oh, don't worry, I thought Patterson was back from vacation, haven't seen those fancy wheels around this week." He smiled.

"No." And she pointed again.

"All right, see you around, good night, Helga," Milburn said, walking out looking over his shoulder.

"Umm, he so nosy, that one," she blurted out, locking the door after he left out.

When Nada arrived home, she was surprised to see Billy had already picked up Peyton from the day care.

"Honey, I stopped by to get Peyton, was there a problem?" she asked, coming in taking off her jacket and laying it on the chair in the nursery.

"No, I just decided to leave early today and spend time with my daughter and wife." He smiled, getting up to kiss her. Billy had anticipated how things would go after Nada came home from having lunch earlier with Annie. Somehow lately those meetings resulted in drama and questions, so he had braced himself and prayed.

Here goes, he thought. How was lunch? he asked.

Nada smiled. "Lunch was great, you know, the usual. We talked about the girls and you and Keith."

"Really, you two can't find anything else to spend girl time on except us?" He smiled questioning.

"It really was kind of rushed today."

"Oh?" Billy asked.

"I had to leave."

"Why, dear, what happened?"

She smiled and walked around the room and stood by Peyton's bed. She was down for her nap and Nada looked down on her tenderly. Billy walked over to her and braced for what he didn't know. "We are having another baby," she said crying.

"Oh my, so that was the moods and all the crying for the past few weeks. Thank you, Lord," he said, running to share it with his staff over the phone after kissing his wife passionately.

She was happy as well and sat down to call her dad and the in-laws with the good news.

Stacy and Clinton, the fashion gurus, had worked their magic on Dillard Patterson all week long, and he had found a swagger Clinton had shared with him. He thanked them for their help with his wardrobe and new 'do. He visited a few of New York's sites with a friend for two days before boarding his flight back to Los Angeles.

"I can't believe you actually did it. You look ten years younger," his female friend expressed, sitting beside him on the plane.

"This is going to blow Milburn's mind," Dillard shared, holding his woman friend's hand, smiling. "I do look good if I say so myself."

"Yes, you do, and very confident. I knew you could do it."

"For you, anything," he said, looking at her sitting next to him waiting for an approval.

"Sure, sure, Dillard," she replied, still looking away out of the window.

This woman who had mysteriously came into Dillard's life and brought new life to him along with a new house, new Benz, Lasik surgery, beautiful perfect teeth, and a new wardrobe. Everyone was buzzing about them when they showed up at the yearly gala. But now, after these changes, what will they say? But he was ready. "Quiet Milburn and I'm home free," he said, riding now down the freeway to Brentwood where he and his new friend both now lived together.

After sharing the news with everyone that mattered to her in Washington State, Nada went to her husband's home office.

"Come here, dear," he said, seeing her come into the room. "I am the happiest man alive right now!" He smiled, holding her tightly in his arms.

"Oh, William, I am too. I'm sorry I have been such a pain these last few weeks," Nada shared.

"It's all worth it," he replied, kissing her and rubbing her tummy, which had not at all started to bulge.

"William, do you think we will have a boy or another girl?" she asked, now sitting on his lap.

"Oh wow, hadn't given it much thought really, just getting myself prepared for less sleep," he said, laughing, then shared an agreeing laugh with his wife.

"Annie said she and Keith have been trying too. I hope they get theirs before Riley gets older so they can grow up together."

"Yes, I missed that when I was growing up," Billy replied. "I grew up an only child."

"Peyton has your hair and skin color, maybe this one will look more like me," Nada mentioned.

"I doubt it. I have a very strong gene, and he or she will look like me," he said, parading around proudly.

"Whatever?" Nada said, slapping him on his chest.

"Dante is calling us for dinner," he said, heading to the nursery to check Peyton before going off to the dining room that the staff had surprised Nada with a celebration for the good news. William stood smiling as well.

CHAPTER 6

DILLARD HAD INVITED MILBURN OUT to lunch as promised and was meeting him at an eatery near the law office. Larvy Milburn hadn't yet seen Dillard's new look since he returned from New York. He hurried along to the restaurant wanting in on all the latest gossip and questions he wanted to know from Dillard. He had noticed Dillard's new Benz, new date, and now a new look Dillard had shared with him when he called. So many questions were going through his mind, and of course, he most certainly wanted to know about the lady Dillard had taken to the yearly function that he never saw coming!

"Hello, Milburn," Dillard said, seeing him come into the restaurant. Dillard held out his hand to greet the surprised Milburn.

"Dillard! Man, you look great. Really, I know we are in Hollywood, but you look like a million bucks, how did you do that?" Milburn was speaking so loudly they were drawing onlookers and Dillard was feeling a bit out of place.

"Our table please?" he asked the waiter who was willing to escort them to a table and from the middle of the floor in the posh establishment. Milburn was still asking questions as they were being seated. "Thank you, please bring two glasses of your best house wine," Dillard requested, sending the waiter off and giving himself some breathing room.

"Does she like it?"

"Does who like what?" Dillard asked Milburn who was looking aside of his head.

"You know, your lady, the one you took to the dance?"

"Yes, she does approve," Dillard replied.

"And does she have a name?" Milburn questioned.

"Yes," Dillard said as their waiter brought the glasses and poured the wine. "Thank you," Dillard said, and a few minutes and again the waiter was gone.

"Well, well?" Milburn tapped his arm, wanting a name.

"Milburn, is that why you wanted to come to lunch with me?"

"Umm, no, not really, but—"

"Okay, Milburn, listen, we are going to order, and I don't want to talk about my relationship with you, okay, anything else is fair game, maybe."

Milburn jerked his head back as if insulted about Dillard's statement. Then he smiled. "Okay, sorry I came on so strong," he said, extending his hand to Dillard across the table.

"Now, how did that case you had regarding that dog come out?" Dillard asked, trying to change the subject slightly.

"Ahhh, oh that was an interesting case, the plaintiff didn't want his pet put down," Milburn replied. "But we had him dead to right."

"Well, that's good, you said the defendant was injured pretty bad."

"Yes, my client had to be hospitalized from the bites he ensued from the vicious animal. So how was New York?" Milburn hurriedly asked as the waiter brought their entrées to the table.

"New York is always a nice time. I go there at least three or four times a year including News Year's," Dillard replied.

"Really, I haven't been there with her yet, my wife, that is. She's always talking about going. When I become as successful as you are, that will be our first trip," Milburn said, smiling. Milburn had been in Los Angeles about ten years and had landed him an executive job. He was an attorney in a law firm in the building where Dillard's successful office was located. Dillard was what you considered an attorney to the stars. So, for him to get a new Benz or anything else for that matter wasn't alarming, but it was certainly out of character for him. Dillard was usually very quiet, had his vintage '98 Benz, he being the original owner, own a condominium in an upscale neighbor in Brentwood, but very low-key and socialized when necessary. Now he was dressing nicer and socializing at big events, new automobile and home, and turning the heads of a few of the women in the building as well these days.

"Milburn, I'm sure you will be just fine."

"So when am I going to be invited to see your new home?" Milburn asked, putting a last bite into his mouth.

"I'll be having something there soon and I'll be sure to invite you and the missus," Dillard replied.

"Well, I guess that's the answer I'll have to accept for now." Milburn sighed. "Are you living alone?"

"Yes," Dillard replied, pouring now a cup of coffee to aid in his drive back to the office after his glass of wine for lunch. He had sat and listened to all of Milburn's past life and probably everything happening in it now. "Milburn, do you think your wife wants you letting me know all that about her, after all, I have never met her longer than five or ten minutes," Dillard stated.

"What? Oh, that's nothing, she talks more than I do," he replied, wiping his mouth with the cloth napkin. "Somehow Caucasians don't mind telling all their business to anyone."

I think you know as much as I care to share about me," Dillard concluded.

"I'll still be looking out, but thanks for the lunch and conversation," Milburn replied with both getting up after the waiter returned Dillard's card and with a signature on the line stood up to leave the restaurant.

Adele sat anxiously at home waiting for Erene, the investigator, to bring her some news regarding her mother. It had been several months and lots of meetings and she had really started to worry that they would never see Rhea Hodges again. She paced across the floor, nervously looking out of the window. Truth be told, she had been thinking a lot about Erene. He was nice-looking, kind of Barry Manilow type by his nose. Tall with brown stylist-cut hair and a smile she thought melted butter.

"But stop daydreaming, Adele, he will be here soon and you have got to settle down," she kept telling herself. "Knowing Attorney Parker, he probably thinks I need a man in my life and sent Erene. Oh stop it, Adele," she repeated, seeing the car pull up to the curve and park. She watched his every move from opening the door to the ring of her doorbell, which frightened her because she was so mesmerized by his every move coming up to the house. Snapping back to reality, she stood counting to ten before she answered the door.

"Erene, do come in, I'm hoping you have good news for me." She smiled, connecting his handshake and returned smile.

"I do," he said, "and if we hurry and if you have time, I'd like to go over there with you to confirm that it is truly her."

"Really! That's not a problem. Where are we going?" Adele asked, gathering her purse and coat hurriedly, smiling from the good news of finding her mother.

Erene stood at the door, and Adele gave him a look, "Let's go," grabbing the doorknob with key in hand and asked, "Where did you find her?"

"Downtown Portland," Erene replied.

"Are you kidding? I'm downtown all the time. Why have I never seen her?" she asked with Erene opening the car door as Adele's questionings just kept coming. "Where?"

"Well, today she was on Congress Street," he replied again.

"Congress Street, what was she doing there? That street is so busy all the time. How did you find her?" Adele asked.

"Wasn't easy, Adele, I asked lots of questions and I'm hoping I'm right about this being her."

"I gave you pictures," Adele said, fearing this trip was all for naught.

"I know, Adele, but people change," he said caringly. Erene had worked at this for years helping families find their loved ones and knowing the person they remember is usually far gone from the one he finds on the street. He drove along answering what he could and keeping Adele's hopes alive.

"How do you know she will still be where you saw her? Was she alone?"

Erene said nothing. He was silent. When he came upon her earlier that morning, Rhea Hodges was lying in a doorway wrapped in an old blanket. She looked to not be moving any time soon and it appeared to be the place a few of the street people used for shelter. Finding a park, he stopped the car.

"Do you see her?" Adele asked.

Erene caught her hand. "Brace yourself, Adele, this isn't a pleasant thing we are about to encounter. You are aware your mother had problems, right?" She nodded sadly. "So you are here to hopefully make things right again, do you understand? Okay?" He came around to her side of the car and they walked along Canal Street. Erene held her hand and squeezed it gently every time she started to ask questions. Two blocks down from the car and as business started to dilapidate, Adele started to get the full picture Erene was trying to carefully share with her.

And just as he thought some of the street people had left and as they walked closer up, Rhea was getting ready to start her day as well. Wrapping up her old blanket, she turned to look at Adele when she heard, "Mama?" Her once-beautiful hair was matted and dirty. Her teeth were almost gone, and "Lord, have mercy," Adele thought, she certainly hadn't bathe since the last time she saw her.

"Ariel?" she asked.

"No, Mama, it's Adele," she said.

Rhea stood as if going over things in her head. Her friend looked on, straightening up his worn-out, torn clothes.

"We's friends, been out here together bout fo months now, gon git us a place to live soon," he added, putting the blanket in the old store buggy used to transport things around.

Rhea smiled. "Malcolm, Ariel, Adele, Hanson, Riggins, and Fletcher, and you're Adele," she said.

"Yes, Mama."

"Gemme a cigarette," she asked.

"I don't have a cigarette, Rhea." Erene squeezed Adele's hand. She sighed. "Okay, let's go home, Rhea."

"Home? I have a home? I told you, Herbert, I already have a home."

"Is I coming wit yall?" he asked. "We's friends."

Adele stayed with the couple, and Erene went back and got the car. After loading the buggy in the trunk, they drove to a shelter and left Herbert and his buggy of things he couldn't part with and he cried as he said good-bye to his friend.

"Did you leave my books in the car?"

"Yeah, Rhea, where is you going?" Herbert asked.

Rhea was going home with her daughter again. Herbert looked to be younger than Rhea but was on some type of drugs for a long time, it seemed, that made him look old and bony!

"Good morning, Keith," Billy said, walking into the office. "Hello, that case yesterday got pretty heated, the jury is sequestered and not at all happy to be there another three weeks at least."

"Really, wow."

"New evidence came in and they have to go through it."

"That's always fun," Billy said sarcastically. "Keith, I'm sure by now you have heard the news."

"Oh, about you and Nada having another baby? That's all Annie has talked about."

"And . . .," Billy said, looking at him.

"Man, I try every chance I get, believe me, but nothing yet, made an appoint with my doctor soon. If it happened once, it can happen again, right?" Keith said, leaving. "I'm heading back to court, Annie is in at nine."

"Okay, have a good one," Billy replied, going to his desk to start work. Billy put in a call to his best friend Glenn in Florida.

"Hello, Uncle Glen," he greeted, laughing."

"Naw, really, congrats, man. Are we trying for another son?" he asked with a smile.

"Healthy will do the trick, just healthy," Billy replied. "How are you doing?" Billy then asked.

"Much better, I have learned to accept that this is my life and where God wants or needs me, and surprisingly enough, it's not bad being in this chair. You know the last time we spoke I shared with you that I had found a church to go to here in Daytona. I was down with Mom and Dad a week ago."

"Oh, I bet that brought joy to your mom," Billy said.

"I'm sure it did. Dad too, but he'd never say it to me but he showed it a lot," Glenn smiled sharing. "I've even met a cute nurse about four months ago." He laughed.

Billy thought about how great it was to hear his friend's laughter again. He was his old self and it lightened Billy's heart to be sharing with him at this moment. "Still chasing those nurses around the hospital?"

"No, we actually met in the produce department at the grocery store, go figure. She helped me pick out lettuce greens for a salad I shared with her I was trying to make."

"And?"

"And she came with me to my family's church service, and again the next night, we had a wonderful conversation over dinner, I even shared the book with her." He laughed.

"You did what? Man, I'm so proud of you," Billy replied.

"If and when I say I do again, I want to be armed with all the ammo that's available starting there," Glenn added.

"God bless you, man, and we'll talk again soon, someone's in my door and I have a busy day ahead."

"Take care, I understand, and congrats again," Glenn voiced, disconnecting the phone.

"Dillard, you are a very handsome bachelor," his houseguest said, walking toward him.

"Why, thank you. I admit I have found my swagger," he teased back.

"Sit, please sit down," she said, heading to the den sofa taking a chair to talk. Dillard sat over in a chair with his legs crossed. "Oh, Dillard, it's not that serious. I just want to say thank you for all the help you are giving me."

"Well, you're welcome," he replied. "But look at me, look what you've done for me. I came from nerd to the most eligible bachelor in Los Angeles, so thank you," he shared smiling.

"Okay, I accept that." She smiled.

"Look, I need something to call you besides friend, a name would be nice," he asked, looking into her beautiful eyes.

"Katia! That's it, call me Katia like the hurricane," she suggested.

"Are you kidding?" he asked.

"No, that's perfect, it's something you will remember, right?"

"Oh yeah, I'll remember that," Dillard said, walking off. Dillard was helping his friend find a new life. He often remembers the night he flew out to another state to get her and bring her back with him. He had moved into a new home she had persuaded him to purchase and was willing to play along with her until she felt the time was right. He would have a hard job trying to keep it from Milburn always coming around the old place and nosing around. But his new home was much farther out on a very quiet but spacious parcel of land. Relieved, he sighed, "Hollywood," his guest wore heavy makeup and beautiful blond hair, and her blue contact eyes were the best Hollywood had to offer. *And* now he's calling her Katia. What some people won't do for money, he thought going into his bedroom.

"Keith has been going to the doctor again," Annie said to Nada as they sat down for their weekly lunch together.

"Really! So, is there good news? I mean, you know, are things okay?" Nada questioned.

"Well, he has been asking about Riley?" Annie replied.

"What?" Nada asked, curiously looking at Annie and putting salad into her mouth at the same time.

"I got pregnant so fast with Riley, but Keith and I were very into each other when we got together. I mean we spent a lot of time together before I got pregnant with Riley."

"Oh, I understood you all married rather quickly, were you pregnant before he asked you?" Nada asked, and Annie didn't seem to mind the questions.

"Keith and I had been together for three weeks when I found out I was pregnant with Riley and he did the right thing, he said, and married me to make me an honest woman, and I love him for it," she said sincerely.

"So why is he questioning it now, did something happen?"

"No, he is just frustrated that we have been trying for another one before Riley gets older, you know, so they can grow up together and play together, but he is still shooting blanks, he says," Annie explained.

Nada had gotten silent. She was thinking about an earlier conversation with her husband, Billy.

"Nada? Nada? Hey, you okay?" Annie asked, touching her hand across the table.

"Yeah, yes, I'm fine, little distracted, I guess. So, I hope things work out for you and Keith," Nada shared.

"Thanks, me too," Annie replied, eating her desert.

"So is Keith thinking you lied to him, you know, not telling him you were pregnant before you slept with him?" Nada squeamishly asked, drinking her juice.

"Oh no, nothing like that, I was dating someone else before Keith, and believe me, if I were pregnant, I would know," Annie replied naively without even giving thought to whom she was replying to.

"I would hope that's not the case," Nada stated, looking directly at Annie. "Because William is not Riley's father, and if that's where you're going, you had better change your tune!"

"No, Nada, I'm sorry, that's not what I'm implying. Keith and I are very happy with Riley. He knows she is his, the doctor shared with him a lot of things factor into having a baby. Some couples try too hard, others don't conceive until after they adopt and get relaxed with a child. His doctor explained about us getting together and how he had longed to be with me, so everything was right, and it happened!"

"Oh, it's time anyway, I have to get over to the day care and get Peyton," Nada said, getting up from the table.

"Nada, I'm sorry if I said something to disturb you," Annie shared, seeing Nada's demeanor now.

"No, William and I are very pleased with our children, we're fine and hope you are too. Lord, have mercy," Nada mumbled under her voice as she walked out of the restaurant.

Their usually hug was left out of this meeting.

"See you soon," Annie yelled as the two went their separate ways.

Adele had been e-mailing Erene and had thanked him over and over for finding Rhea, her mother. She sat in her office wondering if he still had lunch at that restaurant where he used to meet her. "I think I'll just go by and let him know how things are going," she thought, inputting data into her computer. Rhea was doing better.

She had only been with Adele now for two months but she looked amazing.

Ring!

"Social Services, Adele Hodges speaking."

"Adele, Rhea."

"Yes, Mother, how are you?"

"I'm good, but I want to get out today if it's okay with you?"

"Out, where?"

"I'd like to go see Herbert."

"Rhea, do you think that's a good idea? Remember we talked about this. He's not good for you."

"He has got him a place and said he's clean now," Rhea pleaded.

"Rhea, please, I can't get away now, but we can talk about it when I get home okay?" *Buzzzzz.* The phone was hung up and Adele hurried from her desk heading home. "Adele! Where is the fire?" a coworker asked.

"Just heading home for lunch, see you all in an hour." Without stopping, she was gone.

Adele arrived home to find Herbert sitting in her living room. She was livid but walked in her bedroom counting to ten over and over again. She went in the refrigerator and made a sandwich from the roast beef from the night before. Adele sat down in her dining room.

"Hello, Miss," Herbert said, standing to greet her.

"Oh, hello, sorry, I'm in a hurry, how are you?" she said, remembering all the things Erene had shared with her about dealing with addicts.

"I'm here to see Rhea, take hu to dinna, and to let hu see my place."

"Oh so soon. Did you find a job?"

"Ahhh, sort a, a friend of my from a way back hooked me up," Herbert replied. "We been friends a long time. He sho likes Rhea, says she so pretty."

"I really don't think this is a good time for Rhea to go out," Adele said nervously.

"Why she grown, ain't she? Rhea and I got plans tonight," he replied, giving Adele lots of attitude.

"What plans, Rhea?" Rhea walked in all dressed up. She was a beautiful woman even with all her teeth practically gone.

"Oh, baby, don't you look hot!" Herbert said, coming over hugging her and twirling her around.

"I'll be back tonight. Herb, I'll get my coat." And he tipped his brim, accenting the long knee-length wool coat and matching plaid pants, and headed toward the front door.

"Adele, I'll see you tonight, but don't wait up, it will probably be late."

Tears ran down Adele's face. She was sad and mad, but mostly angry about this man's hold on her mother. Rhea came over to hug her before she left. Adele pleaded again with her not to leave but to no avail. Herbert was now honking the car's horn of the lowrider he said he borrowed from his friend now pulling off from the curve with Rhea all gums smiling on the passenger side. Adele wasn't happy at all.

Needless to say, Nada was not in a good mood when Billy arrived home. She had stopped by the university to let them know she would fill in where needed but still wasn't sure of full-time employment. Nada traveled a lot with her husband and loved her mommy role.

"Hello, dear," Billy replied, coming into the nursery where Nada sat on the floor playing dollhouse with Peyton.

"Hi," she said, looking up to kiss her husband's lips as always.

"You sound down, is everything okay with you and the baby?" he asked, reaching to hold her hand and rub her tummy. "Physically I'm fine, had lunch with Annie today."

Billy sighed. "What now? The drama has got to stop. It's not good for you or our baby."

"Look, Daddy, Mommy and I bought a new blanket for my little baby today," Peyton shared, disrupting the conversation.

"Why, that's a pretty yellow blanket and so soft too."

"Yep," Peyton responded and ran out to meet Millicent passing the hallway door.

Billy helped Nada from the floor. Nada walked over to the door looking for Peyton.

"Millie!" she called out.

"I have her, we're going to the garden if it's okay," Millicent responded.

"Fine, thanks," she said, turning her attention back to her husband. "Annie was saying she got pregnant soon after meeting Keith and I asked her if she was sure it was his."

"Why? Nada, don't you trust me? Have mercy," Billy muttered, moving across the room.

"She has been saying Keith had problems in the past and they have been trying with no results and you and she were together before they dated or married," Nada voiced, ringing her hands over and over nervously.

"I thought this had all passed," Billy said, moving around the room. "I'm tired of it and I don't know what to do anymore, that child is not mine!" He had raised his voice and Millicent came and stood in the door.

"Millicent, we're fine," Nada said, looking back at her.

"Oh, dinner is served," she said and walked away.

"Honey, I'm so sorry, please help me get through this, my hormones and pregnancy seems to be leaving me very vulnerable to all these rumors and I can't stand it anymore either," Nada shared, walking over to be wrapped in Billy's arms to cry.

Alfredo François, Nada's father, and Priscilla had decided to marry right away. The two had been dating for about six months after meeting at Mount Nebo, the home church in Washington State, but had known each other about two years. It was not the first marriage for either him or Priscilla, and both wanted a small ceremony at their church with few close friends.

"Perfect timing," Billy thought after Nada shared the date the couple had decided on. "Nada, are the bags packed? Dante will help me get them to the car," he explained, preparing to walk out to the car with the family's luggage. He was looking for a getaway from all the office drama, so the flight to Washington for Nada's father's big day was a God-sent. Peyton was running around playing with the staff while her parents were making sure everything for the trip was now put into the car before heading to the airport. Millicent had picked Peyton up and kissed her good-bye and handed her to her dad as the family all got into the car with Dante, Millicent, and the other staff waving good-bye.

"It will be about seven p.m. when we get there tonight, you call your mother to let her know?" Nada asked William sitting now on the plane. Peyton was asleep for now in her own seat. "Well, tomorrow is Dad's day, and I wish him nothing but happiness," Nada voiced before reclining her seat for the flight to Washington.

The church was decorated beautifully for the wedding vows that were to be officiated by Pastor Edinburg, one of the pastors on staff. Alfredo was dressed in a black tuxedo, and Priscilla had chosen an off-white satin gown for her nuptials to be shared in. Neither wanted a big fanfare with a lot of hoopla; they just wanted to be together and share the life both had left yet to live. Priscilla had her daughter and her daughter's husband and grandchildren coming to be by her side. Her son had also made the trip, thus the reason for the date. He was home on leave from serving in Afghanistan and looked forward to the couple's wedding. He had chosen the military as his career and had devoted his life to it after enlisting out of college. Everyone was gathering together for a wonderful time of friends and family. Tetra and David were hosting the reception at their home after the ceremony, and right now, the church was buzzing with delight.

"Stop running please," Priscilla's daughter yelled to her two children running around chasing each other.

"Hello, Lieutenant," William said, coming up to the tall soldier in uniform.

"Why, hello there, sir, and you are?" he asked with a smile as big as Texas.

"William Parker. I'm Nada François Parker's husband." He laughed.

"Now that's a mouthful," he teased back, "but it is a pleasure to meet you."

"I wanted to take this opportunity to thank you for your service to our country," William said, shaking the lieutenant's hand.

"Why, thank you, and may I ask your profession?"

"I'm a lawyer, sir."

"Well, thank you for your service as well. I had the pleasure of speaking to Mr. François several times, and I must say, my mom's marrying into good company," he shared.

"Yes, Mr. François is a very nice man and I'm sure he will make your mom happy."

As the guys stood talking, Nada walked up.

"And this is my wife, Nada."

"Pleased to meet you, Lieutenant," she said, extending her hand.

"Let's see, don't tell me you are a professor?" He smiled.

"No, I used to be, before I became a wife and mommy of two," Nada said, looking at the lieutenant's puzzled look. "You're right in what you heard, I decided to be a stay-at-home mom and loving wife to my hardworking husband." She smiled.

"I understand," he said, looking down to play with Peyton who had come up standing by her dad's leg.

"I own my law firm, and it was Nada's choice to put her career on hold until our children are older," William explained.

"I am just amazed at the two of you, you complement each other beautifully. I'm still looking, but it doesn't seem to be in the cards for me. I'm married to Uncle Sam, been in since I was twenty-two years old, can't find one who understands the sacrifice it takes," he added, a bit sadden as he confessed.

William gave him his business card, and Nada hugged the soldier as all went to find their seats. The vows were beautifully performed with all the children being introduced to the wedding guest during the ceremony. Nada was teary-eyed as her dad recited the vows to Priscilla and pledged to love and cherish her until death. She stood thinking of her mother who had passed away. "He is a good dad and was a loving husband to my mom, and I wish him only happiness!" She stood crying tears of joy.

The reception was lighthearted, fun, and filled with love. Everyone was hugging, sharing, and laughing together. Tetra had decorated her home beautifully for the day with lots of flowers, glitz, satin, and lace. She knew Priscilla didn't want anything too big, but she did give the reigns to Tetra Parker. Priscilla was a shy, quiet woman who had retired after working as a secretary for the school district and was just glad to find someone to spend her days with. But she thanked the Parkers for making their day so special and welcoming her family into their home.

"Photographs, photographs," David Michael said, gathering everyone together in the family room. "Okay, move to this side, wait, wait, you're shorter, get on this side, come here, okay, put her on your knee, okay, I think we got it. OKAY 1-2-3 CHEESE!"

CHAPTER 7

KATIA SAT WAITING FOR DILLARD to return home from work. She was so glad she had him as a friend. She had gotten herself into a mess and needed his help. He had helped her through a really tough time in her life and she was so indebted to him for it. She *always* said it to him personally that she wanted the best for him. They had met each other a long time ago and were associates for a very long time, so she knew him very well. Katia was always on him to update himself, change his wardrobe, and certainly get an automobile to reflect a successful Hollywood lawyer. So now that she had moved in, she suggested all the changes quickly if he was going to help her through this problem. Standing in the home's beautiful foyer with tall vaulted ceilings and a gorgeous large crystal chandelier welcoming you in, she saw Dillard coming through the magnificent stained glass window of the front door.

"Sylvie Lagger called, says she works at the courthouse?" she stated before sitting down to dinner with Dillard.

"Yes, oh really," he said, smiling. "I met her the other day, so she called, huh? Well, truth be told, I've had my eyes on her for a while, she finally called, cool." He smiled, shaking his head. "It's obvious the new look is working." Katia had created a monster! He already had great personality, gentlemanly qualities, and money. The only thing that was lacking in Dillard was his wardrobe, those hideous glasses, and his vintage though clean car. To help her, he had changed it all, and he had started enjoying the benefits. He and Katia were not an item. She had no romantic or love interest in Dillard, but she desperately needed his help in this matter. So, she played the role, having no one else to turn to. He had been a past friend and knew exactly what she wanted from this arrangement.

An hour or so later after dinner, "So you think she's got potential, she's your type, I mean?" Katia asked, now walking into the parlor room with its beautiful tucked furnishings, holding a glass of wine.

Dillard followed, picking up the conversation regarding Miss Lagger. "Well, sure, I always need a date for something, who knows, it may turn into a love connection," the suave attorney replied, sipping his expensive wine brought up earlier by Katia from the wine cellar of their home.

"Dillard, I'm thinking about going out for a bit tomorrow."

"Really, do you need me?" he asked.

She had not ventured out very far since coming to Los Angeles, not by herself anyway. She had a lot on her plate that took years to clear up. Dillard had worked hard getting things set in place making sure she had covered all the past things legally and she was rewarding him for all his efforts.

"No, I'm going to go shopping, and no, I really don't want to be rushed." She smiled.

"Okay, throw me to the curve," he joked.

"I don't think any woman will ever do that to you again," Katia replied, smiling. "I think you are kinda hot myself," she teased.

Dillard only smiled sitting by the fire, drinking his wine with his houseguest Katia now leaving the room.

The trip to Washington for the wedding was a good break from the office staff, Billy thought, coming out of his office looking around.

"Keith, you're rushing out without saying so long," Billy stated, coming from his office with Keith standing by the elevator.

"Yes, looked in, you looked so busy, I didn't want to disturb you," he replied.

"Oh, I understand, have a good evening," Billy said, going back into his office. Truth is, Keith had been avoiding him lately. Could be he didn't want to be reminded about the baby he and Annie were trying to have, Billy reasoned and chalked it up to that.

Billy asked Dante to please serve dinner outside. "It looks to be a beautiful evening," he requested calling home.

"That's a wonderful idea, do you remember David Michael is flying in today, he is coming to town."

"Oh my, I forgot! I really forgot!" he said, grabbing papers and putting them into his file folders then into his briefcase. "Okay, honey, I'll be out of here in ten minutes tops," he shared, rushing to get off the phone.

"See you soon, drive carefully," Nada said, disconnecting the line.

Nada had, for the most part, put her thoughts of Annie behind her, though every time she spoke with Madison, her best friend, it all came flooding back. Annie was not ever mentioned in their later conversations, but the seed had been planted, and despite prayer, it was growing. She and Billy were so happy with their good news of having another little one to share their love with Peyton, their beautiful little daughter. Nada was also even happier these days because Keith decided that he or Annie would be there to pick up their daughter, Riley, and offered to get Peyton if needed. "We are fine for now," she explained, "but I'll keep you on the list," she remembered smiling.

That night, Billy, Nada, and Peyton enjoyed a wonderful dinner outdoors under the stars. David Michael was the most loving big brother a little sister could have, explaining to her all the stars she took time to ask about with her limited words. "And that one . . ."

David Michael always enjoyed his visits to Maine with his dad, William Parker. He loved seeing his uncle Justin as well, and they usually spent men time together when he came in to visit from California.

Riding back after leaving Justin's condo and a game of golf, David Michael asked, "Dad, you know, after Dana died, I thought I would be torn to pieces for a longer time," he shared.

"Oh, son, I could only imagine, I have lost dear friends and was very devastated by it, you have done well," Billy replied.

"I had you and Grandpa and Grandmother, not to mention that Bible I received."

"Oh that, I remember you telling me about that right before Peyton, your sister, was born. That's funny, son, I had given your mother three bibles, doing our time together, though your mother sent me a really old bible when I was dating Jillian. It was the one I had given her in elementary school."

"Really," David Michael said, thinking about the one he had shared about though his dad never saw it.

"Do you still have it, Dad?" he then asked.

"Yes, I kept it, it was her way of telling me she was all right even though I didn't know where she was, she later told me. That was how Dana's mind worked, son."

They drove on talking about life and Dana. David Michael was in his last year of college at UCLA and had a promising career in baseball. Pulling up into the driveway, he asked, "Dad, if you don't mind, may I see the Bible you have? I find so much comfort in reading the one that was sent me. I could only imagine what feelings yours hold."

"Wow, it's been a while, I keep it on the shelf in my home office. I'll share it with you," he said, walking in smiling with his son into the large estate, his home.

Peyton heard them coming in and ran to her dad, allowing him to pick her up in his waiting arms. He embraced her and gave her a big kiss. "How is my little princess?" he asked, embracing her smiling. She laughed, throwing her head back, pleased with her daddy's jesters.

"Hi, sweetie," her brother, David Michael, shared, kissing her little hand while still in her daddy's arm.

Nada sat in the dayroom hearing them come in with lots of laughter and smiles. "How was the game?"

"Very good. David's game has improved, he almost beat me," William said, sharing a kiss with his wife.

Peyton was now down and off running to play with her toys in another part of the spacious room.

"Uncle Justin did well until the cart girl came by, his mind left with her." David laughed.

"Not to mention he tried to buy everything from the cart," William added. "What's for lunch?" he then asked Nada.

"Let me go and see. I left it up to the staff today. I'll see what Dante came up with while you head to the shower." Nada secured

Peyton, and Billy and his son headed down the hallway stopping in his office.

"It is right here," Billy said, reaching for the book. "Umm wait, I know, I put it here myself." He looked and looked, becoming frustrated. "Millicent! Millicent," he yelled into the wall's intercom.

Everyone came except Millicent. "She's off today, sir," two of the other housekeepers replied.

"Who dust's my office?" he then asked.

"We all do, sir." They didn't know what was going on but they knew this was out of character for Mr. Parker.

"I had a very important book here and now I can't seem to find it," he shared, clearly upset by it. All staff present was looking at each other and shaking their heads, a bit afraid for not knowing what has happened to this important book. Then up walked Dante, his head chef, standing next to Nada.

"Mr. Parker, I think that devil woman took the book when she came through terrorizing the house!"

"WHAT! Dante, are you sure?" he said, looking at David Michael in disbelief.

"Yes, I'm sure, when you and Miss Nada left, you know before you were married. She came looking for you, yelling your name from room to room and I asked her to leave because you were not home. She went into your study and pulled several books from the shelf, leaving them on the floor. I cleaned them up, but I don't know she had taken one or what was in her hand when she stormed out the door leaving with a bang! Sorry, Mr. David," he said, lifting his shoulders and walking off with his head down saddened.

"Not your fault," Billy replied, "you couldn't have stopped her anyway."

"Thanks, Mr. Parker," Dante replied, returning to the kitchen to finish preparing lunch.

Nada said nothing but was relieved that anything about Dana had left her home, hopefully for good!

"Hello, Dad, I sent you those pictures of the book on your phone you asked for."

"I'm sure this is your old bible, which was sent to me," David Michael said, calling now after returning home from his visit in Maine with his dad.

"Hold on, son, I'm pulling them up now. How was the flight?" Billy asked, waiting for his cell phone to open the pic's section viewing the photos.

"Usual not bad," David Michael replied. "I did see Jace, Sonjee's pilot friend."

"Really, are they still dating?"

"Not of late, and Sonjee isn't talking about it to me anyway."

"Okay, son, I looked at the pictures, and yes, that's it. What are you going to do with it?" Billy asked.

"Dad, I'd like to keep it if you don't mind," he said, pausing for a response. "Not sure who sent it, though knowing Dana, she had prepared for me to have it if something happened to her."

"Son, you are probably right, unfortunately we know where she is now," he shared sadly.

"Yes, I hear you. I will treasure it just for that reason," David replied.

"Well, son, I'm glad that part of your mother had a happy ending. The book is where she wanted it to be. With someone who loved her dearly."

"Thanks, Dad, we will talk again soon."

Adele looked so tired coming into her office on Monday morning.

"Good morning, Adele," her coworker said, seeing her sitting at the desk staring into space.

"Oh, morning, Hilary," Adele said.

"Need some coffee? Just made a fresh pot," Hilary explained.

"I do, thanks."

Hilary headed to the break room to get the coffee, pouring Adele a large cup from her desk. Adele had been up waiting another night for her mother to come home. Rhea had caused her nothing but worry and heartache since she found her on the streets again and brought her back home. There were some good days she'd admit, though of late, most days and nights kept her up worrying about if she would ever see her again. The lifestyle Rhea had chosen was winning despite all of Adele's efforts to help her.

"Thanks, Hilary, just another late night," she said. Most of her coworkers in her office knew her pain and sympathized with her plight.

Ring, ring. Her phone was ringing, and another workday had started.

"Hello, Social Services." She smiled, waving to Hilary leaving.

"Adele? Yes, this is Adele Hodges."

"Erene. How are you?"

Adele swallowed hard, surprised by the call. "I'm doing okay, Erene, is there something you have to tell me?" she then asked quickly?.

"Oh no, I was just checking in to see how things were going with your mother."

Adele let out a big sigh of relief. Her first instinct was to say, "Fine," but she wasn't fine, especially not today. "I am tired, she sighed.

"Oh, Adele, is it your mother?" he then asked. "I believe you if you say yes, and I was wondering about it, so things aren't getting better?" Erene asked.

"When she's home, yes, but I can't hold her hand all the time. I'd love to be able to, but I just can't!" Adele replied. "Erene, I'm sorry you caught me at a bad time, let's talk later, I've got to go," she said, starting to hang up the line.

"Wait, wait," she could hear him saying very loudly even though the phone was not up to her ear.

Adele slowly put the phone to her ear.

"Lunch, Adele, we can talk, please," he pleaded.

"Okay," and she hung up the phone.

Ring, ring.

"Good morning, Social Services, Adele Hodges."

"Montello's, twelve o'clock." And the line went *buzzzzzzzz.*

"Good morning, Aunt Doris," David Michael said, coming into her office at the chic boutique.

"Why, hello, David, so glad to see you. Are you shopping for someone?" she said, smiling embracing her nephew.

"Actually, Kara is shopping, I just stopped in so I won't be accused of rushing her with her purchases," he shared, smiling.

"I know how that can be," Doris said, "have a seat."

"Dad says hello, by the way, I was down visiting with him last week."

"Well, that's great, please send a hello back, how are they doing?"

"They are good, expecting a new baby."

"Oh really, that's wonderful. Your dad seems to finally found happiness," Doris stated.

"Yes, I think so. He and Nada seemed to be very good for each other and I absolutely love my little sister," he shared, "and Nada too. I did make a discovery when I was there."

Doris gave her nephew a curious look.

"No, it's not that serious, Aunt Doris. Remember I was telling you about the old bible I got?"

"Yes," Doris said.

"I remember a year or so after Dana's death."

"I received a letter about the same time," Doris recalled, getting up. "I keep it in that box. I take it out and read it when I think of her sometimes," she shared with a tear.

"I understand, Aunt Doris, I read my Bible a lot as well, but I found out from daddy that she had sent it to him when he was still at Harvard. All this time he thought he had it, but Dana had come through one day when he wasn't home and took it from his study."

"What? So, so . . .," Doris searched to find words.

"I know from Dillard Patterson Dana had set up some things to take place when she was about to go to jail for beating Nada."

"So that's where my letter came from, he told me that," she shared.

"Oh, that explains it then," David replied. "She probably had him send me the old book as well. It was precious to her. You know Dad said she sent it to him to let him know she was all right, you know, when he couldn't find her," David Michael stated.

Doris smiled, remembering. "Yes, David Michael, your mother always had a trick up her sleeve."

"Wouldn't that be something if the old book was saying all is well with me," he replied.

"You said she had accepted Christ before she left this world, so that could have that meaning. One never knows the power or work of God," Doris stated.

"Yes, but wouldn't that be something if?" he said excitedly.

"David, don't, please let her rest. We love her and we have fond memories to remember her with," Doris said, getting up.

"I know, Aunt Doris." David Michael got up to embrace his aunt before leaving her office.

"Aunt Doris, they never found her body, did they?"

"David, please? I remember six months after she passed, Dillard Patterson, our attorney, had sent out letters to your dad and Nada, I know it was regarding pressing charges for what she had done to Nada, Billy called and said they were shredding the papers because she wasn't going to hurt anyone else again and petitioned the court to drop all chargers," Doris shared, now thinking over the years that now the conversation with her nephew David Michael had peaked. Her curiosity was running wild and she would have to put in a call to her attorney Dillard Patterson.

Keith and Annie had just returned from vacation in Colorado where his parents lived. He had returned back to Maine knowing now his father was fighting pancreatic cancer.

"Good morning," Billy said, seeing him come in past the receptionist desk.

"Good morning," he replied. "Just flew in last night. Annie won't be back in until tomorrow," he shared.

"Well, how was the trip with family?" Billy asked.

"Okay, could have been better or longer," he shared, forcing a smile."

"Something you need to talk about?" Billy asked in a friend-to-friend way.

"No, and no news on the baby front," Keith replied, walking away to the break room for coffee.

Billy sensed he just needed some space and probably more vacation time. Before leaving, he had been working on a very complicated case that ran for a long time.

"I'll see you round," Billy replied, heading back into his office answering his ringing phone.

Keith had been to the doctor after he had confessed to Billy about him and Annie trying to have another child. In Keith's words, the doctor shared he was shooting blanks. "He had even questioned whether or not Riley was his after all the mix-up he had been privy to in their friends' company. Without telling Annie and he was certainly done with discussing this with anyone except for his doctor, he had asked for a paternity test of his beautiful little daughter, Riley, against his doctor's recommendation.

"Keith, I've seen men wait years for their sperms to produce, which has happened for you. You have a beautiful wife and daughter, why do you question it now, she's what, five?" his doctor asked.

"I just have a need to know to continue working and doing what I love doing," he replied. "I'll see you when I return from my vacation for my results," he had stated in a matter-of-fact tone, leaving his doctor's office two weeks ago. Now today was the day he would find out about Riley, and his nerves in some cases was getting the better of him.

"What's up with Poulton? He's barking at everyone today," one of the attorneys stated, going into a meeting with the boss Billy Parker.

"His vacation was too short I guess. Tomorrow will probably look better for him," Billy teased, heading to his desk sitting down.

Adele rushed along the busy street headed to Montello's for a lunch meeting with Erene. She gave herself some extra time so she would not have to rush. He had some places lined up he thought that might be a better fit for Rhea, and Adele needed all the help available. As she walked along tugging at her skirt she should not have worn to work but was in a big hurry getting out the door, she ran into Mr. Parker and a lady standing outside of the building that housed his law firm.

"Hello, Mr. Parker," she voiced, walking close enough to extend her hand for a shake.

"Why, hello, Adele, it's good to see you. How are things?" he asked.

"Honestly they could be better, though I'm on my way to see Erene now, about help for Rhea."

"Oh, so you found her?"

"Yes, about six months now, but it's been rough lately."

"Honey?"

"Oh, I'm sorry. Adele, this is my wife, Nada," he shared, apologizing for forgetting to introduce her.

"Pleased to meet you, Mrs. Parker," she said, extending a shake.

"I asked Erene to help her in finding her mother," he then said, turning to Nada.

"I love your outfit. Did you buy it in town?" Adele asked. That's the look she wanted but didn't know how to get it.

"I did as a matter of fact. I won't be able to wear it too much longer," Nada shared.

Adele had that *why* look on her face.

"We're expecting." Nada smiled.

"Congratulations to you both," Adele said, moving away. "I can't be late. Oh, and I would love to go shopping with you sometime!" she said, walking fast across the street and down the block to Montello's for lunch.

Billy and Nada stood talking. They had just come from lunch and she was heading to pick up Peyton.

"Sweetheart, you are talking about Erene from church, right?"

"Yes, he's an investigator," Billy replied.

"Soooo?"

"Oh, her mother has a bad drug addiction and has been on the street for some time now, she goes off for days and no one knew where she was, so Adele came to me for help. Justin introduced me to the family when she was going to high school and trying to take care of her younger siblings."

"Really?" Nada replied, wanting more details.

"Look, honey, I will tell you all about it tonight over dinner, but right now, I need to prepare for a client coming in at two p.m.," he said, giving her a kiss and heading into the building.

Nada arrived at the day care running into Annie in the foyer.

"Hello, Annie," she voiced, seeing her standing there speaking with Belle.

"Hi, Keith and I got in late last night. We took a late flight from Colorado," Annie replied.

"So how was your trip?"

"Well, it could have been better, Keith's dad has cancer," Annie replied.

"Oh, I'm so sorry to hear that, we will definitely pray for him," Nada replied.

"Thanks, Nada, we will talk later, got to get to the pharmacy across town, bye," she said, waving with one hand and a tight grip on Riley's hand, leading her to the door.

"I'll get Peyton," Belle said, heading to the classroom with Nada in tow. Phoebe, her assistant, met them at the door. "Here is her backpack, it's so cute," she said, smiling, handing it over to Nada standing at the door.

"Thank you," she said, looking at the children waiting to go out but their parents hadn't come yet, and that wasn't stopping them from heading to the door when they heard Belle coming.

"Keith, may I come in?" Billy asked, walking into his office. "McGuire said you and he had a misunderstanding, is everything, all right?"

"McGuire is sticking his nose in my business and I told him where to go!"

"Keith, can I help, what's troubling you?" he asked, seeing he was upset.

Keith wanted so much to say, "Hell no and get out of my face!" He couldn't. Billy was his boss, fellow attorney, and friend. He was bothered by something and his little girl was on his mind, and Annie should have told him there may be a problem. That's what was bothering him, but he wasn't about to tell William Parker.

"No, Bill, there is nothing you can do, I just found out my father has cancer."

"Keith, I'm sorry, how old is your dad?"

"He's only sixty-four," Keith said, "but if you don't mind, I don't care to talk about it now and I don't really don't want the office to know and start feeling sorry for me!"

"I understand, but we're like family here and you work with a great group of attorneys, but I will respect your decision," he shared and walked out, going into his own office closing the door to pray.

The day went at a snail's pace and the attorneys in the Parker law firm were walking around on eggshells trying to stay out of Keith's way or apologizing over and over again for crossing his path.

"Bill, I'm out," he said, sticking his head slightly in the door before hitting the elevator button leaving.

Billy knew this couldn't continue another day. He called a meeting after he heard Keith had left the building and explained to the guys that Keith was having family problems, and no, not Annie, his dad is ill. "No details necessary, just give him space. Thanks guys." He then grabbed his jacket and said good night for the evening heading home.

"Erene James, please," Adele said, standing by the entrance desk.

"Right this way." She followed him through the busy lunch crowd waiting to sit or be served.

"Hi, Adele," Erene said, getting up to pull the chair out for her.

"Thank you, you're too kind." She smiled.

"May I bring you something to drink?" The waiter asked before leaving.

Adele ordered a red wine, and Erene said, "Nothing for me, but thank you."

The waiter smiled and walked off to get the drink.

"You're driving, right?"

"Oh, you mean that," he said, pointing to the waiter. "Not really, I just don't like drinking with my meal. Pet peeve, I guess?"

"So first, thank you for lunch," Adele mentioned.

"Yes, you sound horrible this morning when I called. I had these brochures in my desk and I think one may work for you and Rhea," Erene replied.

Adele took the brochures and glanced quickly at them. "Let's order and then we can talk about these," she said, giving a tap on the brochures.

Erene smiled at her confident attitude. "Okay, sounds good. So you have been busy with Rhea, what have you done for yourself? You can't help others if you are not being replenished." He smiled.

"Sorry, I know. I'm a sight for sore eyes! I know I need to do something, that's why I'm here. I'm tired though, and I do apologize for my looks and this hideous attire," Adele confessed.

"Stop, don't beat yourself up, it's not that bad," Erene shared, touching her hand.

The waiter came and took their orders and conversation continued. Erene had great information with places that help those with addictions and give out clothes, food, and even shelter if they choose to use the available services.

"Thank you," Adele said, taking another bite from her lunch.

"Oh, it was nothing, I'm glad you are letting me help you," he replied.

"I saw your ring when you touched my hand. Are you married? How do you find time to do this, I mean help people? It requires a lot and a special person," Adele said.

"You are right, it does require a lot of sacrifice." He paused.

Adele sat silent looking at his hand.

"Oh, I am married," he said slowly. "My wife travels a lot."

"A lot?" Adele questioned.

"A lot, and so this is how I busy myself and pass the time," Erene confessed.

"She must really be gone a lot!"

"Yes, sometimes weeks at a time." He looked down sadly. "I get through it. How was your lunch?"

"Very good, and yours?" Adele asked, smiling.

"Good," he said, picking up the tab.

"I can get that, you came to help me," Adele said, reaching for the receipt.

"It's okay, Adele, but thanks, you're a caring person as well."

And then both got up to leave the restaurant.

Annie and Keith sat down for dinner. Riley was now sitting in her booster chair because she was now a big girl, she was told.

"Dinner looks great, honey," Keith said, sitting down to his table.

"Thank you, how were things today at the office?" she asked.

"Why, who called?" Keith stated.

"No one called, I was thinking of you and the news about your dad, I was wondering how you made it through the day. Keith, what's wrong? You seem . . ."

"I seem what?"

"Daddy, look," Riley said, feeling tension from his loud voice at the table. "See," she said, holding up a green bean from her plate in her hand to eat.

He calmed himself. "I see they are very good, see Daddy's eating his," he said, playfully putting some in his mouth and then reaching over to kiss his daughter's forehead.

Annie saw a tear fall from his cheek. "Honey, are you okay? They are finding all kinds of cures, people have lived for years with cancer, we celebrate survivors all the time. Don't give up so quickly," she shared.

"Yeah," he sighed. "Maybe you're right," he added, quietly taking a bite from his plate and giving attention to Riley as they finished their dinner.

"Keith, is Riley ready to go?" Annie asked on their way out the next morning. "How are you feeling? You tossed and turned all night, dear," Annie asked, getting her jacket and Riley's backpack.

"I am fine! And I will take Riley in this morning," he stated.

Annie took a step back when he said it. Clearly this news about his dad had affected him. "Honey, how about if we just call in today and we can take Riley to the zoo. You know how she loves the zoo!" Annie smile nervously.

"No, wish I could, my caseload is monstrous right now, and you know it, but thanks for thinking of me," he teased, kissing her, and both walked out the door together.

Conversation in was the usual pleasant family talk as always as they drove in to work. Annie noticed Keith turned, heading to the office first.

"Hey, did you forget about your daughter? I know you want her in law, but she's got at least a few more years," Annie teased.

"I'm dropping you off first this morning, and here, please pull these files for me," Keith asked, pulling out a list to have ready for him when he returned after getting Riley to school.

"You do have a lot on your plate with this case." She smiled, looking at the list. "I can help, I'll cut out some time and we can work together on it," she said, reaching over to kiss him as they sat in front of the building. "Have a good day," she said, waving to Riley who was secured in her car seat in the back.

Annie walked into the office. It was so quiet you could hear a pin drop as she yelled, "Good morning!"

"Good morning," Billy said, coming from his office looking around. "No Keith today?" he asked.

"He is dropping Riley off, I came in first this morning. He will be here shortly," Annie replied.

"How is he doing?"

"What?" Annie looked, questioning.

"He shared with me about his dad. I know it is tough on him," Billy replied.

"He told you? He asked me—"

"I know, but things got pretty bad around here yesterday and I had to confront him about it."

"What happened? Does everyone know?" she asked, sadden as she sat in her chair.

"No, not really, they just know he had bad news about his dad, but we are like family around here, Annie, you know that," Billy reminded his legal secretary.

"I know, but he is taking this really hard, Billy. I hope it turns out all right."

Billy started to embrace her as he saw her start to tear up. "It will be fine, I'm sure he just needs more time to process," he said, backing away and heading to his office with Nada getting off the elevator after taking Peyton to school now walking to the door.

Annie wiped again her tears and composed herself. "Annie, are you all right?" she asked, standing in front of Annie's desk with just a tiny bulge in her blouse and a concerned look.

"I'm okay, Keith's having a hard time with the news of his dad, that's it."

"Oh! I was kind of surprised seeing you here, I thought you all were not coming in today," she said.

"Nada?"

"Hi, honey, what are you doing here?" Billy asked, disrupting the conversation between the ladies after hearing Nada's voice.

"Sweetheart, you left this at the table," she said, smiling, giving him his cell phone.

"Thanks for bringing it. Can I walk you out?" he asked, wanting the conversation over and Nada on her way home.

"So only Keith is off today?" she asked, now seeing Annie over at the file cabinet.

McGuire came out heading to get coffee. "Morning."

"No, Keith is dropping Riley off and he should be coming through the door any minute now," Annie shared.

"Really? You might want to call him," Nada replied. "I was speaking to Belle and Carrie, both said Keith had called to say Riley wasn't coming in today. So, I figured you and Keith needed some downtime after you vacation," she said, heading off to Billy's office.

Annie looked confused but dialed her husband's cell phone. She spoke with him for about ten minutes and sadly she started her day.

"Is everything okay?" Nada asked, leaving.

"Things are fine, they decided to do the zoo thing without me." She smiled. "I'm joining them at noon." She had not shared that with Keith, her husband, but that's what Annie had planned to do. She knew this news received was really bothering him. She wanted to be there for him, and she needed to hold her daughter and Keith in her arms.

CHAPTER **8**

IT HAD BEEN OVER TWO years since Katia had visited Los Angeles. She was ready for a new outfit or maybe two. She absolutely loved the shoes at Nordstrom's and would have fun finding the perfect pair for tonight with a borrowed assistant for the day. Dillard and she were going to the opera tonight at the Music Center of the Performing Arts. And she wants to dress to impress! From a recommendation from the assistant, she also thought it would be fun to take in the LA fashion district, moving slowly around from store to store. After two hours of looking and shopping, she had the assistant to take her packages to the car. "And come back, we will do lunch," she stated. "Let's find a great trendy restaurant," Katia said, giving the assistant her phone for making reservations if needed.

"The Bodega Hollywood is great, oh, let's do the Bowery, I think it's more to your taste and style," her assistant said, smiling, giving directions to the driver.

Dillard was feeling good these days. What could possibly go wrong? He was on top of the world. He whistled along coming from the parking garage when up walk none other than Milburn.

"Why, good afternoon, Patterson," he said, smiling that sheepish smile.

"Good afternoon, Milburn," he returned.

"Heard you won your last case a few days ago," Milburn stated.

"And that surprises you?" Dillard asked.

"Well, I guess that's why you're paid the big bucks ah guy," he replied, laughing, tapping Dillard on the shoulder.

"Milburn, please, may I remind you that you are in this building as well, you live in Bel Air, you own a yacht, and might

I go on, you get the picture," he said, giving Milburn a "what for" because of his condescending attitude. "Why are you surprised I do well in my law practice?" Everything doesn't need to be pointed out, and especially not by him! Every day he comes up with something to ruffle his feathers, not today. "I have to get in. I'm leaving early tonight going out on the town," Dillard mocked.

"Oh, are you taking that blonde out again? Could get serious." Milburn smiled devilishly.

"It could. Wouldn't that give you something to talk about at the watercooler?" Dillard supposed.

Seeing he wasn't making any ground today, Milburn huffed off throwing a "forget you" wave at Dillard.

"Have a good evening," Dillard yelled to him.

Katia enjoyed her lunch and had let her assistant go, taking her back to her office. She then told the driver she wanted to window-shop on Rodeo Drive.

"Yes, I shouldn't be long, there is another recommended stop. I heard the clothes are fabulous!"

The driver pulled out again on the highway heading to Beverly Hills. Arriving, he pulled to the side allowing Katia to step out on the curb. She walked slowly, gazing into the windows of the unique shops. One sign caught her eye, and before she knew it, she was standing inside looking around.

"May I be of assistance?" a clerk asked, coming over to her.

"Yes, I'm new to Los Angeles and your shop was recommended to me," Katia stated with a stiff upper lip.

Doris Woods, the owner of the Unique Chic, happened to be walking through on her way from lunch.

"Ms. Woods," the clerk said, seeing her go by. "This is a recommended patron coming in for the first time," she acknowledged. Doris walked over, extending her hand. "Pleasure having you here.

If you have any questions that Stephanie can't answer, feel free to ask for me," she said, walking off with her phone ringing needing to be answered.

"Again, thank you, we are glad to have you," Stephanie responded, "we carry many designers and we also have the latest styles." "Good. I'd love to see some of your one-of-a-kind designs, and do you deliver?" Katia asked. "We do, right this way."

"Dillard?"

"Yes," was the reply from the other end of the phone.

"Thank you for calling me back," Doris shared. "The reason I called is to ask you about the items Dana Demato, my sister, left for you to send out."

Not again, Dillard thought to himself before speaking. "It's been over two years, and honestly, I can't remember everything Dana, I mean Ms. Williams and I did together. She always had me sending and buying and ect—"

"Slow down, Dillard, you sound like a runaway train. I know this is something you would have written down," Doris explained. Dillard was quiet. He just listened. "I need to know if there was an old book included in the things Dana wanted you to send out after her death. Better yet, may I please just have the list?"

This is getting ridiculous, he thought to himself. *Why do I have to dig this stuff up again?* "Miss Woods, I will do my best, but it's going to take a while. I have filed those papers away long ago," he replied.

"I'm in no hurry, just let me know when you find it. And, Dillard, I'm sure you have it on your computer files. This is 2012," Doris teased.

Dillard forced a smile as well, but he just wanted to put his past client Dana Williams-Demato to rest for good!

Noon could not get there fast enough. Annie was very busy in the office buzzing around like a bee. She had pulled all the files Keith had asked her to have on his desk and had started her part of the paperwork required for her to type for the case. William and McGuire had also left some documents on her desk for her to record into her computer and e-mail to the court recorder.

"Annie?" She turned to see Billy standing in his office door.

"Yes, William," she said, looking up from her typing.

"You are meeting Keith for lunch, right?" he asked.

"Please have him call me. I have to discuss a case with him. One of his clients called today. No hurry, if he is in tomorrow, he can take care of it himself." He smiled.

"No problem, William, I'll let him know, I'm sure spending a day with Riley, he will realize that his job requires less energy. He will probably beat me to the office tomorrow. That child has so much energy all the time." She smiled her response.

"Thanks, you have a good lunch and tell Keith I said hello."

"Thanks, William." Annie looked at the large clock on the wall that seemed to have stopped moving. It appeared that twelve o'clock would never get there. Since Keith had brought her to work, she had asked Jenin who also worked as a clerk in the building to borrow her car. "William, I'm leaving, I will see you all in a couple of hours," she announced waving, heading to the elevator.

Before she could reach the car, her phone rang.

"Hello, honey," she said, seeing it was Keith calling. "It's funny you called. I was on my way to meet you two. Are you having fun without me?" she asked, excited he had called.

"Oh, I wasn't aware you were coming, dear," he replied.

"I know, I borrowed Jenin's car and was going to surprise you guys." She laughed. "So what part of the zoo are you guys in now? I will meet you, it's lunchtime, you know," Annie shared.

"Zoo, oh, we were there earlier, left an hour or so ago, Riley fell asleep."

"Aww, so cute, did you get pictures? You know how I love pictures," Annie replied, now sitting in the car still on the phone. "Is she still asleep, or was this just one of her catnaps? Can I speak with her?"

"Oh, she is."

"Well, she really had a good time at the zoo if she is still sleep," Annie replied, knowing her daughter. "I'll come home and prepare you and I some lunch. How does that sound?" she asked, still with a smile.

"Sounds wonderful that you're thinking about me," Keith responded.

"Keith, I'm always thinking about you, I love you. Why would you say that?"

Keith didn't answer. He just asked, "How's the office?"

"Busy as usual. Oh, a client of yours called for you, but William said no hurry, you can take care of it tomorrow when you return."

"Okay, Annie."

Annie was just about home as she drove along making small talk with Keith as she maneuvered through LA traffic going home. "So I'll see you two shortly," she said, disconnecting the line, and made a turn on her street giving a sigh seeing their car parked in the driveway. After parking her car, Annie waved to a neighbor and put the key in the door going in. It seemed odd kind of eerie, she thought, standing in her entrance.

"Keith," she called out not very loud, she didn't want to disturb Riley who was probably asleep in the family's great room where she napped. No one answered. She tossed down her purse and jacket and called again. "Keith, KEITH!" Louder this time but still no one answered. She ran into her kitchen and then into the family room. She could see things a bit out of place and some of Riley's toys on the floor. "KEITH! RILEY!" she yelled out in a panic heading to her bedroom. She could see someone had left her closet door open, and yes, there were clothes missing. Her mind was going a mile a minute when she headed into Riley's room and saw drawers pulled out and her favorite toys on her bed was gone.

Nervously she ran back to the front of her spacious home grabbing her purse and removing her cell phone to call. *I just spoke with him!* her mind was saying as the phone rang. Over and over and over! "KEITH, KEITH," she screamed. "What is going on? Did he say he was home?" she thought, trying to remember the conversation they had as she drove. Anger, fear, and hurt all came flooding out at the same time as Annie fell to the floor crying. Then she quickly thought of something. Grabbing her home phone, she dialed her office.

"William, did Keith come to the office?" she asked quickly.

"No, Annie, I thought—" She heard no and disconnected the call heading to her backyard.

"Keith, Keith!" she yelled. Getting no answer, she came back in the house and her phone was ringing. Seeing the ID was Parker and Associates, she didn't want to explain besides she didn't know what to say anyway. Annie headed for her front door looking around.

"Annie," her neighbor called out. She composed herself as she walked over to meet her. This neighbor lived a house or so down from her, and Madeline Bookens always knew what went on in her neighborhood.

"Hello, Miss Bookens," Annie said, walking slowly down the street. Annie needed information.

"You're home, I see," she stated, looking at Annie questionably.

"Yes, just home for lunch." She smiled.

"Saw Keith and little Riley earlier leaving," she said.

"You did?" Annie asked, wanting to know more of what she saw.

"Airport cab picked them up around nine thirty, I'd guess. I was making my way back home," she informed her. "Says he's headed to see his family in Colorado."

And with that, Annie was running back across the street without saying anything to Miss Bookens about the matter.

Ring, ring, ring.

"Hello, Poulton residence."

Without a greeting, Annie asked, "Is Keith there?"

"Keith? No, dear, he called earlier and talked to his dad, says he is on his way, I believe. Hold on, she said putting the phone down.

Annie couldn't hold on any longer. She ran to her storage closet and got the remaining parts of her luggage, heading to her room, pulling out anything, throwing it into a suitcase, and headed out the door. Annie composed herself somehow pulling out the driveway and headed to the law office to return Jenin's car with plans on her mind. William had called back leaving a message of concern, but she would deal with that later, she thought as she drove along.

Quickly getting across the busy LA freeway, she pulled Jenin's car in the employee parking spot and secured her key under the car mat.

"Please help me to remember to call Jenin when I get to the airport," Annie reminded herself. She walked speedily down the street toward a cab spot where one is usually parked. Securing a cab and giving him instructions to the airport, she called Jenin regarding her car. Sitting stuck in traffic now, she called William Parker.

Ring, ring, RING.

"Parker and Associates," he answered. "Annie? What is going on? The phones are crazy today and we need you," he expressed.

"Sorry, you will have to call in a temp. I can't be there today."

"Annie, what's going on? Is there something I can help with?" he asked.

"Honestly, I don't know. I will call you later tonight and try to explain, but right now, I'm not sure myself," Annie shared. It was apparent to Billy that whatever was going on was a family matter and he would wait to be asked in if needed.

"All right, Annie, you take care and please you or Keith give me a call," Billy added.

Annie had a lot on her mind. She had been trying every five minutes to call Keith's cell phone that was only going to voice mail.

Waiting to finally board her flight once again in almost less than a week, her thoughts overwhelmed her and tears came flowing down her face.

"Are you okay?" a stewardess asked.

"I'm fine, just headed to see my daughter," she responded.

"Oh, happy tears," she replied back.

Annie just smiled and sat down in her first-class seat for her ride to Colorado.

Katia looked absolutely stunning in her draped Donna Karen gown she had purchased at Saks as she and Dillard walked into the performing arts theater to see an opera entitled *The Sum of its Parts.*

"How was your day of shopping?" Dillard asked, sitting now, awaiting the opera to start.

"It was wonderful. Your assistant friend took me to the fashion district that was interesting." She enjoyed it. "I visited Neiman's, Nordstrom's, and a cute little shop called Unique Chic on Rodeo. So, there will be lots of deliveries coming." Katia smiled at Dillard. "We even stopped and had lunch at the Bowery," Katia shared.

"Oh really, so now I know you don't mind stepping out on the town, we may embellish it more often," Dillard suggested. "We may even do breakfast at Tiffany's."

"I'd love to," she responded, which surprised Dillard.

Annie wasted no time in heading to the rent-a-car booth. With a thank-you and getting the keys, she put the probably useless suitcase into the trunk, taking her time programming her GPS with the address, and she was on her way. She dialed Keith's cell again.

"Hello," his voice she heard.

Annie wasn't going to give herself away, letting him know she was there. She didn't know what was going on with him. She just wanted to see her daughter.

"Are you home yet? I was going to call you," he confessed.

"I have been trying to call you all day," she said, still calm as not to give herself away.

"Mom said you called."

"I did right after I spoke with you at noon," Annie replied, still driving toward where Keith supposedly had gone to see his father.

"Honey, look, I know by now you have figured out I'm not coming home tonight." Keith sighed. "I had to get away for a while. I was going to explain it to you, but all that talk about babies, I needed a break!" Keith admitted.

"Yes, to be honest, I was quite upset, you left the house in shambles I didn't know what to think."

"I'm sorry, honey, but I have a lot on me right now!" he insisted.

"How's your dad?" she asked to keep him calm, she reasoned.

"Dad's great, so upbeat," he said.

"That's good. And Riley, how is she?"

"Hold on. Riley, it's Mommy," she heard him say. "Say hi to Mommy."

"Hi, Mommy, I miss you, when are you coming? Okay, Mommy."

Annie didn't say much. She didn't want him to know she was there, and a few more turns, she would have her daughter.

"She's off running again with Buck," Keith said, getting back on the phone. "Honey, Riley and I are fine, I plan to spend a few days with my dad and we should be back by the end of the week," he confessed.

"So, you were just going to leave me behind?" She was angry now after knowing Riley was okay but he chose this.

"See, I knew you'd be angry, that's why I didn't tell you my plans," he stated.

"I'm sorry, I just feel you could have shared with me about it and we could have done it together," she said, very calm as not to rile him or anger him.

"Anyway, I'm the one who should be angry. I went to see Dr. Belton yesterday." Annie listened. She was pulling up after the hour drive to his parents' home from the airport. Dr. Belton was Keith's primary care doctor.

"Is that why you're acting this way? Keith, we have a beautiful daughter to raise. We don't need another one," Annie responded, knowing how much he wanted another child, Annie reminded him of Riley.

"All the talk and joy about William's child is daunting sometimes and I feel so left out."

"We will talk when I get home. Someone is at the door, Dad has been having friends drop by," Keith said, ready to disconnect the line.

Annie made small talk, keeping him on the line as Keith came to open the door, opening to "Oh my god, Annie, how did you get here so fast?" he asked.

Annie stepped in and slapped his face before asking. "Where's Riley? RILEY!" she yelled. Riley came running into her arms with Buck, the golden retriever, close behind.

Dillard and Katia sat down at Barney's on Rodeo to a late dinner after the opera.

"Dillard, that was magnificent. You can escort me out anytime for a show of that magnitude," she expressed, sipping her expensive glass of wine.

"I'm so glad you were pleased, it was quite fun," Dillard responded, smiling. He was embracing a whole new world with Katia. Meeting adventures head-on and surprised even himself on the things he really liked doing. She had him going to dance lessons where he was learning the waltz, he sat thinking as he looked at her across the table looking so gorgeous with her whole new look.

"So are you ready for this?" she asked, smiling.

"I'd better be, you look amazing, sexy, and if I didn't know—"

She put her finger across his lips with "Shhhhhhh. Don't ruin the moment." She smiled.

"You're right, think, think, Dillard," he told himself quietly. "Do you remember that client I told you about who has been bugging me about some things her sister left in her will?"

Katia asked, "The one who wanted her mother's portrait?"

"Yes, you remember," Dillard responded. "She called be again, I'm afraid this is going to be the end of me with her naggings."

"Now, Dillard, don't become unraveled, what did she want this time from you?" Katia asked, relaxed being at the end of their meal.

"Some old book or something, and a list, I'm going to go through my archives and see what I can come up with to please her and I'm done!" he stated.

Katia took a big gulp of her now-refilled glass of Dom Romane Conti 1997 wine. "I'm sure you will figure out something, Dillard, right?"

Annie had opted to stay in town and got a room near her in-laws at the Marriott Hotel in downtown Colorado. She and Keith needed to talk and she didn't want to waste time. After spending a few hours with his very sweet but clueless-of-the-matter- at-hand parents, she, Keith, and Riley left to turn in at the hotel in Colorado and would see them tomorrow. Keith was sitting on the couch in the room when Annie called him to help tuck Riley in for the evening. He put down his beer and walked in the room standing by the bed.

"Good night, twinkle toes," he said, smiling, holding back tears Annie could see. He kissed her forehead and wiped across his eyes with his arm and left going back to the sofa.

"Good night, twinkle toes," Annie repeated as they did every night since Riley was old enough to remember.

"Good night, Daddy, good night, Mommy." She turned over, grabbed her stuffed animal, and Annie kissed her forehead and turned out the lights and left the room.

CHAPTER 9

ADELE HAD LOOKED INTO A few of the places Erene had recommended to help Rhea and to lighten her load. Once again finding her on the street, Adele had taken a day off and she and Rhea were going over to see another one of the places that sound like it would fit.

"Nothing is guaranteed," the facilitator of the place called Second Chances explained to the both of them sitting in her office. "This is assisted living, though we will provide all the necessary tools and guide you to becoming self-sufficient," she explained, showing Rhea a brochure.

"So, am I allowed to go out during the day?" Rhea asked, looking at her daughter.

"You are, as a matter of fact, we encourage it," the lady answered. "We have places where you can work during the day. You're free to go and come as you please, though we are very strict on our curfew, you must be in by five p.m. Unless you're employed and it's your work hours, we extend curfew," she stressed, getting up to show them around. "We have family nights and movie nights in this room, and if interested, we have a chaplain in on Wednesdays and Sundays."

Adele looked around as she informed them of the rules and cost. "Our residents clean and have monthly duties and daily chores.

We teach them what it takes to live again," she shared with Adele. "I'll leave you alone for a minute, we have a few openings left, so if you decide to become a part of our family here, you're welcome," she said, shaking their hands and leaving, excusing herself to address a problem in another room. It was one of the smaller facilities Adele had looked into. Being downtown could cause problems because Rhea could head back to her old friends and bad habits, Adele thought as she drove along going back home.

"Well, Mother, what did you think of that one?" she asked.

"I like it. When are you going to take me there?" Rhea asked.

"Rhea, I can take you there, but it's up to you to stay there and get the help I can't give you," Adele confessed.

"So I can go and come as I please?" Rhea asked to confirm.

"The facilitator said they would like you to get involved in something, keep yourself busy, they offer jobs at the different help organizations. You'll be off the street and have a bed to sleep in at night," Adele explained, knowing it had to be what Rhea wanted or it wouldn't work and she was soooo tired.

"Let's give it a try, can you take me now?" she said, acting fidgety to get out of the car and away from her daughter. They had been together most of the day and she hadn't seen any of her friends all day.

"Okay, I tell you what," Adele shared, "we will try it for today, and see if you like it, and you and I will talk tomorrow about it. Does that work for you, Rhea?"

"Does that work for you, Adele? I'm fine where I am. I'll do it for you," she stated, pulling out her cigarette.

"Please, Rhea, not in the car," Adele asked.

"Turn around, hurry, and let me out of here, I need a smoke."

Adele had already headed back to Second Chance, hoping against hope that it would work, but ultimately it was up to Rhea.

"Mother, it's going to be after five p.m. by the time you get checked in," Adele informed her.

"Yeah, yeah whatever," Rhea responded, now getting out of the car and standing under a nearby tree to smoke her cigarette.

Maxine, the caretaker, saw Adele coming back up to her door. "Oh, you're back, so you have made a decision?" She smiled, opening the door. "She will be okay," she said, seeing her talking with two of the ladies who lived there.

"She'd like to give it a try," Adele said, sitting down to prepare the paperwork asked of her by the facility.

"You know, young lady, it's going to be her choice. We have had some success stories and many disappointments. Some just refuse to change, so don't blame yourself, you have tried," she acknowledged, looking at Adele. "How long have you been taking care of your mother, dear?"

Adele almost broke down in tears when she said, "Since I was a young teenager."

"A long time," Maxine replied. After about twenty minutes, she asked Adele to have her mother sign her documents so she could give her copies of her paperwork.

"I've assigned her to Room 4. There are only eight bedrooms in this house and all but two were filled. We cost a little more, but I think if she gives it a go, she will do fine," Maxine said again, shaking Adele's hand, and she walked out to welcome Rhea and have her sign her documents and get her key to her room.

Both walked out the door looking around but didn't see Rhea under the tree. The two ladies had come in because now it was past curfew. Both were sitting watching television. Adele looked quickly in the car she had left unlocked and saw the ashtray filled with coins was pulled out and empty and left on the car seat. Adele and Maxine looked around the grounds yelling her name with no response. Rhea was nowhere to be found!

Billy had finally heard from the Poultons. They were having family issues dealing with the news regarding Keith's father and had gone back to Colorado with as of yet no return date.

"William, I just need to support my mother right now. I hate to leave you in such a pinch, attorney and secretary."

Billy surmised, "Keith, I do understand. We have got it covered. If we have any questions, I'll call, take care and let your father know we are praying for him," Billy concluded, feeling his pain.

"Thanks, man," Keith replied.

Annie had confronted Keith's behavior after tucking Riley in bed. "Keith, what is wrong with you? You can't go off making a decision, taking our daughter and leaving the state! I'm so angry right now."

"Annie, please, lower your voice, you'll wake Riley," Keith asked.

"You'd better be glad Riley is in the other room! You've got nerves!"

Keith sat there while Annie insulted him over and over for his stupid move.

"ANNIE, STOP! You should have told me?"

"TOLD YOU WHAT? Your dad at this point is doing better than you are. That was a stupid, stupid move," she kept saying.

"Talking about a stupid move, marrying you was a stupid move!" he blasted out at her.

Annie walked and peeked in on Riley, closing the door securely from the argument now taking place. Annie was crying and mad because he was being stupid over his father being diagnosed. "So you're sorry you married me, are you sorry we had Riley too?" she asked furiously.

"It's not Riley, I love my little girl and no one is going to take her from me," Keith blurred out.

"Take her from you, who said that? Where are you coming up with this stuff? You are being crazy," she said, flopping on the sofa still wiping tears.

"Annie, I'm sorry, I handled this all wrong."

"You think?" Annie responded, mocking him.

"Annie, just listen please. I was so hurt when I heard about my dad, so when I went to my doctor, bad news is not what I wanted to hear from him. I will really try hard to get through this, but so much has happened already regarding this matter, I don't care to hear another word," Keith tried explaining.

Annie sat trying to read between the lines of what she heard Keith say to her. She sensed that he was upset with her. But what had she done? she questioned, sitting there listening at him lay down plans for her life. "Keith, what are you saying, you want a divorce?" she asked.

"Is that what you want?" he snapped back quickly to her.

"When we left home yesterday morning, my life and my family was intact, I thought. Now I'm standing in another state discussing options. Keith, this is crazy."

"I'll say this, Annie, you should have told me, and if you ever try leaving or taking Riley, you will be sorry! That I promise you! I'm going back and see if I can make a go of Maine but no promises." And when Keith concluded, she knew this matter had very little to do with his father's diagnosis, and whatever he wasn't saying had everything to do with her. Early the next morning, Keith, Annie, and Riley smiling were bidding good-bye to his parents again, going home to Maine, and now Annie was sitting on the airplane trying to figure it out.

"Good afternoon," Keith said, coming into the office with a cheerful attitude and a smile to match.

"Welcome home, stranger," McGuire replied, coming from his office down the hall.

"Hi." The receptionist had looked up from her computer seeing a gentleman walk in.

Billy came to his door. "Well, this is a surprise. When we spoke yesterday, you didn't have a date when you'd be back," he shared, coming over to shake Keith's hand after being gone for a full week. "True, true, but my dad is very upbeat and didn't like my sad face around him," he teased. "He and Mother haven't given up on life and they are doing fine," he said, smiling to feel better.

"Come on in, I was just going through your files, of which you can have back," Billy said, handing the folders to him across the desk. "How's Annie, is she back as well?"

"You know horses couldn't keep Annie from this office, she's spending the day with Riley and will be in tomorrow."

"Oh, okay, that's good to know. I'm going to speak with her about training Abigail Necy. I don't want to get caught off guard like that again. It was absolutely chaotic around here this past week without Annie. She's valuable to this company and so are you, good to have you back," Billy said, smiling as Keith walked out saying very little, Billy noticed.

Adele had sat up late in her living room chair waiting for Rhea to return. Fletcher woke her coming in the door to get ready for school.

"I stayed the night at Justin's, hope you didn't worry. The game went into extra endings and it was late when the game ended," he shared, giving her a cup of hot coffee to get her going.

"Thanks, Fletch."

"So no Rhea again, huh?" he asked before going into his room to shower and get ready for school.

"Fletcher, I don't know what I'm going to do! She left the place before I could even get the papers signed. I'm tired," she admitted, walking off to her room to shower and get ready for her workday.

Busy morning was good, Adele thought, heading out for lunch. As she walked out of the building, she saw Erene sitting in front in his car.

"Lunch?" he asked, smiling from across the other side, beckoning for her to get in.

Adele needed a smile, and Erene was so easy to talk to, she reasoned, getting in, and he pulled away from the curb.

"I stopped by the deli on my way here," he shared, throwing his head back for her to look at the brown bag in the backseat.

"You didn't have plans, did you?" he asked.

"I was going to walk around downtown," Adele replied.

"So she's gone again already!" he voiced because he had spoken with Adele the day she and Rhea were out looking at some of the places he had recommended.

"Erene, I'm so tired." And she broke down crying.

He hurried and pulled to the side of the road. "I'm so sorry, Adele, this is so common, I tried warning you. You don't deserve this," he said, rubbing her head and face and let her cry.

After a few minutes, Adele composed herself.

"There's a park a block over I thought we could go there and eat our lunch. I brought your favorite pastrami on rye," Erene voiced, smiling, lifting his brow for her to agree.

"Sounds good," Adele shared. That cry made her feel better. "Thanks, Erene, for being here," she acknowledged as the two got out at the park and sat on the wooden bench and ate lunch and talked.

Keith had only been gone for a full week, so things for him at the office had started falling back into place. Abigail, the new legal trainee, was bright and caught on quickly, all the attorneys thought.

"Abigail," Keith asked, walking to her desk, "the papers I gave you on the Daniels case?"

"Right here, Mr. Poulton, and I prefer to be called Abby," she shared, smiling.

"Abby it is, and thanks," he said, walking back to his office.

Things seem to have settled down from the past few days, and Abby was doing a great job, Billy acknowledged on his way out. She had been with the firm now for about a month training under Annie, but for the first week had to take a leading role due to Annie and Keith's swift departure. Billy was very busy at the office and still attending night courses at the seminary and wasn't going to be late.

"Good night," was heard by the other two law firm attorneys as they left. Yifat Oren was down at the court today involved in a trial, so closing the office was Poulton and Abigail, the only two left in the office most evenings.

Keith was so busy working on a case that should have been finished up Monday with a settlement and here it was Wednesday, so he had shared with Annie he'd be late and needed to finish it up tonight.

"Good night," Abigail said, putting her head in the door of his office. "I guess you will have to lock her up." She smiled.

"Yes, I guess I will, so how do you like it so far?"

"I like it, you guys are easy to get along with," she cooed.

"Thanks, we try," Keith replied.

"I need to get a schedule for the bus. Since I've secured a good job, I'm going to purchase a new car. The other one has a mind of its own, and this morning was no exception, wouldn't start," she shared, still standing in the door in a cute little business suit. "So I'm headed to the bus stop now."

"Oh look, you're new in town. I'll get you home today. I'm getting ready to leave as well," he said, looking at the files that need his attention on his desk that he should be working on.

"Are you sure? I mean, I appreciate the ride, but—"

"No buts," Keith interrupted her, grabbing his jacket, and headed out the door to his car.

Billy and Nada sat at the dinner table sharing their day and laughing at Peyton's antics as she ate her string beans one at a time.

"Most of them are on the floor," Nada said, wiping Peyton's mouth so she could drink from her cup.

"Wow, aren't you a big girl," Billy acknowledged, seeing how well she drank from her big-girl cup without spilling it. The family time is so enjoyable and so important to Billy he always tried to honor the time by being there on time.

"So how are things at the office?" Nada asked after Peyton finished eating and was taken off by Millicent to be cleaned up.

"Almost back to normal. Oh yeah, Poulton settled that case we were discussing today."

"He did? I thought you had spoken with him and there was no return time?" Nada asked.

"You're right, they were gone a full week. I guess his father didn't want his dome and gloom," Billy shared. "Anyway, I'm glad they are back."

"That was a weird departure. What do you make of that?" Nada asked.

"Sweetheart, everybody handles things differently."

"Yeah, I guess Annie was certainly caught off guard," Nada stated.

"They seemed to have worked it all out and everyone will be back in the office tomorrow." Billy smiled. "Even McGuire is coming back from vacation," he said, walking with Nada to the family room, tapping her growing daily tummy.

"Was Erene at the meeting tonight?" Nada asked.

"Yes, he was, why?" Billy said, getting a throw pillow for her for comfort.

"I had lunch with Nora today. It's rare she's in town, she travels so much. She's flying out early tomorrow, so she was expecting him to be in with her tonight."

"Well, honey, I'm sure they have that all worked out, she was traveling when they got married. There is no children yet, so that's a good thing. Both seem to handle the marriage separation pretty well," Billy informed.

"Yes, I know, she loves it, it would kill me being away from you for a week or two at a time," Nada voiced, showing affection holding his hand.

"They are young and in love, it works for them."

"You're right, dear, I guess you're right." Nada smiled.

Keith arrived home about an hour earlier than Annie had expected him to. Still being positive after their extended conversation the nights before that things had turned around after returning home, she asked, "So did you get that paperwork completed, dear? Dinner is in the oven, and I'm afraid Riley's asleep," she said, walking over to kiss him as he entered.

He gave her a quick kiss on the cheek and headed to the kitchen. "Not really. I'm afraid I will have to go in early tomorrow. It's my turn to take Riley, but do you mind? I'd like to get an early start," he asked, now sitting down with his meal.

"No problem, Keith, I don't mind." Annie breathed a sigh of relief. After the other day, she wasn't going to turn him loose with her any time soon. "So how is the new trainee?" she asked, sitting down at the table to speak since he was not home for dinner.

"Abby, she seems okay."

"Abby already! She must have made a good impression," Annie responded, raising her brows.

"She prefers that over Abigail, and I have to agree, she doesn't look like an Abigail," Keith shared. "All the guys think so far she is doing a good job. It's her first month, I understand," he shared, still eating his meal.

"What do you think, is my job in jeopardy?" she teased, trying to lift a cloud mood in the room.

"Annie, you know the guys love you, you know that office inside out. It will take a special person to fill your shoes," he said, giving her a quick smirk to ease her concerns.

"Why, thanks, honey, I knew you had my back," she said, walking over, gently brushing his hair back on his head, and she left the room to get ready for bed.

Annie had called Keith a couple of times to come to bed.

"Soon, dear, I'm just unwinding," he yelled. Keith had forgiven the situation but had not forgotten what he felt Annie had done to his manhood. He could have gone on through life without children because he was told over and over again it couldn't happen. But he felt Annie had misled him. He sat there thinking about his day. He had taken Abby home without getting permission or letting Annie know as he would have before the news from his doctor to get back at her because he is still angry with her for not sharing that possibilities of him not being able to produce existed.

With "See you tomorrow" to Abby, he was headed to the highway for home. Two hours later, after leaving the office around ten o' clock, he was home now with Annie. They had talked a bit while he ate his dinner she had put in the oven for him. He sat thinking over his day, and with Annie fast asleep, he got in bed and did the same.

Katia sat out on the patio with their 180-degree million-dollar views of LA. She embraced the new lifestyle with total acceptance. Dillard was doing his part in helping her transition into an LA socialite and she fit right in. Her shopping purchases had been delivery, and she was ready for almost any occasion. Dillard she thought was very helpful and kind of cute in his own Dillard way, she smiled to herself, lying on her chaise enjoying the good life.

"Katia," he said, coming in from the office after a long day. "I have some good news, I found the files and the original paperwork for Doris Woods but there's a problem," he shared.

He and Katia had been up late the night before looking through some of his old boxes for the paperwork from years past.

"Problem, what's the problem?" she asked. "You said she wanted the list. You found the list and there is still a problem?" she added, gazing at him standing beside the elevated fireplace on the patio.

"True, that's very true, but she also asked about an old book. And I cannot recall shipping out a book, and there is not one on the list, see," Dillard shared, giving the document to Katia.

She looked over it. "Just add 'and old book sent to my son' and she will be happy, case closed." She smiled, getting up.

"What's for dinner?" he asked, walking into their home arm and arm.

"We're going out," she stated. "I have the perfect outfit from Neiman's I'm dying to wear," she acknowledged.

"That's fine," Dillard replied, "just know we have a big party to go to Saturday in Rancho Santa Fe, a fellow attorney of mine is having a big celebration after winning a major case, so it's going to be fun."

"Really," Katia replied, "and I'm your date for the evening," she teased, smiling.

"Unless you'd like me to ask Sylvie," he joked, knowing she didn't want to hear that name again.

"I'm going to pretend I didn't hear that," she said, walking off to go get dressed for dinner.

Dillard walked into the office of his home putting down his briefcase and laying his jacket on the back of his leather chair. He stood by his large picturesque window view looking at the signed document that had no room on it to add anything professionally or neatly without it looking like an afterthought, he reasoned.

"I'll come up with something. Dana's gone and I certainly can't redo the document. It has her signature on it. How would I get that! Tomorrow, that's thought for tomorrow, tonight I'm going to put that all out of my mind and enjoy another wonderful night out in LA with Katia," he said, looking up to see her walking down the grand staircase in a fabulous rose-patterned gown by Khan.

CHAPTER 10

ADELE WAS MEETING ERENE AGAIN for lunch. A few months had gone by since their last meeting. Months before both had been meeting going out, looking for Rhea on the street. Finding her sometimes, Adele would make sure she had enough food that wasn't perishable, and she loved candy bars. Depending on her mood, Rhea would let her buy lunch for her and a friend at one of the dives in the area. Adele had finally come to realize that she needed to meet Rhea where she was and be willing to take what was left of her life and let her be at peace. She made sure Rhea visited a clinic and just let her live the life she had chosen unfortunately. This went on for close to a year. Erene wasn't always with her physically, but she always felt his heart of caring, she would always remember. One time she came upon Rhea lying under the tracks and had to call emergency services to have her revived. Erene had been such a comfort and a help to her with Rhea who to this point was giving Adele the blues, trying to keep her alive on the streets. Erene encouraged her and listened, allowing her to vent her frustrations and disappointments.

"Erene, what a surprise. I didn't expect to hear from you again."

"Lunch?"

"Sure, I'll see you at 12:15," she shared, hanging up her telephone line and heading into a meeting. She was taking advice from him on taking care of herself, her emotions, and her well-being, you know, some me time. Adele had also planned a shopping trip with a friend to relax. Erene she knew was a Christian, married, and a very loving man. They had talked about all of that as he helped her through the rough patch of life she was in. "What's going to happen to me when Fletcher's gone off to college? I certainly don't want to be an old maid, with no one. I'm young, and fun, and full of life, and I want someone to care and share it with. A man with a caring heart like Erene," she thought, sitting now, listening to another qualifying requirements meeting that takes place every month or so in her department.

Keith was up early and on his way out of the shower when Annie awoke the next morning.

"You are up early," she said, wrapping her arms around his waist. "What time did you come to bed? I waited for you."

He pulled her hands apart and gave her a kiss on the forehead. "Not late, but you were sleeping well when I came into bed," Keith replied.

"Try running around with Riley all day. It's easier to go to the office," Annie said, going in to relieve herself and start her morning routine.

Keith was swallowing down his coffee when Annie came out from her shower with her robe on.

"You are leaving already? Aren't you going to see Riley before you leave out?" she asked.

"I didn't want to wake her, besides I need to get an early start this morning," he shared, picking up his briefcase heading to the door.

"Did you forget something?" Annie asked, standing near the door.

"Oh," he said, reaching over to again kiss her forehead.

"Keith, I'm going to have to talk to William Parker about your caseload, you're being overworked," she teased to get a smile anyway.

He forced a smile and said, "I'll see you at the office," and closed the door behind him as he left.

Annie headed back to the kitchen getting a cup from the cabinet for her coffee. She sat down thinking about Keith's behavior of late, his bizarre trip to Colorado, and his babbled explanation as to why.

As she finished her wheat toast and coffee, she heard Riley. "Morning, Mommy, where's Daddy?" was the first thing out of her mouth.

"Daddy's gone to the office but will be home early tonight," she said. "Let's go and get ready for school," she added, picking her up and heading to her child's bedroom.

Keith wasn't lying when he said he was going into the office early to get a head start on some documents, but what he failed to say was he had also promised Abby he would give her a ride in this morning. Getting on the freeway going in the opposite direction of the office and about an hour drive back to the office downtown, he picked up Abby and they rode in together. Keith and Abby thought it best to keep this between them and defuse questions. What's a ride between friends! Driving to the curb about a block away where Abby had asked him to let her out at a small coffee shop, he drove into the secured parking lot, meeting one of his fellow attorneys coming in early as well.

Letting out a sigh, he said, "Good morning, McGuire, you're early!"

"Yeah, but I could say the same." He smiled back, shaking his hands.

"You're right, been off for a while playing catch-up," Keith acknowledged, with both going up the steps to the elevator to the office.

"What do you think of the new help?" Keith asked.

"She's easy on the eyes," McGuire replied, "and those legs, they go up to her neck," he added with his man talk.

Keith smiled. "She's a young woman with looks for sure, McGuire," Keith stated.

"She's twenty-five and single, we all met her when you were off," McGuire informed, "but seriously, she seems to be a perfect fit for the office, only time will tell and Annie, of course. When is Annie going to give her the thumbs-up?" McGuire asked, pouring his first cup of coffee from the office pot.

"Annie will be in soon, and I better get started," he said, heading to his office to work and wondering when Abby would make her entrance.

"Hi there," Adele greeted Erene sitting at the table in the restaurant.

"Thought we'd change and give seafood a try," he said smiling as she sat down to the table. "Looks like you've been taking my advice," he shared.

"Oh," Adele said.

"You look rested." He smiled.

"Thank you, I did sleep well last night. I was with the family for dinner. We always have a fun time playing games, eating and encouraging each other," she confessed.

"Great, so they are a support system for you?"

"They are, as a matter of fact, the boys saw Rhea the other day, took her to lunch, and talked with her a bit. She still went on her way, but we knew that day she was okay," Adele shared. "Even as early as a couple of weeks ago, we got her to spend the night and go to Fletcher's game at the high school. We had to promise her we'd take her back downtown when it was over. But enough about me, what have you been doing?" she asked. It had been three months since she saw him.

"Pretty hectic, you know, there is always something or someone who needs investigating, and working from my office at the precinct is quite demanding," he replied.

"You're amazing, I told you, and thanks for somehow fitting me in your very busy schedule," Adele shared, giving a caring look across the table.

"A person is required to eat," Erene responded, bringing laughter to the conversation, waving to the waiter to get his attention. "Let's order."

"Good morning. Look who I found," Annie announced, coming into the office.

The attorneys all came from the respective offices to say good morning to a new day, giving her the office hugs and smiles. Keith had come out as well but turned around after he saw Abby standing next to Annie.

"So I'm gone for a few days, you guys panic and replace me," Annie teased, hitting William's shoulder, laughing.

"No, no, we would never replace you, Annie. I'm lightening your load," Billy replied.

"That's it," Yifat Oren confirmed, "lightening your load," laughing, going back to his office along with McGuire whispering in his ear.

"Good, I see you two are getting along."

"Yes, we planned our day on the elevator. Good morning, Mr. Parker," Abby said, going over to her desk to put down her things.

"Good morning," Billy responded. "Annie, can you come in my office for a minute?"

"Sure, William, let me put my things down and I'll be right in," she said, looking over at Abigail Necy. "Be right back." And she walked down the hall into her boss's office and closed the door.

Abby got up from her desk and went down the hall to McGuire's office.

"Good morning, Douglas, do you have any courtroom request that need completion?" she asked, coming over close to him in the chair. She was flirting with him. She was a quick understudy and had his number after the first day.

"Sure do, looking her up from bottom to top, handing her the documents."

"Thanks, Douglas." Smiling and giving a stance in the door, she was gone.

"Trying to start the day, do you need something, anything pressing?" she asked now in Yifat Oren's office. "How's the missus?" she asked, knowing that the first thing he had shared with her when they sat together in the break room was his forty-three-year marriage.

"Thanks for asking, she's doing well, and welcome back." He smiled, letting her know he had e-mailed her about some pretrial agreements that he needed today.

"I'll make them first priority and e-mail you back, sir, when it's completed," she said, smiling and walking out.

Keith's office sat down a bit past the break area of the spacious law firm.

"I met Annie coming up in the elevator," she said, smiling.

"It would be hard not to since she works here," he responded.

"She's pretty," she said, looking for a reaction, he guessed. Abby could tell he was uneasy, looking constantly at the door. "She's in a meeting with Mr. Parker. Is there something urgent on your agenda this morning?" she said, leaning over his desk directly in his face, showing off some cleavage.

"Stand up, please?" Keith said, pushing her up with his arm outstretched. "I need some photocopies, but no hurry."

"Okay, so you'll pick me up at the coffee shop after work?" she asked, shocking him.

What had he gotten himself into with this young lady? Before he could answer, Annie was coming in.

"Hi, hon, I see you guys are keeping Abby busy."

"Yes, I was just saying I need some photocopies but no hurry, not sure what Yifat Oren and McGuire has for her?" he nervously answered.

"I have some pretrial agreements for McGuire, so I'll get on those," Abby replied, excusing herself from the office.

"Riley asked for you this morning. I told her you'd be home early tonight," Annie stated, sitting on the corner of his desk rubbing his hair.

"I'm working diligently to make that happen, so out with you," he said, giving her a peck on the lips and a tap on her bottom, sending her from his office.

Dillard came home to find Katia in his office practicing signatures.

"What are you doing?" he asked, shocked by her actions.

"Calm yourself, Dillard. I know what I'm doing, you need a new document for your client, and take a look, pretty good, huh?" she asked, handing him the redo of the list he had given her a few days ago.

"How did—you are brilliant, Katia," he said, putting the documents aside of each other comparing them. "This will get Doris off my back and close up the questions forever. She will know everything her sister wanted to have done in her last days and she will certainly be happy and, I trust, satisfied," he said, giving Katia a peck to her cheek and dialing his client on the phone walking out of the room.

Annie was very pleased with Abby's efficiency with legal matters in the office. Both worked well together and before noon had gotten the office back on track.

"What's for lunch?" she turned, asking Abby whose desk set in a cove but not far from hers.

"Not sure, maybe meeting a friend," she replied.

"Good, we have some great eating places downtown, we will have to have lunch one day," Annie suggested.

"That's great. I'm just getting settled in, and I'm sure we will have plenty of those." She smiled.

"So, you like the office so far?"

"I do, Annie. So how long have you and Keith been married?" she asked.

She and Annie had that conversation coming up in the elevator this morning.

"Keith and I have been married five years, we have a five-year-old daughter, Riley," she replied, taking the photo from her desk.

"Riley's very cute with her dark curls," she pointed out.

"She takes from Keith's side, his mom is Greek," she informed.

"Oh, that will do it," Abby agreed, seeing Annie and Keith were blonds. "After you've been here for a while, I will take you where I'm leaving to go now," Annie said. "I'm working with McGuire on some legal documents and stopping by the law library, you have a good lunch."

Annie went into Keith's office, letting him know she and McGuire would be out for a few hours and she'd see him when they returned. Abby had worked on some documents for Billy and was standing at his office door.

"Come in, how are things going so far?" he asked her.

"Well, I hope, I'm really enjoying it and I like Annie too," she added.

"Very good, that's important. Annie is a viable part of this law firm and we all treat each other as family," he said. "Have a sit."

She sat down and crossed her gorgeous legs. He was a Christian but no way was he blind to the fact that this young lady was gorgeous. She brought some much-needed life into the place, he thought, that's why he hired her. Nada had helped him with the hiring process, check qualifications, and he was pleased with their decision thus far. He smiled when he saw the resemblance of a younger Annie. But he'd never tell Nada that!

"If there is anything or any questions, don't hesitate to ask one of us," he again reminded her.

"Thank you, sir," she said, getting up, showing off her God-given curves.

"Oh, and, Abby."

"Yes, Mr. Parker."

"I prefer William or Billy," he said, allowing her now to leave his office smiling, leaving the file documents she had brought in.

"Good afternoon, Mrs. Parker?" Adele asked, calling her home.

"Yes, this is Mrs. Parker, how may I help you?"

"I'm Adele. I met you outside of your husband's building and wanted to ask a favor?"

There was silence. Either Nada was trying to remember her or waiting to hear why she called, but most of all, wondering how she got her number.

"Adele? The young lady, Justin's friend, am I right?"

"Yes, Mrs. Parker."

"Call me Nada, what can I do?" she asked again, now knowing who was calling.

"I absolutely love your style of dress, and I was wondering if you could teach me how to dress professionally and young and hip," she asked, with her shoulders squinting, Nada thought.

"Oh." Nada smiled. "I'd love to, that would be so much fun."

"Really, you will? Thank you, thank you so much!" Adele was so excited. "Okay, bye," she said, getting of the phone.

"No, wait," Nada said, quickly stopping her. "When were you planning for us to do this?" Nada asked.

"Oh, when you say," was her response.

"All right," she said, seeing she needed direction in making the decision. "How about we start this Saturday? That works for me," Nada suggested.

"Me too!" Adele voiced, still excited Nada said yes.

"Let's meet at the mall, they have a variety of stores and we will go from there."

"Thanks, Mrs. Parker, see you there by Starbucks this Saturday at noon."

Nada got off the phone smiling and shaking her head, but she was so looking forward to getting out and having a fun day of shopping.

"Lunchtime," she said, leaving the office, heading out the building and down the street around the corner to the small coffee shop for lunch.

Five maybe ten minutes later, Keith headed out also. "I'm going to step out for a minute, shouldn't be long," Keith shared, heading out the office to the elevator and down the street, through the park around the corner to the small coffee shop. He was purposely staying off the street as not to be seen. Abigail had sent him an e-mail stating to meet her at the coffee shop for lunch. He had better squash it and squash it now, he thought, walking in the door of the small place seeing her sitting at a table in the corner.

"I'm having a panini, they're not bad," she advised.

Keith sat down. His shy personality he'd guess had gotten him in this mess or being mad at Annie, his wife. But whatever it was, here goes, "Abigail, I'm happily married. I'm not sure what I did to make you think otherwise but—"

"Keith, just because I asked you to lunch, you think I want to jeopardize your marriage?"

"I'm sneaking around corners and dodging folks, for heaven's sake, we work in the same office and my wife does too! And I don't like it! I can't continue to do this. It was just an innocent ride home!" he stated, looking at her naive smile across the table.

"Keith, calm down, I just wanted to say thank you for helping out, I pick up my car this weekend." She smiled, touching his hand.

Keith looked around. He didn't see anyone that knew him there. It was his first time at the small place.

"Good, that's good," he exhaled. "So Friday will be the last time I'll need you, but I will see you here after work." And she got up and walked out.

Keith sat there, wondering, "What just happened?" He had two more days of this. Her subtle threat had him a bit frightened of what she would do. He ordered a coffee to go and walked slowly back through the park to the office.

Dillard hurried down the street to McCormick & Schmick's for lunch with Doris Woods, Dana Williams's sister. He wanted to personally give her the list he had obtained from Dana's estate file. Looking years younger and sharp as a tack, he made his way to the reservation desk.

"Mrs. Woods, please," he asked, standing, looking dapper in his learned style from the New York gurus.

"Right this way," a waiter, standing stiff with hand behind his back, said, responding to his request.

Doris suggested the meeting place that was blocks from her boutique on Rodeo Drive. Dillard agreed and he opted to bring the document to her meeting at the restaurant on Rodeo.

"Good afternoon, Mr. Patterson," Doris said as he approached the table.

"Good afternoon," he said, returning the greeting with an extended hand.

"My, I see you have been bitten by Hollywood," she smiled stating, looking from his head to feet. Doris had known Dillard for years. He was her deceased sister's attorney when they first came to Los Angeles. "I'm impressed," she added.

"Thank you, I'll take that, it means a lot coming from you," Dillard replied sitting down, getting comfortable at the table. After the waiter brought back their drinks and took their order, Dillard took the document from his briefcase he carried all the time. "And here it is," he said, laying it on the table and slowly pushing it in front of her.

Doris picked up the single piece of paper. "Just like Dana, always scribbling thoughts down, she was always writing in that diary, you know," she said, remembering. "Thank you for finding it. And there it is, the old book she sent to David Michael. Now we know, we can put her to rest," she confessed.

Dillard sat thinking the same thing, hoping this was the final act of material things she would request from him. Dana had written everything out and where she wanted it to go. "I trust this will answer all your questions," he said, taking a drink of wine from his stemmed glass.

"Yes, and again, thank you for your timelessness in getting this to me," Doris shared with a smile, "it means a lot."

The waiter came over with their ordered entrées.

"This looks great," Dillard said.

"It does, it certainly does," Doris replied.

The day went along well at Parker and Associates. Abigail, Annie's new legal trainee, was doing a great job for the law firm. Annie and McGuire came back around three from the court's law library to find everyone still hard at work.

"Annie, I have some questions about this memo and application you left to have typed." Annie stood with arms filled with briefcase and purse after coming back. "When you get settled, no hurry," she added, smiling at her.

"Sure, let me get rid of this stuff and I'll answer your questions," Annie replied, going over to her desk to lay things aside. "So how was lunch? Is everyone still in house?" she said, now standing at her desk after answering the questions Abby had on the client's file. Billy's door was closed, so Annie knew that meant he was in a meeting.

She headed down the hall to speak with Keith. "Hi, honey," she said, seeing he was enthralled in his work.

"Hi, so you and McGuire made it back, I see," he said, getting up from his desk.

"Did you get lunch?" she asked.

"Why?" he snapped back.

She looked displeased of his comeback. "I just asked because if I'm not here to remind you, you won't eat!" she responded.

"Sorry, honey. I'm tired, I guess," he said, realizing and checking his attitude.

"Precisely why you're heading straight home tonight, right?" she suggested. "Can I help with anything?" she asked.

"No, Abby helped type the medical records and accident reports I needed."

"Good, she seems to be on top of things. I'm pleased so far," Annie acknowledged, looking at the reports she had processed for Keith's client. "What do you think of her?" she asked, now putting the file back together and looking at him.

"Why does it matter what I think? If William hired her and you like her work, she seems to get along with everyone, what's to think?" he said, skirting the questions Annie was posing. "She seems fine, let me get back to work," Keith said, kissing her as she left.

"Oh, I'm leaving at five today," Annie reminded. "You know I have to get Riley on time and I hope you're home for dinner," she said, smiling, walking out the office. She met Abby coming from McGuire's office.

"Hello, Aunt Doris, how are you?" David Michael said after his aunt had called him.

"I'm good, and how are your classes going?"

"I can't complain. It's going better than I envisioned with baseball and everything," David added.

"Books first, right?" she proposed, still with a smile.

"You sound like my dad," he said, laughing aloud across the phone.

"Speaking of your dad, how is he?" Doris asked.

"Dad's fine, they're awaiting a new arrival in less than six months and have their hands full with Peyton," he shared. "I had a wonderful time on my last visit. What's happening with you, Auntie?" he asked, turning the conversation.

"I just had lunch with Mr. Patterson."

"Dana's old lawyer, why? What happened?" he asked anxiously.

"No, nothing to be alarm about," she paused. "Remember the old book you received?"

"Yes, yes, what about it?" David quickly asked.

"I got the list from Dillard your mother had given him and that was one of the items on it," she confirmed.

"So Dillard sent it to me on Dana's request?"

"Yes, that's correct. So, our mystery is solved," he affirmed.

"Yes, David, now Dana can rest," Doris shared, "she can now rest."

Annie and Abby sat at their desk laughing and talking at the end of the day. Billy's client meeting was long over and he was now having a meeting with his fellow attorneys in the large conference room. Looking up at the clock after hearing the noise and the *tat-tat* of feet coming down the hallway before realizing it was five o'clock.

"Thanks for all your help, it was a good day today," she said to Abby, gathering her things to leave. "Keith, walk me out," she said, giving him a box she needed to take home. With "Good night," she headed to the elevator with Keith. He didn't say a word all the way down. "You're quiet, did you guys have another one of those chew-out meetings?" she asked. "You're awfully quiet," she added.

"Just have a lot on my mind, that's all," Keith replied.

"Dr. Belton," Annie asked, getting into her car looking around. "I wonder what kind of car Abby drives?"

"What?" Keith stated.

"Just seeing how she rolls, what she likes, it's a woman thing, I guess, see you at home," she said, giving Keith a kiss and closing the door, pulling from the lot.

"Katia, Katia, I'm home!" Dillard announced loudly coming into his sitting room.

Katia was sitting with a bottle of expensive wine waiting for him.

"Well, how did it go?" she asked.

"Like a charm. I'm happy, she's happy. Win-win!" he said, removing his jacket. Picking up his glass, he asked, "Do you mind?"

"Not at all," Katia replied as he leaned over and gave her a passionate kiss.

Keith sat in his office trying to wait out William and Douglas in going home. Yifat Oren had made his exit at five thirty along with Abigail, who had text him back she was waiting at the coffee shop that closed at 6:00 p.m. He walked around pretending to make copies and arranging papers in the supply closet. The small flask he had in his suit pocket was empty. About a quarter to six, Billy announced his departure and McGuire did likewise. Right on their heels was Keith, seeing them pull from the underground space. He quickly got into his car and up around the corner getting Abby and off he went.

CHAPTER 11

"SEE YOU IN THE MORNING," he heard Abigail say as she got out of the car closing the door.

How could he keep doing this? He only did it because he was mad at Annie. It had gone too far and Abby was threatening now to tell Annie if he didn't show up. He'd have to make up a lie to get out of the house early tomorrow morning. "This has got to stop. Annie will get suspicious. She knows what I am working on. Nothing has happened between us. I will just have to explain to Annie what happened. Why did I go to lunch with her? Annie's going to be mad! I can't tell her, Friday can't get here fast enough, then this will be over," Keith thought out loud, speeding across the highway to make dinner with his wife and daughter. Annie had called and left a message on his cell phone.

Adele sat in Starbucks waiting for Nada. She was so excited about shopping and updating her wardrobe. That's what a coworker had said. "Adele, you should think about updating your wardrobe." Sipping on her frappé, Nada walked in.

"Adele?" she asked, walking toward her. Adele could now see clearly she was pregnant with child and gave her that look.

"Don't worry. I'm good for about two hours before I fatigue. I have on my shopping shoes and I will be fine," Nada said, giving her a come with the wave of her hand to the stores. Nada had thought all night about where they would go. She knew Adele worked for a living and she was young girl well twenty-four. "Okay, tell me what we're doing today?"

"Well, I want to get some outfits like business suits and—" she replied.

"Okay, this is what we're going to do, what, you're a size 6, I'm guessing," Nada asked, walking to BCBG. "We're going to start with the staple pieces and build you a week's worth of outfits to start," Nada explained, "once you learn the concept, the sky's the limit."

"Staple?" she asked.

"Yes, Adele, basics are things every woman needs in her closet. Follow me," she said, interlacing her arm in hers and heading into the store.

Keith hurried speedily across the highway to get home before dinner was over, taking a swig of rum he now had under his seat before going in. He walked in seeing Riley and Annie still sitting at the table.

"Sorry, honey," he said, sitting down to prepare his plate after putting down his work things.

"Hi, Daddy," Riley said, vying for some attention. He kissed her and sat down, playing with her while Annie warmed dinner for him.

"What case are you working on? I saw you had the Frandue case nearly completed when McGuire and I left at noon," she remembered.

"Yes, but a new one came in, and now that I caught up, I can spend more time with my daughter," he said, continuing to play with Riley.

"So you're good, all caught up?" she asked again as he ate.

"I'll go in early tomorrow, finish the week strong and settle back into the good life." He smiled at her affectionately.

"So another early day, you're going to work yourself out of a job," she teased.

"Dinner is good, sweetheart," Keith said, changing the subject matter.

Annie could feel Keith was being evasive, but after the week she had gone through with him, she was glad he had rebounded from whatever Dr. Benton had shared with him that caused him to spiral. Annie just wanted it to be over.

Billy had spoken with his parents about coming for a visit, and the plans were to come around Peyton's birthday. So now that she was a bit older, she would better understand it, and Nada had planned a big day for her little girl. She was turning three and so full of life, besides being spoiled rotten by everyone.

"Mom, yes, we are looking forward to having you and Dad visit," he said, speaking with Tetra after her call to his office. "Seminary is challenging as expected. Dr. Stewart, one of the instructors, has been helping me out with questions I'm having," he informed after she asked. "The office? The office is good, we just hired some help for Annie and things seem to be okay. Yes, that will allow her more time out and away from the office. Yes, Mother. Nada is very joyful these days, being a mother agrees with her. Yes, she is very active in the church, she lunches with friends, and of course, she has me," he teased across the lines with his mom. "She hasn't stopped talking and planning since we decided to give the party this year. Tell Dad to ship his clubs. I'm sure we will get in some golf this week while he's here. I know, Mom, you and Nada will have so much stuff in that nursery Peyton nor the baby will have any room to play," he added, laughing with her. "I love you, love to Dad," he said, disconnecting the call.

Adele couldn't wait for tomorrow to come. She was like a fifth-grade girl on the first day of school. Nada and she had so much fun shopping on her budget with outfits that flattered her body. Nada showed her how to pick out sets of clothing that went together, be it color, texture, or pattern it works. She was so nice Adele thought now looking at the wardrobe she had purchased,

"What will I wear?" She was not overwhelmed by the prices at the stores Mrs. Parker had suggested for her. Nada had taken her to stores within her budget and everything went well. She showed her how to pick out "staples" until today Adele didn't know what that was. Every girl needs the basic black dress, pants, a jacket, and voila, the combinations are endless. Of course they picked out a business suit and a pencil skirt and a couple pair of shoes this time, one pair is a cute little wedge style.

"I didn't know I could look like this on my budget! Thank you, Mrs. Parker. I can't wait until we shop next time! I can't wait until tomorrow! What will I wear?"

Jumping in bed and pulling the covers over her head, she said, "Good night."

Keith was up very early tiptoeing around as not to wake up Annie. His razor fell to the floor while he was in the shower and it woke Annie. She lay there pretending to be asleep while Keith moved carefully getting dressed. Grabbing his suit jacket, he headed out of the bedroom.

"Keith, you're up and dressed already, what is it, 6:30 a.m.?" she asked pretending to be sleepier than she really was.

"Honey, I shared with you I had to go in early today," he said, reminding her of a conversation they had.

"Yes, but you're leaving without kissing me even after last night," she said, giving him a reminder of their passionate night together.

"Honey, you're right, that was incredible," he said, coming over, hugging her tightly and kissing her closed mouth.

"Morning breath," she said to let him understand why she wasn't kissing him as usual. "I will make it up to you later today," she added.

He wanted this day over and he wanted all the trust in his relationship back. Most of all, he wanted to be free from guilt as he stood by the liquor cabinet sneaking a drink to deal with this Abby. He went into Riley's room and gently kissed her forehead and left out the door. The law firm didn't open until nine, but Keith wanted to be in before anyone else could see him coming in with Abigail Necy. As he pulled up to her place, he noticed the time was 7:15. He sent a text letting her know he was outside. He sat there without hearing a response and sweat was now messing up his nice starched professional-cleaned shirt as he stole his first swig from the refilled flask he now carried. Just as he was opening the door to go and knock, Abby emerged smiling. "Sorry, couldn't decide what to wear today, forgive me please," she cooed, getting in, showing off her shapely legs. With the clock ticking down, Keith was now behind the time he had set for himself. The traffic slowed to almost a stop as the time was approaching eight o'clock.

"We will be fine," she voiced, sitting smug in the passenger seat.

"Oh, when I get you to the office, I suggest you call a friend, or someone you know! I cannot take you home!" he shared, finally getting a clear lane to proceed in. He hurried along down the highway to his turn off. Now downtown, he drove to the coffee shop and pulled to the curve in front. It didn't open until 8:30 a.m. "Get out!" He didn't even look again at her nor look back when she hesitantly got out, leaving her pricey pink-patterned briefcase in his car. Keith was breathing hard as he parked under the law firm in his assigned space. Looking in his backseat, he noticed the case.

"How can I get that hot pink case up without being seen?" he thought, running up the steps to the elevator with it covered under his coat.

"Good morning," he said, meeting others who worked in the building as well. "Please don't let McGuire or Oren be here yet," he said out loud, putting his key in the door. He hurried and put the expensive case down on Abby's desk and ran to his office, closing the door, quick drink from his flask, and Keith started to work. It was 8:31. Annie usually arrives at 8:45.

"Good morning," he heard from the guys coming in after seeing lights on and the coffee brewing. He also heard Abby and Annie come in as well.

"There it is. I was worried I had left it at the coffee shop." Abby heaved a naive sigh, taking the case from her desk smiling.

Katia was very happy these days. This new lifestyle she had chosen by being with Dillard wasn't so bad. And she knew he was sweet on her. She liked him, all right, but she was in love with his success, his drive, and his personality. Now that she had him dressing and looking the part, they could move on to the next steps, she reasoned, getting dressed and waiting for him to arrive home. Tonight was the big gala in Rancho Santa Fe. More shopping deliveries had come this week, and her wardrobe was growing fabulously.

"What gown shall I adorn myself in tonight?" she thought, looking through her enormous bedroom-sized designed closet space. She was now in a private place, living a very good life. She needed to get involved with something because some days went by like watching paint dry on a wall. She needed something to do! She had sat down earlier getting facts from one of the *Forbes* magazines Dillard subscribed to. She wanted to be well versed on all parts of Los Angeles if the conversation came up tonight. Noting that Ranch Santa Fe is one of the most expensive zip codes in the United States, she was very impressed. Dillard was feeling trust from her as well taking her around his friends and fellow colleagues. Katia had impressed him by helping him with Doris Woods, a client, and now she's going to be his eye candy tonight, walking around on his arm. She had to be well informed and well versed, believable to those she encountered tonight as a seasoned LA icon. Dillard had shared they were A—listers, and Katia was excited to be able to complement Dillard in his world. Her dress was an original from Saks Fifth Avenue on Rodeo Drive. A Gucci feathered dress costing over eight thousand dollars paired with ankle heels accented by diamonds. Her gorgeous blond locks of curls bounced beautifully around her dazzling blue eyes as she walked down the stairs to the parlor to wait her date for tonight.

Nada showed up in the office about eleven thirty. Today was the girls' lunch day at their favorite Italian restaurant.

"Nada, would you mind if I ask Abigail to join us today?"

"No, that's fine, as a matter of fact, I was going to suggest it," Nada responded.

"I'll ask. I think she is in Oren's office," Annie said, going down the hall.

Nada walked along to Billy's office.

"Hi, honey, I think I see a waddle," he teased.

"Awww, honey!" She sighed, walking into his arms.

"So it's girls' lunch day, huh."

"It is, and we have asked Abigail to come along."

"Good," Billy replied.

"Oh, Adele is meeting us as well, she wants me to see her in one of her outfits she bought," Nada confessed.

"Honey, that's why I love you," Billy shared, kissing her as they stood talking in his office.

Abby was standing in McGuire's door.

"Fix your skirt," she whispered loudly to her.

"Oops, just coming from the ladies' room, we've got to install a full-length mirror for us," she suggested, twisting her skirt in place.

"Hey, it's girls' lunch day, want to go with us?"

"Us?" Abby whispered.

"Nada and I, we lunch every other Friday, you're welcome to tag along," she said.

"You and Mrs. Parker?"

"Yes, now do you want to go? Get your purse. I'm going to let Keith know I'm leaving, he has been so busy today," she said, walking down the hall around the corner to his office.

Keith again played all is well. He certainly didn't want Annie having lunch with Abby and now Nada! What this woman might say plagued him. OMG! went through his mind as he swigged from his flask. While at lunch, he texted Abby, begging her to please be quiet about him and he would take her home tonight as promised. Keith sat in his office hearing his intercom.

"Poulton, can you please come to my office?" Billy asked. He was concerned about the late hours he was working and wanted to offer help if needed. Keith did not answer back. He just got up and headed into the office. "Keith, how are things?" Billy asked.

"Look, William. I don't want to talk about me, or babies, or having babies!"

"Hold on, hold on, Keith, you're on a runaway train."

"I'm tired of being the talk of the office, poor me!"

"Is that how you feel? Is that why you've been working yourself to death and staying hidden?" Billy questioned.

"You walk around bragging about your baby this and your baby that!"

"Wait, Keith," he said, getting up to close the door. Getting closer to him, he could smell the alcohol on his breath.

"Keith, can I help? I mean, what's going on? You're going off on me, and what have I done?" he asked, looking at him now slumped in a chair.

"I saw Dr. Benton when I got back from Colorado, so no good news there, and I don't think ever, so let's just stop asking me if we are having another child okay!"

"I understand, I didn't mean to make you feel bad. I'm so sorry, man, that's the last thing I wanted to do," he said, embracing Keith who was bawling like a baby standing in his office. "Sometimes we are so happy for ourselves we forget about others. You and Annie mean the world to me. You have a beautiful daughter that God blessed you with, and if He sees fit, He will give you another, but it will be His call. And I will let you tell me," Billy shared, heavy-hearted. He didn't realize the effect the conversations and questions they were having about Annie and he having another child was causing a problem. And Billy felt bad.

"My dad is in good spirits, and my mom is staying strong, thanks for asking," he said, sitting, blowing his nose and wiping his eyes with the Kleenex from William's desk. "I'm so happy for you and Nada. I'm sorry. I just have a lot to deal with right now."

Billy stood there with his fellow attorney and friend whom he saw almost every day and he still wasn't sure what to say or do. "Why don't you and Annie plan a vacation? We have Abby here now and the two of you could get away and relax and talk."

"I'll think about it, man," he replied.

Billy thought he looked close to a breakdown. Keith was a social drinker but never at the office. Clearly something was wrong. "I'll have Nada get Riley, she can stay with us, and we don't mind caring for her while you two have some time together," Billy stated. "We are her godparents, after all," he teased to bring a smile. "That's final, you speak with Annie and let me know Monday morning. If you need me before then, please call," Billy asked, giving the now-standing Keith an embrace.

"Thanks," he said and walked out, down the hall to his office. Billy closed his door and prayed, pouring out his heart for a friend. Believe it or not, the ladies all got through lunch without drama! Nada and Adele left the restaurant together after their lunch. Nada complimented her on her new look. The outfit she had chosen to wear was very flattering, Nada said to her, "very age appropriate."

"Thanks, Mrs. Parker." Adele felt independent and confident as she strolled back to her office after saying good-bye to the ladies and Nada.

Annie and Abby were coming back from lunch just about the time Keith had reentered his office again. Annie had brought him lunch and was headed to his office with it.

Dillard looked suave in his black Valentino tuxedo standing in the foyer of his home waiting for his date to come from the powder room.

"I will never understand how a woman can be dressed and still be late," Dillard voiced, looking at his Breitling watch on his arm.

Before long, Katia in her lovely gown walked out to the foyer and both walked together to the Maybach parked in the driveway.

"No limo?" Katia asked, standing at the Benz door waiting entrance.

"No, not really, different crowd," Dillard replied. "Most will drive themselves, you'll see. Oh, and Milburn will most likely be there."

Katia had met Milburn briefly at a smaller annual function given by the law firm.

"Maybe this will be our lucky night and there will be no Milburn, she said sitting content in the passenger seat of the smooth riding automobile.

"So is it safe to say you're happy here in Los Angeles thus far?" he asked, making conversation as he drove the I-5 highway to Rancho Santa Fe.

The day had come to an end. Annie was very busy as were everyone in the law firm. Billy came from a meeting on the second floor to find Annie saying good night to everyone and leaving to go and pick Riley up from school.

"Did you speak with Keith?" he asked with Abby looking on from her desk.

"Excuse me?" Annie replied.

"Can you please come into my office for a moment?" he asked for privacy.

"Sure, what's going on?" Annie asked, coming in and closing the door, sitting down.

"I spoke with Keith while you all were at lunch."

"Yes, about what?" Annie asked. She didn't want to go through this again. She and Keith had promised not to talk about their problems in the office. *Now what?* she thought.

"I suggested you all get away for a bit, just you and Keith.

When is the last time you all had time to yourself?" Billy asked.

"It's been a while, not since Riley was born, if you're saying alone," Annie replied.

"I know you have noticed he is under a lot of stress with his father's illness and other things," Billy stated.

"What are you talking about, William, you're scaring me," Annie confessed. "Keith has been bothered by what Dr. Benton shared with him. He wouldn't tell me, but I promised him I wouldn't discuss it with you or anyone in this office, he hates that!" Annie said, getting up.

"I know, I know, Annie, I'm so sorry. I missed seeing what it was doing to him to talk about having babies."

"Did he tell you?" Annie asked, looking up with eyes filled with tears. "I have been walking around on eggshells since we got back from Colorado with our baby. He says things are fine, but he has poured himself into work and leaves early and comes home late. Honestly, I don't want to set him off again."

"I suggested to Keith that you two get away for a while. Nada and I will be glad to care for Riley, and you two can relax and reconnect," Billy said as a friend. Still speaking, there was a knock on his office door.

"Come in," Billy said, opening the door to Keith standing in it now.

"Abby left, she said good night, and I'm leaving as well. It's 5:15 p.m. I thought you had left to pick up Riley, what are you two talking about?" he said, smiling very calmly but clearly upset.

"I'm on my way now," she said. Leaving with "Good night, and have a great weekend," she jumped up from the chair and was gone.

"Keith, I was asking Annie about Abigail's work this week, how she's getting along with everyone and her work performance," Billy lied, but he did not want to set Keith off either. "She seems to get along with everyone, and I didn't have to tell her over and over again about drafts or corresponding documents I needed," he confirmed. Do you think she will be able to run the office if Annie's gone for a week or so?"

"She knows her stuff, but of course, Annie is the best at what she does, so if she's happy, I'm happy," Keith ended. "And, Bill, I'm going to talk to Annie tonight about your suggestion," he said, shaking his hand, and with a "Good night," he was gone.

Billy could see he was still not himself, but at least he didn't smell the liquor on him as much. Keith got in his car looking around suspiciously as he drove out of the parking garage up the street around the corner to the coffee shop, picking up Abby, and off he went. He was feeling pretty good, though after emptying his flask to cover the guilt of lying to Annie. He had gotten away, it was Friday and Abby was getting her car this weekend, and he could go back to riding in sometimes with Annie.

"Keith, thank you so much for bringing me home today. I thought I'd have to take a bus or ask McGuire."

"McGuire? Why would you do that?" he asked, showing vulnerability, and Abby felt she was getting to Keith too, so she jerked a bit harder.

"Yes, McGuire, he is pretty cute," she teased, tapping his leg as Keith drove along.

"McGuire, you're kidding, right?" he asked, looking at her as she played the naive card for all it was worth.

"You said you weren't going to bring me home, soooo I . . ." Abby just smiled without finishing her sentence.

The traffic was heavy as they slowly rode along down the highway with Abby getting her claws deeper into him with her adolescent flirting.

"I enjoy your conversations, you're very smart, you know," she said, rubbing down his face as she spoke. "But McGuire is older."

"And that means what?" he asked, engaging the question, taking the exit to her townhouse. "So you're saying he's older and . . . ?"

"Oh, never mind, you're a married man. Don't get your panties in a bunch," she joked, laughing.

"Tagless briefs, if you must know," Keith responded. "And I can run circles around McGuire any day!"

"Really," she said, pulling her skirt up, showing her thighs while claiming to look for a paper in her case. "Oops, sorry about that," she explained.

Keith had swallowed hard looking at her body and trying hard to concentrate on the road and she knew it! After an hour of riding down the freeway with Abby's flirting ways and naive jesters, Keith pulled to the curve in front of her condo.

"Well, thank you, Keith, may we have lots of years together," she said, getting out the car and blowing a kiss. Her gorgeous legs and seductive walk had him sitting there gazing. He had not started the engine, waiting for her to get to the door.

"Annie, I got to get to Annie," he thought to himself, looking back to pull from the curve. "What? Not again?" He backed a bit to park his car and got out opening his back door and took out the pink case and headed to the door. He couldn't go home with that in his car. He'd really have some explaining to do, more explaining than being an hour late already. Just as he walked to the door, Annie called, "Yes, honey, stuck in freeway traffic," he said, standing at Abby's door with the case. He should have rung her doorbell, put it down, and left but . . . "I left later than I wanted to avoid traffic, so, honey, I'm trying, I love you and I'll see you as soon as I can."

"Okay," she said. He disconnected his phone, ringing Abby's doorbell.

"Who's there?" Abby asked from the closed door after a few minutes.

"Keith, you left your case again," he replied, holding it up to the peephole.

Abby opened the door, and when Keith arrived home two hours later, Annie was sitting on her couch waiting. And upset!

Katia and Dillard mingled around through the party. "Caviar? Champagne?" waiters asked, moving around the large spacious home from room to room serving each guest.

The open bar was a blast as some wanted other delights for the pallet.

"Dillard Patterson, I'm glad you made it." Looking up, Dillard saw Chad Berington, the attorney whose home they were in.

"Great space you have here, Chad. Thanks for the invite. This is my date, Katia Norfen."

"Pleasure to meet you," Katia replied, with him kissing her hand.

"Things have changed for you, Dillard my man," he said, admiring the beautiful Katia with envy.

She entwined her arm around Dillard's smiling as Chad's wife, Lola, joined the conversation.

"Very lovely home you have here," Katia said to Lola, engaging her in the small talk being had.

"Thank you, and you are?" she asked, reaching her hand.

"Katia, Dillard's date." She smiled, extending to connect hands.

"Well, it's a pleasure to have you in my home, hope to see you again, though one never knows with Dillard," she said, smiling, walking away to meet others, taking Chad with her.

It gave Dillard confidence and he stuck out his chest feeling good Katia had chosen him.

"Congrats on your win," Dillard voiced loudly over the crowd, moving away to another room. "Sorry about that, you seemed uncomfortable?"

"Quite the contrary," Katia acknowledged. "I'm very content. Lola seems to have her hands full with Chad though," she added. "Again, thanks for inviting me," she said, pulling Dillard into the room filled with laughter, joy, and dancing.

CHAPTER 12

NADA WAS BUSY AT HOME still making arrangements for all the things she wanted for Peyton's party. William had said they would have a big party this year because she was older and could get some enjoyment out of it. Peyton was turning three years old.

Ring, ring. Nada heard Millicent say the telephone was for her as she moved around picking out an outfit for Peyton's big day.

"Hello, Mrs. Parker?"

"Yes, Adele?"

"Yes, I'm sorry to bother you, but I just wanted to thank you again for all your help, I feel so different," she timidly said.

"Confident, independent, beautiful," Nada said, helping her find the words she thought described her today.

"Thank you, Mrs. Parker."

"I'm glad you called, Adele, I was going to call you."

"You were?"

"Yes, I'd like to treat you to a hair makeover to complete your look. My treat," Nada added.

"Oh, Mrs. Parker, I can't."

"It will make all the difference in the world. You have done so much for everyone else, please let me do this for you, meet me tomorrow, Saturday, at 02 Salon on Congress."

"Are you sure, Mrs. Parker?"

"I am very sure, see you then," she said, hanging up before Adele could change her mind.

Annie walked into the kitchen after being up late getting things in order with Keith. He came in and apologized over and over for being late. He hurried in their bedroom making himself comfortable, trading his slacks and dress shirt after showering for sweats, and rushed to read a bedtime story to Riley before she went to sleep to diffuse Annie's anger. He talked so sweet to Annie and discussed the conversation he and Billy had at the office. Keith felt so guilty. How could he let that happen? This woman had singlehandedly made him cheat on Annie! He was determined now that this was over. *It's done!* he thought as he made Saturday morning breakfast for his best girls.

Annie walked up to him scrambling the eggs in a pan.

"You were a beast this morning," she flirted, kissing him on his neck. "I don't know where that came from, but let's disagree more often," she teased, making him feel guilty but blushed at his wife's complimentary teasing.

"I give what I get." He smiled, moving her aside so he could put the eggs on the table. "Get Riley," he said, pushing away her playful advances, "our breakfast is getting cold." He smiled, trying to prepare all the plates for breakfast.

Annie went to Peyton's room. "See, Mommy." Peyton had dressed herself for school. Well, she had a skirt from one outfit and something with red in it from another outfit. Her shoes were on the wrong foot and her frizzy hair had a green scrunchy barely hanging from it over her eye.

Annie laughed to herself before calling Keith to bring the camera. "See, Daddy, I did it all by myself," she said proudly. Both parents raved their approval to her standing looking at herself in the mirror.

After a wonderful breakfast and family time around the table, Keith, Annie, and Peyton walked to their neighborhood park. He catered to his best girls all day long. He loved them. He laughed with them and enjoyed the entire weekend that included Peyton's birthday party on Sunday with all their friends. Yeah! Keith was being the perfect father and husband one could ever ask for.

Adele met Nada as promised. It was her regular appointment as well.

"Good morning, Mrs. Parker, and this must be Adele."

"Yes," Nada said, going over to take her appointment seat.

"Well, pleasure to have you," Marco said with his strong Italian accent. "Come this way, Emillo will be doing your hair today. What were you thinking about having done?" he asked, sitting her over in the assigned station.

Then he looked up to see Nada standing, holding a hairdo she had gotten from a magazine.

"This, Mrs. Parker, are you sure?" Adele laughed.

"Yes, this is a perfect 'do for a twenty something to wear. You will be the envy of your office," she teased with her standing, waiting for Emillo to get things ready.

"Okay, we start by putting some life into your hair," he informed.

"All right, it will be nice," Nada said, waving, going back across the shop to her assigned station and black stylist.

Sunday, Annie and Nada were standing out by the jump house disguised as a big pink princess castle featuring all the Disney princesses.

"Well, Annie, what do you think of the new legal?" she asked, looking at the girls jumping around inside the castle.

"She's efficient, and knows her job well. William says that was one of the reasons you all hired her."

"True, but how is her personality around the office?" Nada asked.

"She gets along with everyone, even grumpy McGuire." They laughed.

"Let's sit for a minute, Annie, I'm exhausted. I'm having fun, but you know when you get halfway there, the body changes and everything goes south," Nada shared.

"Whoa," she said, moving to sit in the nice comfy outdoor furniture on the lawn.

"So I must say, finding someone to stack up to you wasn't easy," Nada confessed.

Annie just smiled with a "Thank you."

"Yes, that was key. William shared you would be very hard to come close to for proficiency, let alone trying to equal. So, our hope is that Abigail will make your job easier and lighter for both of you. You can have some much-needed time off without the guys losing their minds when you are out for a day. And you're not feeling guilty when you need to do something with Riley or Keith for that matter," Nada stated.

"Thank you both for thinking of me. Abby has done a great job these past months so far, all the guys seem happy with her, so for now, she's a keeper," Annie expressed, hearing, "Mommy, come see what Peyton and I can do," her daughter said, running back to go inside the castle with four other little girls behind her.

Most of the girls were from the day care Peyton and Riley attended. Others were from the couple's church where they attended services regularly. Tetra and David Parker, Peyton's grandparents, had just arrived from Washington State and had been in town a week already. She stood for a moment looking at the girls playing around the small entrance to the castle. Riley she hadn't seen since she was very young and now told she was five. Tetra smiled at her and walked over to meet the group of mommies near Nada.

"Hello, ladies," Tetra said, coming out to see all the festivities going on. She was Nada's mother-in-law and Billy's mother.

"Hi, Mom, so glad you guys could come," Nada said, getting up to hug her.

"Sorry we're late, we were out on the boat with the Mitts and traffic was delayed on the Five, we would have been here sooner. Hi, Annie."

"Hello, Mrs. Parker."

"Hello to all," she said, looking around the circle of women who had joined Nada for lots of fun, food, and festivities. And a happy birthday too!

Katia left walking down Melrose from her Zumba class she had enrolled in to ease her daily boredom. She came prepared to walk and enjoy some of the sites for the day. Stopping at the Johnny Rockets diner for a burger she thought would be fun. She had already past Paramount Studios as she strolled down the made-famous boulevard, meeting and greeting with hi's and hellos. After enjoying her burger, she walked down to La Cienega Boulevard and enjoyed shopping for antiques in the quaint little shops. She spent time browsing the unique boutiques historical to the area.

Ring, ring.

"Hello, darling," she answered, greeting.

"Well, someone is in a good mood. How was the workout?"

"Fantastic," she responded.

"Just got in from my meeting, what time are you back?" Dillard asked.

"Shouldn't be much longer, paying to have some items shipped home. Why?"

"I was going to start the bar-b for tonight if it's still a go, you know what we talked about last evening," he reminded.

"Yes, yes, Dillard darling, I remember. Oh, and please put champagne on ice," she added, disconnecting the line.

Tetra walked into her son standing over the barbeque pit speaking with his dad and another dad, she guessed. His blond hair was a prominent feature to his looks.

"Hello," she said, walking up, giving Billy a peck on his cheek. "Mother, so glad you let Dad bring his clubs," he teased. He and David had played golf earlier in the week. And David had already said how he had sent his clubs by Fed-Ex because she said it wasn't necessary to bring them.

"Oh, now you have clubs, right?"

"I do, Mom, but a man is used to his own clubs."

"I'm sure David will play the same game with clubs from here as the ones he play with every week at home," she shared, laughing.

"Dad, she got you on that one, I'm just saying," Billy teased with everyone enjoying the rub. "Mom, I don't recall if you've met, but this is Keith Poulton, Annie's husband," Billy said, introducing her to the thought stranger standing by her husband, David.

"Pleasure," she said surprised, giving him a very obstinate look. "I met Riley and saw Annie by the castle, those girls have not stopped jumping long enough to eat," she teased with him.

"Oh, so you met Riley, yes, she's a handful," he said, squeamishly excusing himself quickly before Tetra could reply to the conversation.

Billy stood with his mom and dad removing the last pieces of kabobs from the grill.

"Son, I need to speak with you," she stated in a motherly tone. David, knowing his wife, made an excuse and quick exit away, meeting other guests mingling around the large yard space designated to the party.

"William Parker." Billy didn't have a clue what his mother was going to say, but he knew it was serious because she called him by his first and last name. "What are you thinking? If you are thinking at all," she asked, looking at him. "I'm not here to start trouble, God knows I'm not," Tetra expressed.

"Mom, what are you talking about?" he asked, waiting whatever she was being dramatic about.

"How in the world do you keep getting caught in drama?" she asked.

"What drama now?" he asked, looking at his mom sadly. "Did Nada say something to you already you've been here, what, three hours?" he stated, a bit teed off this whispering had started again.

Looking up, he saw Annie and Keith coming toward them. Keith was carrying Riley who was crying because she was not ready to go.

"Great party, Bill, will see you Monday," Keith said, shaking Billy's hand. "Thanks for the invite, and nice meeting you, Mrs. Parker," Keith said, wanting to be so far from this situation as possible.

"Oh, you all are taking her from the fun?" Tetra said, rubbing her head as she lay on her dad's shoulder.

"Keith, are things all right? I mean, you don't have to leave," Billy said, feeling bad they were leaving and concerned regarding their meeting Friday during lunch hour.

"No, man, we're fine, Riley will be fine." Riley wasn't happy and they hurriedly made their exit from the Parker's home.

Billy was now a bit upset and somewhat confused and went to find Nada.

"Sweetheart, things are going well, don't you think?" she asked as he walked up to her in a comfy wicker chair. "I hate Riley had to leave," she said.

"Yes, Keith came by as they were leaving. What happened? I mean, we haven't cut the cake yet?" he asked, astounded by the Poultons' departure.

"I know, that's what Annie was saying as Keith just pulled Riley away, saying they were leaving now," Nada replied. "Riley wasn't happy. I offered to bring her home," Nada shared, rubbing her tummy. "I really don't know he was very persistent, so I just backed off," she added. "Got a bit noticeable by others."

"So what did you say to Mom?"

"Mom, nothing unusual, why?"

"Oh, I don't know, something's weird, and I guess we will get to the bottom of it!" he responded, walking away.

Annie brought up the first question as she and Keith had sat silent almost all the way home. Riley had cried herself to sleep in her car seat secured in the back.

"Okay, I think we need to talk," she started.

"Talk about what?" he asked, driving along to their home.

"About what just happened? You pulled Riley and I away from a perfectly fun party and she is really sad," Annie said loudly.

"We talked about this, Annie. I said when I feel uncomfortable in a situation, we would leave, you agreed, right?" he asked, turning the corner now to their home.

"Uncomfortable, at the Parkers' home?" Annie asked, still trying to find an answer for her husband's abnormal behavior lately.

"Too much history there, Annie, too much, and that's all I'm going to say. If you want to go back there, you go right ahead, but I'm staying home," he said, parking the car and getting out.

Annie sat for a minute wondering what to do. Keith had opened the back door to get Riley from her seat.

"What are you going to do, Annie?" he asked sternly.

"I'm staying home, Keith," she replied.

He unhooked Riley and put her on his shoulder carrying her in the home.

"No one is going to take my little girl," he thought, walking her into their home.

Annie opened the back door on her side to get Riley's toy and a tote she carried with an extra outfit for changing. Looking down, she saw a shiny object under the seat. She reached down and pulled out the flask.

"Where did this come from? I haven't seen this since before Riley was born. He promised, he promised," she thought to herself, closing the door and walking in with it in her hand.

Tetra and David were getting ready for bed in their son's guest room of his home.

Knock, knock, they heard and responded with "Come in, we're decent."

It was their son, Billy, and he needed to talk. Tetra looked at him and hugged him tight.

"Have a sit, son," she said with her and David following suit.

"Mom, Dad, it's so hard," he said. "I've poured myself in the ministry, I'm studying at the seminary, I pray, I pray daily for strength fervently, and the devil still finds ways to sideswipe me," he shared, very heavy-hearted.

"Where is Nada?" Tetra asked, looking at the door.

"She's in bed for the evening, that's why I thought this would be a good time to come speak with you both. I told her I had some work in my study."

"The devil doesn't stop working because you start praying, he works overtime," Tetra informed him.

"How, or what can make this rumor go away? It's like a termite eating away every chance it gets. I don't know what to do, it has started affecting lives."

David knew the pain his son was feeling. "Son, you are going to need to confront the problem, lives may become disheveled now, but in the long run, God will see it through because he already knows," he said, looking wisely into his son's eyes.

"Mom, what are you thinking?" he asked, confronting her suspicions.

"I don't know for sure, and it's my first meeting with Mr. Poulton. But it's very obvious to me that he knows and is uncomfortable that someone else will find out."

"Knows what?" Billy was still clueless.

"Billy, you really don't know, do you?" she asked, holding his hand.

"Mom, please, this is so unsettling. I'm trying so hard to keep my wife happy with these pregnancy mood swings and all the personalities at the law firm, I just need straight answers and not whispers," he explained, pleading for an answer.

"I can't answer all your questions, but I can put one to rest," Tetra said, looking at her son. "Riley is not Keith's daughter," she said.

"WHAT? Mom, what? How does this keep happening? Does Nada know?"

"Can't say, she's has suspicions, I'm sure. You have got to tell her. It was before you met her. I'm only going on a mother's intuition, and this time, I'm so sorry. But I hate how long it took us to find David Michael. I hate to lose out on another one," Tetra said with a heavy heart.

"And Annie, oh my god, Annie!" Billy gasped.

"She should know, but I don't think she knows," Tetra added. "But you need to let Nada know what's going on first, above everything. She is your help, and the Word is true."

"What have I done? I can't believe this is happening again! Lord, have mercy!"

Tetra and David held their son in their arms standing in the middle of the room crying and praying for comfort through what he knows is going to be a test for the ages!

"Keith, what is this?" she asked, walking into their home. He was coming from Riley's room after laying her down to continue sleeping.

"She is really tired, she didn't squirm at all when I put her down."

"Keith, you promised, you promised me after Riley came that you would give up drinking."

"Annie, calm yourself, I found that in the garage Saturday when I aired up the tires on Riley's bike. My intent was to toss it out," he said, "honestly. The reason I chose to leave was I've shared with you that I don't want to talk about babies or having babies, and, honey, I have been really trying. You see I attempted the party," he said innocently to her.

"I'm sorry I went off on you, but you're acting so bizarre lately I figured—" Annie concluded, holding up the silver bottle.

Keith walked over to her and took the flask, throwing it in the trash. Walking back to her, he said, "Honey, Riley's asleep," smiling, pulling her to the master bedroom of their home.

The Parker family sat around the breakfast table Monday morning. There was a lot to discuss and think over. Billy's parents thought it best if he and Nada talk things through without interference from them and had decided to cut the visit there shorter than planned and go home.

David, his dad, breathed a sigh of relief. He shared his son's pain after having had an affair himself that caused the family pain and produced a child out of wedlock. When Nada brought Peyton down to say good-bye to her grandparents, it was evident she had been crying.

"Nada, are you going to be okay?" Tetra asked.

"I will, I'm committed, but it hurts if I'm being honest."

Peyton was playing with her small toy. Millicent had fed her breakfast and helped Nada get her ready for school. Peyton was riding in with her dad.

"Honey, we'll talk when I get home, should be early, okay?" Kissing her and hugging her tight, he headed to the door.

Her in-laws hugged her and went out behind their son.

"Call me if you need me," Tetra said to Nada as they walked to the door.

With good-byes shared and "Please let me know," both cars left the driveway of the estate.

Adele was the morning talk on her floor for weeks around the watercooler. Her short sassy locks enhanced her beauty tremendously. Not to mention the makeup gift Nada have given her and had shared makeup techniques to live by. She was complete from head to toe. She had a bounce of confidence as she moved throughout the office building from task to task. Some of the guys even took noticed more than once.

"Adele, you look fantastic," Hilary, her coworker, voiced one day regarding an outfit she was wearing. "You look like you just stepped out of a magazine." She laughed, sharing in her delight.

"I know, I look like a manikin, don't I?" Adele asked, moving around her desk.

"Well, if you mean very put together, yeah," she informed.

"Thank you."

"Excuse me, I'm Mason, human resources department," he said, standing now by her desk.

"See ya later," Hilary said, moving away waving.

"You are Adele, right?"

"Yes." She smiled.

"I'd like to know if you would join me for lunch?" he asked confidently, waiting an answer from the beautiful Adele.

Keith and Annie rode to the office together more often much to her surprise. They would take Peyton to kindergarten and pulled in the underground parking the same time as a small sporty hot pink mini coop driven by Abigail Necy most of the time.

"Oh, so that's what she drives," Annie said, getting out on her side of the car one morning.

"Good morning," she yelled about three stalls over.

"Good morning," Annie replied loudly.

"Good morning, Keith, cat got your tongue?" she teased, walking up with the couple to the elevator.

"I said good morning, sorry you didn't hear me," he continued, pushing the button with all three heading inside.

"Like your outfit, I'm ready for another girls' shopping day," Annie added, changing conversation.

"Sounds great, how was your weekend?"

"It was good, a few Fridays ago after work was great, but the weekend was good," Abby said, looking at Keith who wanted to get out of the elevator quickly.

As soon as the door opened, he bolted out quickly heading down the corridor into the office while Annie and Abby made small talk walking slowly down the hall.

C H A P T E R **13**

ADELE THOUGHT IT WOULD BE fine. After all, he was a coworker and they had talked occasionally when she took paperwork downstairs for processing. He mentioned they would go to Montello's, which was her favorite place to have lunch and not far from the office. Mason was very preppy and geeky at the same time, Adele thought as they walked down the street to lunch. He drove one of those fuel-efficient cars and loved his iPod he carried everywhere. His oversized glasses were very fashionable in which he sported different colors to coordinate with his clothes. Adele laughed at his jokes and his outgoing personality, and she liked that he shared. He had been trying to ask her to lunch long before now, but she was just moping around the office most of the time and always in a hurry. Seeing her that morning, he decided to pounce early. One of the guys mentioned Hilary's friend as they convened in the conference room and Mason feared competition. Now his wait was over, they were on their way through the doors to enjoy an hour, well, forty-five minutes due to walking time. Since Mason had made reservations, the two were soon heading to a table, seeing a familiar face sitting across from them.

"Hi, Adele." She looked to see Erene and a woman sitting with him.

"Oh, hi," she said, looking at Erene and glad he saw her in this outfit. It was one of her favorite purchases made. "This is my coworker Mason, we are here for lunch," she confessed, anxiously standing by her table.

Adele was twenty-four, just learning life. So perfect for Mason, he thought, who was twenty-five and thriving in life.

"Adele, this is my wife, Nora."

"Pleased to meet you," she said, walking over to shake her hand. Nora coldly showed her the fork, indicating she was eating, and her attitude showed she did not want to be disturbed.

"Sorry," Adele said, going back raising up her shoulders and a quick wave shyly at Erene.

Soon the table across from them was occupied by someone else. Adele relaxed and enjoyed a lunch full of good food and laughter. She even said she'd do it again as the two went their separate ways once in the building.

Billy had thought hard about confronting Annie and Keith about his suspicions. The first thing he wanted to settle was that Nada was all right and had forgiven him if their suspicions were true. He knew if it was true something would have to be done with Annie, best he could figure was she would have to get another job because Nada would insist.

Nada was always on the bubble after all the rumors that now could be true, if a mother's intuition was true, and Billy knew his mother well and she wouldn't fret if she didn't think it was true. But since it was yet to be confirmed, they treaded lightly on the matter and a few months had gone by.

He kept a close eye on Keith's continuing bizarre behavior with him and the office staff in general and questioned him several times about it, Annie, and their marriage, but all as a friend. From Keith, he got the baby-talk answer and his father wasn't getting better. Annie seemed to be okay. She had reasoned that Keith's behavior was due to the report he had received from Dr. Benson, so she tried everything to keep him satisfied. The thought of him not being able to have another baby was weighting heavy on him, and she suspected his drinking had started again.

"Annie, can you please come to my office?" she heard William over the intercom. Not long after that, she returned to her desk getting her briefcase and heading to Keith's office, letting him know she would be out for a while at the courthouse with William.

"Why do you have to go?" he questioned to the surprise of Annie.

"Keith, it is my job, I've done it hundreds of times, you know that," she said, looking at him almost in shock.

"You guys spend a lot of time together lately since that birthday party," he reminded.

"Wow, that's out of left field, birthday party? What does that have to do with the price of a goat?" she stated. "You are aware we are working on the Sandursky case and I'm the experienced legal in this law firm, so I accompany William on all these. That is not new!" she explained, angry she had to.

"Well, whatever, Abby is just as good, he could take her, she has to learn," was his response.

Annie looked at her husband and walked out the door of his office.

"Oh, no kiss!" he yelled. She turned and went back and kissed him. He made the kiss last longer than Annie wanted and she walked out a bit angry, but she had a job to do and she had to be at the top of her game today.

Adele sat at home reading a book when she heard a knock on her door one evening. Looking out, she could see it was Erene. Fletcher was spending the night with Justin and a friend after coming from a sporting event that ended very late, he had shared with her.

Smiling, she opened the door. "To what do I owe a visit tonight?" she asked, letting him in. "Good evening," she said. She noticed he wasn't his usual self, but he was probably tired, she thought.

"Hello," he responded.

"Can I get you something to drink? I just made some lemonade, pretty good, I'm told," she teased, sitting down and making the gesture for him to do the same.

"Where is Fletch?" he asked, looking around.

"You know Fletcher, he's out, why?" she asked.

Erene seemed so distant, she thought. "When was the last time you saw Rhea? You know, your mom?" he then asked sadly.

"NO! NO! NO! This isn't about my mom. Why are you here? Tell me! Tell me!" she screamed, pounding his chest knowing Erene being here this time of night was unusual.

"I'm so sorry, Adele, but they found her body down by the tracks," he said, coming over to her and wrapping his arms around her.

She pulled away. "NO! NO! Can't be. Fletcher, Riggins, and I just saw her Thursday after work, she was fine, she was fine. We took her some lunch and kissed her. She was fine," she said, falling to the floor on her knees weeping the saddest sobs Erene had ever heard. He got down on the floor in front of her and again he wrapped her in his arms to comfort her. He let her cry all night and release all the pain she felt for the loss of her mother.

McGuire had given Abby some work to do for him on a case he was actively working on and had stopped by her desk on his way in from lunch making small talk with her. Abby by nature appears to be a very friendly and a bit flirtatious girl most of the time around men. She's very professional and well versed in her job as a legal secretary. She was one of many temporary applicants that even came close to Annie's experience as a legal. That was a crucial criterion in the decision to hire her made by Parker and Associates' human resources department. She had worked at a very large law firm before moving to Maine and knew the ends and outs of the business. But coming in so soon and finding leverage of which to secure a top spot in the prestigious law firm was icing on the cake!

McGuire was butter in her hands. He was an older attorney who had been around for a while unprecedented in the courtroom. On his second marriage of a few years, he was an avid smoker, always trying to quit but loved the social life and was often the talk of office parties. She knew he loved her legs and she played it up for all it was worth with him.

"Okay, Douglas, they are all completed, here ya go," she said so coyly, smiling at him.

"When will you be getting out with us in the courtroom?" he asked.

"I figure soon, I've been here about three months, fast learner, and I'm looking forward to helping you guys out in court," she replied, touching his shirt cuff enough to make him want more.

"Ahhhww." Clearing his throat and walking up to the desk where the two were standing was Keith. McGuire went instantly into attorney mode. "Thanks, Abby, great job," he said, making reference to the paperwork he held up in his hand, walking away lifting his brows to Keith.

"William's not back yet?" he asked.

"Should be back soon, William informed me that he would return around two thirty," Abby replied. "Are you worried about Annie?" she asked.

"No, not at all, Annie and I have a great relationship," he boasted.

"Yes, but you and I both know that—"

"Shut up!" he interrupted whatever she was going to say. "I don't want to hear that ever again," he whispered lowly but she knew he meant it.

"Ooooh, someone's grumpy," she said, reaching for his arm. He slapped her hand away and walked off. Abby sat at her desk thinking soon she would have that top spot all by herself.

They next two weeks, Erene stayed by Adele's side despite long hours at work and his marriage. He came by every evening after work hours except the nights when Nora was in town, which meant he was there a lot. His wife, Nora, traveled and was out of town most of the week. He had seen her and the family through the funeral plans and comforted her and the family of Adele as a friend. "Thank you so much for being here. I'm not sure what I would have done," Adele shared, sitting on her couch at home. "I couldn't believe all the extended family we have," Adele started, "they were coming out the woodwork. Mother could have used some love from some of them. I was so angry when they all wanted to be there for us after they read in the paper about our mother. Where were they when she was trying to raise us, why didn't they come to help her when they found out about Dad? They had to know they were his siblings. She was out there all alone." Then she broke down crying again.

"I'm sorry you have been here and neglected your own life. You are such a caring man. I'm going to get it together," she said, wiping her eyes, trying to stop the flow of tears. "Mason called and I finally spoke with him. Hilary had said he wanted to come by, I didn't want company then," she confessed.

"All of what you're going through is okay, you have a right to grieve, you lost your mother," Erene responded.

"I know, but I've shut off all my friends," she added. "Oh no, I don't mean to say you're not a friend." She smiled.

"Good, I see a smile, and that means you're headed in the right direction."

"You have been closer to this family this last year than all those so-called educated relatives. They were trying to impress us with all of their accolades and accomplishments, their successful careers, nice homes and fancy clothes, and all I wanted was an answer, did you know our mother and that we existed before today? The two who had come to help set up an elaborate celebration for Mother but really disguised for themselves didn't even care about us or her or they would have showed up before now. No, they didn't live in this part of Maine, but right down the street in Bangor. Jude Hodges showed up at the small funeral as well with his boyfriend, if that wasn't a slap in the face to his children," Adele miffed. "Things between him and Malcolm, my older brother, got a bit heated. I asked Malcolm to walk outside and cool off and respect Mother. Jude Hodges is a jerk and Rhea was better off without him in her life. So, Erene, thank you for standing by us and our choice to have a small gathering at the cemetery, it was people who knew her." She walked over and gave him a shared hug. "And if Ariel or the boys want to get in touch with Jude's family, they can go right ahead, I'm done," Adele said, getting up going into her refrigerator to get something for the two of them to drink.

"Hey, guy," Fletcher said, coming through the door greeting Erene.

"Hello, how are you?" Erene replied.

"Much better today. I'm improving, how's my sis doing? She's been so sad lately," Fletcher voiced.

"Rightfully so, but I did get a smile out of her," Erene noted.

"Good, been here long?" Fletch asked. "How about a game of chess, you have time?" he added, hanging his backpack on the hook near the door.

"Sure, that sounds good as long as Adele doesn't mind us disturbing her tranquility."

"I'm sure she won't mind," Fletcher responded, taking out the game table from the hall closet to begin play.

"Oh, I saw her friend at the Apple store checking out the latest gadgets they are going to release soon. He wasn't alone, so I might want to keep that to myself for now," he noted. "Your move," he said, looking up at Erene sitting across the table.

William and Annie came walking through the door shortly before two o'clock.

"How did it go?" Abby asked, seeing Annie come back to her desk putting her briefcase down.

"Went well from my end, but I've done this with William so many times I kinda know what to expect." Annie smiled.

"Would you be mad if I said I can't wait to accompany one of our attorneys to court," Abby squeamishly asked.

"Not at all, that's what I as a legal secretary look for, the big challenges of the job. You'll get your turn," she said, going down the hall to Keith's office.

Abby ran down the hall in the other direction into William's office to ask more questions to further help her advance in his high-status law firm.

Tetra and David had just returned home from midweek service. She went into the kitchen to prepare a light snack for them before bedtime.

"Honey, I'll bring the tray into the great room and *20/20* is on channel 713, be there in a minute.""

"Yes, you remembered that news story I wanted to watch, thank you, dear," he replied, heading to his study to put their bibles on the desk and then to his great room, turning on the television and finding the designated channel.

"Service today was so rich in spirit. I love when Dr. Wang teaches, he's a little Asian fireball for the Lord," Tetra confessed, bringing in the tray with fruit and a half croissant sandwich for each of them as they sat down to watch one of their favorite shows. "He draws a clear picture so vivid and heartfelt," David added.

During a commercial, Tetra brought up the dreadful situation that both had purposely ignored since their return home from visiting their son in Maine.

"David, what do you think will happen with that child?"

"Oh, I have prayed so many nights about that, dear, it's so hard to know what God has planned for her. We don't even know, for sure if it's Billy's child and God only knows what Annie's going to do when she realizes her mistake?" he replied, adding to the many questions both had.

"I just pray God gives Nada peace with whatever the outcome, I know it's not easy," Tetra confessed.

"Nothing's ever easy when it comes to relationships."

"You are right, David, but she can rest in the fact that it wasn't an affair, and hopefully realize that it wasn't Riley's fault and take it out on her for her mother's oversight."

"Now, dear, we don't know. Nothing has been confirmed about whether or not she belongs to Billy or Keith."

"You're right, you're right. I'm just hoping and praying that whatever the outcome, it doesn't take years to get an answer."

"Let's leave it in God's hands, and when he's ready, whatever happens, we will support Billy and Nada," he concluded as both returned to looking at the end of their program before heading up to bed.

"How did it go today?" Keith asked, sitting at the dinner table with Annie.

"The usual in a high-profile case, did a lot of runaround for docs, but overall, it went well," she replied, sitting across the table eating dinner.

Riley was in her high chair she still used to be high enough to sit at the big table with her mom and dad. "We had birthday cake today at school."

"You did, was it good?"

"Yep, it was Peyton's cake and we had lots of balloons too."

"Wow. I know that was exciting." Keith smiled, wiping the sauce from the spaghetti from her face.

"Yep, and we had all colors, all colors, red, blue . . .," she went on, her face beaming naming the colors that were limited to her at her age.

"And what was your favorite color?" Annie asked.

"Ummm, pink," she laughed. "I like pink, 'cause ellow is too hard for me," she surmised, having a challenge saying *yellow*.

"Today was Peyton's birthday again, but we didn't have a princess house," she said, making a sad face to her parents.

"Ah, but you still had fun with all the balloons, right?"

"Yes, Daddy! Lots of balloons," she said, stretching her arms up and out to demonstrate. "Can I get down now? I'm finished, see?" she added, holding her bowl up.

"Okay." Wiping her hands and again her face, Annie took her down to go and play with her toys for a while. "Did you talk to Abby about today?" Annie asked, now turning back to their conversation.

Keith had to tread lightly not knowing where Annie was going. "What do you mean talk to Abby?" he stated.

"Whoa, Keith, you're being way too serious, she just asked when I got back today, how it went, and you brought up the same question, that's all, that's it," she said, now questioning again his behavior. "You went from zero to ten in less than a minute. Do you want to talk about it?" she asked, looking at him across the table.

"Talk about what, Abby? Now how did she get in this conversation?" he said, looking at Annie and fidgeting with his fork in his finished spaghetti plate. "I have absolutely nothing to say or talk about concerning Abby," he stated again.

"Is she saying something or doing something I should be aware of? I thought the two of you got along well," Annie commented, keeping her eyes on Keith making shrewd gestures to what she was asking.

Afraid now of what Annie might ask next, Keith said, "She says she can't wait to go with one of us to court, I've shared she's not there yet," he lied.

"Now, dear, I hope you didn't discourage her," Annie replied, softening her tone now. It gave Keith breathing room. The room had got a bit small. "For someone her age, she's quite good. I'm very impressed with her work ethics and her knowledge as a legal," Annie confessed. "Sweetheart, I know you're probably thinking of me, concerned about me being pushed out or pushed aside, I get it, but I'm fine. She's a nice young lady and I can leave the office in good hands knowing she values what I value in the law firm," she added, getting up and kissing him with "Help me clear the table."

Dillard and Katia were becoming an ultimate couple showing up around Hollywood's elite due to Dillard's status as an attorney to some elite clients. Her fashion sense had landed her in a few of the magazines as Dillard's trophy girlfriend. Her beautiful tanned skin and blond hair, blues eyes, were envied by a few, but the devotion to Dillard surprised most, which led to marriage conversations. Dillard had met her one day for lunch and they sat eating sushi at Yamashiro's in Hollywood when in walked Larvy Milburn and his wife, Roslyn.

"Hello," Milburn voiced, now standing over the table.

"Why hello," Dillard returned.

"Wish I would have known, we could have made it the four of us," Milburn stated, inviting himself into Dillard's lunch space. "This is one of our favorite places, oh my wife, Roslyn," he added, pointing and introducing her to Katia. Dillard guessed he knew her.

"Pleasure seeing you again," Dillard said, trusting they were moving on to their table.

"Place is sure crowded today," Milburn stated, looking around vying of an invite to sit down. "Sorry, I didn't make Berington's party, heard it was a blast," he said, still making conversation over Dillard's lunchtime and table.

Dillard looked around for whomever was in charge and going to find a table for Larvy and his wife still standing in the aisle. "It was very nice, but did you make your reservations, they are really good about accommodating you here," Dillard brought up again.

"Yes, but I saw you guys sitting here at this big table, you're close to the front," he shared.

"Yes, not much time, just grabbed the first table available at this hour," Dillard stated, wanting Milburn to go and wait wherever in front he was supposed to. Katia smiled at the couple standing, knowing Dillard had no intention of having them sitting at his table. Soon up walked a waiter.

"I found you a table, right this way," he said, indicating to follow.

"I guess I'll see you at the office."

"Yeah, unfortunately," Dillard mumbled under his breath, shaking his head yes. "Whew, so glad to see the Calvary, that man always finds ways to irritate me, and I couldn't sit through his question-and-answer period for an hour," Dillard said, smiling at Katia.

"I know, that's why I texted under the table into the restaurant manager and asked them to find the Milburns a table asap!" she said, holding up her phone to show him as they left following the waiter.

Dillard shook his head smiling. "Genius!"

C H A P T E R **14**

BILLY AND NADA HAD DISCUSSED, prayed, and cried about the situation at hand. Nada had asked him over and over about his love for Annie and how he feels now.

"You guys work so close to each other every day, what if something happens?" she questioned, sitting again discussing their future.

"Sweetheart, what Annie and I had was long over before you came. If there were more to it, I would have married her and not you," he painstakingly explained, trying to make her understand there was nothing to worry about.

"But you didn't know she was with child when you left her."

"I didn't know, Nada, I didn't know, and honestly, we still don't know. Nothing has been confirmed. How do we approach this delicate subject without hurting families?" he asked, holding his hand on his wife's tummy. "Soon you and I will bring another child into this family, into this world with God's blessings. I most certainly want all this behind us. If Riley is my child, I have to trust that it is what God wanted for me. I have read over and over, Nada, in the book of Isaiah, 'For my thoughts are not your thoughts, neither are your ways my ways, saith the Lord.' Believe me this is the last thing in my life I wanted to have happen. I had to watch my mother go through this kind of hurt, and I certainly did not want you too. That's why I wanted to be sure before I got married, but I'm finding out nothing is sure," Billy said, feeling the weight he was now carrying.

Nada held him close. "Honey, we will get through this, our children will be fine."

"Nada, I'm so sorry. I never want to hurt you. I love you, please forgive me." Laying his head on her tummy, he cried fervently.

Katia sat out sunbathing by the pool. Her already-tan skin was glowing in the beautiful sunshine of the day. Dillard stood for a moment in the doorway admiring her gorgeous and shapely figure in her bikini.

"Good evening," he said, coming up to her.

She sat up a bit startled. She didn't hear the door as he came home. "How long have you been here?" she asked.

"Long enough to see a lovely flower," he replied, smiling.

Katia smiled back at his comment. He touched her arm, leaning over to kiss her. Then he rubbed it again, feeling a place where a scar had healed looking at her.

"Oh, that's nothing that a good surgeon can't make go away," she responded. "I've shared with you what happened and that is a result of it," she said, showing him another scar near her side. "Yes, I was hurt pretty bad, some counted me out, but I being what I am, was able to help myself. I'm a fighter if you haven't figured that out already," Katia added.

Dillard raised a brow and shook his head. "And thanks for the reminder, I will have to make an appointment soon to take care of that, how was your day?" she asked, putting her wraparound on her waist and both heading into their home arm in arm.

Billy sat in his office early one morning before anyone arrived. He had read his bible as he had been accustomed to and was heading to get his cup of coffee from the break room across in front of the conference room. It had been about two months since his daughter Peyton's birthday party and he still had not confronted Keith of his suspicions. Keith, he noticed, was acting strange with him sometimes, but it did not interfere with office flow and his work for the clients, so Billy kept quiet.

"Lord, does it matter who raises her?" he asked himself, pouring the coffee. "Why can't we let bygones be bygones? And I wouldn't have to cause a disruption in the workplace. It's going to surely have a domino effect. Who will stand?" His thoughts were screaming from inside as he headed back to his office and in walked Keith through the door. Billy noticed he was by himself.

"Good morning, no Annie this morning?" he asked, greeting him near the front desk.

"Drove in by myself today, have an errand to do after work, Annie will be in usual time," he replied, heading to his office.

"Keith! May I speak with you for a moment in my office?" Billy asked loudly as Keith was walking away.

"Sure, do you mind if I get a cup of hot coffee before I get there?"

"No, not a problem, just made a fresh pot," Billy replied and headed into his office and sat behind his desk.

Keith did not want to talk to Billy about anything. He had been avoiding him since the party. Mrs. Parker, his mother, gave him such an eerie feeling he just wanted to be rid of it all, he thought walking back in his boss's office with his coffee to talk.

"Should I sit?" he asked, looking at Billy.

"Sure, enjoy your coffee. I just need to talk to you as a friend," he started. "How are things with you and Annie?"

"What do you mean, what has she said?" Keith replied, getting defensive.

"No, she hasn't said anything, but remember when you and I talked about the both of you taking some R&R for a while?" he asked, reminding Keith of the conversation they had months ago now.

"Yes, Annie and I have discussed it and we plan to take time off when we are ready," he reacted.

"Well, I was just thinking if you guys were worried about Riley, Nada and I will be glad to keep her while you two take some time for yourself," he said slowly, careful to choose the right words.

Keith was up from his seat. "We don't need anyone to keep Riley, we are fine. Stay out of my business, Parker!" And he walked out of Billy's office in a huff.

Adele was back in the swing of things after her mother's funeral. Few months had passed and she was still making time for the occasional lunch with Mason. His quirky personality the girls just loved. Adele thought he was kind of cute as well. She was starting to feel like maybe they were ready for the next level. She had been busy raising her brothers and caring for her mother she had forgotten about Adele. She had made several trips monthly to her favorite stores, and now her wardrobe was tight! Very fashion forward, trendy shoes, the latest handbags, adorned her every day. She looked her age and was so full of life.

Adele saw Mrs. Parker at the hair salon at least twice a week. She loved her new 'do that bounced and behaved so beautifully. Seeing Nada often, Adele confided with her asking her advice on all girl matters. "Thank you, Mrs. Parker, for everything," she'd say. Her confidence had gone through the roof, yet her caring heart kept her humbled and attractive to a few of the single young men around town.

She strolled happily down one morning to human resources with a document from one of the personnel files. As she stepped off the elevator, she was met by Mason and a friend by introduction as Angel. He was trying to inspect her jaw with his tongue if she had to guess. He moved away from her quickly to apologize to Adele. And Angel exited into the elevator.

"No apology needed, the document is on the counter." And she pushed the button waiting to walk in.

"Adele, lunch?" he asked.

"Sorry, I have a lunch date." And she was gone. She had almost started to care. She was visibly upset as she walked back to her desk to dial a friend. "Montello's at eleven thirty, see you there."

Billy had called and shared with Nada what had happened and asked her to pray about the situation as well.

"God," he thought, sitting behind his desk, "please instruct me in what to do." Pushing through to keep things moving in his law firm, he kept his cool.

Everyone had come around nine o'clock and the office was its usual buzz. Keith did not discuss what he had asked him about, which Billy found abnormal behavior with Annie, and his next step was to call Annie in his office. Keith heard Annie's name called by William over the intercom. It was nearing noon and he had gone back to his office that morning and spiked his coffee from another flask he kept in the inner pocket of his suit. He was quickly by Annie's desk.

"Abby, are you busy now?" he asked, sounding hurried.

"Not really, is there something you need me to do?" she asked, waiting to hear his request.

"I'm taking my wife out to lunch and I want to make sure you can cover things while we're out," he said, looking at Annie who was waiting to go into William's office but he was holding her arm.

"Sure, enjoy yourselves, I will be fine," Abby replied.

He looked at Annie, letting go of her arm smiling. She smiled back at him sheepishly and walked down the hall to William's office. Keith looked at his watch and went back to his office.

"Yes, William?" she said, a bit loud because it took her a while to get in his office after the request. "Sorry, I was getting a document out," she lied, sitting down in a chair near his desk with her electronic tablet in hand. "I'm ready," she noted.

"How are things going?"

"Abby is wonderful, she's bright and energetic, very professional."

"That's good, so she's working out okay?"

"That would be a yes," she said, smiling.

"Good to see you smile, haven't seen it in a while."

"Been busy, I guess," she replied, moving around nervously in the chair.

"In a hurry?" he asked, looking at his watch. She had just came in.

"My hubby is taking me to lunch today, that's all, sorry. He just surprised me as I was coming into your office," Annie confessed.

"Oh, I see, well, don't be late, and I'm glad Abby is working out."

"Thanks, William." And she was gone.

Soon Billy heard Abby say, "Enjoy your lunch," and they were out for lunch, he hoped.

Katia was now feeling self-conscious about the scars left on her body. They were wreaking havoc on her bikini look, she felt. Honestly, they really went unnoticed. She had found a surgeon in Beverly Hills and was parking her car to go up for her appointment.

"Hello." It was Larvy Milburn's wife. "Katia, right?" she yelled, hurriedly getting out of her car waving her arms running over to her.

Katia looked, trying to remember her name and hesitantly getting out of her car.

"Roslyn Milburn, my husband is an associate in the building where Dillard Patterson practices," she said, clarifying the weird behavior.

"Oh yes, Roslyn Milburn, I remember," she said, extending her hand and ready to move on.

"Are you going up in this building?" she asked.

"Not sure. I'm looking for a doctor," Katia conferred, omitting the name.

"In this building, there are four doctors: Dr. Noglk, he's a dentist; Dr. Flinch, optometrist; Dr. Baggley, surgeon; and Dr. Willis is a plastic surgeon."

"Thanks, wrong building, you have a nice day," she said, hurrying into her car and pulling away at the befuddled Roslyn.

Her appointment was with Dr. Willis, but there's no way she was going into that building with the national inquiry on her heels. She's got to find another one.

Adele walked in and asked to be seated with instructions of who she was waiting for. She ordered a wine cooler to relax and sent a text to her sister.

"Hi, is this seat taken?" Erene asked, standing over the table.

"Funny, how are you? Long time no see," Adele said, welcoming him in.

"So what have you been up to?" Erene asked. "You look gorgeous and rested." He smiled.

"Why, thank you, I try," she teased, feeling confidently beautiful with her newfound self.

The waiter, seeing Erene now at the table, came over and took their orders and left.

"So how has life been treating you?" she asked.

"You really want to know about my boring life?" he joked.

"Yes," she replied, shaking her head, smiling.

The two got along so well. Erene was a thirty-eight-year-old Christian married to a very strong-willed woman who traveled all the time. He was an investigator for the local precinct in midtown and is known by many to have a very caring heart. "Give that case to Erene, he's the only one who cares," was the joke in his office. He was so glad for Adele she had come through a rough patch in her life and had started to flourish.

"How's Fletcher and the rest of the family?"

"They're good, we are survivors, thanks to friends like you," Adele replied.

Both enjoyed their lunchtime.

"Thank you, sir, for joining me today, I needed a lift," she confessed at the end of the meal.

"I somehow sensed that when you called, can I help?" he asked, now knowing a bit more about the invite.

"I'm wonderful and thank you as always for being there." She smiled, touching his hand.

"Maybe I'll stop by sometime this week, Fletcher beat me mercilessly in the last chess game. He owes me a rematch," Erene delighted.

"He would love that, I will let him know," she said as the two walked out of the restaurant after a wonderful lunch.

Keith had a client in Billy's office when they returned from lunch.

"Sorry, lunch ran a bit over, Mr. Bets, right this way. Thanks, Bill," he said, showing Mr. Bets now to his office for the scheduled meeting.

"Annie, may I speak with you?" he asked, standing in the main hall.

"Yes, William," she said, putting down her doggie bag on her desk. She walked into his office.

"Close the door, please. How was lunch?" he asked, sitting behind the desk.

She just laughed blushingly. "Good, lunch was great!" Annie replied, a bit embarrassed.

Billy didn't want to pry; obviously it was an interesting lunch.

She seemed happy with the outcome, no need to push. "Annie, I need to ask you about Riley?" he started.

"Riley, what about Riley? Did the school call?" she asked, excited.

"No, nothing like that, I understand you and my wife had a conversation about Riley a while ago," he asked gently.

"We have had a lot of conversations where the girls are concerned, William. Can you be more specific?" she asked, smiling, trying to figure out what her boss was speaking about.

"If I recall correctly, this conversation took place at an Italian restaurant during a lunch hour," he said, looking at her, trying to say without saying.

"Oh, that conversation about rather or not you were—" She stopped in midsentence; everything that had happened of late came flooding back to her mind. She sat stunned.

"Annie, Annie, are you all right?" he asked as she got up and opened the door and walked out in a daze.

Billy watched her behavior the rest of the day, concerned, but you would never know from Annie the conversation they had ever happened.

When she arrived at the school's day care to pick up Riley, Nada was waiting to speak with her. She saw Nada and broke down crying on the sofa bench in the waiting area.

"What have I done, Nada, I'm so sorry. I didn't know, I honestly didn't know," she cried.

Nada put her arms around her and walked with her to the ladies' room down the hall.

"Annie look, look at me, you didn't know, how could you tell him! I was so angry with you and then I got angry with my husband, and sweet little Riley is in the middle of this mess. Keith's a basket case trying to keep your secret."

"WHAT? Keith, what do you mean?" she asked.

Nada had her undivided attention. "Keith knows."

"Is that why he's been so crazy lately? Am I the last to know, why someone didn't tell me!" she said loudly.

"Tell you, you should have been the one to tell us. You're letting your little girl think she's Keith child when in reality, he knows she's not," Nada confessed, knowing. "And I have to deal with that truth." Nada was at a breaking point, now finding a comfy stool in which to sit.

"Okay, stop, you are saying my husband knows that he isn't Riley's father. I don't believe you!" Annie stated, looking at the grieved Nada. "I'm not sure what you and William are up to, but

Keith is Riley's father and that's all I'm going to say about it. End of story." And she walked out to get her daughter and go home.

Nada had secured Peyton in her sit and watched Annie pull from the curb without another word to her about it.

Katia decided to go shopping since she was out anyway heading to Rodeo Drive to window-shop all the beautiful stores. As she walked along down the sideway, she found herself in the Unique Chic Boutique.

"Hello, Miss Norfren, it's good to see you," a clerk said, greeting her warmly. "We have our new designs that just arrived this morning, would you like to take a look?" she asked, escorting her into the showroom of originals.

"Why, hello, so glad to see you two, it's been a while since we got together as a family," Doris said, seeing David Michael and Sonjee, her daughter, walking through her Beverly Hills home. "Russ will be down in a minute, let's go into the parlor."

"Glad to have an invite for some real food," both the college students agreed.

"Good to see you as well, Aunt Doris," Michael replied with hugs all around.

"So school's good?" she asked them.

Both were in their last year of college at UCLA.

"Great," David Michael said, taking a hors d'oeuvre from a tray on the buffet.

"How's Finley?" Sonjee asked, looking around not seeing him.

"Finley, well he is off at a church social tonight, and no, he is still running from the ladies," she said, sharing a laugh from the two young people who were near and dear to her. "You know, David, ever since I received that list from Patterson, I've been trying to put together the last days of your mother's life," she confessed.

"Aunt Doris, are you still investigating?" he asked, knowing she was always looking into something.

"Well, yes, kind of, I just always thought that if we had found her, then it would be a closed case," she added. "In the police report, it stated they found her shoes, a torn stained blouse over by the path where she supposedly fell to her death," Doris informed.

"Didn't they locate her car?" Sonjee asked.

"They pulled the car out about two days later, but remember, that vet had told them about how she went over the cliff in the car was a bit confusing."

"That was a horrible way to die," David said, sitting, shaking his head.

"They never located her cell phone, I don't know if she ever tried to call anyone or who if anyone did she call," Doris said sadly, thinking of her sister Dana who had been shot and driven over the cliff in the Atlantic River a little over two years ago now. "Since her body wasn't found in the car, she must have fallen out on the way down. They did identify it was her blood at the scene. Anyway," Doris said sadly, "I truly miss her and she will always be in our hearts."

Everyone got up heading into the dining area for a family meal with hopefully lots of laughter to accompany it.

Annie waited up until about nine thirty for Keith. He said he would be working late after getting back a bit tardy from their lunch rendezvous, which she thought was very romantic. He had called about eight thirty when she was putting Riley down for bed and she was still waiting to talk with him about William and Nada's suspicions. "Had William spoken with him? No, he wouldn't dare." Annie woke up and called the office at around ten. She knew then he must be on his way home. "Does he have suspicions he's not telling me about. But what was all that sweet talk and lovemaking in the afternoon if he thought that to be true? I can't call William and Nada to ask where he might be, they are probably mad with me too." Her mind was racing a mile a minute and Keith still had not come home.

"I went on Rodeo again today after running into Roslyn Milburn when I arrived at the doctor's office," Katia shared with Dillard. "So needless to say, I will not need his services. That woman stood there less than five minutes and had shared everything one needed to know about the whole building." She laughed with Dillard.

"I believe it, they are truly an inimitable couple. So you may want to look further out and be careful the Milburns are always watching," Dillard teased back as both relaxed in the beautiful Brentwood home. "So how did it go at Unique?" he asked, smiling.

"Not bad, the owner happened to stop in while I was in the design showroom."

"How did that go?" he asked, looking curiously at her.

"Well, very well," Katia responded, smiling, "there are so many gorgeous fashions."

Billy and Nada had shared their unbelievable day and now sat in their room having breakfast the next morning.

"This seems to be getting worse, not better," Billy voiced, putting on his tie getting ready for work.

"I agree, I thought Annie would at least be reasonable about this whole mess, it's her oversight!" Nada said, a bit upset, Billy could tell.

"Now, sweetheart, the last thing we need is you getting upset in your condition. Both now seem to feel threatened about us taking their child," she shared.

"I don't know if I wouldn't be the same way," he acknowledged.

"Billy, you're probably right, I have no more tears to shed over this one, we just have to trust in God. The more we get involved, the worse it gets, I've noticed. God has his own timing, his own way, so we are agreeing right now that we will move aside and let him do it, agree?" Nada asked, sitting up in bed to hug her husband. "That sounds very wise, and I totally agree," Billy said, hugging and kissing her before leaving for the office.

Keith had waited until Annie left for the office before he went home, showered, and left quickly for the office as well. Once again, his flask had gotten the better of him and caused him to stray. It had become a fixture in his inner jacket pocket and he had filled it again before leaving home. His dad's pancreatic cancer was getting worse, Annie was closer to finding out the truth about Riley, and he was feeling less of a man to her. Their afternoon rendezvous did not ignite or excite him and he had went to a familiar place for the rush he felt he needed.

"What will I say to her?" he thought, pulling in the garage of the law firm, and looking around, he noticed Annie was arriving as well. "Deep breath, Poulton," he said to himself, getting out of his car.

"KEITH!" she yelled. "Are you all right?" she asked, running over to him. "I didn't know what to think, what happened?" She was touching him and asking him caringly about why he had not come home. He felt so bad he almost started to be honest and tell her the truth until she spoke. "Honey, I know you're going through a lot with your dad right now, your mom called."

"My mom, did something happen?" he asked, now thinking the worse in regards to his dad.

"Well, they took him to the hospital last night, but she says he is still in good spirits and he is ready for whatever happens," Annie shared, holding him around his waist walking in.

"Good morning," the smiling Abby passed by them cheerfully. "Is everything all right?" she asked, moving quickly into the elevator.

"We are fine," Keith replied. "You go on up, we will be there shortly," he responded to her.

She waved, hit the button, and closed the elevator's door. Annie and Keith stood talking things over a few more minutes before going up. He loved his father dearly and really had accepted the fate of this dreaded disease his father has, but right now, he was using this sympathy card for all it was worth. And if the truth be told right now, it held his marriage to Annie. He despised Abby, but the flask made it all go away and he just couldn't put the flask down to save his own life.

Everyone and everything in Parker and Associates went along as a usual day. With everyone doing what everyone does, respecting one another, staying out of each other's space and face, satisfying the clients.

"God, you get your glory," is how Billy started his routine morning prayer of the day. Amen.

"Hi, guy," Billy called Erene on his cell phone. "Just calling a reminder about the brotherhood tonight seven o'clock in the main sanctuary."

"Oh, you're right. I'd better call Don," he shared.

"No, Don called me and said Frank tagged him, so you're going to have to call someone else, he's already been tagged." He laughed.

"Well, yes, he has really stepped up his game, he was always a sure one, not complaining that's growth, thank God," Erene said, laughing with Billy. "Man, I will see you this evening, I'm going to pull over and go through my contacts to find someone who hasn't been tagged yet." Erene laughed. "Moving forward, I'm going to call these brothers when I wake up in the morning every other Tuesday just to get a tag. Love the system though, talk to you later," he said, disconnecting the phone from his fellow church brother after his reminder to attend the meeting.

Keith and Annie went home after a long day at the office with their daughter, Riley, for a great family evening according to Annie. Good night.

The month ended intact despite of everything going on at the Parker law firm. Keith was still fooling himself with the bottle; in disguise, it was making him a better man. Billy continued to pray for answers of a direction of which to take his suspicions, which he couldn't believe his mom had not called him once about in the past two months. Annie was being so focused on Keith she hardly noticed that Abby was moving up and taking on the task of executive legal secretary right in front of her. Oren was Oren, did his job, and went home. McGuire had something he was hiding, Billy suspected, but it was not affecting his clients or the office, so it was his secret to keep. Another week had finally come to an end, it was Friday. Yes, that one, the one where all the ladies lunch together at their favorite spot. Not really having a conversation with Annie since the bathroom debacle, Nada initiated the call.

After hearing the greeting, she said, "Hi, Annie," calling into the office Friday morning.

"Hello, Nada. William is in a meeting, do you need me to let him know that you are calling?" she asked, knowing in her condition this could be that call.

"No, I was calling for you," Nada replied. "It's our lunch Friday, did you forget?" she asked, very cheery.

"Huh, not really, I didn't know we were still going to have these?" she said, talking slowly and questioning.

"Why not, has something happened I don't know about?" she teased.

"Well, no, I don't think so," Annie said, contemplating. "Abby is saying she can't go today, she's headed downtown with McGuire, so I guess that just leaves me," Annie added. "I will speak with Keith, see what our plans are and I'll call you back," she said compromisingly to Nada.

"Sounds good, look forward to seeing you," she said, disconnecting the line.

Annie made her way down the hall to Keith's office. Abby was standing in the door.

"Excuse me, lady," she said, playfully pushing her out of the way. "Nada wants to do the girl day thing today, do you mind?" she asked, flirting with her husband by his desk. Abby waved bye and left.

He was trying to be patronizing and keep her happy. "That sounds fun, why not?" he asked.

"I don't want you to be upset with me. You know what happened the last time those two interfered, you didn't come home all night," she reminded him, kissing him as she sat on the corner of his desk.

"Well, sweetheart, we work for these people, and frankly, they are very nice folks to work for. We have great careers. I really don't have a beef with them as long as they don't discuss you and my daughter to me!" he stated, brushing his hands off.

"Keith, are you sure, 'cause I'm sure Riley's name is going to come up."

"Riley has asked about Peyton lately, you know, they always played together. It has been what two months, month and a half since anyone of them have said anything to us about Riley, maybe, just maybe, they are minding their own business, go enjoy yourself," he told her, kissing her passionately.

Annie still thought Keith was covering because he was not fertile and couldn't make any more children. She still didn't know that he knew about Riley. Or just didn't want to know! Happily she was soon out the door after a call to Nada to let her know she was meeting her at the restaurant.

"Glad you came," Nada greeted, seeing Annie come toward the table.

"Oh my." Annie smiled. "Haven't seen you in a while, you have grown," she said, speaking of her now very pregnant body.

"Yes, that's why I called, because traveling isn't a thing I take lightly these days," she confessed.

"How is Peyton taking the arrival of the baby-to-be?" Annie asked, shocking Nada she brought up the children.

"Truthfully it's not reality for her yet, another month and we will see," Nada said, only giving short answers. Hesitantly, Nada asked about Riley.

"Riley is great," was her stock answer given.

"Ready to order?" Nada then asked, looking around for the waitress or waiter. Nada was tired of waiting and playing Annie and Keith's games. If Riley was Billy's child, she wanted to know. She didn't want all this uncertainty hanging around her children especially her newborn coming into this world. This was affecting her and her husband's relationship. Even though they pretended many times that it wasn't. She knew that Billy and she had made a promise to stay out of it. Honestly she was doing everything in her power not to ask Annie about Riley's father as Annie sit across the table smug smiling with her. Could it possibly be someone else's? With her backup plan in place, Nada ordered her lunch and shared careful conversation the whole hour of lunch with Annie. She had been by the school that morning when taking Peyton to day care, purposely seeing Riley and conveniently having a swab to secure in a small plastic bag in her hand for a paternity test of Riley.

Katia had put finding a plastic surgeon to remove the scar abrasions from her body scribbled on a notepad near her bedside. It wasn't really noticed unless she was touched or she told you about them. These were her little secret, something she was glad to put behind her. But most of all glad that scars was all she kept from the incident that caused them.

"What should I wear tonight?" she thought, looking in her huge walk-in closet. "Oh, I know, that lovely gown I bought from that cute little shop on Rodeo Drive. It will be prefect for an art showing tonight on Mulholland. Dillard will love it!" she surmised, floating around the room humming a happy tune, getting prepared to go out for the art show and dinner while Dillard in tux waited anxiously at the foot of the stairs to see what she would dazzle him with tonight.

The two had an odd kind of relationship, less romantic than the tabloids painted it to be, but Dillard liked it because it ran Milburn crazy trying to keep up with most of the things written and frankly maybe 40 percent true.

Dillard and the beautiful Katia walked into the Pasadena Museum of Art on Union. The crowd of elite art dealers and buyers and guests were admiring the beautiful art pieces displayed for this evening's event. There were tall handsome waiters moving around the crowded room with champagne and caviar for all who attended the gala affair.

"Look at that masterpiece, Dillard," she remarked, seeing an Alfred Gockel painting on display.

"The movement, the lighting is absolutely breathtaking. Gockel was so careful with each brush stroke," he pointed out to Katia who was very impressed with his knowledge of the arts.

They moved around from piece to piece when up walked a couple standing beside them.

"Hello, Patterson," she said, surprising Dillard.

He looked at Doris Wright. "Pleasure seeing you here," he said, taking her hand and giving a gentle kiss to it. "You remember my husband, Russell Woods," she asked.

"It's been a while," he said, shaking his hand as well. "Oh excuse me, this is my date, Katia Norfen."

"Pleasure," both said, smiling.

"If I'm being honest," Doris said, "it was your gown that caught my eye." She smiled.

"Why, thank you, it is gorgeous, isn't it?" Katia replied, touching the gown's material, showing off her Elie Saab design.

"Rodeo," Katia shared, putting her finger over her pooched lips. "Shhh."

"I know." Doris smiled. "I'm the owner of the Unique Chic," she admitted, surprising the couple delightfully.

"Well, what an honor to have met you, and I love your boutique!" Katia added, smiling, very pleased for the encounter. Dillard gave a nod and walked in another direction. Katia smiled.

Annie and Keith enjoyed a nice early dinner at home after playing with their daughter, Riley, and hearing all about her day at school. It wasn't alarming she had seen Aunt Nada today because both she and Peyton attended the prestigious school together. Riley was all tucked in and Annie was heading into the bath before bed when Keith announced he was going out to the store for milk.

"Honey, are you sure? I just bought a gallon of milk," Annie yelled from the bathroom where she was running the water into the tub.

"Yes, I'm sure, shouldn't be too long." And he was gone.

"What?" Annie asked to an empty of Keith house.

A quick swig from a hidden flask in his car, he pulled out of his driveway. He knew Annie wouldn't trip unless he was gone longer than an hour and a half. He could cover that with a lie, he reasoned, speeding now on the highway. Where he was going was forty-five minutes from his house, so time was of the essence. Seems every red light was causing him to stop and wait and it was wearing in to his time. As he pulled up to his destination, he noticed a car he recognized from the license plate.

Ring, ring.

"Hello," the voice said.

"McGuire, I was just checking. Maggie called, said you were working late," Keith stated to his fellow attorney.

"Yeah, I should be out and home soon, some last-minute docs needed for tomorrow morning," he lied.

"Yeah, all right. If she calls again, I'll let her know," he said, hanging up, mad his rendezvous was spoiled. Angrily he headed home stopping by the corner market to get the gallon of milk he had poured down the sink before leaving home. He lay coldly in bed beside his wife who wanted his attention, but his heart just couldn't make it happen, not tonight.

"Hey, Nada Jean," Miss Manuel said, calling her former neighbor and dear friend from Washington.

"Why, Ms. Manuel, how are you? Good to hear your voice."

"Girl, you sound like yo daddy. Hahahaha." She was laughing so long and hard saying she was now crying.

"Miss Manuel, why do you say that and laugh about it?"

"Yo daddy ain't told you?"

"I guess not, what's going on?" Nada asked curiously after hearing Miss Manuel's laughter to tears.

"Nada Jean, yo daddy got me leading a song for the kawi [choir]."

"Why, Miss Manuel, that's wonderful!" Nada acknowledged.

"Ah, huh, that's what he says, I ain't been in front of the church since I was a li'l girl, I'm satisfied putting on my big hat and sitting in the pews looking holy." She giggled.

"Now, Miss Manuel, you'll do a fine job. Daddy said you were coming along a while ago," Nada confessed.

"Okay, Nada Jean, yall can put me out there if yall want to, but I sure could use some support 'cause I can't stop these old legs from shaking." She laughed, making a joke about herself.

"Is Miss Ross gonna be there?"

"Oh yeah, I finally got them people to set her up with the van pickup from the church. All they have to do is make sure she's showered early and she dresses herself. I wasn't very nice when I talked with them, but they got my point. Hazel has been ready the past two Sundays 'cause I ride the van when it picks her up, they don't want me to go back up in there," she threatened, causing Nada to laugh silently at her antics.

"Now, Miss Manuel?"

"You have to stay on 'em though, Nada, you really do," Miss Manuel concluded again, laughing, speaking about the rest home Hazel Ross's daughter had put her in after her mother's fall.

"How's my Peyton?"

"She's good and spoiled," Nada answered.

"And Jeffrey?"

"Jeffrey?"

"ain't that's the name you picked out for the new one?"

"Now, Miss Manuel, you know better than that," Nada replied, hearing laughter and knew Virginia was teasing her as she hung up the phone laughing as well. Nada didn't really like traveling late in her pregnancy, but she certainly had to make an exception for Miss Manuel. She had grown in the Lord a lot since Nada first met her years ago.

CHAPTER 15

ADELE WAS FEELING GREAT AS she left for work. What a wonderful time, she thought heading to her car thinking about the fun she had with her family over the long weekend. She had parked farther out so that her car would be in the shade most of the day.

Looking down at her cell phone, she heard, "Hello there." It was Erene leaning against her hood.

"Well, hello, surprise, surprise, didn't expect to see you," she said, smiling.

"I know. Nora had an unexpected trip, just came from the airport seeing her off and thought I'd say hi," he replied.

"Well, if that's the case, you can take me to dinner," she joked. "You need my company," she added.

Erene laughed at her antics and her tease. "Montello's will be closed at the dinner hour," Erene said. "Is that the only place you know to eat?"

"No, but knowing you, that's the only place you will let me take you," he commented.

"Okay, stop teasing me. I just had a wonderful day at work, so don't rain on my parade," she voiced in a sassy tone.

"Adele, I am so proud to see the improvement you have made since we met," he said, giving her a brotherly hug. "And you smell good too," he thought to himself standing, looking at the attractive young lady in front of him.

"Say, let's get out of this parking lot. I do have a roof," Adele shared, opening her car door starting her car.

Erene got into his car and followed her home.

Keith was up very early the next morning letting Annie know that he was driving in early by himself. He came in loving and kissed her after preparing to head out the door.

"See you at the office," she said, smiling after he tapped her behind and left.

He drove hurriedly across the highway, but he wasn't headed to the office. He turned on an exit about forty-five minutes from his home. He had one thought in mind after seeing McGuire's car parked there last evening. He couldn't call McGuire out because he was doing the same thing. He and now McGuire were both caught up, and for him, there was no turning back. He got out of his car looking around before heading to the front door knocking.

After a few times, "Who's there", he heard from Abby.

"Keith," he replied, standing anxiously with anticipation of seeing her. As soon as the door opened, he pounced quickly heading inside.

He arrived at the office just before Annie did but pretended to be involved deep in his work when Annie came in to see him after she arrived. Oren came up to Annie with some documents he needed processed and she smiled a wave at Keith and went to her desk.

"Hey, how are things going?" McGuire asked, passing down the hall putting his head into Keith's office door.

"I should be asking you? What were you doing out so late having your wife worry?" Keith joked, raising his brows.

"Man, I was here late, you know how that happens, but thanks for the cover, she didn't even bring up the call to me. Thanks, man, I owe you," McGuire said, heading back around to the meeting room with Billy.

Truth is, his wife hadn't called. Keith was just verifying his suspicions of where he was, and a bit teed at what he knew was probably going on.

Erene rode into work the next morning. He had spoken with his wife who had called, knowing the hour he is up in the morning.

"Good morning, sweetheart, you sound tired, did you rest well?"

"Yes, the usually stay up a bit late watching a movie on television, but should turn in early tonight," he added.

"Love you, I'm on my way to a conference meeting and I'll call you tonight at home okay."

"All right, have a good day," he said, disconnecting his call.

"Good morning, sleepyhead." She smiled across the phone.

"Oh sorry about that. I did go to sleep on you. I will need a rain check, that was a great movie," Erene replied to Adele.

"Hey, no problem, I know you work hard all day, it's probably hard for you to stay awake watching a movie. Fletcher was nodding a bit too, it is long. It has to be a weekend movie night." She smiled.

"Yes, for sure," he said, thinking it would probably never happen. Nora is home most weekends and she wouldn't have Adele and Fletcher over to their home, who was he kidding. Erene enjoyed them. He could relax around them and be himself, didn't have to put on airs like most of his and Nora's Christian friends, thinking they were better than most. "You have a good day."

"You too, Erene," she said, hanging up, walking into her office for the day.

Nada was mailing the envelope to the address she had gotten from a television program. She wasn't going to share with Billy until she was 100 percent sure either way. She was determined to be quiet with Annie still working around her husband after the discovery.

"And, Lord, have mercy, you're going to have to guide me," was her prayer. "I know all this happened before I met my husband. But Annie's saying she didn't know. I don't mind sharing Billy with a daughter, but if Annie thinks she's got rights, she's wrong! A week, it will all be clear in a week. I hope I last that long," she added, rubbing her tummy, and waddled to her bedroom.

"Dillard, good morning," he heard a voice following him through the covered garage.

Without looking back, he replied, "Milburn, good morning, very cheery for this time of day."

"Is my voice that distinct?" he asked, coming up to Dillard standing in the aisle.

"Well, Milburn, I took a guess of who would be that interested in me this early and the lot fell on you," Dillard joked.

"Haha. Roslyn saw your lady friend the other day downtown. What's her name?"

"You can't remember, that's a good thing," Dillard replied.

"Oh, I remember. Katia Norfen. Is she from here?"

"Milburn, how many times have I told you to mind your own business?"

"Why are you so interested in my affairs?" Dillard asked as they walked into the building of the law offices.

"So she's looking for a doctor. What's up you want to share? Are you two really serious?" he asked and pissed Dillard off.

"Milburn, I'm not going to stoop to your level and answer that, but I'll say this, if you even look like you want to ask me about Katia again, please don't!" he stated, walking off.

"Ummmm, interesting, he's very touchy about Katia Norfen. What is she up to, and where did she come from? There have been lots of things happening these past months," Milburn thought, heading into his office for the day.

Against everything right, Erene went by his favorite pizza spot after work. He knew he had to pick up Nora from the airport at nine as he walked out the Pizza Hut with a large hot pizza and two bottles of soft drink.

"Good, Fletcher should be home by now," he thought, looking at his watch. "And if I time it right, we can watch the entire movie before I have to get Nora from the airport," he surmised, driving along to the Hodges' home. Getting out and knocking on the door, "Pizza delivery," he teased, seeing Adele at the door.

"Hahaha," she laughed at him, inviting him in. "How did you know I was wanting pizza? As a matter of fact, I was just about to go out myself and pick one up," she confessed, taking the sodas to the refrigerator. "So I wasn't expecting company. As a matter of fact, I just got in from the salon."

"Your hair is beautiful," he said to her, smiling.

"Thanks, I love it," she said, dancing around, playing with it running her fingers through it. "You and Fletch have plans?" she asked.

"I thought we could watch that movie I missed a few weeks ago, where is he?"

"Maybe in his room, I haven't been home but a minute. Sit, I'll see if he's asleep in his room, he's been training on the cross-country team, so that's where I find him most days," she said, heading up the stairs to Fletcher's room.

Before opening the door, Adele read a note he taped on the outside of it. "Gone to a game with Justin, be home late, Fletch." Adele went back down to give Erene the news.

"Sorry, no Fletcher, tonight. He's out with Justin."

"Okay, not his fault. I should have called him," Erene admitted. "Well, since you did bring pizza, and I'm hungry, and if you're willing to share your pizza with me, I'll watch the movie with you."

She smiled at Erene being a playful twenty-four.

Erene thought about it. He enjoyed her bubbly personality, but was very careful to not lead her into taking his caring for something else. He is married, you know.

"Good we are alone, I want to ask you about men," she said, getting the movie set on the television after plates and glasses for both to eat and drink from.

"Men? I'm not sure I'm the one you should ask," Erene confessed.

"Well, you are older, right, thirty-three? Did I guess right?" she asked, ready to hit Play on the Blu-ray.

"Close, I'm thirty-eight, and I still don't consider myself as knowing men."

"Anyway, I have spoken with you about Mason more than once, right?" she said, looking at him smiling. "He's, ummmm, he likes to tease a lot, and I'm not sure where he wants to go with it," she confessed.

"Are you sure you want to talk with me about this?" Erene again conferred.

"Who would you suggest no mother and certainly no father, at least you care," she admitted, taking another bite from her slice of the delicious pan-crust pizza. "I really need someone to talk to about things like this," she shared, being deep in thought. "I don't want to make the mistakes my mother made, I'm so afraid of letting myself feel anything for anyone. Can I tell you something?" she asked naively.

Erene felt uncomfortable and didn't want to listen but was sitting there now. "I have never really been kissed by a boy or young man like that."

"Like what?" Erene asked before realizing what she meant. He looked at the screen and the scene was being played out before him. Innocent enough, the actors had on their clothes. "So have you and Mason ever went out on a date? You know, talked with each other besides work?" he asked.

"Maybe once, but when he brought me home, I just got out of the car and ran in the house. I did call him on my cell to say good night. He didn't seem too happy with me the next day at work. Not sure what he was expecting, but I've watched enough movies to know he only wants one thing," she said.

"All men are not like that, Adele."

"Have you tried those dating services, Christian dating, Match "dot" com, to find someone compatible?" The movie had been on but the conversation was so intense little of the movie content was seen.

"I think I've set my expectations too high."

"Why do you say that, you're a beautiful young lady, full of life and bright, and caring beyond your years," he said to make her smile and to stop her from beating up on herself.

"You see that, but I don't think others do."

"Ah, Adele, come here," he said, holding her in his arms. "You will find that right person that will love you and care for you, no doubt in my mind. We will try the movie again another time, okay?" he said, pushing the remote to turn it off. Erene stood up from the sofa, preparing to leave after looking at his watch. He still had an hour to kill before the airport run.

"Let me get the remaining pizza wrapped for you," Adele said, hurrying in the kitchen to get plastic wrap from the drawer.

"No, it's okay, you and Fletcher enjoy it," he replied, walking now to the front door to leave.

"Thanks again, Erene, for listening, I needed it," she shared so heartfelt that before Erene realized what was happening, he had wrapped Adele in his arms and was kissing her passionately and she was returning the favor.

After a few minutes, he hurried out the door and to his car without stopping to look back at the house. Adele for sure knew she had been kissed for the first time and he knew with a doubt he had been kissed too!

Nada sat waiting for Billy to come home from the seminary that evening. She had received the envelope in the mail with the news regarding the paternity test she had sent off to be verified.

She was afraid that her husband would be mad at her for doing it, but she was not going to sit around and let Annie have her way either. She should know who she slept with. How could she put a child through that? It's crazy, she thought, packing her ready bag for when the time comes to head to the hospital. She had called her mother-in-law but decided not to share the news even when it was apparent that's what Tetra had referenced in conversation.

"I spoke with Daddy and Priscilla earlier this morning. They are planning a trip after the baby comes," she said to Tetra, changing subject.

"Oh, that's nice, maybe we will all be there together again," Tetra replied, delighted about the news of her father's visit. "You heard about Miss Manuel?" Tetra asked.

"She called me laughing," Nada said, "but Dad says she's really pretty good for the song he chose for her."

"She'll do fine," Tetra affirmed, smiling.

"Mom, I hear the garage going up. Billy's home, I'll call you tomorrow," she stated.

"Okay, give my love to Peyton and Billy," she replied, disconnecting the phone.

"Hi, honey, how's my girls?" he asked, coming in tired but joyful his day had come to an end.

"Good day, Peyton's asleep, you'll see her in the morning."

"Yes, I know classes will be over soon, and I won't have to miss her on any night," he acknowledged, knowing she's usually in bed by the time he gets home on Tuesday and Thursdays. "So what filled your day?" he asked, getting comfortable sitting beside Nada in the comfy chair.

"Honey," she said.

Billy knew that tone. "What has happened now, Nada? Oh my god," he said, looking up to the ceiling. "I know we promised. We promised, what did you do, Nada Parker?" he said, getting up looking at her sitting there deviously.

"What did you say to Annie or the Poultons? To anybody? What did you say!" He didn't want to go through this. They had made a promise to let God guide this. "Now what, Nada, tell me," he said, exhausted with his past.

She slowly pulled the envelope from behind her back.

"What's that, Nada? Where did you get that from, Nada?" He was kneeling in front of her on the chair.

"Billy, I'm sorry, but I just couldn't go on not knowing if Riley was your child. You have to understand where I'm coming from, you work closely with this woman every day. How much can I take?" she screamed, crying.

"Honey, please stop crying. I'm sorry you have to go through this mess. I'm so sorry. What did you do?" he asked again, calming her down and wiping her tears.

"I got the results of Riley's paternity test today," she replied, holding up the sealed envelope.

"Paternity test, when? How? Nada, what have you done, you promised," he shared, walking around the room holding his head.

"It really doesn't matter when or how, I've got it, and that's all that matters. Are you going to look at it?" she asked, holding her tummy. She still had about a month and three weeks but she was feeling the stress of this situation bearing on her.

"Why, you already know," he said, sorry, frustrated, angry with Nada for being disobedient to a promise.

"I haven't opened it. I waited on you, but if you're not going to open it, I will because I want this over and I want Annie out of your life, and your office!" she said, walking off to her bedroom up the spiraling staircase of their estate with the envelope still sealed in her hand.

Only two days had passed since the last encounter when Milburn walked into Dillard's office to apologize.

"I apologize for inferring that Katia was just eye candy for you, it's obvious to me after your reaction that she's more," he stated, extending his hand for a shake.

Dillard looked at this man who he found nosy and annoying but extended his hand accepting the apology. They talked law for about ten minutes before Milburn headed out the door, stopping.

"I guess I'll see you at Wheatfield's in a couple of weeks," he asked, looking around and smiling.

"Oh, that's right, I do have it on my calendar," Dillard responded.

Wheatfield was a judge who was retiring and was having a gala retirement party. Dillard didn't attend all the functions, but this one was one he was expected to show up for.

"Wheatfield doesn't take kindly to being stood up." Dillard laughed. "So I will probably be there," he joked.

Milburn waved and walked out. Dillard had accepted his apology, but he was going to keep Milburn on a short leash. Friends close, enemies closer!

Annie had taken a backseat to Abby who was now doing all of the process work for William. She was trying very hard to appease Keith and his strange behavior of late. Billy had stayed away from the Poultons and their drama as long as it didn't affect the office in any way, and so far so good. He did notice Annie was pushing things asked of her to Abby, and Abby loved it. She had that fire Annie used to have about her job, he thought, coming in one morning finding the files he needed for work already on his desk.

"William, I'm leaving early today. Abby has your itinerary and she'll do fine assisting you in court today," she shared, standing before his desk.

"No doubt she will, but this is the second time this week you have to leave early, is something wrong?" he asked.

"It's Keith's birthday and I'd like to get home and start a special dinner for today," she said standing, smiling at Billy.

"Sounds romantic like things are on track again," he said as a concerned friend.

"Now, William, what are you talking about, Keith and I have a solid marriage, good night." And she walked out of the office. She headed to Keith's office where she found him chatting it up with Abby. She kissed him and shared she would see him at home and she was gone.

Oren was returning from court and McGuire wasn't far behind heading into his office. "There's cake in the break room, guys, it's Keith's birthday today," Abby said loudly as they passed her in the hall.

Billy just needed this day to be over. He was going home and hopefully end this Annie saga in his life. Nada went up to bed the night before and laid the sealed envelope on her nightstand, which he had looked at when he left this morning, and it was still sealed. He prayed that whatever was in it that God would give him the needed strength to bear.

Dillard left the office like any other day. He got on the highway and into the crowded traffic heading home. He loved his privacy and felt very secure his home was safe and out of the way of people just dropping in uninvited. As he drove along the highway humming to a song, he was being followed.

"I know he's up to something, and I couldn't find anything on a Katia Norfen," Milburn though out loud, driving along behind the Maybach to find out what affluent neighborhood Dillard lived in Brentwood.

Annie and Keith shared a wonderful evening together. She had hired a babysitter for Riley right across the street—Madeline Bookens, a sweet elderly lady who talked to Riley almost every day. It was a weeknight, so the plans were to go dancing on the Friday night at a trendy dance spot in downtown.

"It was wonderful, sweetheart, thank you for preparing my favorite dinner," Keith said as Annie was leaving to go and get Riley from the sitter. "Are you sure you don't need me to go with you?" he asked.

"No, it's early, she is still awake, I know, we like to make a game of it getting home," she shared, "be right back."

Keith looked at his watch. It was only nine o'clock and his birthday wasn't quite over yet. He stood in the door watching Annie and Riley playing as they came down the sidewalk.

"Wheeee," he said, picking up Riley and spinning her around until he almost fell with her.

"Keith, be careful, you're gonna fall with her," Annie yelled, reaching for the both of them.

"Oh, be quiet, she's fine, aren't you, sweetheart?" he replied, walking her into the house.

Annie took her after kissing her daddy good night and prepared her for bed while Keith sat on the sofa watching television and stealing shots of whiskey from his birthday stash.

"Keith, are you coming to bed?" she asked after getting Riley all tucked in. She had adorned herself in Victoria Secret lingerie to end the evening.

Keith was not a man to wait. There was no playing around. He had built it up in his mind and the romance had walked out the door. After speeding like a rabbit through a carrot patch, Annie lay there looking at the ceiling and Keith snoring next to her in the bed. She got up and showered and put on her pajamas and got back in bed looking at the clock. It was only ten thirty.

After about an hour, Keith was awake again. He looked over at Annie who was sound asleep and probably a bit tired after his misplaced lovemaking. He put on his clothes and left. At about twelve forty-five, Annie heard him coming back into the house. She just lay there pretending to be asleep as he eased his way back into her bed.

"Hi, guy, haven't seen you in a while," Fletcher said, calling Erene on his cell phone.

"Been so busy at the precinct, unfortunately, and took on more responsibility in the brotherhood at the church, so how's cross-country?" he asked, smiling across the waves.

"It's coming. I ran five miles the other day, so it's coming," he bragged. "I didn't mean to beat you up so bad in chess that I'd never see you again," Fletcher teased, laughing.

"Oh, not at all, just busy, do you want to do a pickup game at Lennox Park? I saw a few guys up there when I drove by."

"Sure, sounds good. I'll see you in a few." Disconnecting the cell phones, Fletcher was out the door.

Erene was only up the street, so he backed around the corner and parked. He was having another night without Nora this week and was glad Fletcher had called. He sat on the bench and called to tag one of his brotherhood brothers regarding the meeting tomorrow when he saw Fletcher drive up. He and his brother Malcolm had done a nice job fixing up his 1998 Honda Civic. New engine, chrome rims, but still waiting that illusive paint job he talked so much about.

"Hi, guy, you are all right? Adele says hi, and glad you're all right," Fletcher said, coming up sharing a fancy handshake with a somewhat-older man.

After chatting a bit, they played two games of basketball with other guys at the park before deciding to go out to eat.

"Let's take Adele, do you mind?" Erene was trying to stay away from this woman. He knew his Bible, and he knew himself, and he was better off away from her company for sure. He thought of that kiss that was now three weeks ago! "We can go to Pero's, love their steaks, I'll buy," Fletcher said, surprising Erene. He was a very responsible young man. Adele had raised him.

Erene followed Fletcher home to shower and they agreed on taking one car, so he headed home to do the same. He called Nora but she was only available on voice mail. He got back in the car and drove to the Hodges' home. Adele hesitantly went along. She was thinking of that kiss too! Fletcher had shared with Erene that she had started moping around the house again and she needed to get out even if she was just with friends. With reservations made by Fletcher, they were quickly seated and enjoying their steaks when up walked this cute little girl.

"Hi, Fletch," she said, cute as a button.

"Hi, what are you doing here?" he asked.

"Having dinner with my parents over there, I saw you come in," she said, looking at the table.

"Hi, Adele." She smiled. "And this is Erene, our friend."

"Oh, hi," she replied. "I'm Amanda."

Erene nodded his head.

"Do you mind if I sit with you guys, I drove myself here," she confessed.

"Do you guys mind?"

"No, no." Both shook their heads.

The four sat laughing. After forty-five minutes, Amanda's family came by the table to say they were leaving and remember it's a school night as each finished their meals with Amanda now highlighting her day of purchasing her first car.

Fletcher was proud paying for the meal and Erene left the tip.
"Thanks, Erene."

"No, thank you, that was the best steak I've had in a while," he admitted, getting up to leave.

"Fletcher, did you drive?" she asked.

"No."

"I can take you in my new car. We were here celebrating me getting it. I'll take everyone home," she said, smiling.

"No, I drove, I'm good." Erene smiled. He had not had that kind of fun in a while.

"Erene, can I trust you to bring sis home, I am going to check out Amanda's wheels." He laughed, hugging Adele and a high-five to Erene, they all walked out together.

Adele got into Erene's car and buckled the seat belt, and he closed the door going to the driver's side.

"Great times, great steaks," Adele said, riding along heading to the highway.

"I agree, what plans do you have for the week?" he asked, trying to make careful conversation.

"I have hooked up with one of the match services, and tomorrow, there is speeding dating at Petrolii's."

"Petrolii's, pretty fancy," Erene said, looking over at Adele's beautiful smile and her funny laughter, which is contagious.

Both rode along, being careful not to mention the kiss or the last conversation. Erene enjoyed himself even if he was ten years older than Adele and Fletch was in high school, he viewed as a little brother. Everything with Adele was carefree, naive, and innocent. She had him and he knew it but fought by staying away. He pulled to the side of the street and parked in front of her home. He looked to see if Nora had called back or left a message, nothing.

"Thanks, that was fun," she admitted, sitting in his car.

"So what happened to Mason?"

"He is still there, still looking fly, and let's just say, not my type, I think I want a more mature man, just saying." She smiled.

Erene got out and walked around to open her door as she got out. She closed the door and leaned back on the car to answer a question about the speed dating he had asked about. As he stood there in front of her smiling at her antics, she put her arms around his neck and it just happened.

Billy and Nada had finished up dinner on their patio under the stars of the sky.

"Well, William, we can't prolong the agony. I spoke with your mom today."

"You didn't tell her about this, did you?"

"No, I didn't, but I wanted to," Nada shared. "She knows, William, she's just waiting for confirmation from you," she added.

"I learned that it doesn't go away, and, Nada, you promised to stick by me no matter what?" he asked.

"William, that goes without saying."

"Oh today was Keith's birthday, so we had cake in the office."

"That sounds like fun. Did Annie do anything special for him?"

"Yes, she left early again to go and prepare a special dinner."

"She has done a lot of that lately according to you," Nada chided.

"Yes, not good, but anyway, here goes," he said using the letter opener on the envelope to break the seal. He pulled out the single-page document from the envelope and bowed his head down.

"You are the father, is that what it says, William, you are the father!" Nada got up and left the table and went up to her bedroom to cry.

Billy sat out under the stars and prayed to God for mercy! "For my thoughts are not your thoughts, neither are my ways your ways, saith the Lord. For as the heavens are higher than the earth, so are my ways higher than your ways, and my thoughts than your thoughts."

Nada needed a getaway and asked Billy the next day if she could go to Washington for the women's annual day service at Mount Nebo. Millicent loved taking care of Peyton and it was only an overnight trip staying at her in-laws' home, so Billy didn't need to worry.

"Honey, are you sure you'll be all right?"

"Yes, William, I'll be fine. I just need a breather from this," she said as she packed her bags for traveling.

Getting to Washington State, Nada enjoyed a delicious dinner prepared by her dad, Alfredo, the Parkers' chef. She needed encouragement from her mother-in-law and shared the conversation she had with William the night before the news and standing by her husband. Nada and Tetra shared a comforting hug after prayer and went to bed.

The next day at 3:00 p.m., all the family went to Mount Nebo's Annual Women's Day service. It was high energy and spirit felt as Nada sat enjoying it with her in-laws and her dad who not only is a great chef but also the senior choir director. When the choir featuring Virginia Manuel as lead singer finished singing, most attending were on their feet, clapping and praising in the presence of the Lord. After service, Nada walked up to Miss Manuel and hugged her and praised her singing.

"My, Miss Manuel, you really blessed us today and you said you were afraid," Nada added.

"You know what, somebody bet-ta call Yolanda Adams and warn hu, 'cause Virginia Manuel is now on the mic!" she said, sharing a laugh with a few besides Nada who heard her.

C H A P T E R **16**

E RENE FELT SO GUILTY THURSDAY night after picking his wife, Nora, from the airport. He had beaten himself to a pulp mentally all week but couldn't stop calling Adele each day since that last night just to talk. They would call each other at lunch or after work, it felt so comfortable. Truth is, Adele had blocked out the fact that Erene was a married man. And the way he was reciprocating, he had forgotten too. They had only to this point exchanged passionate kisses. "God forgive me."

As Nora and Erene rode home together in the car, Erene asked, "Nora, wouldn't it be nice if we had a family, you know, a child?" He smiled, looking at her sitting next to him.

"Now where is that coming from?" she questioned.

"You're gone a lot, and it would be company for me and someone to love and care for," he explained.

"Really, Erene, we have gone over this before, I'm not ready for children and neither are you, if you're being honest, how did this come up anyway?" she asked again, laughing sarcastically at him.

"We talked about it the other night at brotherhood."

"Really, one hundred men in a room and that's all you guys could talk about, always putting the women in the kitchen," she stated.

"Huh, how did you surmise that from what I ask?"

"Children plus caring, plus housework, equal kitchen," she laughed.

"Whatever, Nora," he scolded.

"We have been married four years and you already want to tie me down with children," she reprimanded. "And now you're complaining about my traveling, I have an important job," she stated, looking squarely at him.

"Forgive me, I do understand that you have an important job, you travel to important places, and you have met important people. I get it!" he said, speaking of how low on the important list, he felt.

"I know you missed me, dear, I missed you as well. I'll make it up to you again for a while anyway," she whispered in his ear as he drove her home.

Armed with the confirmation, Billy had to find the right time to speak with Annie. He didn't want a scene in his office from Keith, and a week had passed since he found out. Nada was heartbroken by the news but really she knew. All the signs were there for years when she looked back over them. She had prayed, they had prayed, and Nada was determined to stay by her husband knowing how this came to be. "God can do whatever he wants, whenever he wants, however he wants, and with whomever, thank you for helping me to accept that." Now Billy needed to talk to Annie, who had totally blocked out everything and focused on Keith, and Billy was concerned about that too.

"Annie, can you please bring an iPad tablet and come into my office?" she heard that Friday after she returned from lunch with Keith and Abby.

"William, I'm sending in Abigail, is that all right?" she asked.

"No, Annie, I need you, thank you." And he disconnected the intercom button.

Annie hunched her shoulders and smiled at Abby.

"I'll let him know you can handle any job in this office now, don't worry." She smirked, going into her boss's office.

"Close the door please," was William's first request.

"I gave Abby the Beeferton case, she knows all about it," she explained why Abby should be the one in here taking dictation.

"Annie, I don't want to discuss this office."

"I'm not going to discuss Keith with you, he did drink a bit too much at lunch today, but I was there and Abby too."

"Yes, well, I'll get to that later," he replied.

"But I don't want to discuss, Keith. I want to talk about Riley."

"Riley! What happened, did the school call, is she all right?" she asked, getting up to run out.

"Calm, Annie, none of the above. She's fine at school, I'm sure. Annie, why didn't you tell me about Riley?" he asked again.

"William, what are you talking about? Tell you what?" She looked at him strangely, and it was what he wasn't saying that confused her. "William, if you don't just come out and say whatever you're not saying, I'm going to leave this office," she stated, standing with her hand on the knob.

"Who is Riley's father?" he asked.

"William, why are you asking me this, you know Keith is her father," she believed.

"Annie, no, he's not, and you didn't tell me, how was I supposed to know!" he shared with a heavy heart.

"William, no, William, you're not saying, you're, you're not saying," she kept repeating herself and backing up from the edge of his desk. "How do you know, who told you, who did this, why?" She was crying hysterically and Billy caught her in his arms to calm her down. She stood there wrapped in his arms and cried for minutes. "I didn't know, and then I didn't want to know," she cried. "Does Keith know? Did you tell him?" she asked.

"No, I didn't tell him, but I think he knows," Billy confessed.

"This can't be true, just can't be," she insisted, walking around his office.

"Annie it's true, I'm sorry, things would have unfolded differently, concerning Riley anyway," he said.

"William, I would have never married Keith, if I had known, you must believe me," she pleaded.

"It's okay, I'm just concerned for the child. I'll leave it up to you to tell Keith," Billy clarified.

"What about Nada?" she asked, looking.

"Nada knows," he said, giving her a Kleenex box from his desk to clean her face from tears.

She sat there in his office sadly. "I'm sorry, William, I am so sorry. I didn't mean to hurt you," she added. "How long has Keith known about this?" she asked, looking up from her chair.

"I don't know, that you will have to take up with him," Billy said, going back behind his desk.

Annie got up after clearing her head and wiping tears temporarily from her eyes, going out the door, saying, "William, I am truly sorry."

"Annie?" She looked back quickly. "Your tablet," he replied, getting up handing it to her as she left.

Milburn moved swiftly in and out of traffic trying to keep up with Dillard's Maybach. This mysterious woman who had come into Dillard's life was turning heads at all the functions and he wanted to know if she was old money or new. Milburn had done some detective work, but Katia Norfen's identity couldn't be found anywhere he looked, and that led further to his curiosity buildup. Milburn had photographs spread across the seat of his car that he had taken with his long-lens camera for weeks now as he made his way through traffic. He knew Dillard lived in Brentwood and was headed that way. Milburn didn't want to miss a turn or following him would be over.

"She is very polished and loves to dress." Milburn's wife recognized many of her fashions in the photographs he had taken. Milburn wanted the address of Dillard's home more than that he wanted to be invited in. Dillard was a recluse and now he was living the life and secretly Milburn envied it. He has been married for twenty-six years to the same woman, very outspoken, a bit headstrong, and not bad as a looker, but certainly not a Katia, he thought going on behind Dillard.

After almost two hours in heavy traffic, Milburn saw the zip code he had been looking for: 94513. He pulled over a bit watching Dillard turn into a gated driveway that stretched way back on several acres of beautiful property. The home he could see in the distant was magnificent. The more he saw, the more obsessed he became with finding out about Dillard and Katia. He wrote down the entire address and took more photos before leaving. There's no way he was going to get on the property without setting off an alarm. He would need an invite, so he started up his car and headed home.

"Annie, you've been so quiet since your meeting with William, is everything all right?" Abby asked, sitting at her desk processing documents.

"Things are fine," she lied, "just concerned about me giving off the work and my loss of passion for the job, that's all." She wasn't going to tell Abby the truth especially after William had assured her only he and Nada knew about Riley.

"So what's going to happen now?" the concerned Abby questioned.

"No worries, Abby, did you get the files Oren requested processed and also McGuire?" Annie inquired.

"Oren, I just took his files and put them on his desk, and McGuire's I'm working on now." She smiled.

"Good," she said, gathering up her case and purse to leave. "The traffic was horrible yesterday getting across the freeway to the day care, I was almost late picking up Riley, so I'm going to try and beat that five p.m. rush," she shared, standing up by her desk. "Will you please let Keith know I'll see him at home, he's in a meeting with Matterson." Annie headed to the door and was surprised when Abby stopped her by running over and giving her a hug. "Huh, what was that?" she asked, looking at her a bit puzzled.

"Awww, I just felt you needed it," Abby replied, standing shyly with her hands behind her back. "Goodnight."

Nada was sitting in the parlor waiting for William to come home from the office. She knew they had discussed telling Keith and Annie about her daughter, Riley, and she was waiting to see how it went. Hearing Dante speaking with Billy, she knew he was in the home, probably putting things down in his study.

"Good evening, sweetheart," he said, as always entering to give her a kiss upon arrival after seeing her.

"Hi, honey, how did it go?" was Nada's question very quickly. "What did Keith do?"

"Honey, slow down, it wasn't that easy," he said, sitting next to her on the beautiful settee adorning their parlor. "First of all, I didn't speak with Keith because I didn't want a confrontation in my law office. That could have gotten real ugly. However, I did call Annie in my office and spoke with her," he shared.

"And what did she say?" Nada's demeanor had changed somewhat.

"She was surprised, a bit annoyed and angry because I implied such a thing that could ruin her family," he added.

"Angry?" Nada was sitting straight up on the sofa.

"Now, Nada, please stay calm, please."

"I mean what about you, what about me? I had asked her a while ago and she denied it and she's angry?" Nada was livid.

Billy held her to calm her down. "Dear, honestly I think she was very surprised by the news myself," he said.

"Surprised, you think a woman would know who she fathered a child with!" she responded.

Billy wanted to say it was either Keith or him, but he wasn't going to open that can of worms on his wife, no way! "Well, anyway, it's up to her to tell Keith, and we will continue to pray and see what God has for us to do in this matter," he concluded. "So how's my son today?" he added, rubbing Nada's tummy.

"Your son, who told you? I wanted to surprise you," Nada confessed.

"No way, I was worried about being the only male around here surrounded by all things pink." He grinned. "But now I can think football and baseball and golf." He laughed, helping Nada up heading into the television room to watch an animated movie with Peyton before bedtime.

Annie had cried all the way home after putting on a front in the office most of the day after her meeting with William. She sat on her chair in her bedroom. She had tucked Riley in and read her a bedtime story while thinking about how she was going to confront Keith about the news. She wondered if he knew. Maybe that's why he's been acting so bizarre lately. And tonight was no exception. It was 8:00 p.m. at night and he was still not home from the office.

Whatever, she had bigger thoughts right now. "How is Nada reacting to the news? What is she saying about me? My job, how can I work with William knowing what I've done?" She was going through a barrage of questions over and over in her head. "Oh, my husband, what if he knows? Will he still love me and accept me and Riley? Is that why he's drinking again? What have I done?" she screamed loud sitting in her room before crawling into bed and crying until she fell asleep.

Katia did most of her shopping from home consulted by a fashion expert and always delivered to her home. She did enjoy the interaction of people and would go out window-shopping every now and then. She loved the smell of restaurants and coffeehouses as she strolled along Melrose. Often finding herself on Rodeo at Nordstrom's, Macy's, and other posh shops along the drive.

She loved being out, unaware to her she was being followed by a detective hired by Milburn, and when she entered the Unique Chic Boutique on Rodeo Drive, Roslyn Milburn with instructions from her husband did as well.

Seeing Katia across the boutique, Roslyn quickly made her move. "Hi," she said, startling Katia. I'm sorry, didn't mean to frighten you, Roslyn Milburn," she shared, reaching out her hand.

"Oh," Katia paused, "yes," reluctantly connecting her hand.

"I just seem to keep running into you."

"Yes, that sure seems to be what's happening," Katia agreed but wasn't happy.

"You shop here a lot, it's one of my favorite places," Roslyn shared, looking around lost, Katia surmised.

Katia was trying all she knew how to end the conversation and move on, but Roslyn just kept jabbering about anything. Doris noticed from her office window the stance of her customer and walked out to the floor seeing her clerk had not greeted the patrons upon arrival as policy. Before long, a clerk ran from the back.

"Just me this afternoon, Mrs. Woods, nature called, I do apologize," she said, coming over. The clerk looked at Katia, just browsing. "Help her, I think she may be a newcomer," she shared, moving far away from her and her conversation.

"Hello, sorry about that, I am the owner, Doris Wright, extending her hand." Katia graciously connected with a smile. "I apologize for my clerk's absence, I could see the lady was bothering you," she confessed.

"It's all right, really it's okay." Not wanting to say much to her, Katia shied away from Doris. "Pleasure meeting you," Katia said before Doris remembered her voice, or the way she delivered that line. They had met at the art show a month or so ago.

"Enjoy the rest of your shopping." Doris smiled, walking away seeing Katia did not want to be bothered and the clerk was amazing Roslyn with the fashion closet on the tri-floor of the boutique.

"Hello, Patterson," Doris greeted, calling him on the phone after returning to her office.

What now? Patterson thought to himself, *I thought all this was over with this sister stuff.* "Yes, Mrs. Woods, what can I do for you?" he asked.

"Really, I'm just saying hello, saw a friend of yours in the boutique, Miss Norfen, you remember the one wearing that fabulous original gown at the art show," she said, reminding him where they met.

"Yes, yes, I remember, she loves your fashions, what can I say," Dillard confessed.

"The lady has exquisite taste, Patterson, I'll give you that."

"She does, she does," he again agreed. "So normally I don't even bother looking at who is purchasing for my patrons, but I did notice your name and I know you, so you are apparently okay with the amounts," she voiced.

"Doris, not you too, if you have lived in LA for some time, you would know my family. Judge Patterson was my dad, lost him a while ago. He serviced in the judicial system in LA for many years. He invested his money well. He lived the American dream and left all his children sufficient enough to move ahead, I chose law, anyway, this call could have been avoided," Dillard explained. "No need to be concerned with my finances, I'm fine," he remarked.

"I know and I'm only one of your clients," she teased. "And good, she appears to be a very nice lady, hope things work out for you. Although today it seemed like she didn't want me in her face," Doris interjected, joking with her lawyer, "'cause it could have been Roslyn Milburn, oh, I'm just rambling, and thanks for reassuring me," Doris concluded.

"Wait," she heard Patterson say just as she was about to hang up. "Did you say Milburn?"

"I did, Ms Norfen seemed to be put out by her conversation with her."

"Is she a regular patron at your boutique?" Dillard asked, curious she and Katia had met up again.

"Didn't appear that way, why do you ask?" Doris questioned.

"Interesting couple, the Milburns. I will have to share them with you one day." He laughed. "Her husband is a fellow attorney in the building," Dillard shared with Doris Woods who is a client of his for years.

"Oh I see, must be that new impressive zip code, Mr. Patterson," she said, still looking at her inventory sold and shipping delivery sheet on her desk. "It makes me proud to have you on my team as an attorney," voiced Doris before disconnecting the phone.

"Someone else is on my back," Dillard murmured, going back to the files he was reading over.

Annie didn't mention Keith's late-night rendezvous to him the next morning. He had gotten up and showered and was heading to the kitchen for his morning coffee when she decided to greet him. "Good morning," she said, starling him somewhat because she usually sleeps soundly.

"Oh are you awake?" he asked, coming over to the bed, rubbing her hair back from her face. She moved back on the bed and he sat down playing affectionately with her nose and smiling. "How's my sleepyhead this morning?" he asked, smiling and playing the devoted husband role.

"Keith, I have to ask you something?" she said, not buying into his playfulness, pushing his hands off of her face.

"Abby told me about your meeting with Parker, is that why you're pushing me away?" he asked, a bit teed at her posture toward him.

"Abby told you what about my meeting with William? I've been a little distracted, Keith, with all the drama we have in this house right now, and it is reflecting in my work, he noticed that," she confessed but was lying to his face.

"What drama, what are you telling him?" he asked, standing looking down at her sitting on the bed.

"I'm not telling him anything about what's going on in my home, but you are aware of what's going on," she stated, focusing on him pacing the room. "Keith, ever since you took Riley and left that day a few months ago, you have been acting very strange, you're drinking more again, and staying off later than usual, and you're not always at the office," she blasted out.

"And, Annie, what, you think I don't have a reason for the things I do? My father is dying with cancer, remember?" he responded back loudly.

"Right, and there is nothing we can do to fix that, Keith, but you're ruining this family with your actions," Annie criticized, getting up and putting on her robe.

Keith laughed sarcastically. "I'm ruining this family? Really, that's what you're thinking? I have to live with you, grinning around your boss, and kissing up to his wife after what you've done!" he blurted out.

"Keith NO, why didn't you come to me and tell me". She sat on her bed crying.

"You should have told me, Annie, you should have told me," he repeated, going out of the bedroom.

"Keith!" she yelled. "I'm sorry, I didn't know, I really didn't know," she said, falling over on her bed and crying as he continued out the bedroom and soon the front door.

Dillard and Katia sat at a posh restaurant in Beverly Hills near his office. Katia had stopped by to have lunch with him after her Zumba class.

Ring, ring. His cell phone in his coat pocket was going off. He looked at Katia. "Excuse me, this is a client. I won't be long, I promise."

"Good afternoon, Doris?" he answered. Looking at Katia, he whispered, "It's Doris Woods," and went back to his caller. "Yes, what can I do? I'm having lunch, busy day," he shared.

"I'm sorry, won't keep you long, I do understand. I'm not sure what relationship you have with the Milburns, but you're right, when she left the boutique the other day, there was not a lot I didn't know about you and your lady friend," Doris explained. "Mrs. Milburn is quite the talker."

"What did she tell you, Doris?" he asked, distraught by the thought of his business being put in the street.

"Nothing incriminating," she explained, "mostly gossip and busybody statements of all the new changes you've gotten done to yourself since meeting Miss Norfen. The new Benz, another home, you know, busy stuff. Anyway, I'm calling as a friend, Dillard, that woman would make a better friend than an enemy, I'm just saying," she said, smiling.

"Thanks for the call, Doris, really, thanks for the call." Dillard disconnected the line and Katia noticed immediately his mood had changed.

"What happened? What does she need from that estate now?" Katia questioned, knowing this client of Dillard's pretty well now.

"No, this was a friend call," he explained after allowing the waiter to place their entrées on the table and move away.

"Oh," Katia paused, putting a bite of her meal into her mouth.

"The other day when you ran into Milburn's wife at her boutique?"

"Yes, what about it?" she asked curiously.

"Well, it appears Miss Milburn decided to give Doris and her clerk a history lesson on knowing us," he clarified.

"Oh, no!" she gasped. "What is up with those people?"

"I'm not sure, but I guess I'm going to have to invite them over to find out," he said, lifting his glass to toast with Katia.

Adele had contented herself that who she wanted to care about was Erene even though he was already taken. She had convinced herself that life was not worth living without him in it. So she'd share his time without question. He on the other hand was trying all he knew how to stay faithful to his marriage, and to this point, he was losing. He had taken on more responsibility in his brotherhood group of his church and pleaded continually with his wife to have a child for companionship while she traveled but to no avail. He knew every time he spoke with Adele, it was wrong because he had begun to care for her. It wasn't right. She was young, innocent, and full of life. She made him laugh again and smile and brought so much joy into the fading existence of his lonely days. Scriptures upon scriptures were recalled to his mind that often steered him from dialing her number and going by her office or her home. He sat having a brown bag lunch in the park near her office and his phone rang. Yes, his caller ID read Adele Hodges.

"Hi," she greeted after he answered. It had been three weeks since he last spoke with her. "I miss you," with another line said.

Erene didn't know how to respond. "Adele, what are you up to these days?" he asked, cheerfully breaking the ice.

"There you are." She laughed. "How have you been? Haven't seen or spoke with you for a while. Fletch says he played ball with you yesterday?"

"True, I have seen Fletcher."

"Ooooh, I see, then it's me that is the problem," she teased, smiling across the phone.

"You're not a problem," he said, but clearly she was for him.

"Then why are you avoiding me, I'm not going to hurt you?" she continued to tease and flirt with him over the phone.

"I know, Adele, look, if things were different, oh well, I have to go, take care." And he disconnected the phone.

After work, Adele went shopping. She found that to be her new outlet for stress. Mason was still toying with her affections and every other girl in the huge county building where both were employees. Angel was his go-to girl. She kept up drama. She had a child for another guy who she said wasn't any good yet she was always sneaking around with Mason. Everyone in the office knew her stories. She was always throwing stones and hiding her hand. But most had her number! Adele had canned the dating services for now and had focused on the only man she cared about—Erene James.

He had helped her and she had fallen for him. So off she went to the mall and the Victoria Secret store where she ran into Nada.

"Hi, Mrs. Parker," she said, seeing her standing looking at a lingerie.

"Hi, Adele," she said, giving her a friendly hug. "This is a nice store," Nada said, smiling.

"Yes, since you have inspired me with all the new fashions and I absolutely love my new 'do, I thought I'd throw myself into the dating scene. I've been getting a few looks lately," she explained.

"Oh, I see, well do be careful, there's a right way and a wrong way to make that happen," Nada added.

"Yes," she replied, looking down at her stomach smiling.

"Oh very soon, I'm here getting a new piece to wear after my arrival this month," she shared. "I know you're not there yet, but a woman has to remember to keep your husband satisfied or someone else will," she said, giving the young Adele some womanly advice. "Enjoy your dating, be careful and have fun. Oh, and look over there, I saw some really cute sets for your age." Nada smiled, going to the counter to make her purchase and waving good-bye as she waddled from the store.

Annie drove into work alone after taking Riley to school. She had cried and cried all night, and her tears were all gone, she assumed coming into the parking garage of the law firm. She looked at her watch. It was close to 9:00 a.m., and she hurried getting her case from the car and up the elevator of the building and quickly into the office.

"Good morning," she said, seeing Abby at her desk smiling.

"Cutting it close, aren't you?" she asked, smiling.

"I did, the traffic was horrible and I almost didn't come in today. But we have a new case to process and get ready for William. I know it's going to take both of us working to get it done," Annie confessed. "Is Keith in his office?" Putting her case on the desk with her purse, she went down the hall to his office. She walked in and closed the door. "Keith, let's agree to talk about this tonight at home please. I really don't want to air this all out here in the office," she asked, looking at him busy working on a client's file.

"Sure, Annie," he replied, not even looking up.

"Keith?"

"I said okay, now please let me do my job," he stated, "and close the door behind you when you leave."

Annie knew he was pissed and she didn't know how to get into his graces.

Dillard went back to his office after the lunch with Katia in Beverly Hills. He purposely walked by Milburn's office just so he would call out to him as he passed.

"Dillard, my man, how are you?" he heard as he passed through the beautiful terrarium growing inside the building's entry space.

"Why, hello, Milburn, I'm great. I was just thinking about you."

"Me, you're thinking about me?" Milburn inquired, looking and pointing at himself.

"Yes, Katia and I are having friends over Friday and we'd like you and Roslyn to come. I shared with you I'm a man of my word, so this is your invite to my home," Dillard said, waiting an answer. "No hurry, you let me know and I'll get the address and direction to my home," he added, walking off down the steps to his office smiling.

Milburn was on the phone to Roslyn immediately and soon called Dillard to let him know he'd be there at 7:00 p.m. sharp.

Erene left the church brotherhood meeting at 8:00 p.m. sharp and said his good nights to the guys he see each week. The meetings were really helping him stay focused on his marriage and the guys talked about all kinds of issues and scenarios in relationships. No topic was off-limits. The group range from the young men in high school to newlyweds in their twenties, middle age, and a surprisingly amount of elderly men who shared their wisdom freely. Many often quoted the wise king Solomon when making a point from the book of Proverbs. And just today, Deacon Abom brought in Proverbs 7:5, "That they may keep thee from the strange woman, from the stranger which flattered with her words."

But another Tuesday without Nora, he decided to stop by an ice cream parlor near his home for a sugar cone. He walked in, being a regular there with Nora, the clerk greeted him by name.

"Hello, Erene, what can I get for you?" the clerk asked as soon as he entered.

"The usual," was his answer, and as he turned around to sit and wait at a table, in walked Adele standing behind him. She knew his schedule and tonight he'd be leaving the church heading home this way. She didn't know he would stop for ice cream, but he had, and she just played along.

"Hi there, may I help you?" the clerk asked her before turning to give Erene his ice cream. He headed to the door. "You're not eating it here? I could give you a to-go container," the clerk suggested.

"No, I'm good," he explained, hurrying to leave from the ice cream spot.

Adele sat after she ordered. "Your order, miss," the clerk voiced with her getting up to take it from the clerk whose line had gotten longer.

Adele went out of the parlor looking around for Erene. She thought he had gone and she walked toward her car.

"You must be careful out here by yourself," he said, coming out of the shadows and frightened her. She pushed him playfully on the chest and dropped her cone with a scream. He held her tight, saying, "I'm sorry, I'm sorry," laughing the whole time. To him, she smelled so good, she was soft and warm, he thought, standing next to her now smiling 'cause he startled her. Then he took a bite of his cone and kissed Adele and she kissed him back standing out by his car in the dark of night. "You're a ways from home. What brings you this way?" he asked.

"I was missing you, can you believe that?" she said, flirting with him sarcastically. They stood talking for a few minutes in the dark with only the lights of the ice cream parlor breaking through the night's dark sky. Before long, she had persuaded him into following her home since Fletcher was spending the night at a friend's house just to continue the conversation.

Abby left with McGuire and Oren to process documents at the courthouse. William and Keith had just finished up an interview of a new client in William's office.

Ring, ring.

"Hello, honey," Billy answered, "it is, it's time, okay I'll meet you at the hospital, tell Dante to drive carefully," he advised.

Shaking the client's hand leaving Keith standing with him and grabbing his briefcase, he was gone.

"Yes, Mr. Lampler, we look forward to helping you win your case. Mr. Parker's wife just called, they're expecting a new arrival," Keith smiled, informing him.

"Oh, makes sense the quick exit, I've been there," he replied.

"Yes, yes, we all have," Keith found himself saying as he shook the new client's hand as he left.

"Where is Abby?" he asked, standing now at Annie's desk.

"She's out with McGuire and Oren," Annie replied.

"Oh, that's right, Bill wants her to have this one, I'll leave a note on it on her desk," he said and leaned over on Abby's desk to write on a Post-it.

"Keith, are you going to be angry with me all night as well? William just left to meet Nada at the hospital, so it's just you and

I here for now. Please let's talk, she suggested, looking at him now standing by her desk.

"I honestly don't know what you want me to say. I married you, to do right by you because you were having my baby. But none of it is true, do you even love me?" he asked, looking at Annie.

"I'm sorry, I didn't know, and I do love you, Keith, and your daughter, Riley, as well."

"I hate Riley has to be punished because of you! You should have known. You deceived everyone including Bill. I can't imagine the conversations he and his wife are having. So how do you propose we move forward with William now knowing that Riley's his daughter, Annie? You have humiliated me and made me feel less than a man and I don't know what's going to happen," he said, walking off to his office.

Annie put her head on her desk and cried.

Every encounter Erene had before this night was simply a kiss. But he was very vulnerable tonight and Adele had gotten her way. When he left her home sometime during the night, he knew he'd be back again. He didn't care if it was wrong. She made him feel alive. She cared for him and held him in her arms for as long as he wanted her to. She was there in the flesh and he didn't want to stop. No matter what he knew, he was going to spend his alone days with Adele.

Proverbs: 7:13 says, "So she had caught him, and kissed him, and with an impudent face said unto him, 14: I have peace offerings with me; these days have I paid my vows. 15: Therefore came I forth to meet thee, diligently to seek thy face, and I have found thee. 16: I have decked my bed with coverings of tapestry, with carved works, with fine linen of Egypt. 17: I have perfumed my bed with myrrh, aloes, and cinnamon. 18: Come let us take our fill of love until the morning; let us solace ourselves with loves. 19: For the goodman [wife] is not at home, she has gone for a long journey: 20: She hath taken a bag of money with her, and will come home at the day appointed. 21: with her much fair speech she caused him to yield, with the flattering of her lips she forced him." All this was floating around in Erene's head as he drove home that unfaithful night.

CHAPTER 17

D ILLARD AND KATIA HAD PLANNED a small dinner party at their home just to appease the Milburns and get them off their backs. They were making their lives more exciting than it really was!

Dillard had nothing to hide, but Milburn was so sure he did and he wanted to know everything about his fellow attorney.

"How did he get a woman like Katia?" he really wanted to know. He and his buddies were talking about her from the last social gathering near the infamous watercooler. She was beautiful. She was a big step up from Sally who worked at the courthouse in the files department. And Dillard had landed her. Couldn't be, he doesn't have enough money to get a woman like Katia that they could see, they all agreed. It must be something else. And why did all of a sudden he change his ways, new car, house, looks, everything, 360-degree turn around within a year, and it was bugging the heck out of Milburn. No matter that the Milburns lived in a prestigious neighborhood, drove fancy cars, owned a yacht, rubbed noses with the elite, but Dillard, no!

Milburn would be all right with it if he didn't know Dillard was a black man 'cause you couldn't tell on sight. When you first meet Dillard, you immediately think he is Caucasian by nationality. What you call "very high yellow" in the south. His very thin, wavy, and balding hair was what we blacks call "good hair." His skin was very pale; yes, he looked all of Caucasian, very articulate, well-groomed, educated, savvy, and a total gentleman. One would mistake him easily for the other side. But proud of whom he was, and quick to correct you, and Milburn had been a recipient of his correction a few years after meeting him in courtroom. He was fierce in the courtroom, attorney to the stars, impressive client base, seemed content in life. Dillard was just staying in his lane or wheelhouse, wasn't moving quickly up social ladders, or rocking any boats, not even trying for that matter. He wasn't very social with anyone other than his clients, no steady woman to speak of, but was certainly a threat in the courtroom and knew the law.

Now he had landed a gorgeous Caucasian woman who looked to be making headways with Dillard. She had brought him out of his shell and fixed him up, and Milburn felt a bit threatened by him. Was it her money he was spending? Oh, to be a fly on that wall, he thought driving up to Dillard's very nice home in Brentwood he had purchased about nine months ago.

The parents had all made their way to Maine to see the new arrival. David Michael had come immediately when he heard that his stepmother had gone into labor.

"Hi, Dad, I should be there at three fifteen, don't worry, I have a car waiting. I'll come directly to the hospital," he shared, excited it was a boy.

Now everyone was sitting in the waiting room to get their turn at seeing William and Nada's son, Trevor Jonathan Parker.

"Dad, did I look like this all wrinkly? Look at his fat cheeks," David Michael said, laughing with his dad as both stood outside the nursery window. "Wow, so many little guys, they outnumber the girls, look," he said, counting the pink and blue blankets they used to identify easily. "I brought him a baseball, Dad."

"You did? Way to go, son." They stood for about twenty minutes before relinquishing the window to other family members to view that included Millicent and Dante. Everyone was happy and so glad Nada and the baby were doing well. When they left for the Parkers' estate, Billy's parents, Nada's dad and his wife, Priscilla, David Michael, and Billy left flowers, gifts, and well wishes in her hospital room. Everyone anxiously waited for the day that Nada would be returning home; for Billy, it would be a long two days. Tetra, Billy's mom, was very proud of her new grandson and couldn't wait to see her granddaughter, Peyton, who had stayed at home with one of the staff at the estate.

Annie had got the news via a text William had sent out to everyone. He was so excited that he now had a son with Nada. He had just saw David Michael off again after he spent two wonderful days with him and the family bonding with his little brother, Trevor.

"I'll call when I arrive, Dad, and give Trev a fist bump from his big bro," he said, smiling before embracing his dad and getting on the plane going back to Los Angeles.

Annie was watching a movie with Riley when she heard Keith open the door.

"Keith! Keith! Are you leaving?" she yelled from the family room where they were watching the video.

"Yes, going out for a while, shouldn't be long." And he was gone.

Looking at the large clock on the wall, it read 7:00 p.m. Annie had been trying to talk their situation through, but he was done and won't consider the matter at all.

"What is going to happen? Are we going to be a family again? What is Billy going to expect now if anything. And Riley is in the middle of this mess and it's all my fault," she uttered.

Keith crept back in about 10:30 p.m. Annie just lay there pretending to be asleep. She had not one tear left to shed in a long, long time. This treatment by Keith had been going on for about six months and she had dealt with being hurt, angry, neglected, lonely, compromising, and now she didn't feel anything, nothing at all. But Annie knew she couldn't continue this. She had to look out for Riley. She couldn't pretend at work anymore, and wherever he was leaving to go in the middle of the night hadn't been addressed at all. "I'm going to just leave and raise my daughter by myself," and about that, she started to cry deeply.

Dillard had spoken with one of his Brentwood's neighbor who was willing to help him with his dinner party. He had just returned home after a meeting with him and everything was a go.

"Should be fun," Dillard voiced, leaving the high-profile actor's home in his neighborhood.

The big day had come for the party.

"See you this evening," Dillard said, seeing Milburn in the parking garage leaving work.

Milburn smiled and hurried out of the garage quickly. Dillard smiled. When he arrived at home, things on the other end were going as planned. Katia was in her element giving instructions to the hired help for the evening, and the food smelled and looked delicious. The decorators for the party had done a fabulous job with all the décor. Dillard wanted to make this evening very memorable for the Milburns in every way. Katia adorned herself in a gown from Neiman Marcus, and she as always looked stunning. The first to arrive were two dear friends of Dillard's. They were just young bucks when his dad practiced law. Both retired and Dillard wanted the knowledge and notability to impress the critic Milburn.

"Good evening, George, so good to see you this evening," he said, greeting a dear friend.

Soon in walked Howard Stuns, another fellow retired lawyer and former marine. He showed them in and sat talking about old stories and the new law with Dillard laughing and having a wonderful time. Before long, the place was rousing with guest, including the Milburns. They had arrived, seeing Bentleys pull in, and a least two Rolls Royces, and other fancy cars as they pulled up to Dillard's home.

"Wow," Milburn thought, "this is old money Dillard affiliates with. I'm impressed," he shared with his wife who was gasping over the gowns the women were wearing. They were in great company, each thought going through the door of Dillard's amazing Brentwood home.

"So glad you could grace us tonight," Katia said to Roslyn Milburn, sipping on champagne looking out at the Hollywood sign far in the distant from the balcony.

"Oh, this is magnificent, dear, thank you so much for the invite, you have a lovely home," she replied, looking around at the guests.

"Come let me introduce you to a friend, she's in the fashion industry, a designer. She's designed a lot of the red carpet A-list celebs," Katia shared, walking her over by a table inside the home.

"Oh really, and I'm Roslyn Milburn, a great honor to meet you." She smiled, shaking hands.

"I'll leave you two to talk, where is Dillard?" she asked, walking away leaving Roslyn awed.

Dillard was moving around the crowd but mostly watching Milburn wandering around looking at everything. He and Roslyn had made their way to another part of the house away from the crowd of guests Dillard had invited to his home. As Dillard approached the two coming down a wide corridor of his home, Roslyn turned toward the sound of the crowd, leaving Milburn to face Dillard alone. Milburn went through two beautiful French doors and stopped in Dillard's study, which was off-limits, but what the heck, no harm, Dillard thought, going in surprising him.

"Oh, just looking for a room to relieve myself," he lied.

"Oh, you made the wrong turn," Dillard responded. "But I understand, this is a big house, one could easily get lost," he added.

"I have seen that portrait before somewhere," Milburn said, looking and pointing aside the wall scratching his head trying to remember.

"Yeah, I remember, downtown at the courthouse! What are you doing with this guy in your home?" he asked sarcastically. "I mean, I love my career job as well as the next fellow, but come on now, to bring them home, that's a bit much," he said, shaking his head at Dillard as he spoke.

"Milburn, if you were anyone else, I'd be offended, but it gives me great pleasure to tell you that this is a portrait of my dad," he said, pointing and smiling. "And yes, that's exactly where you saw it."

"NO! You're telling me Judge Patterson is your dad? But I thought—" he said, looking shocked at what Dillard was sharing. "Ummm, umm, okay, you got my attention, so you're really a man of substance," Milburn admitted, shaking Dillard's hand.

Dillard didn't want to shake his hand nor go into his life story and certainly didn't want Milburn running through his home being nosy. So drop some truth along the way and it all comes together, Dillard surmised. "Now let's go this way to the men's room," he said, showing Milburn from his study and down the hall. The Milburns were very glad Dillard had invited them to this wonderful dinner party with their high-profile friends. The bubbly was flowing, the caviar was endless, the fashions were to die for, and the five-course dinner was fabulous. The invited guests present were treated to a performance by one of Dillard and Katia's friends who were also on the guest A-list at the party. She delighted the crowd with a Barbara Streisand song, which happened to be the one played at the Milburns' wedding. She was accompanied by her pianist on Dillard's splendid black baby grand piano in his great room. Dillard had done his homework too! Milburn even sat and talked with George and Howard being amazed at some of the cases he had only read about early in his practiced career. He had a great time and left with a newfound respect for Dillard. Realizing now he was old money! Milburn had also saw a woman's portrait in another room as he roamed through the house, which he now believes was Dillard's mother.

When the evening was over, Dillard thanked George and Howard, his true friends, for coming. He was very pleased with his neighbor's daughter who had come to sing for his party. His celeb neighbor had recommended her when he and Dillard met to set up the party. She lived in the Hollywood Hills. Dillard and Katia walked into their parlor putting their feet up and letting out a big sigh.

"I think we did it," she said, smiling at Dillard.

"Yes, which goes to show, you can do anything with actors in Hollywood!"

Adele was having coffee in the break room with Hilary when Mason walked in.

"Hello, ladies," he voiced, getting him a cup of coffee. "Adele, have you seen that new movie we talked about that's coming out this month?"

"No, no, not really, haven't been out a lot lately."

"Oh, I saw you at the steak house with that guy you're always with," he stated.

"You saw me and Fletcher and two other people, right? That's how things get confused," she returned.

"Yeah, yeah, anyway, what's the chance you'll let me take you out this Friday, my treat?" he asked, hoping she accepted his apology.

"I'll have to see, but right now, it's a no," she said, getting up with Hilary about to laugh as they walked away.

"I know you didn't just say no to Mason?" Hilary laughed, going behind her desk.

"I did, Mason is very immature and the things he does are so juvenile," she added, going back to work.

Sitting now at her desk, she dialed. "Hi, Mrs. Parker, congratulations on your new arrival," Adele called the hospital to congratulate Nada.

"Adele, thank you, he is so perfect. When I'm up on my feet, we'll have to do lunch or something."

"Sounds good, Mrs. Parker."

They talked a few more minutes before Adele hung up the line and called her sister to let her know she and Fletcher would be by for dinner.

William had his See's candy pops that read, "It's a boy!" He was handing them out to everyone in the building on his way up to his law firm. "I can't believe I got one on my team?" he expressed, laughing. "Love my girl Peyton, she's all girl and all pink. Trevor is going to have trucks, and baseballs, and manly stuff," he said, slapping a high-five with Oren as he entered the office.

"Good morning Abby, good morning, Annie," he said, heading into his office on cloud nine.

Annie had driven in again by herself and went into Keith's office closing the door. She wasn't long in the office when the door opened and out walked Keith going into the men's room. She stood waiting for him to come back to his office. After a few minutes, she went back to her desk and Keith came out of the men's room. This went on all day with him leaving a few minutes after she did at 5:00 p.m. Annie was home waiting for Keith.

This couldn't go on, she was going to confront this tonight! She had made up her mind. Keith came in about eight thirty. She quickly got Riley in her pajamas and laid her in bed with a favorite video to watch. She walked in the great room. Keith was standing in the refrigerator looking for something to eat.

"Keith, your dinner is in the oven," she said. Annie noticed he was quite tipsy and stumbling. "How did you drive like that, Keith, how many times have I warned you about drinking?"

"Annie, are you talking to me? I'm having a blast!" he mumbled, sitting hard in the chair and almost dropping the plate to the floor. "Ooops, that was close," he said, leaning over his plate, losing more food on the floor than he's putting in his mouth.

"Keith, where have you been?"

"Dancing." He laughed.

"Keith, I don't believe you."

"Good. I don't believe you either, hahaha."

She was feeling so humiliated by his antics. She sat silently on the couch while he struggled eating and completed his meal. He got up with the plate and almost fell. The plate broke, shattering all over the floor.

"I'm sorry, Annie, you lied to me," he said before throwing up on the kitchen floor all the food he had just eaten.

Annie hurried to clean up the mess, seeing he had fallen asleep on the sofa in the family's great room. She went to bed and let him sleep it off, throwing a small blanket over him. His drinking was getting worse, she thought going to lie in her bed. After about two hours, she stood in the kitchen door hearing him moving around the house and then opening the refrigerator and hearing the pop of a beer can opening. She just stood there. Then he came toward the room. Annie hurried and lay back down. She wasn't going to let him go out in that condition if that was the plan. He sat there for a minute and dialed his cell and went into the shower. Soon Keith was dressed and headed to the door. Annie lay there. She started to stop him, but no, she needed to know where he was going, he tiptoed out, closing the door quietly behind him. Annie checked and rechecked Riley to make sure she was asleep and quickly got in her car following her husband. She wasn't fuming, but she was determined to find out where he went when he leaves in the middle of the night. She curved through the LA traffic, close behind Keith. He moved quickly through the heavy traffic and across the freeway before turning off at a condo about forty-five minutes away. Annie turned off her lights and eased up to the side street. His mind was on one thing so she really didn't have to be a detective on this one.

She looked at the address. "I know this address," she thought to herself. "That's Abby's address," she added, now upset she had been betrayed. He walked up and knocked and was soon let in. Annie sat there crying, mad and hurt. "How could she? How could he?" She started her car up and parked it in front behind Keith's car, the exact spot. Then she got in Keith's car and drove home. She would have words with him when he returned, though she thanked God Riley had slept through the whole thing.

Milburn wasn't sharing anything with his fellow attorneys around the office or watercooler. Usually he led the conversations when the guys talked about Dillard being a sugar daddy, or his new car, or new woman. But Dillard had let him into his world, and though Milburn never said, Dillard had made a friend for life.

"Naw, he's pretty cool," they heard him saying more than once.

"So who dropped you on your head?" a fellow attorney named Cole asked, standing by Milburn's desk.

"He's not that bad, the guy gets misunderstood," Milburn responded.

"He certainly has sold you a bill of goods," Cole boasted.

"The guy is a good attorney and march to his own drummer, but that is not a reason to put him down."

"Okay, Milburn, whatever you had at that party really influenced your brain, but okay I get you like the guy now."

"Like I wouldn't say like, he is an odd duck, but I respect him and his girl Katia, very easy on the eyes." Milburn smiled, looking at docs of his client walking in.

Annie sat waiting in the underground garage for Abby to arrive at work. She wanted to confront her but not in the office. She looked down at her watch on her arm. She had gotten there early and had left Riley with her neighbor across the street. Keith hadn't got there before she left home either, but as always, he thought Annie had taken Riley to school. Soon she saw her car driven by Keith come into the garage. Abby wasn't far behind. Keith and Abby parked and both got out. They talked a few minutes pointing at the camera in the garage. She could see they didn't want to enter together. "Why?" Annie thought, they just spent the night together as far as she could tell. Keith had on the clothes he changed into when he left home the night before. Keith grabbed his briefcase from the backseat and headed into the elevator while Annie stood counting the ticks of her watch.

"Good morning, Abby."

Abby turned, shocked to see and hear her. "Keith just went up, did you see him?" she stuttered.

"Why were you with my husband, Abigail?" Annie asked, angrily looking at the frightened Abby.

"I came in my own car, Annie, clearly you are mistaken," she responded.

Annie stood in front of Abigail and slapped her with an open hand so hard that Abby stumbled to the side about to fall.

"I can't believe you, Annie, he came after me. You should be mad at him, not me. I'm not married," she informed Annie.

Annie looked at her and walked to the elevator going up to the office. She was clearly at a breaking point. Angry, hurting, and betrayed by someone she trusted and loved. Annie walked into William's office.

"Good morning," he said, looking up as she entered.

"William, I am really sorry I hurt you and your wife. I wish you and Nada and the children the best."

Billy could see something was wrong and she was clearly shaken.

"Annie, are you all right? Have a sit," he suggested.

"Riley and I will be just fine." And she walked out of his office. By now Abby had made her way in and sat at her desk. Annie said nothing, just walked over and slapped her again, knocking her from her chair before leaving the office.

Billy hurried over to Abby. "Are you okay, what's going on around here?" he asked, astonished at the happenings.

"I'm okay, but I think she's upset," she replied, rubbing her face from the sting Annie had inflicted.

"You think she's upset, she just assaulted you." Then he ran after Annie, meeting her at her car pulling from the garage. "Annie, what is going on?"

"William, I said I'm sorry, please get out of my way!" she asked as the tires squealed.

William stepped back upon the sidewalk. He knew not to mess with a woman's wrath.

Billy hurried back up to his office and went to Keith's office.

Keith looked up as if surprised to see him. "What's up?" he asked, smiling.

"I know you just got here, but are you aware of what Annie did?" he asked, concerned with her behavior.

"Annie? I came in by myself today, what happened and when?" he asked as if he didn't have a clue about anything.

"Annie was just here, Keith, and she assaulted Abby and left," he informed him. Billy knew it was impossible for Keith to see what goes on in the front of the office from his location in the office, but maybe something happened before Annie left home that he was aware off.

"She did what? Is Abby all right?" was Keith's question.

"Abby seems okay, she says she's okay, but I'm asking about your wife?" Billy stated, a bit teed.

Keith stood up, realizing Billy was not in a playing mood and wanted answers. "Look, she's mentioned being envious of Abby a few times. She sees you're giving her more leeway, she may feel a bit threatened when it comes to her job here at Parker and Associates, maybe that's it. We have discussed it a few times," Keith lied to Billy's face.

"No, Annie's job was never threatened. We were giving you and her breathing room to live your life. This firm is growing by leaps and bounds and she was her 24-7, and I wanted to spare her of that," he said, flopping in the chair in Keith's office.

Keith turned his head to keep Billy from seeing him smirking at what clearly was a lie. "Look, I'll speak with her after she calms a bit," Keith responded. "I know Annie and she will be fine after a day or two and it is that time of month," he added, "if you know what I mean," again lying to further his cause. "Where is Annie now?" Keith asked as Billy sat, holding his head baffled.

"She left," he replied.

"Was she in her car?" Keith asked.

"Yes, why would you ask that?" Billy looked up, wondering.

"Just asking trying to figure out what's going on with my wife," he said as if concerned.

Billy got up. "Let me know if I can be of help." And he walked out.

Keith sat back behind his desk smugly thinking to himself. Milburn had taken a sit in the courthouse library after being shown where to look for the information by the librarian behind the desk. He was there looking up information Dillard had shared with him about his father. He found out that Dillard had four siblings and he was number four of five Patterson children born to Agness and Bernice Patterson.

"Same photograph on the wall at Dillard's home," he said, now taking his time to see all the intricate details he had missed. "Wow, I mean really, that's amazing what his father accomplished during those years being a black man. Well, I must admit, I really wouldn't know he was black had Dillard not told me," Milburn thought, looking through the large book that held all the information about past judges in the judicial system. "It's true this guy was telling the truth." He looked again at the picture of his wife, Bernice. She looked different, not as pretty as the one in Dillard's home, but women tend to take more photographs than men. "They are always changing," he reasoned, closing the book after an hour and leaving from the library.

"Did you find the information you were looking for?" the librarian asked, seeing him leave.

"I did and thanks for all your help."

Annie had gone back home for the day. She ignored all the phone calls coming in from her cell and home phone. She had fun playing dress up and any game Riley wanted to play for the day. She was determined not to let Keith's infidelity get to her. She had been such an independent woman. Sure, she had her eyes on William Parker, what woman didn't. She dated him for over a year, but she settled and fell in love with Keith and now he had strayed.

"Okay, you could say it was my fault. I should have known I was pregnant when Keith and I got together. But if I would have known about being pregnant with William's child, there is no way I would have let him go!" She was angrier about that than she was losing Keith. "I had the opportunity to marry the man of my dreams and I fell victim to Dana Williams, his mean ex-girlfriend, and ran away to another man. If only I would have known," she sat thinking after Riley was down for a nap.

Annie sat planning where to go and if to spend some time with her dad who lived in Augusta where she was raised. It would be good for Riley to get away from all this hostility. Annie had been putting up with what she deems as Keith's mess for months now and she wanted it to be over. How could he? she again thought, walking into her room to pack a suitcase. Then the big D word popped into her mind. "Divorce," yes, that's the one. The same one she faced as a child. A very bitter divorce for her parents when she was eight years old. It all came back as vivid as yesterday while she stood taking clothes from her closet to leave her husband. She fell on her bed and began to cry. Is this something she wanted to go through? Did she really want to end her five-year marriage? She had invested five years into this man and now divorce was probability? "How could he do this to me? I trusted him!" she thought, sitting up on her bed. She put the suitcase from her luggage set pack in the closet, she ran across the street and asked her neighbor Miss Bookens if she would come and stay with Riley until she wakes and she would be back. She had to run to her office. She hurried across the freeway trying to get to the office before he left. She saw him leaving the garage when she arrived at 6:30 p.m. Oren wasn't far behind, so she knew they had a late meeting together to hash out some details on a case Oren was working on. She was held up at the next light, and Keith was out of sight, and she pulled over to the side of the road in tears.

William had stopped by at the seminary and turned in an assignment he had been working on. He wanted to be excited about how things in the ministry were going for him. How God was leading and guiding all of his decisions and directing his paths. He prayed fervently for his law firm, his friends, and certainly his family, lifting them up to God. As he walked into his home, he was greeted by Peyton running to him.

"Daddy, Daddy!" She was so happy. "Baby," she then said as he walked into the nursery where Nada was with his son, Trevor. Billy leaned over and kissed Nada and then his son who was in her arms.

"How was your day?" she asked, looking at him.

"I will tell you about the office over dinner, but right now, just let me hold my son. No, this way, Peyton, as this arm covered." He smiled.

Over dinner, Billy shared about the incident in the office between Annie and Abby. He felt so bad.

"We never intended to push Annie out," Nada voiced. "I certainly did not want Annie in the office with you before I knew the truth, but we were trying to help," Nada again voiced, taking the plates from the table.

"I don't know, this is a big mess, and now Annie stormed out, I don't know if she's coming back?"

"Well, what about Riley, has that even been settled?" Nada asked.

"I have shared with her, she came in and said she was sorry for hurting you and she left. Keith was there all day, so we will see what tomorrow brings," Billy shared. "Should I speak with Annie?"

"Sweetheart, look, if you had not just got home from the hospital, that might have been my suggestion, but no, I really don't think that's a good idea," Billy concluded.

"So this thing with Riley is just going to be squashed and this child is never going to know that you are her daddy? That's not right!" Nada believed.

"Look, I'm not sure what's going on with Keith and Annie, but I really want a stable home for Riley, and now that we know the truth, we can't just stand by and do nothing."

"I'm convinced now more than ever that Annie never knew about the pregnancy. She loved you, she would have never married Keith. Now maybe it's the best thing if she leaves, but I don't want Riley to suffer for her mistake. Keith and Annie will have to sit down with us, and collectively, we will come to a decision," Nada expressed.

"Honey, do you believe that's possible?"

"Anything is possible." She smiled, looking at him.

When Billy turned in that night, he prayed mightily for God's hand to guide the matter before them.

Annie started her car back up again and headed back on the freeway. She drove along and decided to go by the popular bar where she and Keith and some friends stop sometimes for drinks in the evening. After being there for just a few minutes, she found out from the waitress Keith had just left by himself and said he was heading home. She paid quickly for her ginger ale and left. But something was saying he didn't go home over and over again. She decided to listen and headed toward Abby's condo since she was closer to it than home at this point. Arriving in front, she saw Keith walking up to the door. Then she noticed another car she recognized to be McGuire's.

"What is going on?" she thought, sitting across in her car out of sight. She saw Keith standing on the porch arguing loudly with someone at the door. This went on for about ten minutes, she figured, before a loud slam of the door. Keith angrily walked away from the door and got in his car and swerved away, almost hitting cars as he left.

Erene enjoyed a weekend with his wife, Nora, who was heading now to the airport to attend another business meeting out of town.

"Sweetheart, we had a wonderful time and I'm truly going to miss you," she shared, being one of the last to board her flight.

Sharing a kiss, she was gone.

"How can I keep doing this? I love my wife, I do," he said, ignoring the ringing cell phone in his pocket. He was having an affair, and he knew it was wrong and quoted every scripture verbatim as proof and still he couldn't stop wanting the touch of this younger woman, Adele, who he was deeply involved with now. Before even he realized it, he was at Adele's door and again she invited him in.

Dillard had finally, he thought, gotten Milburn out of his business and the parts he had volunteered to him he was fine with.

"Howard, how are you, sir?" Dillard asked after getting a call from his dear friend. "He did?" Dillard asked. "You enjoyed a great lunch and you got a chance to see the ocean from his yacht. Good, don't mention it, enjoy the ride, he is quite a colorful character," Dillard said, sharing a laugh with his retired friend.

Katia decided to do her shopping online for Unique Boutique for fear of running into Roslyn Milburn again. She loved the boutique's designers, which were comparable with Neiman's designs.

"Hello, this is Miss Norfen," she greeted, answering the phone.

"Yes, this is Doris Woods from the Unique Boutique."

Katia cleared her throat. *What did she want?* "Yes," she replied quickly. "I just wanted you to know we got a new shipment in today from our Europe designers, they are the latest designs, and I'm personally calling all my elite patrons to let them know," she shared delightfully.

"Why, thank you, Doris, that's kind, I will certainly give them a look." And she quickly hung up the line.

"Wow, I must be tired, just the way that lady said my name gave me chills," she said to Russell, her husband, dialing another number on her list.

Annie got on the freeway behind Keith as he drove along like a madman going in and out of cars while changing lanes. She was scared for him and just knew he would get pulled over by a patrol car before he reached home. Luckily, he was going in that direction and the car seemed to be driving itself. After several grueling minutes, Keith pulled up in the driveway of their home, stopping short of hitting the garage door. Annie wasn't that far behind, but he had entered the house before she pulled up to their home and going inside. She could see he was intoxicated and shouldn't have been driving.

"Keith, what is wrong with you? You're going to hit or even kill someone driving in your condition!" she exclaimed, looking at him slumped in a chair. He looked up and smiled, pulling the flask from his pocket and turning it up to his mouth.

Annie walked over and grabbed it throwing it on the floor. He was wasted and she was wasting her time trying to talk to an inebriated man. Within minutes, he was asleep, and she went across the street and got Riley thanking Miss Bookens.

"Oh anytime, she's such a dear," Miss Bookens replied. "Now is everything all right with you?" she then asked Annie.

"I'm fine, he's home now, and thanks again."

"Mommy, is Daddy home?" Riley asked as she skipped across the street holding her mother's hand.

Roslyn walked into the Unique Chic smiling at the clerk as she greeted her coming in.

"Good afternoon, is Doris Woods in?" she asked, looking around.

"Miss Woods? Sure, but is there something I can help you with?" the clerk asked, smiling back at her.

"Well, Mrs. Woods called me the other night about a new shipment from Europe, and oh, I would be glad to help you with any questions you have, Mrs" she asked, waiting to hear the woman's name.

"Roslyn Milburn, and I would like to speak with the owner please?" she stated, very sure of who she wanted to deal with.

As not to rile the woman, the clerk said, "I'm not sure if Mrs. Woods is in her office at this time but I'll certainly check for you, Mrs. Milburn, and let her know you'd love to speak with her on a matter." She went off the floor, leaving Roslyn looking at a designer scarf displayed beautifully laid out on a table.

After a minute or two, out walked the clerk and Doris who chose to come out to speak with this patron.

"Good afternoon, Mrs. Milburn, how may I help you?" Doris asked, reaching out her hand.

"Oh, thank you so much for the call, I have this gala at the hospital to attend and I'm sure I will find the perfect gown for the occasion," she voiced, excited Doris had called.

A bit taken by her reaction to a phone call, Doris uttered a little before her response, "So glad I called, it's important to me to keep my clients satisfied," she added.

"I tell you, I was at Katia's home a few weeks ago and I loved that gown I was wearing, it was so unique, and I was complimented more times than I can count. That says a lot to me," she confessed.

Doris did catch the name Katia in her ramble and she continued on describing her evening and the gown she absolutely loved.

"I did want to ask you about a designer I met there, wondering if you carried her designs?" she asked, looking curious as she spoke. "Do you mind if I call you Roslyn?"

"That's fine, all my friends refer to me with my first name." She giggled.

"Come this way, I have a book in my office, if she's anything in the fashion world, her name will be in there," she replied, escorting her into her fabulously designed office of the boutique.

Roslyn's mouth was agape at the beautiful accents and drapery fabrics Doris had used to decorate the space. She stopped, noticing a portrait of a woman on the wall.

"Sit, please," Doris suggested, getting the book out.

But Roslyn's mind was now wondering off to the need of seeing her husband and nothing else mattered.

"Okay, what was the name you were looking for?" Doris asked, looking at her patron who had clearly been distracted by something. She gave the name to Doris who quickly found the designer's name. "Yes, as a matter of fact, we do carry a few, I'll be glad to show you."

But Roslyn made an excuse to leave and with "Yes, I met her at the party Katia gave," she left the boutique.

Doris was now thinking that Dillard was certainly right about the Milburns being interesting people. Dillard and Katia had done their homework well, knowing the Milburns would check things out. So whereas the designer was real, the woman she met at the party was an actress called in for the party. Yep, you said it, Hollywood!

CHAPTER 18

NADA HAD CALLED HER MOTHER-IN-LAW and again shared everything about Riley. She knew Tetra had gone through a similar incident with William's father and needed her advice.

"I'll be glad to help you, Nada. I do understand it's hard when a woman invades your marriage space, let alone there is a child involved. Though your situation is much different than mine, we share the same concern, the child. So if you've prayed about it, and I know it takes lots of prayer, I'll do my best to help you by speaking with Annie on your behalf because no matter what, Riley's my granddaughter too," she admitted. "Nada, God will bless you, he always does. I know it doesn't look that way now, but I assure you, if you hold on, it will come to fusion," Tetra shared with a heavy heart. "How are my grandchildren?" She smiled, changing the subject.

"The children are fine, Mother Parker, and I look forward to seeing you soon. I will have David draw up the paperwork to present to Keith and Annie."

"Love you, dear, kiss Billy and the children for me," she said, disconnecting the line.

Ariel sat waiting at the bistro for her sister Adele to meet her for lunch. They were very close especially after their mother's passing last year though less than a year ago.

"Sorry, traffic," Adele announced, running up to the seat across from Ariel at the table.

"I ordered, for time's sake." Ariel smiled back. "So how's life, you were not at the last family dinner a week ago, what goes?" Ariel inquired jokingly.

Adele said, "Huh."

"*Huh* is not an answer. Are you still seeing Mason? Pretty cute," Ariel agreed.

"No, not really, I mean we are friends."

"So is there a guy?" she asked as the food was being sat in front of them.

"I'm hitting the dating scene a bit, why are you asking all these questions?"

"Why are you being so offensive?" Ariel snapped back. "Fletcher said you were out the other night when I came by, and you've never brought him by, so I was being nosy, okay?" she confessed.

"So that was all the family had to talk about over dinner was me? You all must get a life," Adele teased. "Actually, Hilary and I were out. We went saw that movie about dating," she lied.

"Yeah, that would be hard to get Fletch out to see that one." Ariel laughed, drinking from the soda straw.

Then a doctor Adele assumed walked by with a slight wave. "What do you think you would be doing had you married Justin Parker?" Adele asked.

"Who knows, Justin's a man still on the move, I hear," Ariel shared. "Still not married, and I guess having a blast with his life."

"Are you still angry with him for breaking up with you?" she asked.

"I'm happy with my life, and my marriage and child," Ariel said. "I don't have time to concern myself with woulda, coulda, or shoulda." She chuckled again. "I only know that no one should feel the hurt of being betrayed by another, so watch out, sis, that ain't pretty."

"Ain't, Ariel? No, it ain't," she said as they laughed continuing on with their lunch together.

"So are you coming next Wednesday to prayer meeting? Riggins is teaching, he's pretty good. I was surprised to hear him Sunday as he spoke across the pulpit on grace."

"Really, oh I hate I missed that," Adele said. "He and Becky are still together, right?"

"Yes, they are such a cute couple. I wasn't going to bring it up, though I have noticed your absence lately in service," Ariel expressed.

"Just a bit busy," Adele replied.

"Are you kidding, the county never works overtime," she teased.

"That's not the only life I have." That's the only time she had to spend with Erene was during the week when his wife was out of town.

"I'll try to do better, I know it would mean a lot to him to see me," she admitted, smiling, feeling proud of her brother.

"You're the one who started me going, remember the boys used to get on that bus with the faces on it. And you started going, and when I was going through that terrible breakup with Justin, you pointed me in that direction and I found my husband and the rest is history," Ariel confessed, embracing her younger sister as both stood to leave.

"Give Gabe a kiss for me."

"I will, love ya," Ariel said, heading back into the hospital where she worked.

Annie had let Keith pout around the house all weekend. He would argue with someone on his cell phone and then played a while in the yard with Riley as Annie kept a watchful eye. Nothing between Annie and Keith got solved over the time she had taken from the office and Keith couldn't wait for Monday morning.

Annie had reasoned leaving the marriage was not a thing she really wanted even after Keith's infidelity. She reasoned in her mind that she had driven him to it and forgave him for his indiscretions with a stern warning not to do it again.

"See you at the office?" he asked pitifully.

Abby had said she wanted nothing to do with him if Annie didn't come back showing she had forgiven him. Some nerves, right? "Keith, we can work this out if you're willing," Annie explained, looking wanting to badly for marriage's sake. He kissed her and smiled and walked out the door.

"See you at the office."

Annie had spoken with William and had set up a meeting time for Monday morning. She hurried to the day care where she kissed Riley and left heading to the office. Her thoughts were racing a hundred miles an hour as she pulled into a Starbucks drive-thru for a latte to calm them. She was so angry with herself for the oversight of her pregnancy and now the man she married over William was having an affair with her coworker and trainee. Annie sipped her hot latte as she sped through traffic.

"Wow, all this is really happening to me," she thought. I usually just blended in with things going on. "A fairly quiet life really, most of my excitement came when I was dating William for over a year. And I'm so mad at myself for not knowing I was carrying his child! I missed out on the man I truly love and now what chance do I have? He's married with two beautiful children and really has made it clear that I am not the one. If I had only known about Riley, I know he would have done the decent thing and married me!" she went on reasoning her losses as she pulled into the parking garage of the law firm. She looked over at the assigned parking stall where William's Jag with his personalized license plate displayed always parked. "This could have been all mine," she whispered to herself, pushing the button to go up to the office.

The building usually didn't get started until nine o'clock. The lights were on in the foreclosure department, Annie noticed, as she made her way to the double doors of Parker and Associates. Looking around, she saw Oren's light on in his office and she assumed Keith was probably in as well. He had left home going there. McGuire's light was off. Annie knew he was in court all week, so that wasn't a surprise. She made her way down the wide hall to William's office, tapping slight as she walked in.

"Good morning, Annie, it's good to have up back, have a seat," he greeted her coming in.

She nervously took a seat smiling, saying good morning in return.

"Annie, let me start by saying I'm very sorry if I pushed you to this," Billy shared. Annie was confused a bit but listened. "Keith explained how you felt pushed aside or not appreciated around here, let me be the first to say that has no truth whatsoever," he stated. Annie was fuming that Keith had lied and made William feel it was his fault what happened with Abigail. "You are very vital to this office, but, Annie, what were you thinking when you assaulted Abigail? You know how many cases we have won that dealt with assault?"

"William, I'm sorry that happened in your office. I really didn't mean to cause you to feel pushed and think your job was in jeopardy."

"We are growing, and I needed more hands and you work selfishly in this firm, but I do recognize that you have a life and a family too!" he again pointed out. "But, Annie, you can't do that, I'm glad you two worked it out and she's not pressing charges. I'd hate to think what could happen."

Annie was angry and so close to tears because of Keith's lying and Abigail. "If she even looks like she wants to be upset about anything, oooooh, it would not be good at all," Annie thought to herself, listening to William. "I know with the news of Riley, which caught us all by surprise, and we are working on getting things cleared up with that, I understand you are under a lot of pressure. How is Keith's father?"

"It's day to day, I spoke with his mother and she's preparing for the day, she tells me." Annie wiped a tear, Billy thinking it was for her father-in-law and family.

"Annie, it is my intent to take care of Riley, you know that, right?" he asked.

"William, I know you're a good man, a decent man. I'm so sorry all this is happening and I guess my fault, but I'm sorry for Riley, I'm sorry for Abby, and right now, I'm just thankful you're not sending me out the door," she confessed, wiping tears.

"Annie, I was looking out for your interest when we hired Abigail, she's a good paralegal and she's training under the best and that's all it was. We need you both to keep this firm on top," he said, getting up from behind his desk to shake her hand. "New start?" he added, extending his hand.

"Thanks, William, and I am open to speaking with you and Nada about Riley," Annie responded, going out of his office to her desk out front.

Roslyn hurried across the freeway of LA as fast as she could. She had spoken to her husband's secretary and knew he was in a meeting and couldn't be disturbed unless it was an emergency.

"Kelly, let him know I will be there in about an hour looking at this traffic, but it's vital that I speak with him when I get there," Roslyn explained, disconnecting the line to concentrate on the heavy traffic.

When she walked into her husband's office about an hour later, he was shaking the client's hand. He introduced Roslyn to his client and had her wait in his office. Roslyn stood anxiously in his office as he instructed his secretary of the paperwork that needed to be processed for the client and went into his office closing the door.

"Now what are you so excited about?" he asked, smiling and giving her a peck on the lips.

"Honey, listen, you are not going to believe this!"

"Then why are you going to tell me?" he teased.

"No, honey, really listen, it's about Dillard Patterson."

"Dillard, where would you be to hear something worth telling about Patterson?" he questioned, curious now.

"Well, it is kinda about him," she changed after thinking more about what she was about to say.

"Okay, okay, okay, whatever just tell me," Milburn stated, anxious to hear whatever it was.

"I told you about the call from the boutique in Beverly Hills, you remember?"

"Roslyn if you don't get to the point," he repeated, hearing her muddled through the parts that didn't matter.

"I went in today to ask about the designer I met at Dillard and Katia's party. Well, I got an invite into Doris Woods's, the owner's, office and you will not guess what I saw?" she said, teasing Milburn who was not laughing and not wanting to play her guessing games.

"Roslyn, if you're holding me up from my next client to tell me about a new gown or a new designer, I'm not going to be happy," he shared with his hand on the knob to open the door and kindly tell her to leave.

"No, Milburn, no, honey, remember when you and I were wandering through Dillard's home and we saw those portraits?"

"Yes, Roslyn, I remember, he told me all about that. That's his father." Milburn sighed. "Is that it?"

"No, remember the beautiful lady we saw?"

Milburn nodded, wanting her to go on get to the reason she was here.

"I saw the same portrait in Doris Woods's office, now how about that?" she said, giving him a what for.

"You saw what? Are you sure? Maybe she's a sibling of his, there were five children. You saw this where? And you're sure it was the same portrait?" he asked, rubbing his chin thinking. "Okay, and the woman's name is what?" he said, going behind his desk getting all the details to check out. "Roslyn, I may just have to buy you a new gown for our next social gathering from the Unique Chic Boutique in Beverly Hills," he said, giving her a kiss and sending her out of the office smiling with her head held high.

Annie walked out to see Abby now sitting at her desk. She jumped, a bit taken Annie was there.

"Don't worry, Abby. I'm not going to slap you, but I will say this, if I see you and Keith anywhere together, I will not be responsible for my actions," she stated. "You and Keith have lied to me and on me and I'm not happy at all. So if you want to keep this job, I suggest you leave my husband alone and find a man who doesn't belong to anyone to sleep with," she voiced, waiting for Abby to answer. "Do you have a problem with that?" Annie asked, looking meanly at her.

"No, no. I understand," Abby stuttered.

"Good, I know you're a smart woman. What's on your agenda for today? I have some docs to process for Oren," she said, walking away to the ladies' room, leaving Abby to sigh blowing out air. The nightmare was over for now.

Adele and Erene had taken a day off from work to attend the small county fair together. Since Nora was home on the weekends, it was the only time the two could get away. Sitting having lunch after a fun morning of viewing the displays and simply life of the Cumberland County fair, both were enjoying barbeque and roasted corn on the cob.

"Why, howdy," a male voice said, smiling at Erene.

"Chuck, hey, what are you doing down this way?" he said, seeing he was a coworker from the precinct.

"Nothing much, got me and Fleckner walking around checking things out, pretty quiet though, I must say," he said, looking at the young lady with him.

"Oh, out with my sis," Erene lied to him, "about to get her back home before she's missed." He laughed.

"I hear ya, have a good one." And the guy walked away.

Both quickly finished their meal and headed away from the fairgrounds. They enjoyed the Maine Country band that was playing as the two left after meeting his buddy from the precinct.

"I think this would be better if we just keep this inside," he said, looking at her across the car as he drove.

"Wow, I would never think I'd be the other woman! Let alone your sister," Adele responded back, laughing.

Katia still had not got around to finding a surgeon to rid her of her scars. She sat thinking about her life and how it had almost come to an end. "Thank God for my know-how, it saved my life to be knowledgeable to take care of myself, it could have gone really bad," she remembered, lying out on her veranda thinking over her life.

"Hi," she heard Dillard come in. "So, what did you find to do with yourself today?" he asked, giving her a refresh on her drink and fixing one for himself.

"I was out by the university taking pics, weather was prefect today for that," she shared.

"Yes, but do remember the Milburns," he said, laughing.

"I think we have satisfied them for a while," Katia boasted. "Roslyn's chasing fashion designers now." She laughed.

"Yes, I sure hope so!" Dillard replied, getting up to go in to make himself more comfy from his office attire.

Later that day, Annie met with David and Tetra in Billy's office in Maine. He had flown his parents in to handle the situation regarding the matter of Riley. Keith Poulton, Annie's husband, was certainly invited but refused the meeting and left the office, he said, for the day.

"Let's go in here, no one is scheduled for it today," Annie advised, showing David and Tetra into the large conference room of the law firm.

"Well, Annie, I hope this doesn't mean there is a problem with your marriage since Keith isn't joining us?" Tetra asked, looking at her.

"No, Keith isn't happy this came up, he is the only father Riley has known. If you must know, this meeting infuriates him, how can you all just do this to us? If I'm honest, he's not at all on board with this action, but he knows Riley's not his daughter and he's not going to fight a losing battle, and yes, he blames me for it all but wants what's best for Riley," she acknowledged, surprising Tetra and David because Billy had said she was okay with the meeting. Annie took a seat at the long maple-colored table.

"I'm sorry it has to come to this, Annie. William said you did agree to a meeting."

"I did agree to a meeting with William," she replied sternly.

"I see, well he asked us," Tetra confirmed.

Annie held up her hand. "It's okay. I know it was my fault. I should have known my own body. I'm still beating myself up for it. Mrs. Parker, you know how I loved William. I would have done anything to marry him," she confessed.

David excused himself from the meeting. It got to be too close to home for comfort, so Tetra let him off the hook because Keith wasn't there anyway.

"Annie, I'm sorry my son has brought another child into this world, single, unwed, I mean, but not even knowing the child was conceived? It is such careless behavior on his part. Oh, I have spoken with him in length and he knows my feelings on this matter! But you two were dating, he really got blindsided by this one, Annie, you should have told him. Instead you married someone else," Tetra acknowledged. "He has started a new life with a wonderful wife and now two children from his marriage, I'm not sure what you're expecting from this?" she added, looking at Annie, concerned from feelings she still had regarding Billy. "I can't honestly say I understand how this happened or I can't be mad at you, because you're married to someone wonderful too, I've heard," Tetra continued speaking. "Correct me if I'm wrong, it was your understanding that Keith was the father. Am I right?" she asked, looking for an answer from Annie.

"That is true, Mrs. Parker, but I would have never married anyone else had I known William was Riley's father." She sighed, wiping a tear.

"Annie dear, you must be careful, it sounds as though your husband is just a side note right now," Tetra voiced, interjecting from Annie's thought.

"A side note, that's better than I was thinking," Annie muddled. Tetra stood now, looking at Annie. "It's really unfortunate that this has happened and there is no reverse button to change things, so you will have to pass it and move on with your life."

"My life was fine before you all started poking around in it!" Annie expressed loudly. "I'm not sure which one of you did this, but you've turned my world upside down," she specified, wiping tears as she spoke.

"Annie, your husband made the discovery himself, that's precisely why I wanted him to join us. We are just doing our part and taking responsibility for our part in this, even though we never knew about Riley in the first place," Tetra shared, teed at Annie's innocent behavior for her part. "You're young, you and your husband can have plenty of babies if you chose to," she added. "He will make a wonderful shared father for Riley as well."

Annie just smiled. There was no need to share about Keith with her. *Let's just get this over,* she was thinking, sitting there at the mercy of William's mother. "Mrs. Parker, can we just get started with what you and William want from me?" she asked, feeling a bit ashamed of this whole thing besides being defied by her.

"What William and I want from you?" Tetra repeated, a bit taken with her question. "William wants to make sure Riley, his child, is taken care of. I'm here out of concern for his wife and children because they asked me to assist in this matter. Now what we want from you is to read and sign if you agree with what William has proposed in this document," she said, pushing it over in front of her on the large boardroom table. "I would really like to have come to Maine for the enjoyment of my granddaughter and new grandson, but I am sitting in front of you and we are faced with paternity, and for that, we are here," Tetra explained, clearly unhappy with her attitude tapping her fingers in front of Annie on the papers.

Annie pulled out a pen and scanned each document signing it. "Didn't you want to share it with your husband, Keith, or have more time to read it and ask questions?" Tetra inquired. "William has asked for visitations and other request," she added, letting Annie know she should read over the documents before signing them. "He'd like to be a part of her upbringing," Tetra explained since Annie carelessly signed the documents in front of her.

"Mrs. Parker, the fact that William allowed you to come here today tells me he has thought this through very clearly, and if I have questions, they would be addressed to William who is not here! You being here is letting me know that whatever is in these documents are final and so the rich and powerful win again!" she said, turning her head as she spoke.

"Annie, I'm sorry you feel wronged, but we can't go on with life and let that child not know her father. We didn't do this. You did. You have to understand that," Tetra shared. "You can't be mad and upset with us because of your oversight. Am I correct?" she said, standing now getting her composure in the matter.

"Mrs. Parker, William is an upstanding man and willing to do what's right or make it right. I can't ask for anything else, this is not about me, it's for Riley," Annie said, getting up and looking at Tetra, allowing Tetra's extended hand to be a somewhat friendly end to this conversation and she left the room. Tetra later shared with Billy that he'd better watch out for Annie. "You have not seen the last of her!"

Nora had arrived a bit early at the airport and was waiting for Erene to pick her up after she called.

"Hi, Nada, how's the repeat of motherhood?" she asked, calling her at home.

"I'm wonderful, you and Erene should give it a try, you'll love it." She laughed, speaking to a friend and fellow church member.

"Child, you are sounding like Erene, has he been speaking with Billy about that, nothing is off-limits with the brotherhood?"

"Really, he probably wants company, you're always traveling," Nada stated.

"True, that's precisely why I don't want children, I love my career," Nora shared and added, "I don't want to be tied down," again sharing a chuckle between friends.

"Well, whatever works for your situation, I'm no marriage counselor," Nada confessed. "Are you and Erene going to attend the charity function at the church?" she then asked. "It's for young couples. William and I are going," she teased.

"When is it anyway? Erene mentioned something about it a week or so ago."

"Nora, you better get yourself together and decide between your husband and your career."

"What! Erene and I are just fine, we're still honeymooning," she teased back.

"Okay, there are a lot of women in our congregation that would love to have a good man." Nada laughed.

"Now, Nada, you know there are a lot of ladies in our church who would just love to have a man!" she said, laughing loudly regarding her statement.

"Girl, anyway, you home?"

"At the airport waiting for Erene, got in early this week."

"That's good," Nada replied.

"I guess, but I leave a day early, on Thursday this week," Nora added.

"Honestly I hope you guys can come to the function, it's usually lots of fun," Nada shared sincerely.

"I am putting it on my calendar right now, Mrs. Parker, kiss them babies for me," Nora remarked, disconnecting the phone seeing Erene pulling up to the front of the airport after her early call for a ride home.

Annie arrived home to find Keith sitting in the family room watching a football game. Riley ran in and hugged him and kissed him telling him all about her day. Annie wasn't sure who was at home today, was it the sweet man she married or the lush that had started drinking, making her life a living hell. Lately it changed from day to day.

"Hello, honey," she said, coming to him and planting a kiss on him as she entered with totes and briefcase in hand. Putting them down smiling, she went into the kitchen to see what she'd prepare for dinner.

"Annie, I made dinner for us," he said, taking Riley's sweater off and getting her prepared to sit at the table.

"You did." She smiled.

"Well, it's my version of dinner, there are limits, so we've got fried chicken, mac and cheese, and a green salad," he said, now standing in front of the refrigerator taking out the salad.

Annie said, "Okay, that's fine, let me go in and change from this suit and I'll be right back."

Keith and Riley started playing again hide-and-seek by the sofa until Annie came back with her hair in a ponytail and her sweats on for comfort. She took the plates from the cabinet and set the table putting the fried chicken and other entrées in the center of it.

"Daddy, put me over there," Riley asked, pointing to the side next to Annie.

Everyone now sitting around the table, Keith said grace and everyone began to eat.

"Honey, you did a great job frying the chicken," Annie acknowledged because he did that, well, it's just been a while.

"How did the meet go?" he asked.

"As I thought it would, no surprises," she replied.

"So what we discussed is pretty much how things will be?" Keith asked, wanting to know about moving forward.

"William is really just looking out for Riley long-term, making sure of her college fund, a monthly allowance, and stability. No, he's not asking for sole custody, or taking her from our home at all. He would like to see her and share some time with her. When she's older and can understand, things will be explained to her, just like you and I discussed," she explained, taking a bite of her salad with raspberry vinaigrette, Keith's favorite dressing.

"So my little girl can still be my little girl?" he asked, smiling and reaching over, making a funny face at her.

"Yes, and I'm so sorry for causing you so much pain, but the drinking, Keith, has got to stop!" she shared, looking at him.

"I know, Annie, I was under so much pressure wondering what Bill was going to do when he found out about Riley. I just knew he'd try and take her from us. She's my daughter, I was there when she was born and I bandaged her little knees when she falls, I couldn't bear losing her," he said, confessing to Annie about changing.

"And what about that Abby situation?"

"What Abby situation? I'm not going there today with this mess! I told you there's nothing there, I was only trying to get back at you for hurting me," he said, starting to get riled by her accusations.

"Okay, but, Keith, I saw you there with my own two eyes, just confess and let's start with a clean slate."

"Annie, I have searched and searched for answers to forgive you for deceiving me about Riley. I know you where dating Bill before I came, so I gave you the benefit of the doubt of not knowing."

"Daddy, can I have some more cheese?"

Still speaking, he gets up and puts more mac and cheese in Riley's plate and sat back down talking with Annie. "I have been so mean to you, it has taken all the life from me. "I'm not the person you have turned me into," he confessed. "Now you want to stone me. Even the Bible says the woman was caught in the very act before being stoned," he stated, getting up and leaving the table.

"And you were caught!" Annie yelled.

Milburn whistled around the office all day. He was annoying his secretary who mentioned it speaking with a clerk at the receptionist desk.

"Whatever it is that has got you dancing on the moon should be bottled," Cole said, laughing. "You're killing your sec with that whistle."

"Sorry, habit, when I'm feeling good about something," Milburn responded. He had now started looking into Doris Williams-Woods's background and just wanted to know if or how they were connected. He just needed to know more about Dillard Patterson for whatever reason. He was on another hunting expedition!

"Was she Dillard's relative, or maybe a sibling? Why would they have the same painted photograph in their home, coincident maybe, there must be a connection, umm, worth checking out," he thought to himself, sitting at his desk looking over some information he had discovered. He sat reading the information, finding Doris Woods, the owner of the Unique boutique, was married less than five years ago to a Russell Woods. He was a nose-dived corporate executive who fell after the fall of Enron Corporation. She came from a small town in Oregon with her sister and settled in Los

Angeles and opened the boutique two years later. He was very interested in what he found in his search.

"Oh look, she got her money from an inheritance and Dillard Patterson is her attorney. Oh, now that makes sense, but what about this personal-looking portrait? Who is that woman? I remember helping Dillard bring a portrait like that up to his office, didn't get a good look at it though he had it covered, said it was for a client.

Interesting," Milburn pondered. "Oh my, she had a sister who was killed in Maine, a Dr. Dana Demato-Williams, ummm." He read on, finding out about her tragic death and her son David Michael Parker who resides in Los Angeles and attends UCLA.

"So, let me understand this, oh look, Dillard was her attorney as well, there's history here," Milburn reasoned. "Somehow I'll need to see what role this portrait plays, if any, in connecting the dots in finding who this lady is who's bringing Dillard all this fame and glamour. I guess I'll make a visit to the boutique in Beverly Hills, Roslyn always appreciates a gift."

"Why hello," Doris said, seeing Sonjee and Jace coming into her office at the boutique. She hugged her daughter and then her on-again, off-again boyfriend whom Doris liked. "I love that hairdo," Doris said, touching the bouncy curls flowing in the style.

"Oh thanks mom, it's one of Aunt Dana's old do's very becoming, right?" Sonjee asked, admiring herself in a gold-trimmed mirror Doris had on the wall.

"It is. I guess Dana will live forever, she is always appearing everywhere, her antics and mannerisms," Doris stated. "Yeah, she was a classy lady, and I still want to be just like her," Sonjee added. "I know she could get away with most anything, remember how she hid in plain sight from Billy posing as a neighbor."

"David Michael was telling me something about that."

"She really should have been the actress in the family," Doris smiled. "Now what's going on with you two?" she asked, looking at Sonjee and then Jace. Jace was a pilot and his schedule Sonjee, her daughter, didn't like at all. "Jace, so glad to see you," she said, giving him a motherly hug and smile to welcome him.

"Good to see you again, Mother," he teased, looking at Sonjee smiling.

"Whatever, we just stopped in meeting David Michael and Kara at Universal Studios for some fun."

"Wow, that's funny, Finley and Russell just took a group of young boys from the church there about two weeks ago, had a blast," Doris shared.

Sonjee smiled. "That's just like Finley."

And she decided to look around the boutique for a minute, as Doris enjoyed questioning her soon-to-be son-in-law. "So how are the friendly skies these days, haven't seen you in a while."

"Oh, I know, Sonjee is so mad at me. I'm trying to get my LA run back. I lost on a football bet for a year."

"Jace, no!" Doris gasped.

"True, but lesson learned, I miss Sonjee a lot, and she almost dropped me from her Facebook page, she was so mad. Excuse me, someone is texting. Babe, it's David Michael, he wants us to meet them at the gate near Mulholland," he said loudly, she had stood looking at dresses.

"Its' Sonjee, Jace, but okay, love you, Mom, we will be by tomorrow before Jace takes off again," she said, with both giving her hugs and waving, leaving the boutique.

C H A P T E R 19

ANNIE HAD SETTLED IN FOR the weekend enjoying her family. Keith tried over and over again to let her know he was sorry for his behavior of late, but wasn't going to confess to his infidelity because he felt she had pushed him to it. Resting now in the fact that Riley wasn't going anywhere, his family would still be intact, he wanted only to proceed with life. Besides, the last two times he tried to visit Abby, Doug McGuire was there and she wouldn't let him in, saying she feared what Annie would do and she loved her job!

Doug was only there to see he didn't come in, well, anyway that was Doug's story and he was sticking to it. So away with her and now Keith has to win Annie back, but it was proving not so easy. Annie had come to the realization after being hurt all those months, even though she felt most of it was her fault, her feelings for Keith had gotten misplaced, and now did she really want to fight for a marriage that was secured only by Riley? She cringed when Keith tried kissing her affectionately. Even though Keith would not confess, she knows he was having an affair and she didn't know if she could forgive that. She was now the one pretending in the marriage. She loved William, and now she knew she always would. Adele left work hurrying home to meet the family at church.

It was a Wednesday night and she had called Erene earlier that day and shared with him not to expect her tonight. She would be with her family. Wednesday had become a sure thing for the both of them even though it was wrong.

"Riggins is bringing the Bible lesson tonight at his girlfriend's church and I kinda promised I'd be there," she said after he called her before she reached home.

240

"I understand, but I'll miss you," Erene replied, "and I guess it will be a TV dinner and turn in early," he added.

"Awww, now you're going to make me feel bad," Adele voiced.

"No, really it's okay, enjoy yourself, talk to you soon," he said, hanging up. *She's going to church,* he thought, *this is so wrong what I'm doing, why didn't I meet her first?* All these questions were going through his mind.

Ring, ring.

He jumped up to answer his phone. "Erene, hello, brother, this is Caleb, just a tag reminder about the brotherhood this week."

"Ah okay, you got me, thanks, see you there, and I'd better get a tag in, everyone's starting earlier this week," he teased, disconnecting to make a call to another member of the brotherhood who hasn't been called this week.

Katia had just received an order that was delivered to her home. Dillard had shared there was a charity event coming up soon and she wanted an original gown for the occasion. She had just hung the gorgeous gown in her closet before sitting down looking at photographs she had taken while strolling around different parts of LA. She went through great pains and put them away securely in an album she kept under the bed.

"I need to take an excursion," she thought aloud to herself. "I need to get away for a while. Dillard seems to have things settled now with the Milburns, so I'm hoping they will stop nosing around, no telling what they can pick up with their snooping." Katia's thoughts were interrupted by her intercom buzzing. She got up and, pushing the button, answered, "Yes."

"Katia, this is Larvy Milburn."

She stood surprised. He had come out to their property uninvited. "Yes, what can I do for you? Dillard's at the office," she answered. She was not going to open the locked security gate at the entrance to her home to this man.

"I was in the area and wanted to ask you about a gift for my wife, Roslyn," he acknowledged, still standing speaking into the intercom.

"I'm not sure what I can do, but I'll give you a call tomorrow," she said, "I'm busy."

"Thank you and sorry to bother you," he stated, getting back into his car, and she hurried into Dillard's office looking at the security camera as he drove away.

She quickly went in and called Dillard and shared the story with him.

Erene and Adele decided to meet the next day for lunch at the city park not far from where she worked. There was a craft fair going on with lots of people so they could enjoy each other without being noticed as being together. Adele was so cheerful all morning knowing she would see Erene at noon. She was concerned after hearing the Bible lesson last night, but he had initiated the call and she wasn't going to refuse it. She hurried from the building and walked quickly up the street. An hour lunch tends to go by really fast as she came upon the activity going on in the small park. There were a few food vendors out ready to sell their wares and lots of crafts of all kinds were represented by the folks who had set up the booths to sell the goods. Adele ordered burgers for the both of them and took her number and then left, waiting until it was called. Being there a bit early, she decided to walk around looking at the beautiful crafts on display. She spotted something that was sparkling on one of the display tables and walked over to see it.

"Hi," she heard, walking up being greeted by the vendor behind in the small booth.

"This is gorgeous," she said, picking up a necklace from the table.

"Oh thank you, it's handmade by me," she boasted, smiling.

"Really, it's gorgeous, I've seen the high-end department stores jewelry and this is comparable to it," Adele confessed, looking at the clasp and the detail to the work she put into it.

Reaching out her hand, she introduced herself. "I'm Tawny and this is my passion," she said, holding her hand out moving it slowly across all the jewelry in the booth.

"I absolutely love this piece. Can I afford it?" she asked, holding it up in her hand looking at Tawny regarding the price.

"Hello," she was startled by Erene walking up behind her.

"Oh, you frightened me," she said, turning around to hit him gently in his chest. He smiled and apologized as she heard her number being called over the loudspeaker through the air. "I already ordered our lunch, they are calling my number," she said, putting the necklace back on the table with "I'll be back" and hurried toward the food truck.

Erene started behind her and stopped. "You go ahead. I'll find us somewhere to sit," he said, looking at the crowded little park filled with people enjoying the craft fair. When she was far enough away, he went hurriedly over to the booth and not only purchased the necklace but earrings and a bracelet was also part of the set. Not having enough cash on hand for the surprise purchase, Erene quickly used an app from his phone to buy the gift for Adele and surprised her by presenting it to her as she sat down to the little wooden table and bench with their burgers.

Annie was up with a new attitude about life as she took Riley to day care before school. She drove to the office, stopping by to get her morning latte from Starbucks near downtown.

"Good morning," she announced, coming into the office.

"Good morning," was returned by Oren and Abby who were looking at files in the computer.

Abby held her breath until Annie sat down at her desk and logged into her computer to start her day.

"Is William in?" she asked, looking at Abby.

"He is, just came in about twenty minutes ago," she replied.

"Good." Getting up, Annie went down to William's office.

"Good morning, William," she voiced, walking in and asked about the Bitterman case she had been processing docs for last week.

"Yes, I had a meeting with Mr. Bitterman yesterday at his office and we have some issues that need addressing, so yes, continue processing those papers and fax copies to Welty in the recorder's office. Thanks, Annie, and welcome back," he said, seeing a smile on her face.

"Thank you, I'm not sure if you heard, but the meeting with your mom went well," she shared.

"Good," Billy responded, not wanting to get into it now, just too much for a work environment. "Please close the door behind you, I have a conference call at nine thirty."

Annie got the message and went out closing the door behind her. She passed Keith's office. "Fresh coffee, can I bring you a cup?" she asked, going from office to office along the back. Keith and McGuire both said yes; Oren refused, holding up his V-8 can he drinks every morning.

"Well, good morning, Doug, how's life?" she asked, smiling at him.

"Good, Annie, life's good," McGuire smiled, wanting her to end the questions.

"And how's dear Maggie? I'll have to ask her out to lunch soon," she said, leaving his coffee and heading to Keith's office putting his coffee on his desk with a smile before going back to her desk to work. Billy and Nada had discussed Annie and the office more than once.

They had long passed the jealousy thing and now it was up to Annie as to what directions things went in for Nada's comfort. She hadn't been out of the house to socialize since having her son, and the ladies' lunch Friday was approaching.

"Hello, Annie, how are you?" Nada asked, calling into the office.

"A bit busy today, but that can be good sometimes," she responded with a smile in her voice.

"True, very true, and I'm glad you're in good spirits after last week," Nada added.

"Nada, thank you and William for helping me out with Riley. Keith is happier that things are settled and I guess I am as well," Annie shared.

"Annie, it was the right thing to do for Riley. I have no ill feelings toward you as long as you stay in your place with your husband," Nada stated. "Now are you guys up for lunch Friday, I know I've missed two Fridays, but I have a beautiful son to show for it," she expressed joyfully.

Annie had got Nada's message loud and clear and she wasn't going to jeopardize being around William for anyone, so if it meant she'd have to kiss up to his wife to keep her job, she could do that! "What time are we meeting Friday? I'll let Abby know," she asked. *Wow, I'm as bad as Abby when it comes to thinking about being with*

William, she murmured to herself. "Okay, see you then," she said, disconnecting the line and inputting something in her computer before turning around to speak with Abby about lunch.

Dillard stopped in to see Milburn after getting the phone message from Katia earlier that day.

"Why, hello, I knew I'd see you today," he said sarcastically as Dillard walked up.

"And why would you make an assumption like that?"

"Because I stopped by your home earlier, had a client out your way," he replied.

"Well, one doesn't usually come by unless invited, so what was the need?" Dillard questioned again, now taking a chair available near his desk.

"Well actually, I'm trying to get Roslyn a gift, I'd like to surprise her and I thought"—making an open-hand gesture with his hands—"I could get help from Katia."

"Katia?" Dillard asked.

"Yes, why not? Roze says she is very informed on fashion and has friends in the industry," Milburn shared, looking for confirmation.

"So you thought armed with that you'd just stop by?" Dillard questioned, puzzled he had done this.

"Look, I know you're a private kinda person, but hey we've rub noses together over dinner, I just thought—" he said, looking at Dillard shrugging his shoulders.

"Well no, that doesn't give you a leg up on anyone else, frankly, you frightened Katia coming by unannounced," Dillard shared. "So a call next time would be more appropriate," he advised.

"Okay, so maybe you can tell me, remember that large portrait I helped you bring up from your car?"

Dillard turned his head puzzled and said, "Yes, the one I said I didn't need your help on but you insisted. Yes, I remember it was for a client."

"Yes, you told me that," Milburn said. "Then what's the question?" Dillard asked.

"Was the client Doris Woods?" he asked and almost knocked Dillard from the chair after hearing his question.

Dillard then jumped up and asked, "Why have you been snooping in my business, who told you Doris was a client?"

"Is she a sibling?" Milburn was now standing poised though he had Dillard on the ropes. "You said the portrait was an original."

"And?" Dillard snapped.

"And Mrs. Woods has the portrait in her office and there is one at your home as well," he confessed, smiling deviously. "So either you're running a scam on Mrs. Woods and who knows who else or you're lying about the portrait being your mother?" Milburn stated. "I don't recall telling you about a portrait of any woman at my home," Dillard recanted, getting his composure.

"I assumed," Milburn specified, "it was an old portrait as well."

"This time your assumption is wrong and you have gone way too far for my comfort." Dillard didn't want to further Milburn's curiosity that was clearly becoming a nuisance to him and now Katia. "Look, Larvy, I'm not sure what you want from me or with me. I'm just a very successful lawyer who wants to be left alone. Doris Woods is a very dear friend, and yes, a client. She has a very private life and I respect that. If you must know, and for the record, it's really none of your business, we share more than just a lawyer-client relationship, and I will leave you to ponder that. Please stay away from my home, my office, and my noneventful life until you started snooping in it," Dillard acknowledged, walking away knowing there would be way more questions than even he wanted to deal with after this conversation.

"Hi, Aunt Doris," David Michael voiced, coming into her office at the boutique. "A few friends and I had lunch right up the street and I thought I'd stop in," he added.

"Well, it's always a joy to see you, how are things going?" she asked. "Well, classes, baseball, and life not bad, and you?"

"Good, my health is holding steady, and Russell, of course, has been a true help being husband and friend, not to mention my business partner, so I'm all right." She smiled, giving her nephew a tap on his shoulder. "Have a seat, if you have time, actually I was just thinking about you, well, your mother just came across my mind."

"You know she loved clothes and all things fancy and expensive," Doris shared, speaking with her nephew whose mother was her sister that had passed on.

"I know, Sonjee is always rocking her style!"

"Dana was the belle of the ball always and the master of disguise when she didn't want to be found," Doris remembered fondly.

"Funny you should say that, the other day, Kara and I were leaving baseball practice, she says to say hello by the way," he said, stopping looking at a text from Kara. "And this lady Kara said sounded like Dana, she was a photographer, great camera equipment she was using, but when she got closer, it was clearly not her," he admitted to his aunt. "I guess she will always be around us in something, a song, a voice or action," he said.

"You're right, even in fashion. I received these gowns in the other day from Europe and I know one definitely had Dana's style written all over it. It takes a certain lady to pull that look off and she certainly had that," Doris confessed.

"Yes, that is true," David said, getting up and turned looking at the portrait of his grandmother.

"You think she had the same qualities as Dana?" he asked, looking at his aunt.

"From what I remember and from the few pictures and information Dana shared about her that she had located in an old box, I'd have she to say she was quite a lady!"

He smiled and said, "I'm glad I still have you," acknowledging with a hug.

"And I you, I'll see you and Sonjee Sunday, right?"

"Oh yes, we couldn't miss Finley's birthday."

"It's brunch right after service and then the concert at the Roxy Theater."

"You got it! Love you, Auntie."

Annie, for the sake of keeping her job at the firm, played the wife role with Keith all day long. She never let on to anyone that things were very rocky in the Poulton home.

Abby wasn't talking either; Annie had warned her if she did. Abby quickly found her a date for the Octoberfest event the whole office was invited to, and Jeff Suds, her date, had come by a few times since the big misunderstanding so things appeared normal. Nada kept a close watch even though she fully trusted her husband and made her weekly lunch dates with the women in the office.

"So, Annie, how's the workload now since having Abby what almost a year now?" she asked one day at lunch.

"Abby has really stepped up to the plate. She learns fast, very fast," Annie said sarcastically.

Nada didn't get the joke, but Abby did and cringed about the thought.

"Oh, okay, so that's a good thing," Nada questioned, looking at Abby then Annie.

"Yes, as far as work in the office, we are fine, and Abby has a man and things are much better," Annie confessed, smiling.

"Okay, I see where this is going now." Nada smiled. "That is always a good thing! So is he coming to Octoberfest with you?"

"Yes, Jeff is so cute, isn't he, Annie?"

"He's your age and, yes, handsome." Annie nodded. "Unmarried, and single," she added, going on making a joke about her relationship fitting.

"Good, I'm glad all is well at Parker. I ran into Maggie in the Louis Vuitton store last week shopping with her daughter. I can't believe how she has grown, just graduated with her master's, time flies," Nada shared.

"McGuire has a daughter my age?" she asked, surprised.

"Yes," Annie replied, looking shamefully at her.

"Really, I never knew he was that old," Abby responded.

"He and Maggie just celebrated their forty-fourth anniversary last month. I look forward to William and my fifth," she confessed, enjoying laughs with the ladies over lunch.

"And you and Keith?" Abby asked.

"It was seven for us this year," Annie confirmed.

"Well, ladies, I'm glad there is love all around the table. You ladies are wonderful and I'm glad we can share our lives outside of the office," she said as everyone finished up the meals. "I have new pictures of Trevor, he is growing so much, I know, two months already." She smiled sharing her photos with Annie and Abby.

Erene hurried from the precinct getting into his car. A briefing ran longer than expected and now he was fighting the highway traffic to be on time for the weekly brotherhood meeting at the church. Hurrying across the freeway, he pulled in about ten minutes late, already meeting Silas, a fellow brother, coming in as well.

"Good evening," Erene said, extending his hand. Silas shook his hand tight and held on trembling. Erene felt the emotion as both walked in quietly sitting down because prayer had started. All the men were gathered and the group was about seventy-five to one hundred men of all ages. The noise level after prayer with everyone greeting one another was music to God's ears of the fellowship shared. Erene took time with Silas as clearly there was a burden he carried.

"My wife left me," he said to Erene as the meeting was under way with the week's announcements being read before the lesson. Tonight, William Parker was teaching and the brotherhood was excited. Silas was devastated and jumped up and ran to the front asking for prayer. Some now looked wondering what the heck was going on. Erene ran to his side to aide him. "MY WIFE LEFT ME!" he yelled out.

Some of the devote men including William who led the prayer laid his hands on him and begin to pray. It was an unscripted time of devotion to God. This man had come to the end of his rope and needed a touch from the master's hand, was said by William as he petitioned to God on his behalf. That was the lesson for the evening. Fervent prayer for a fallen brother who had strayed to the arms of another and his wife had found out and left him. Many there left disappointed about what had happened because the lesson, they say, was not for them. Erene knew for sure it was his lesson that walked through the door with him tonight, and like Jesus, he wept.

Annie had ignored Keith for the last time this week without him finally saying something to her. She had been getting into bed and going to sleep or stayed up until he had fallen asleep, and tonight, he decided to confront the problem.

"Annie, are you still upset with me about what you think happened? And exactly how long do you think I'm going to put up with it?" he asked, getting ready to go to bed after reading a book to Riley and saying good night to her.

"Keith, what are you talking about? You know how busy we've been at the office. I'm usually so tired I can hardly get myself showered and in bed, not to mention Riley," she said, making an excuse for her behavior.

"Really, that's what you're using to turn your back on me every night for the past two months so far and I don't like it!" he stated, putting on his pajama bottoms, which he slept in every night.

"I didn't complain when you left me here and went off to do whatever you wanted for hours and come back when you thought I was asleep, but oh, that's my imagination, I guess?"

"Annie if you're not going to forget or forgive what you think I did, what do you think is going to happen to these seven years we have spent together?"

"I need time, Keith, you say you haven't been unfaithful and I think you're lying. Abby said you are the one who initiated it, you came on to her. I guess she's lying too?"

"I know Abby didn't tell you that, you want something so that you can continue to be upset and treat me vile," he again stated, turning over in the bed with his back to Annie.

She was fine. Now another night of him being mad meant she didn't have to deal with him touching her! And that was just fine with her.

Dillard knew his best move was to tell Doris Woods about the portrait he had painted from the original portrait Dana Williams had made of their mother. He had shared with Katia about the Milburns seeing it in their home and did not want her to hear about it from them. Besides, he needed to explain what the portrait meant to him. He and Dana had a very close relationship as lawyer and client and he wanted to share with her something she never knew about the two, which led him to having an artist paint the portrait for him to keep.

"Katia, do you think Doris will understand and not be angry?" he asked, sitting out on their veranda one evening.

"I'm sure she will be filled with questions, you just must have an answer for each one," she replied, thinking now concerned about the encounter to take place today in Beverly Hills.

Dillard sat nervously at the table off to the side of the posh restaurant he had invited Doris Woods to meet him. Cool, calm, and poised attorney in a courtroom but now he was on edge about what he had to tell his client and friend. Looking up from his *LA Times* newspaper, he had secured to keep himself occupied. When she arrived, he saw the headwaiter escorting her to their table.

"Good afternoon, Patterson, so kind of you to invite me to lunch," she stated as he stood taking out the chair so that she could sit down. "Thank you," she said, adjusting herself in the quaint chair and laying her clutch purse on the table.

"That's what friends do occasionally, Doris, sit and chat." He laughed nervously.

"Look, Patterson, I've been your client for, what, more years than I can count or as long as I have been living in Los Angeles and you have never initiated a lunch, I'm saying." She smiled. "So what's going on?" she asked, looking for something to drink.

Dillard nodded to the waiter and ordered non-alcohol wine and he hurried off to bring the best he shared with them. Dillard was a social and an occasional drinker but he knew Doris didn't indulge, so he was going to please her today no matter what.

"Well, Doris, I know it's hard to keep anything from you too long," he started, giving a slight laugh. "I know you remember the Milburns?"

"Yes." Doris was listening attentively as the waiter returned, pouring the fine wine in flute-style goblets and walked away. "The Milburns, so this is about the Milburns, they must really be interesting to warrant a lunch at Enoteca Drago?" She chuckled, taking a sip from her glass and the appetizers Dillard had ordered.

"Doris, please, anyway the Milburns came to a party at my home."

"Oh I see, and of course there were a lot of high-profile folk around and I had opened my home to all the guests including the Milburns, one of the fellow attorneys in the building where my office is," he explained.

"Patterson, I really don't want to sound sarcastic about this story, but it appears so far that it's going to be a long one, so if you don't mind, let's order and then we can get to the point I hope," she asked, looking at him stumbling around the point, he still hadn't made after fifteen minutes on rambling and the appetizers were half gone.

After about twenty minutes, their entrées had been delivered to the table and Dillard again began to explain about why he invited her. "The Milburns are very inquisitive people and, for some reason, interested in me!" he continued. "They like some others wandered around in parts of my home that I had in my mind to be off-limits, like my home office and library to name a few," he shared. "And I found him and her in my study looking around touching things and—"

"So, Patterson, what? Did they steal something, or break something?" she asked, trying to get something from this boring story.

"No, nothing like that, they were nosing around my home and found a portrait of a woman I have in my home library," he finally said.

"Yes, and?" Doris was now getting impatient with Dillard. "And when Roslyn Milburn was in your office a few weeks ago, she saw something and ran and told her husband, who came to me about it and I wanted you to hear it from me first," he spurted off quickly.

"Okay, Patterson, so whatever you're not saying has something to do with what Milburn's wife saw in my office, is that what I'm hearing?" she asked, putting food into her mouth from her plate.

"Yes, that's correct," he responded.

"That doesn't make sense, because the only picture I have on my wall is a portrait of my mother, why would you or anyone be interested in that?" she asked again, looking for answers.

Dillard gave a big sigh watching Doris continue to enjoy her meal in spite of the conversation. "Okay, Doris, listen, I have a portrait in my home of your mother," he finally said, "and Larvy Milburn threatened to tell you about it and I wanted you to hear it from me."

Doris sat looking at him with her mouth wide open, pondering what she finally heard Dillard say. "You what? After all the trouble you said you went through to find the portrait, you have one as well, how many of these original portraits did Doris purchase?" she asked, making parenthesis signs with her fingers regarding *original* and looking questionable at Dillard.

"No, Doris, it's nothing like that at all," he assured her.

Doris pushed the almost-empty-anyway plate to the end of the table and placed her napkin across it staring across the table at Dillard. She reached over and filled her glass and took a sipped of her wine. "Go on, Patterson, you have my attention now," she stated.

"Doris, the portrait of your mother has a story I'd love to share with you. First note, the portrait meant the world to me because it was hand-painted by my brother Millard, no, we're not twins. He was named after Millard Fillmore, the thirteenth president of the United States, he was an older brother. Great artist in his own right. Ah, anyway, he was petitioned by Richard Demato to paint your mother while on a getaway in Europe. He only had three weeks in which to paint her before he and Faye, your mother, came back to the States and Millard later shipped the finished portrait to Mr. Demato who was a prominent businessman who lived in Washington State. My Katia fell in love with the portrait of the mysterious woman and I wouldn't dare tell her I had to part with it, so I had a replica made for myself and you have the original hand painting from 1965. I purchased it from the estate sale after the Demato's death knowing the story of it."

Annie, again wanting to stay in Nada's graces, had accepted an invite for girls' day with Nada at the estate. William and Nada had built a state-of-the-art workout room for her to get her body back in shape after the babies. So instead of their usual Friday lunch, they met at her estate for a workout session including lunch. Annie had decided to keep Abby close to her and used the leverage against Keith who still never admitted to an affair with Abby, but Annie knew different and was glad now that it happened for some crazy reason. Nada had just conferred with Dante about her menu for the ladies and letting him know it would be about six ladies besides her there.

"I love that," she said, looking at the scrumptious salad Dante had put together for their meal after the workout.

"Thank you, ma'am, I know it's your favorite," he replied, smiling.

Nada looked at her watch before hearing Millicent going to the intercom to say her guests had arrived. After a few minutes, Nada came into her parlor to find Abby, Annie, and two other ladies who had followed Annie up to the estate with them.

"Why, good morning, everyone, welcome to my home," she said, smiling, "ready for a workout?" She laughed, embracing the ladies in Nada fashion. Nada was very down to earth and warm and those who knew her were surprised to know she was, after all, the William Parker's wife. Annie was looking around as the ladies who had not been there before oooood and awwwed about the size of the estate and its beautiful décor.

"You are?" Nada asked. "Cherly and Stacey from accounting department," both added. "Good, welcome, is this your first time here?" she asked being polite. Their action kinda said it was. "So we are still waiting on two more, am I correct?" she again asked. "No problem, there is juice, water, and those who must have coffee or something to eat before the workout in the adjoining room, please make yourselves comfortable until the others get here and then we will go to the gym," she explained.

Cherly nudged Stacy. "She has a gym here!" she said, laughing quietly to herself seeing Nada leave the room. Everyone headed to the beautiful laid-out banquet table in the other room talking to each other.

"Can you believe this home?" Stacy asked, getting a glass pouring fresh juice for her to drink.

"I've been here several times," Annie shared.

"Really, so you know them that well?" they asked, looking to hear more about this fabulous place.

"Yes, I've known William long before he and Nada married, and he lived here," she confessed. "I was here during the big renovation of the magnificent home, some of this is my idea," Annie boasted to the ladies void of Nada in the room.

"What, are you serious? They asked you?"

"William asked me, we were dating at the time," she again let slip out.

"And you let all this get away?" Cherly expressed.

"This place is a place I dream about in my dreams. I don't know anyone who lives this way, except on television," Stacy added.

Abby hadn't been there but she had heard all about it on the ride in with Annie who knew intimate details about the renovation William had done long before marrying Nada. Abby was keeping Annie happy and getting her footing with Nada because she wanted to secure her position at Parker and Associates, and she felt if Annie wanted to, she could make things bad for her. Annie thought the girls' actions were a bit childish, but hey, understandable. Annie stood listening, upset now because this could all have been hers, and now knowing about Riley, it may be someday, she thought getting a croissant and latte before sitting.

Nada came back with Trevor in her arms. "Ladies, I'd love for you to meet my son, Trevor Jon Parker," she voiced, smiling.

The ladies, including Abby, hurried to stand and aww the handsome little Parker, the CEO's son. Annie was in her own world and slowly came up and touched the child's hand.

"They grow so fast, don't they?" she shared, being the only other mother in the room of young ladies.

Standing smiling and talking for about fifteen minutes or more, the other two young ladies had finally arrived. Millicent came in and took Trevor as Nada again welcomed the last two ladies to her home, allowing them to partake of the goodies prepared for them before showing everyone to her awesome work gym William had built for her.

"So, if you had not been heckled by the Milburns, I would have never known about the portrait?" Doris asked.

"You wouldn't have known about the story of the portrait, Doris, you have the original portrait," Dillard again reminded.

"And Katia, what was her interest in the portrait?"

"She loved the clothes she's wearing and colors Millard chose to express the sex appeal and artistic flare but still being very classy," Dillard explained. "Your sister Dana found me here in Los Angeles from my brother's painting. She had not found the small copy of the photograph Millard used at the time of the painting. It was in an old box of her father's papers she finally received after Mrs. Reeves's celebration due to Demato's untimely death. When Dana came to me, she was a very naive and a bit troubled young lady with a child. She said she found me in the yellow pages here in Los Angeles after reading through some of Richard Demato's papers. At that time, she wasn't aware he was her natural father because he had adopted her with his wife, Victoria. That's when I found out about my brother's painting and it had no value to Dana, so I purchased it from the estate, which he had left to her. She also hired me to be her attorney and I have been working for this family since then," he shared humbly. "She did mention she had a sister, which I later found out was you," he stated, continuing with his story. "It wasn't until years later that she found out about her mother, Faye, and Richard Demato being her real dad. I felt as a friend I would tell her about the portrait she had clearly forgotten about. She came to my office one day regarding a simply matter and inquired about a photograph she had recently found and wanted a painting made from it. It was then I shared with her about the painting and why I purchased it from the estate, but since she just had to have it, I let go of it," he shared sadly. "It was probably one of the last things my brother did," Dillard added, saddened. "He died in 1967, he has some paintings displayed in several famous buildings around Europe, I enjoy them from time to time. After Dana passed, I bought the portrait back from her estate. So, Doris, there you have it," he said, waiting for her response.

"Thanks for lunch, Patterson," Doris responded, getting up graciously, and stood up to leave out of the exquisite restaurant. "That's it?" he said, looking for more.

"I'm overwhelmed by this heartfelt love story on so many levels. Thank you for sharing." Reaching over with a hug, she was gone.

CHAPTER 20

ERENE WAS DEALING WITH THIS Adele thing the best way he knew how. He poured himself into work and avoided her calls. If she came by the precinct, he usually made an excuse, and some of the guys were getting suspicious of her frequent visits. "James, that young lady was here again," one yelled out. He had tried again speaking with his wife about having a child and her traveling so much, which he felt had led to him stray. But really being young and a Christian man, he really couldn't blame Nora for what was happening, but he needed her help and she was laughing it off every week as she left for her important job with the important people. Adele had his heartstrings and she was winning him over big-time! She was there to speak with anytime and not by a phone call. He could actually touch her when he had a bad day, she cared for him, and he mattered. It was what he wanted his marriage to be! Why he hadn't met her first, he thought heading to another brotherhood meeting for strength.

As Erene rode along in his car, a song from Luther Vandross came of the radio. "The Closer I Get to You" was sounding so tender in his ears. He was torn between his wife and the woman he knew in his heart that he loved. He pulled his car over aside of the road.

"Oh my god, help me to do the right thing. I'm torn and confused, my head says one thing and my heart is saying something else, please help me through this time of decisions." He sat there pondering over his life and his marriage and Adele. He pulled himself together and got back on the highway and went to the meeting that had already started. He was there physically, but his mind was so far from the activities taking place.

The ladies had a wonderful time and the lunch meal was five-star, Dante was told by Cherly as they sat around after the workout together.

"So everyone got showered and got the gifts I left for each of you?" Nada asked, seeing everyone laughing and enjoying the meal prepared.

"Nada, the machine that deals with the abs I'm going to dream about tonight, it whipped my behind," one confessed.

"I agree," another voiced, holding up her hand.

"What about that instructor on the video? I wanted to hit her from where I was standing," Abby shared, laughing.

"Yes, yes, she made everything look so easy," another chimed in.

Annie wasn't saying much but agreeing so she wouldn't stick out too much.

"Mrs. Parker, this was wonderful, thank you for inviting me," Abby said.

"Me too," another added all around the table.

"You're all welcome, it was my pleasure," Nada replied, finishing her meal. "It sure made my workout more enjoyable and I didn't have to suffer through the pain alone," she confessed, slapping a high-five with one of them.

With gift totes in hand and hugs and good-byes, everyone went to the foyer of Nada's gorgeous estate.

"Annie?" Everyone stopped and looked back before continuing out the door as Nada stood waving. "Annie, are you okay? You seemed to be bothered by something," Nada asked.

"Oh no, that was a real workout, girl," she said, not wanting to give Nada a bad impression of what she was really feeling.

"Good, anyway, I'm not sure how you feel about this, though I was wondering about having Riley over next weekend if you don't have plans?" she asked.

Annie looked puzzled at the question. "Somehow for Riley's sake, we are going to have to get past our feelings," Nada said.

"You know what, let's talk later. Abby's waiting," she said, smiling, "And take care." She walked back into her home as Annie pulled off from the driveway.

Doris was so very curious about everything Dillard had shared with her over lunch as she sat that night at dinner talking about it with her husband, Russell.

"So you really got a history lesson on that old portrait you thought was just a whim of Dana's spending, huh, babe?" He chuckled, eating dinner.

"Wow, did I. It is something. I see it in a whole new light. But now I want to know more about my mother and Mr. Demato and their romance," she shared. "I'm going to call David Michael, there are some questions I want to know about that old book he got and all those boxes of stuff she wanted kept for five years. Somehow I don't think this is the end of the story yet," she said, looking away curiously into the air. "And who knew, Dillard Patterson was somehow tied into this old mess. The story is still unfolding long after Dana's death. I know she's up there wondering what I'm going to do with the information I have received. She's right, I want to see how this all comes out. Maybe there is something to tell me what happened to my dad? I wondered if Dana knew, she was always so secretive about her findings. Well, really, I wasn't interested after I became successful myself. But maybe it's time I did? Just maybe Dana's talking to me from the grave," she said, looking at Russell with questions.

"Well, you know Dana. If she wanted you to know something, she'd go to any lengths to get you to see it," he confirmed. "Any lengths!"

Adele was in love with Erene and she hated the fact that he was married. Not only was he married, but he was a Christian and aware what he was doing was wrong.

"Erene, I'm so sorry," she acknowledged one day as they sat at lunch. "I didn't mean to fall in love with you, you're so caring and kind I wouldn't dare hurt you," she admitted, looking with those big doe eyes across the table.

"Adele, it's not all your fault, I knew better. I should not have gotten you involved. I'm the one that's sorry, and even sorrier that I have to say we must stop," he stated, leaving Adele looking at him shocked.

"Why? Did she say something?" she asked him, holding his hand across the table.

"No, no, Nora doesn't know. I can't keep hurting you, and what's going to happen if she finds out?"

"Erene, please don't go, I don't know what I'd do?" she pleaded sadly.

As they continued talking, Fletcher came in the dining spot where the two were having noon lunch.

"Hey, you two, what's happening?" he asked, talking loud with a small crowd of friends who had come in to eat.

"Hi, guy," Erene said, getting up shaking a friendly hand and a hug to.

"So you two decided to leave me out?" he joked.

"No, had a minute between cases and thought I'd touch bases, haven't seen you guys in a while," Erene lied.

"True, so where ya been, the missus keeping you inside?" he teased with Erene, his friend.

"Something like that," Erene replied. "Look, I'm going to let you and your sis talk, I've got to get back," he said, getting a sad look from Adele as he got up and let Fletcher and a friend of his move into the booth.

Adele got up and followed him out looking as he kept walking. Erene never looked back. He just walked out and got in his car parked on the curb and drove away. Adele knew he was right but it hurt. She came back in, got her purse after giving Fletch money to pay for his friend's meal, and she left.

"Okay, Aunt Doris, so here's the last box of Dana's stuff you asked for," David Michael said, coming in with a heavy box of papers, putting them in Doris's home office. "So, Aunt Doris, Mr. Patterson said his older brother painted that original portrait of Grandma Faye?" he asked, searching for questions after hearing the long tale as well. "So what do you think you're going to find in those old dusty boxes you had me to bring over from my basement?"

"Honestly I have no idea. But it seems Dana is talking to me," she shared.

"Really? You think that way too? Sometimes something will happen and I'll say that's a Dana," he shared, remembering things about his mother and her ways. "I know I enjoy reading the Bible she gave me when I think about her. I remember the night she scared me being in our apartment when I came from baseball practice, but that was the night I led her to Christ," David Michael confessed. "Aunt Doris, do you really believe she was saved?" he asked curiously.

"Yes, I do, if you believe what the Word says," she confessed, "and God doesn't lie. So I believe we will see her again," Doris believed, confirming with her nephew. "Oh yes, about that, do you remember exactly when you got the book?" she asked.

"I don't, but don't worry, I never threw away the shipping wrapping. I'll get it to you as soon as I get home," he said. "I just wanted to keep it knowing she had touched it, kinda creepy, huh?" "No, David, that was your mother and she had her ways. God knows she did. I didn't always understand her reasoning for most of what she did, but I also didn't have to live with her in that home," she said, opening up to her nephew about his mom.

"So you guys didn't grow up together?" he asked.

"No, not until we were teens, we came to know each other only by mishap, I thought, now I know better after learning about the ways of Jesus," Doris added. "Oh believe me, I had my own hell, but we survived by God's grace. I had Finley to prepare something for us to eat if you have time in your day. I'll share some of our stories if you'd like to hear them," she asked, looking at David who had grown into a handsome young man.

"Sure I'd love to, do you mind if Kara stops by in an hour or so?"

"I'd love to see Kara. Let's go this way," she motioned, seeing Finley standing in the door directing them in the dining room.

Annie had gone across the street to Mrs. Bookens's home and got her daughter, Riley. She had left her there so she could go to the Parkers' home for girls' day out.

"Thank you, Mrs. Bookens," she said as she left going back across the street.

Keith was home as well after being out with the guys from the office on the golf course.

"So how was your game today?" she asked, making small talk after getting Riley settled looking at one of her favorite videos.

"My game was good, on the greens every time and my putter was on fire." But he laughed. "So was everyone else today," he said, coming over being affectionate, kissing the back of her neck.

She stood and cringed at his touch. He felt it but chose to ignore her action.

"What would you like for dinner?" she asked, moving to the kitchen to start preparing the meal.

"Whatever is easy, Annie, but I do want to talk with you about a getaway for us," he said.

"For us?" she asked, taking lettuce from her refrigerator.

"Yes, you and I. I was telling Bill about it on the course he said they'd be willing to keep Riley, and I think it would be good as well, you know, small steps," he stated, looking for her response. "But you and I need to renew our marriage relationship, and I think time to ourselves, we can talk about the issues," he added.

"You have been doing a lot of thinking involving me," Annie chided. "I don't have a problem with the way our relationship is going," she shared, now cutting tomatoes for the salad she was making.

"We have no intimacy, Annie, how can you say you're fine with it?"

"Because I am," she replied.

"You seem to be pushing me to another woman, I'm startingto believe that's what you want," he lashed out.

"I didn't push you a few months ago and you did, now I'm the cause, you're pathetic," she smirked.

Keith walked away, leaving the room hurt and feeling bad about Annie's reaction to his suggestion. He wanted to take her away and start rebuilding their marriage and family again. He wanted forgiveness and restoration from her. But he wasn't willing to confess and this is how things went most days, he on one side and Annie on the other putting up a good front for friends, family, and coworkers.

Katia and Dillard were discussing his lunch with Doris Woods over lunch at Caffé Roma in Beverly Hills.

"So now we have to wait and see what those nosy Milburns do after starting all this mess," Katia acknowledged.

"She seemed pretty bummed after I shared with her about the portrait," Dillard added, eating his Italian ordered meal. "Well really, I'm not sure what she was thinking, but if she is anything like her sister, it's not over," he shared, being her attorney for a while now.

"Well, you did well explaining the portrait and how you came to have it, didn't you?" she asked, sipping her wine with a bite from her pasta plate.

"Well, Katia, the truth is always easy. What I'm not sure about is how she will handle the truth," he thought. "For sure Doris isn't at all like the Dana I knew, but I know before you say anything, people can change," he concluded.

"Dillard, you had better brace for the monsoon I believe is coming."

"Why do you say that, Katia?"

"Doris Woods is the same one that helped in finding her sister, you told me, after she had been avoiding family for years, right? I don't think she is going to stop just because you told her your brother has passed. She will find out how and exactly when and where he was when it happened. She's going to search until she finds his significant other, child, or anyone associated with him," Katia laid out what she believed would be Doris's action.

"So you're telling me another lunch or dinner date is in my future?"

"I'd bet on it," she said, finishing her second flute-style glass of fine wine.

William had called a meeting with his fellow attorneys in his firm to discuss some of the cases each was working on.

"Yes, I have just about completed that one, the jury should deliberate tomorrow," Oren clarified to the group.

"Good," William stood saying. "I am very pleased with the progress we are making in our firm, we're one of the top firms in the country," he added. "Good job to you all," he said as they got up after the encouraging pep talk from William Parker, the owner of the firm.

"Keith, may I speak with you for a moment in my office?" he asked as both walked from the conference room down the hall to Billy's large office at the end. Billy closed the door after both were inside. "I just wanted to know how things are going after the news of Riley? I mean it was a surprise for me and I'm so sorry, but I didn't know, you have to know that," he confessed.

"Bill, I believe you, Annie should have known she fooled both of us," he acknowledged.

"Yes, but are you two able to work through it? Nada and I are. It's tough, but I never knew especially since she married you. I had no reason to think Riley wasn't your child," Billy kept explaining.

"Billy, Annie and I are going to get through it. I love her and she said she loved me, so we will work it out," he admitted. "I'm trying to convince her to go away for a while, you know just her and I and give you family time to know Riley," Keith shared. "She hasn't said yes yet, but I'm still hoping, we are heading out to lunch, I'll let you know," he said, shaking Billy's hand and he left the office with Annie for lunch.

Adele moped around the office keeping busy most days. "Adele, you better be smiling, we get our bonuses this payday and we are going shopping. You've promised to show me those shopping tips you've learned so well," Hilary expressed.

"Hill, you know I'm always up for shopping. I'm just not feeling my best this week, but we're good, what day?"

"Friday, after work, we will go straight to the mall, okay!"

"Okay, no problem. I'm heading down to the resource department so I'll have to see Mason, thanks for giving me that boost," she said, pretending to be happy, but clearly Erene was on her mind.

Adele loved Erene so much she was going to respect his decision even if it was hurtful to her. She was going to wait for him because she knew he was her soul mate. Yes, he was married, but his wife didn't really love him, she was never around and never put him first. What kind of love was that exactly? Erene deserved more, and Adele was willing to wait for the man who had her heart in spite of his commitment right now.

Annie had again laughed off Keith's suggestion to get away for a while and talk things out. She was willing to play the all-is-well role for the office to keep William from being suspicious of her intentions of getting him back someday. She played the loving devoted wife at the office, which quickly turned spiteful and cold after the office hours. Keith had tried everything to get back in her graces except owning is infidelity with Abby who had moved on with a guy named Jeffrey who resided in the same building and worked at another firm in town. Besides, he really loved Annie. He was so confused and hurt after he found out about Riley that he did something stupid and cheated on Annie to hurt her. Now she's so unforgiving of him after he accepted and forgave her. Annie was sitting on the floor coloring with Riley in the family's great room when Keith joined the fun.

"Can I color too?" he asked playfully with Riley, his daughter.

"Yes, Daddy, here," she replied, giving him a bright color from the box.

"The picture is finished, Keith, you will only ruin it if you add another color," Annie stated, snatching the picture looking at him in disgust that he was even considering sitting down with her and her daughter.

"Annie, I just wanted to have fun," he said still smiling as to not let Riley know about the mood change in the room.

"Daddy, you and I can color this one," Riley said with the child innocent and knew nothing of what was going on.

"Next time, sweetie, you and mommy can hang that one on the refrigerator, I'm going out for a while," he said, kissing her forehead and walked out the door.

Doris wasted no time in getting started with her research of the portrait and the family's past. She had taken one of the boxes to her office at the boutique and wouldn't you know in walked Larvy Milburn. Doris watched from the camera in the back as he conversed with the clerk out front.

"So you're looking for a special gown for you wife?" the clerk asked.

"Yes, she shops here, so I'm sure I can find something she will love," he shared, looking around the boutique.

"Color, any particular color, sir, you have in mind?" she asked, finding his wandering eyes very disturbing.

"Good afternoon," Doris said, coming out noticing the guy but knew exactly who he was from Dillard's description.

"Good afternoon," he replied back, smiling because he knew he had found the person he was looking for.

"Doris Woods, how may I help you?" she asked, diving right in.

"My wife, Roslyn Milburn, shops here, and I was curious about a gown she had seen here in one of your catalogs in your office?" he said, smiling from ear to ear.

"Roslyn Milburn was in my office?" she said just to play devil's advocate for a moment.

"Yes, I'm sure this was the boutique," he believed, pulling out his cell phone. "Yes, the right address and Doris Woods, the owner," he added.

"Well, it sounds like you're in the right place, did she happen to get the designer's name?" she asked again, stringing him along.

"I'm afraid she didn't or I forgot to ask, I'm trying to surprise her with it," he quickly said with a sheepish grin. "But If I saw the catalog she saw it in, in your office, I'd know," he then added to his already nosy demeanor.

"Well, Mr. Milburn, as a rule, I don't usually take clients into my office, but since you're a friend of Dillard Patterson, my attorney, I'll make an exception," Doris explained, showing Milburn into her office off to the side of her posh boutique.

"So you are one of Dillard's clients, well, I'm very pleased to meet you," he said, coming in and finding a seat to look directly at the portrait he had come to see.

"Yes, Patterson and I have known each other for a long time, let me get the catalogs," she said, walking around her desk to get them from the shelf on the wall. "Look, Mr. Milburn, I wasn't surprised to see you here, Patterson said you might show up."

"Really, he actually told you I'd be here about the original he probably sold you!"

"He did. Dillard's that kind of a man, very honest, can't say that about most lawyers I've encountered," Doris added.

Larvy drew his head, quickly surprised at Doris's statement. "Well, did you know he has your original in his home?" he probed.

"I have the original, that I'm very certain of, now would you still like to buy a gown for Roslyn, or are you finished with your search?" she asked, extending the catalog she was holding in her hand.

CHAPTER 21

ERENE HAD FOUGHT WITH ALL he had and so far was winning the battle of infidelity. Nora was so busy with her career she never even suspected a thing. Besides she was never in town. She worked as a resource specialist for a Fortune 500 company and loved all the hype that went with it. The two had only been married for two years, and all Erene wanted was for her to have a child to what he considered would seal the marriage.

"Nora, look, my son and I could be watching the play-offs right now," he said, teasing her one weekend as he sat watching the game on television.

"Erene, there is no guarantee you'll have a son," she replied.

"Okay, my daughter, girls are making names for themselves in sports, look at Ali's daughter, or Mia Hamm in soccer, I won't complain about a girl," he shared, playfully kissing her softly on her lips.

"Honey, remember we agreed five years in, right?" she said, pushing him away and heading to get her laptop and sat on the sofa where she spent most weekends when home.

"I know you're not going to do work, we only have the weekend these days," he stated, coming over playfully again.

"Honey, I'm just looking at some charts I have prepared for a PowerPoint presentation," she replied.

"And if it wasn't that, it would be something else," he said, leaving out the door to his garage.

Nora didn't follow. She just had a "he'll get over it" attitude and continued looking at her charts.

Erene stood outside talking to a neighbor in the front yard about the game when his phone rang.

"Hello," he said, seeing it was William Parker calling. "Good evening, sir, how are you?" he said, greeting his caller warmly.

"I'm wonderful, Nada has got me helping her with this call list for the couples' night out." He laughed. "And I'm calling the guys who I know are watching the game and won't talk long about it," he explained, laughing the whole time.

"Really, it's halftime and I'm out talking with my neighbor until the game starts again, but yes, Nora and I, sure put us down, she'll be in town," he said with certainty.

"Good, enjoy your evening."

"Thanks I will. I should be able to get a few more calls in before the game starts again," Billy said laughing, hanging up the line.

Erene walked back in just before the game had started up again.

"Billy called while I was out."

"I didn't hear the phone," Nora responded.

"No, he called on my cell, just about the harvest couples' night at the church. I told him we'd be there."

"When is that?" she asked.

"In two weeks, the second Saturday, so put it on your calendar," he shared.

Doris had finished going through the box by the end of the day. Russell had come through for lunch and was waiting to hear what she had found. Most of what she found in this box was information Dana, her sister, had share with her already. There was also a dairy labeled #4, indicating there were possibly more somewhere. She did find something interesting in the letters her mother had wrote to Richard Demato, and it was a name of a woman she called her friend, "Judy." They did everything together. She called her "her partner in crime." "I bet she has stories," Doris thought. And there was also someone named Dornelton, who Faye, her mother, mentions as well. Doris wrote the names down in a book she had started. She kept notes for further search. She knew she would start her search in Oregon because that's where she was from and grew up until she was seventeen. Why hadn't she looked at the name on her birth certificate? It had no meaning to her, and she had a new life now and wanted to forget about

Oregon. Wow, could she really go back there again. What would she find? Is it worth it to dig up, or should she just leave things alone? Doris sat thinking to herself before hearing her clerks saying good evening, leaving the store. She got up and put papers into her briefcase, and with the box in hand, she headed to her car to go home.

Annie called Keith for dinner after his hour away to go and cool off, she surmised. He came in and sat at the table with his family to eat the dinner Annie had prepared.

"Annie, this has got to stop, the way you're treating me is not right. I don't deserve the treatment you are giving me," he said, starting to eat his dinner after the said grace.

"You're going to bring this up over the dinner table?" she asked, looking mean at him.

"Okay, I'm sorry, I did it. I admit being with Abby, if that's what it's going to take to get forgiveness from you. I'm sorry, Annie," he said, almost in tears.

"Daddy, what's wrong? Don't cry, Daddy," Riley said, looking sad at Keith who was clearly sorry for his behavior with Abby.

Annie jumped up and took Riley from the chair and took her in the family room and turned on a movie. She walked back into the kitchen. "Why are you putting on a display after your action with Abigail?" she said loudly and caused Riley to come screaming and crying from the family room. "Now see what you have done!" she said harshly, grabbing Riley up in her arms.

"Annie, I'm so sorry, you have to forgive me. I love you." He got up and left the room.

Annie calmed Riley down and took her in the bedroom and began preparing her for bed by putting on the pajamas. Keith walked back into the bedroom to say good night to Riley.

She cried out to him, reaching her arms for him to hold her. "Daddy, Daddy, please, Daddy," she pleaded, but Annie held her tight and wouldn't let Keith hold her.

He turned again and walked out the bedroom. After Riley fell asleep, Annie came into the family room where Keith was sitting in front of the television. It was 8:00 p.m. by now and dinner was spoiled for everyone.

"Keith," she said calmly, "you can start preparing the divorce papers on Monday morning or I will. Riley is not going to go through this because you messed up," she stated.

"Annie, we both messed up, why don't you just forgive and we can try and work on our marriage. I love you and I really don't want a divorce."

"I do!" she acknowledged and walked into the couple's bedroom preparing for bed.

Keith followed, pleading with her to change her mind. "I admitted to you, Annie, now you have to forgive me," he cried out.

"I don't have to forgive you and I won't!" Annie stated. Annie ignored Keith the rest of the evening and got in bed, turning her back to go to sleep.

The next morning, both were found shot through the head with a gun Keith had just bought less than a month ago.

Doris had started in on another box when Finley came in with her breakfast. Russell had left for the office and to get ready for a big donation drive they were having today.

"Madam, how are you doing finding about all this family information Dana had?" he asked.

"Finley, I've only scratched the surface. I think that Dornelton Hawkins, the man on my birth certificate, never met the man that I know about. I couldn't find a death certificate on record, so I'm going to go to Oregon to see if I can find him."

"My lady, you're really going to open yourself to that? Are you sure?"

"Yes, Finley, I am. I have lots of questions and someone has the answers," she believed.

"Do you want me to come with you, my lady?" Finley asked, standing up straight in front of her.

"Finley, you'd do that for me?" she asked, hugging him around the waist.

"I would, my lady, for you," he responded.

"That's very touching, Finley, but Mrs. Parker is going to go with me," Doris shared.

"Oh really, Tetra Parker is going to accompany you? Oh you will be fine." He sighed, relieved she wasn't going alone.

"But, Finley, there is something you can do for me," Doris said, taking out a surveillance video she had brought from her boutique.

"Shhhhh, just look at this and tell me what you see, Finley, I know I can trust you with this," Doris explained.

Finley looked a moment at the video of two women standing in Doris's boutique talking. He looked and looked, and Doris was watching his reaction when she heard, "Oh my god, she's done it again!" Finley expressed to Doris.

"Shhhhh, not a word, Finley, not a word."

Doris was sure now her suspicions were confirmed. She had also found out other information about Dillard's brother from an investigative report she had received as well. His alternative life had banished him to Europe with his lover due to family acceptance, She read. Most of his paintings were of people and he was well known there. Doris had read about her mother, Faye; she just wanted to know her life before Dana came along. She was three years older than her sister, Dana, and she wanted to know how she got stuck with those people, who were they, and why was she there? Questions, so many questions were going through her mind as she continued going over the papers and letters Dana had put together in chronological order as best she could after reading them.

By 9:00 a.m. Monday morning, police cars were all over the street. Riley had woken up and went into her parents' bedroom. She tried over and over to wake up her mommy and daddy before going across the street with blood on her pajamas and hands to Mrs. Bookens's home.

Mrs. Bookens opened the door when she saw her in pajamas before noticing the blood on them. "What happened?" she screamed, frightened for the child. "What happened?" she asked, looking on her for injuries from having so much blood on her clothes.

"I couldn't wake up Mommy," she cried.

"Where is your father, Riley?" she asked, now hugging her to comfort her.

"I couldn't wake up Daddy either," she replied.

Mrs. Bookens turned on the television and, as quick as she could, put Riley in some other clothes. Her hands were shaking so much. The clothes were much too big for her but free from blood. She tuned the television to one of Riley's favorite cartoons before leaving to go across the street nervously as she walked. She approached the house seeing the door wide open. It was opened no doubt from Riley when she left, Ms. Bookens imagined, as she walked closer.

"Annie! ANNIE!" she called out, louder each time. As she walked now further into the spacious home, she called out again heading to the bedroom. "Annie? Keith?" she yelled, still no answer. Then she walked into the bedroom and almost fainted seeing all the blood spattered against the wall and in the bed. She ran back to the living room screaming and breathing heavily as she ran as fast as her legs could carry her home. She immediately dialed 911, explaining the situation that had taken place. Annie and Keith were lying on the bed in their night clothes and the suicide note from him was on the dresser. Mrs. Bookens sat holding Riley in her arms after calling William Parker and Associates where the two worked while hearing the police arrive across the street.

Billy arrived about forty-five minutes to an hour after the call. The traffic getting to the Poultons' home was heavy not to mention the shock of the news was quite overwhelming. As he drove along, he reflected back to high school and Dana Williams's adoptive mom and dad. That horrible day.

"Oh my god, I should have seen this coming? My god, my god," he cried out, driving along heading to the scene after their neighbor called to inform him of the matter. By then, it was breaking news on television and radio. "I'd better call Nada before she hears it," he thought, dialing the phone.

"Hi, sweetheart, how's your day?" she asked.

"Nada, there has been a terrible thing done," he said for a lack of what to call it.

Nada felt the tension in his voice. "Honey, what's wrong, are you all right?" she stated, fearing the worse and that something had happened to him.

"No, honey, I'm fine, but Keith and Annie was found dead this morning," he started out.

"Is this the breaking news on the television?" she quickly asked. "Where is Riley? Oh my god!" she cried out, clearly shaken from hearing the description of the case now being televised on the television.

"Riley? I hadn't thought about Riley. I'm just about there, they have everything cordoned off. I'll see what I can find out and call you back," he shared.

"Billy, I'm on my way." And she hung up the phone.

The information Billy had taken down from Mrs. Bookens after she called had him now standing on her doorstep ringing the doorbell. She had just returned inside after speaking with the lead detective giving them information until asked again if needed.

"Yes, may I help you?" she asked, coming to the door.

"I'm William Parker, you called me about the Poultons?" he said, letting her know why he was there.

"Yes, they worked for you. I kept their daughter sometime," she acknowledged.

"Yes, their daughter, where is she? Is she over there as well?" he feared.

Before another word was spoken, Riley came streaking from the room almost falling down in Mrs. Bookens's oversized blouse she was wearing. "Uncle Billy, I couldn't wake up Mommy and Daddy," she cried out, running to him.

He picked her up in his arms tightly, holding on to her crying silently.

"I'm here, Riley, I'm here," he acknowledged as Mrs. Bookens looked on, relieved for the child.

Tetra Parker had just heard the news aired on television and was on the phone speaking with Nada. No names had been given out, though she knew the affluent neighborhood Annie lived in was stated where the murder suicide took place.

"Yes, Mother, Riley is okay. I just spoke with Billy," Nada shared.

"Oh, you know me, every time I hear about something happening in Maine, I think I always know the people." She laughed.

"Mother Parker, you knew this couple," Nada said sadly, "it was Annie and Keith."

"What? What happened? Oh my god! That's why you said Riley's okay? Oh my Jesus." She was clearly torn by the news.

"I don't know anything yet, I'm waiting to hear from William. He told me it has been a mess over there for the past two hours or so since their neighbor called him at the office," she shared with Tetra. "And asked that I not come. He'd get Riley to me," Nada added.

"Oh my god, that child? That sweet, innocent child. Call me when things settle down. I'm turning off the news now." You could hear the emotion in Tetra's voice. "I'm going up to pray, oh my god," she said, hanging up the line from her daughter-in-law.

Abby and the associates at the law firm had also got the news about their fellow attorney and his wife. They were surprised to hear about trouble between the Poultons because they never showed any tension around the office that was earth-moving, each thought. Abigail sat crying at her desk with her head in her hands.

"You never know what someone is going through," Oren stated, looking around the room at McGuire, Abby, and some others gathered after getting the news from Billy to confirm that it was truly Annie and Keith.

Police had labeled it a murder suicide, since a note from Keith was found on the dresser in the couple's bedroom.

Nada walked from the living room to her nursery and back up to her bedroom several times nervously waiting for her husband to come home. She could have been over there by now, she thought, looking at the time again and again. She had called and gotten his voice mail when she grabbed her purse and informed Millicent she was leaving to go and meet Billy. When she got down to the garage, she heard William pulling in the driveway as she watched from the garage door. All she could see was William under the wheel as he stopped and got out. Nada ran and hugged him tight.

"What happened? Where is Riley? Is she all right?" she asked quickly, knowing the situation.

Billy held on to her crying. He had gone through an ordeal and it was truly bothering him. Broken though relieved, he stated, "She's okay, she's asleep on the backseat. I'll get her out. Could you please get her some clothes to put on? We weren't allowed back in the home to get any of hers," he shared with Nada. "And we will be right in," he added, going to the passenger side of his car as Nada went back to get Riley some clothes her size to wear.

William walked in and took Riley to Peyton's room. She was very familiar there, she had spent nights and birthday parties with Billy and Nada, they were family, and she was comfortable. Waking up after being taken from the car and seeing now where she was, her whole countenance changed.

"Hi, sissy," she said to Peyton smiling at one another.

Billy's grief for a moment was subsided as he watched the two girls being playful with each other. Nada came back with clothes and changed Riley before leaving the girls to play as she and Billy went out into another room to talk and comfort one another.

C H A P T E R 22

DORIS HAD RUN A CHECK on the man named on her birth certificate. And since there was no death certificate that Doris could find, she had made up her mind that she would try and find him for closure. She didn't want or certainly need anything from him at this point in her life but had questions about her mom that maybe he could answer. Her mother would be sixty-eight if she was still living, so it's possible he could still be alive if he was close to her age, Doris reasoned as she prepared for her trip to Oregon for answers.

As she sat looking over some documents in her home office, her phone rang. "Mrs. Parker, how are you?" she answered, greeting her caller.

"Hello, Doris, I'm sure by now you have heard the horrible news out of Maine," she began her conversation.

"Honestly, Tetra, I haven't been near the television, I'm so tied up in these papers of Dana's," she replied.

"I see, well, the reason I call was to let you know I would be glad to accompany you on your trip, however, I can't go if it's next week," Tetra explained. "There was an incident today, I'm sure you will see it on the news. A couple from Billy's office was murdered today."

"What, that's close to home, for sure," she stated.

"Yes, Keith and Annie Poulton both worked in Billy's law firm."

"Are you kidding, so you knew them, what happened?"

"It appears to be a murder suicide, he left a note," Tetra confirmed.

"So, I guess no one saw that coming? I mean you never know what a person is facing, are going through," Doris added.

"Annie was a very sweet girl, she's been working for the firm close to ten-plus years, she and Billy even dated," Tetra confessed.

"It was just unfortunate what happened, but we will never know what went on in the home that night, the child is fine though."

"Child? They had a child in the home when he shot her and himself?" Doris asked, surprised.

"Yes, apparently asleep in the other room, and Riley found them and tried to wake them, I heard," Tetra said.

"Oh now that breaks my heart to think what that child will remember from that night."

"That's true, Riley's five and I'm praying mightily for that little girl."

"What's going to happen to her now?" Doris asked, curious now.

"Billy has contacted her grandmother, Annie's mother, and she should be there by the end of the week. She's there with Billy and Nada until then," Tetra shared.

"Okay, Tetra, I'm on my own schedule, so let me know in a week or so if things are working out for you and William and I'll schedule my flight," Doris suggested.

"I will, and thanks for the prayers," Tetra closed her conversation, disconnecting the line.

After two weeks of moping around the office, Adele needed a pickup and she headed to her favorite international salon and stylist. She and Hilary had been out shopping and the new outfits she had purchased were still hanging in her closet with the tags still intact.

With lots of hi's and waves of the hand, she walked in speaking loudly walking through the door. She wasn't feeling joyful, but that's what was expected of her because that's what she usually did upon arrival.

"Adele, how are you?" she heard someone say coming from the direction of the dryers.

"Oh, Mrs. Parker, hello, I'm okay," Adele replied, walking over near where Nada was sitting.

"How's the dating coming along?" Nada asked.

"Huh, okay, not doing much these days," she said.

"A young professional lady like you should be out enjoying the world," Nada cut in. "God's way though," Nada added. "We have a young professional group that meets at our church on Wednesday nights, wait, let me see if I have a card."

"Here is the address of the church, call me, I'll be there with you if you choose to come," Nada added, smiling.

"Adele?" her stylist said, looking for her in the front seating area.

"Coming, thanks, I'll think about it," she said, taking the card. Billy and Nada had a planned meeting with Mrs. Mater, Annie's mother. She had arrived from Colorado after his call regarding Annie's death and her final arrangements, and her granddaughter Riley Poulton. William had sat up a meeting at the office for the two of them including Nada, his wife, was attending to discuss Riley, Annie's child. The case which wasn't that difficult to put together because of the very detailed note Keith had left behind. He states clearly she was planning to divorce and leave him. Other documents including divorce papers not yet filled out were found in Annie's desk that also confirmed his story. Abby was busy trying to keep things together at the prestigious firm in the middle of the unwanted publicity and news media very present there.

"Morning," she said, looking at Abby behind the desk working feverishly on documents.

"Good morning," she said, looking up at this curly blondish gray-haired woman with a strong Southern drawl voice.

"I'm here to see a Willie Parka," is what Abby heard coming from the lady looking to be late fifties, early sixties, not sure.

"William Parker," Abby said, smiling, "You must be Hanna Mater, Annie's mother, so sorry for your loss," she acknowledged, coming from behind the desk to escort the woman to the conference room legated for the meeting place.

"Why, thank you," she replied, looking at the large office space and windows all around.

Abby, seeing she wasn't much for conversation, showed her to the room and informed William she had arrived.

Hanna sat looking at the long table with papers in front of the chair at the end. She had never visited her daughter's place of employment and thought how nice it was as she looked around hearing the soft elevator music in the air. It was just she and Annie, and Annie had grown up with her father for the most part. Annie had left home after graduating high school in Colorado and moved to Maine. She put herself through college, while working graveyard shift at a hospital to pay her tuition. It was a big payday when she landed the job for Parker and Associates law firm. The firm at the time was just starting up by William Parker who himself had just passed the bar and wanted a firm of his own after working for others in the area. He saw Annie, he hired her. That was so long before Nada came along. The two dated a while before his fiancée Jillian was taken in a plane crash in 9-11 and long before his now marriage to Nada. Annie became a staple and an asset to the company.

"Good morning, Mrs. Mater," William said, coming into the room extending a hand and then a hug. It surprised Hanna, and William could tell she felt a bit uncomfortable. "Have a seat," he said, sitting at the head of the table. "I'm so sorry we are here," he began. "And Annie was a friend," he added. "Did you find the accommodations we made for you in town acceptable?" he asked, prolonging time for Nada to arrive.

"Way more room than I need, but it's real nice, thank ya," she replied, speaking of the Maine Hilton Abby had set her up in for her stay. William had never met Hanna and was a bit surprised because Annie was elegant and well-spoken, to say the least. "Annie was my only daughter," she shared. "I told her to stay wit that man," she said, "when they got together, he was nice, and den when she called me oh round the end of this month 'cause the check she usually sends me was not there, so when I called her, she says she was gon leave him." Hanna appeared a bit upset, but William wasn't sure why.

"Keith worked here as well, Mrs. Mater, we thought they were a happy couple, they appeared to be," William added.

"I told her she was being crazy, she had set hur sights on a married man, then says she leaving this man after he married hur," she again informed. "She sent me a check every month and it was never late before, I don't know what I'm gon do now." She actually started to cry.

"Mrs. Mater, I'm sure you won't have any worries. Annie has insurance policies and you are the beneficiary along with her daughter, Riley," he said.

"Oh, that's right. I can't keep no child, I'm sick. I'm always going to the doctor for something," she said, then she coughed hard and loud.

"Are you all right?" Billy asked, not wanting to touch her again without her permission.

"Trying to quit them cigarettes," she confessed. "So you say she got a policy?" Hanna perked up after wiping her mouth.

"Yes, and where would you like to have her final arrangements made?" he reminded her.

"Is that covered in her policy?" she asked, looking at William.

"Mrs. Mater, if you like or give me permission, I will honor your wishes with sending Annie to Colorado or wherever you want to lay her to rest. I'll have my secretary make all of the arrangements. We loved Annie here," he suggested, seeing that it was all about money and he understood Annie was her sole support.

"I told her father about this, but he cain't come, 'cause he worse off than me, I'm afraid. So if that's something you kin do for my Annie, okay," Mrs. Mater said.

Tetra prayed mightily for her family and the situations now taking place with her newfound granddaughter. She didn't know if little Riley would stay with her son and his family or go to live in another state. Annie had her will and kept everything up to date. Being a legal secretary certainly afforded her the know-how to keep things of that nature current. A part of her job was to accommodate many of the clients in the law firm with the service.

"David, I pray things work out for that child," Tetra said sitting, having breakfast with her husband one morning.

"Wow, I talked with that young man the last time we were at our son's home. There was never an indication of him doing this kind of thing, and I shared it with our son because he was beating himself up over not stopping it," he said, drinking from his coffee cup. "It couldn't be prevented unfortunately and only God knows. I just feel so sorry for Annie, Keith, and Riley. This was a horrible tragedy. William said Keith's body was shipped back to Colorado, his mother and sister are making arrangements for his final resting place. His dad is still hanging on in spite of his condition," David added, "and his wife says he was up and walking around their home."

"I heard William is meeting with Annie's mother, so let us pray for the outcome there," Tetra said, concerned for losing the child.

Adele had opted for her bouncing short funky-style hairdo. She had found a way to pull herself up from the moping and determined in her mind that Erene would be hers one day and she was willing to wait. She thought it would be a good thing to do the church dating, less risky, and besides, she could pull the abstinence card if the person started wanting more than just dinner, or talk. Armed with the address, she asked Hilary to join her Wednesday at church and to be a part of the young professionals.

Nada had made her way downtown to her husband's office for the meeting with Mrs. Mater, Annie's mother.

"Sorry, honey, Millicent was busy and so I was waiting for her before I left," she came in explaining her tardiness. "Mrs. Mater, I am very sorry for your loss," she shared, coming over to speak and express her condolences.

"Why, thank you," she said, looking at her wondering who she was coming in.

"I'm sorry. I'm William's wife, Nada Parker, and a friend of Annie's also," she said, taking her seat at the table.

"Oh I see." Hanna smiled.

"Nada, Mrs. Mater and I were just discussing where she wanted to lay Annie to rest," he said, looking at Mrs. Mater.

"Well, Annie spent most of her life here with yall. I don't know anybody who matters to her in Colorado. Her in-laws lived in another city 'bout hundred twenty miles or so from us. And since she was planning on leaving him, I doubt seriously if I want her buried with him," she responded, shocking Nada, but Billy had spoken with her and wasn't a bit surprised at her reply.

"Your daughter deserves a proper heartfelt burial, she was a likable lady and a friend to a lot of people right here in Maine," Nada expressed.

"Well then, that's it, we will just have something for her here as soon as possible 'cause I can't be way from home too long and traveling I don't really lack," Hanna shared.

"That's fine, Mrs. Mater, I'll have Abby get right on it," Billy said, leaving out of the room to speak with Abby about plans.

"So did you and Annie have a good relationship, Mrs. Mater?" Nada asked, making small talk until Billy returned.

"We got along, 'cause we didn't see each other much, it seemed to work for us. Buster, her stepbrother, is always out hunting somewhere when she's around," she replied.

"So you're just lost in the big house all by yourself most of the time?" Nada asked, trying to see how Riley would fit in.

Hanna laughed before saying, "If you call a trailer big, I've got one. And I'm fine with it. Just me and my dog Buffer, we love our trailer park."

"You are aware Annie has a child, aren't you?" Nada asked, a bit afraid to confront the question.

"I do, but I heard she has godparents, I'm hoping we could work something out with them, you know, she doesn't even know me, haven't seen her since she was a little something, bout four years ago now," she explained, looking around.

"May I get you something to drink, coffee, soda?"

"I'll take a pop," she stated, smiling.

Nada smiled. She knew she meant soda because that's what they call soda in Louisiana.

"Coke, ma'am?"

"That's fine," she acknowledged, smiling as Nada walked out. Billy and Nada both walked back into the room together.

William was glad to hear what Nada had shared with him about Mrs. Mater regarding godparents as he stood by having Abby draw up a document regarding Riley. Their aim was to have this child with as little interruption in her life as possible.

"Mrs. Mater, Annie's insurance policy is quite substantial and will cover all funeral expenses, any care for you and the child," William shared regarding the documents he laid out.

"Okay, but before we get into that, I'd like to talk to the godparents 'cause Annie said if something ever happened to her that the child had godparents," she said, taking an envelope from her purse. "Annie sent me this bout two months ago and told me to put it in a box she left for all my important papers. Now if it means

I don't get no money, then that's how it's goin' to be, 'cause I know that's what Annie wanted." She was sure. She handed the envelope to Billy.

He was shocked but nodded her permission to take out the contents being a papered document he held securely in his hand. William read and began to shed tears, Nada could see.

"What's wrong?" Nada asked as Billy handed the document to her to read for herself. Annie had specified that if something ever happened to her, Riley Poulton was to go to the custody of William and Nada Parker, her godparents. The document was dated and signed with a seal the day Riley was born. It had been prepared by Keith Poulton and signed by both of them.

"It was already in place," William thought, getting up to hide tears of sleepless nights and uncertain decisions.

"Mrs. Mater, we will honor Annie's wishes, and for you, I'm going to give you all of the money Annie has coming from one policy I know of which is $200,000 from this law firm alone. There could be more and I will certainly make sure you get every penny owed to Annie," he informed to her surprise. "When everything is settled, you will be able to live as well as you'd like for a very long time," he shared, hugging her in spite of herself. "Don't ever worry about Riley, she will be fine as well," he shared, hugging Nada and thanking God. Nada was shedding tears of joy as well.

By Friday, Mrs. Mater was headed home, pleased that her daughter, Annie Poulton, was laid to rest and the funeral arrangements and kind words from those who felt the loss and knew Annie were heartwarming. William had also flown Annie's father in for the funeral, even though he is a very ill man, carrying his oxygen tank with him for breathing.

"Thank you all, I hadn't seen Bud all dressed up with a haircut and every-thang in a long time, me neither for that matter." Hanna smiled.

She didn't ask to be introduced to Riley, but she gave her a hug and shed tears with the Parkers who promised to keep her informed about Riley. She thanked them for honoring Annie's request as she and Bud boarded the plane back to Colorado with less worries of living due to the dollars now in her bank account.

Doris had questions and had gone down to Dillard Patterson's office. Parking and getting out of her car, she ran into Larvy Milburn.

"Good afternoon, Mrs. Woods," he said, seeing her walking through the beautiful terrarium garden leading to Dillard's office.

"Why, good evening, sir," she replied. "How was the social and your beautiful wife's gown?" she asked smiling as he extended his hand to her.

"My wife was the most beautiful dressed woman at the event," he beamed, accepting her connected hand of friendship.

"Please tell Roslyn hello," she said and waved, going on her way and avoiding a long conversation.

Dillard was expecting her. She had called, so seeing her coming through the window, he got up opening his office door.

"Hello, Doris," he greeted, and she smiled, returning a smile and a nod of hello coming in. "Have a seat, can I get you something, water, Coke?" he asked before going back behind the desk.

"No, thank you, I'm just coming from lunch with Russell and wanted to ask you about Dana before I take my trip back to Oregon."

"Oh, that's where you were born I understood from your sister?" he stated but with a questioned look on his face.

"Yes, that's correct, I was." She paused. "What I wanted to ask you about is a box of papers Dana had?"

Dillard's mind was now going a mile a minute because he and Dana had collaborated on a lot of things together when she was putting together her family history.

"Did you guys by chance find out information about a man named Dornelton Hawkins?" she asked.

Dillard sat down at his computer. "Now since I knew you were probably going to ask me something regarding Dana, I pulled up these old files from some archives I have. Dornelton Hawkins was the brother of Judy Hawkins McNeese, your mother's best friend," Dillard informed with Doris hanging on every word.

"Judy? Her name came up a lot in the letters," Doris commented.

"Okay, she had two brothers, Dornelton and Marcus. Marcus was the suave and debonair one who was a lady's man, according to our reporter. Faye had eyes for him but so did all the ladies.

Dornelton was more the homebody and looks hadn't caught up to him yet, kind of scrawny, quiet, big Coke bottle glasses, and always reading books."

"So what happened, how did Dornelton end up on the birth certificate looking like that?" she asked, surprised after hearing the story.

"He liked Faye a lot and he knew his brother wasn't deserving of her, he said, she was real nice, not like some of the other girls. So he decided after graduation from high school to enlist in the military. When he returned home after boot camp with his uniform and muscles to match, he asked her out. She couldn't believe he was the same puny little guy who had left almost two years ago, but he convinced her, and before he left to go to Vietnam, Faye, your mother, was in love and pregnant."

"So go on." Doris was intrigued.

"He never saw the baby or knew about a baby for a long time, besides Marcus was still in the picture. But after about a month of putting Marcus off, Faye wasn't yet showing but decided to tell Marcus, the player, she was pregnant and he dumped her and never came a calling again. She just continued with school and got a job working for an insurance company as a clerk temporarily until she could no longer hide the pregnancy. Of course after nine months, she delivered a beautiful baby girl. Needing to care for you and no one to turn to, the very beautiful Faye went to a nightclub so she could work at night while Judy kept you. There she met an older Caucasian man who after seeing him for about three months she convinced him to take care of her and as far as we know until her death. Dornelton was injured severely in Nam and feared dead. Faye had a good thang, is how she described him to Judy. She vowed to stay with her sugar daddy until Dornelton return if ever. Years later, he came back home with lost limbs and put in the veterans hospital in Oregon. Really unable to help himself, he gave up hope of finding Faye. Judy tried to find Faye or the baby because he had moved her to an upper-class neighborhood and made her swear to leave that life behind. Dornelton was disabled and knew she'd never want him anyway," Dillard read from his notes.

"Wow, so how in the world did you and Dana find out all this detailed information?" she asked, looking at her attorney.

"If you're willing to go the distance and put in the research, you can find out just about anything," he shared. "Though our best resource came from Dornelton himself," he said, looking waiting to see her reaction.

"He's still alive?"

"It was seven years ago. Dana said you wanted nothing to do with her discoveries so . . ." He smiled.

"I remember that conversation, and you're right, I didn't want a thing to do with any of those folks in Oregon! Unbelievable, just unbelievable, now you're telling me possibly this man could still be alive."

"I haven't found a death certificate yet," Dillard shared.

"Yes, I know. I went that route first and now that I have this information, I've got to see where it leads. I know it brought closer for Dana," Doris said, taking a Kleenex tissue from her purse to wipe a tear.

"Are you going to be all right?" Dillard asked.

"I will and thanks, I'll be in touch on what I find so you can archive those files hopefully the last time," she said. "Now, Patterson, is there something else I might want to know that you haven't said already?" she asked, pulling her chair closer to his desk.

"I'm not sure, but I'll make you a copy of the entire report and you can take it with you, it's only about seven to ten pages," he added, getting up to get them from the printer in the other room.

"Thanks, I appreciate this, and tell Miss Norfen I said hello." Doris smiled, going out of the office.

Billy and Nada were determined to transition Riley into their family with little to no friction on her. A month had passed since that awful tragedy and Billy and Nada had sat up a few nights when all Riley wanted was her mommy and daddy. They were taking the family on an outing after Nada and with Millicent's help in getting the children dressed would be on their way.

"Why, don't you girls look beautiful," Billy said, seeing them run to the dayroom where he was sitting waiting for them.

"Daddy, Daddy," Peyton said, running to jump in his arms. Riley, being a bit older by three years, looked around.

"Come on," he yelled to her from across the room with a smile. She ran and jumped in his arms. "Love you," he said and kissed her cheek. Peyton mocked with a kiss on the other cheek and both girls began laughing.

Standing with both girls in his arms, he saw Nada and Trevor made their way down the stairs for a day out. When they arrived at a familiar play area to the children, Nada and Billy sat near the area and let the girls run free. There were other children there having fun in the sun, sand, and slides. A lady came up showing her little child how to slide down.

Riley ran over to Nada. "Mommy Nada, she looks like mommy," she said innocently.

"Yes, but your mommy is in heaven, right?"

"Oh, I remember, Mommy is an angel," she expressed smiling, running back to play.

Billy looked up from playing with his son, Trevor, in his stroller. "She'll be fine," he said, giving Nada a hug of encouragement. She had shed tears every day for Riley's loss.

"Honey, you know how much I like helping young people I find myself getting more and more involved every day with their lives," she said, now sitting watching the girls laughing and having fun.

"I think that's a great ministry to start pursuing further," he commented.

"I have been sitting with the young professionals the past Wednesday nights and they are really trying hard to apply the living Word to their everyday lives. I know it isn't easy especially with all the temptations they have today," Nada shared.

"Dating, abstinence, marriage, children, commitment, the list goes on," Billy agreed. "So if they could hear from those who have gone through what they're facing, it may cause a different decision to be made on their part."

"Yes, and that could make a big difference. I'm praying about it. My heart right now is to see Riley through this time."

"Yes, but, honey, if you haven't heard me say how much I appreciate what you are doing, caring for my child and now your child, I just want to say heartfelt thank you!" he said, reaching over for a hug. Trevor squirmed. He was asleep reclined in his stroller. Billy got up with the ball and ran over to the girls playing. He stood Peyton out on the grass and called for Riley to join the circle. What fun they had chasing and kicking and running after the ball. Everyone was exhausted after returning home.

Millicent, loving her job, ran to meet them at the door. She loved helping Nada with the children. So it was baths and early dinner before being tucked in.

"Good night, Milly." Riley smiled. "Night, Me-I," Peyton mocked again what her big sister said and both giggled hiding under the covers.

"Good night, sweet dreams," Millicent said, leaving as Billy and Nada came in with a book before kissing them good night and tucking them in.

Wednesday had come and Adele and Hilary had arrived at the church with which Nada Parker had invited them to.

"Adele, what room are we looking for in here? This is a huge place, we will certainly get lost trying to find the room where the young professionals are," Hilary voiced as both walked in.

As they entered the foyer, Minister Billy, Erene, and two of the deacons were discussing moving the room around to get ready for the harvest fest.

"Hello, ladies, can we help?" he asked, seeing them look for signs as they walked toward them.

Erene immediately knew it was Adele hearing her voice.

"Mr. Parker," she greeted.

"Oh, Adele Hodges, how are you, dear?" he said, giving her a brotherly hug.

"I'm fine. Hi, Mr. James," she said, smiling. "I wasn't aware you went to this church?"

"It's Erene, yes, I am a member here, but hello and hi," he said, shaking Hilary's hand.

"Oh sorry, this is my friend Hilary Cass. Your wife, Mrs. Parker, invited us to join the young professionals tonight, are they here?" Adele asked, ignoring the relationship jitters felt between her and Erene.

"Yes, they are down that hall and through that door in the Prayer-Stone room. Erene, will you show them? I'm going to show Roger and Bert the room where the tables are, have fun," Billy yelled, walking the opposite direction.

Erene was speaking softly to Adele, asking her what did she think she was doing here. Hilary seemed excited about the whole thing of meeting a Christian young man.

"Prayer-Stone, here it is," Hilary said, opening the door.

"Go in, Hil. I'll be right in," Adele said. "Erene, what do you want from me? You said you wanted Nora!"

"I do, Adele, and I'm so sorry."

"I'm sorry too, Erene." And she went into the Prayer-Stone room a bit teary-eyed.

CHAPTER 23

ERENE TOOK THE INVESTIGATION OF the murder suicide to heart. What would lead someone to kill another? he sat questioning himself. He had gone over to the scene and was sick to his stomach seeing the blood spatter left in the bedroom from the shootings. He had heard them speaking about the note the husband had left on the dresser. How he had found his wife's diary and how she was planning to leave him. He wrote he had given her plenty of time to change her mind, but it seemed she never would. Then Erene thought about the child who had found both of them the next day.

"Lord, have mercy!" he thought, riding home to prepare for the harvest celebration at the church after picking his wife up from the airport.

When he walked into his house, it saw the message light blinking on the phone. He took off his blazer and walked over hitting the button. "Hi, honey, please don't be mad, I won't be able to make the harvest fest tonight I have an important meeting early tomorrow morning, but I'll call tonight as soon as I get in. Love you, honey. I know you know, it's Nora."

He flopped on the sofa exhausted from his workday. He had committed to coming and was on for the opening prayer.

Oh well, it's not the first time he thought Nora had stood him up with her traveling. He exhaled, getting up and walked over, turning on his Sirius radio to break the silence of his quiet home.

"The Closer I Get to You" by Luther Vandross was playing and his mind went immediately to Adele before changing the station shaking his head. He had prayed pouring his heart out to God for forgiveness. He had also asked Adele to forgive him and he repented and moved on. He dialed Nora his wife's hotel room first. She was out of town for work and left a message knowing she was still out at the office. Then he dialed her cell phone.

"Hi, honey, just a minute," she said, probably answering from a meeting. She was always in meetings, it seemed. "Honey, okay, I just stepped out. I left you a message at home."

"Yes, Nora, I got it. I was just calling to hear your voice and say of course I love and miss you, but I'm heading out to the harvest fest anyway tonight and I'll call you when I get in," he shared with a smile.

"Aww, so you are going to attend the couples' affair without me?" she asked, innocently-sounding.

"Well, Nora, you leave me little choice, but really I'm used to it by now, don't you think?" Erene replied with a forced laugh.

"I'll make it up to you, honey, I promise!" she expressed.

"That sounds wonderful, Nora, I don't want to keep you away from your meeting too long, love you," he said, ending the conversation before going in to the shower, eat, and head out to the harvest fest by 7:00 p.m. with church friends.

Doris, armed with more information about her past, continued packing her bags for her flight to Washington and then a drive to Oregon with her friend Tetra Parker.

"Hello, Mom," greeted her caller as she stood in her closet.

"Sonjee, hi, how are you doing?"

"Mom, I'm good, just down visiting Jace's parents. Will stop by when I'm back in LA," she confirmed.

"That sounds wonderful. I will be back by then," Doris said.

"Back? Where are you, Russell, and Finley headed to now? You guys travel more than Jace and he's a pilot!" She laughed.

"You're probably right, but no, I'm going with Mrs. Parker to Oregon," she shared. "Hoping to visit someone there who I've never met," she admitted.

"Mom, it sounds like something you need to do, just be careful and keep in touch."

"I will, dear."

"And, Mom, I'll be praying for your trip as well," Sonjee shared lovingly. "Love you, Mom," she said, disconnecting the line.

"My lady, dinner is on the table and Russell is sitting waiting for you," Finley said, coming to her door.

"And you, is your service set up as well?" she asked, entwining her arm around his as they walked toward the dining room. "I have something to share with both of you," she added smiling at Finley, her butler and friend.

Fletcher sat in the car waiting for Adele to get her coat, she had yelled from the closet. It was family night and it was a vow each family member had promised to keep. It was a very special night tonight. Hanson was coming in on leave and everyone was so excited. He had not been home since their mother's funeral and could only stay a short while. This visit would be for two weeks, and the family had plans for the whole time he would be with them. Ariel, their older sister, had set everything up at her home, and Malcolm, the oldest, Riggins Fletcher, Adele would all be putting their arms around Hanson who had been deployed to Iraq and now would come home to visit his family.

"Malcolm, I'm on my way," Riggins said, calling his older brother.

"Oh good, are you bringing Sasha?" he asked.

"Yes, she will soon be a part of this family," he answered.

"I was just wondering 'cause Becky wanted to come."

"Sure, that shouldn't be a problem, just be ready. I'm hitting the freeway now and I can't wait to see Hanson," Riggins expressed, smiling across the airways.

Adele was in the car and "If This World Was Mine" by Luther was playing on the radio in the car. Fletcher commented on the old song playing. "I'm going to use that line," he said, looking at Adele smiling.

"Fletcher, you're too young to know how deep that song really is, you might want to do some 'Baby, baby' by Justin Bieber." She laughed. Adele was remembering this was one of Erene's favorite CDs that he used to play for her.

"Bieber, huh, baby, baby. Baby, oooh! Baby, baby, baby, wish you were my . . .," Fletcher echoed driving down the road to the freeway with his sister in tow singing along.

Katia and Dillard were all decked out. She in a pricey Vera Wang gown and Dillard's fancy tuxedo also from the Wang collection for the gala award banquet one of his clients had invited him to. The limousine parked across the front door to let the two off in front of the Leonard H. Goldenson Theatre in downtown Los Angeles, the driver got out opening the door in front of this huge crowd of celebrities out for a fun evening.

"So, Dillard, do you think you have satisfied your client Doris Woods and those nosy Milburns?" she asked as they walk past many A-listers and celebrities heading to the red carpet event.

"Hello, hello, excuse me, why you look so lovely tonight," was heard has they walked in to find the seats as guests of the award attendees.

"Has it ever been your desire to walk on the red carpet, Katia?" "I don't know, I think I probably would make a great actress if that was a passion of mine," she expressed back, smiling seeing their numbered seat and row.

"Speaking of acting, Doris Woods said to say hello. She tried the Hollywood scene years ago, I read in some documents my once-client Dana Williams, her sister, had entrusted to me," he shared.

"Oh." Katia looked a bit puzzled. *Why is she sending hello to me?* she thought to herself. "She does have a fabulous boutique and I'm there a lot, well, I was until that Larvy Milburn and his wife invaded our space," she voiced, teed with the thought.

"Look, really, I believe all that is now behind us, we are moving to the future," he said, tapping Katia's hand as it laid on the arm rest of the comfy theater chair for the evening.

"Really?" she questioned smiling, wanting to believe a new start for her again and no more hiding.

"Yes, the Milburns are satisfied that I'm not a shyster, and most of all crook." He laughed. "And I think Doris is going off on her own adventures in life and so"—he smiled gently—"here we are," he said, looking at the large curtain being drawn back as the annual Emmy award show begins.

Billy and Nada had kissed the children and headed out to the harvest fest being held at their church. It was an annual event and all the members loved it and most boasted about the large turnout each year. Women loved it because they could pull out those evening dresses and beautiful gowns very seldom worn out. The men even appeased their wives by adorning a tuxedo for the evening to earn points with them. Arriving at the mega church and entering, the Parkers saw Erene standing speaking with two other guests going in.

"Good evening, so glad you could make this evening," Billy shared, tugging his lapel of his very nice tux.

Erene hugged and greeted Nada, saying hello to the couple.

"And where is your lovely wife, Nora?" he asked.

"The million-dollar question," Erene replied. "She wasn't able to make it tonight," he added sadly.

Nada felt his pain, hugging him again, and walked off leaving Billy to talk with him.

"Man, are you going to be all right tonight?"

"I am, but what I've decided to do is say the prayer to open and I'm going to go and meet Nora, hope you don't mind?" he questioned.

"I certainly don't mind, when are you planning to leave?" Billy asked, still standing in the foyer of the sanctuary's door.

"I was thinking I would open up first, I'm on the prayer, and then I would just quietly leave, but I wanted you to know," he shared with his minister brother and friend.

"Erene, you know I'm aware of your struggles with your wife's traveling and she seems to be the one who isn't willing to change, so, brother, do what you feel is right for you in keeping your marriage intact. A secret rendezvous is very romantic," Billy shared.

"Yes, I'll surprise her and go to her. She's always coming home and usually it's the same old thing," Erene agreed. "Billy, thanks for the idea. I love her so I'm going to do better to understand her side of this traveling, thank you for helping me see another way." He walked off smiling, heading to the front of the banquet hall to start the evening after many more guests joined in. "Thank you, Jesus!"

Ariel greeted all of her brothers and sister with a warm hug and big smile. She and her husband had gone to the airport early that morning to greet Hanson, their brother, who was coming in from Iraq. There were lots of well wishers at the airport waiting to greet the servicemen from several branches home and to thank them for their sacrifice to the America, our country. Fletcher was first in the airport's corridor behind Adele because he had also made the airport trip by himself that morning meeting Ariel and her husband standing waiting also. After what seemed a long time, there suddenly came lots of screams and yelling. *Hoorah!* could be heard as a group of servicemen entered the airport lobby.

"Well, good seeing you again, little brother, I think you have grown on me," Hanson said standing, looking so dapper in his beautiful white navy uniform, hugging Fletcher tight and laughing. There were tears of joy, laughter as hugs and kisses were exchanged from the groups gathered and their families. Hanson got in the car with his younger brother, Fletcher, and everyone headed to Ariel's home. What a joy to have everyone together again. Ariel had prepared lots and lots of food, yes, pizza, hugs, kisses, and storytelling of yesteryears and growing up. They shared fond memories of their mother, Rhea, and sad remembrances of what they went through as children but big smiles were on their faces when each looked around the room and could see the next one that came behind them. Fletcher, being the youngest of the siblings, stood up smiling and declared loudly, "We did all right, didn't we?" lifting up his nephew Gabriel, Ariel's son.

The beautiful transformed room of the church was set for the harvest fest. The fall colors were on display. Gold, rust, and oranges popped out all around the huge space. The couples expected to be there were about three hundred. It was a great event for the church, and everyone especially the ladies looked forward to it each year. It was a chance to see the spouses all decked out in their Sunday best. Brilliant stemware sparkled against candlelight and table settings of white trimmed with gold. The committee had done a magnificent job, Billy shared, standing with Nada smiling as the two were escorted to their table with the pastor and his wife. The couples were smiling and laughing and ready to enjoy an evening filled with love.

"Five more minutes and we will start," Erene said, looking around, "I see a few empty tables," then stopped to point. "See," he said as a couple took one of the spaces that were empty. With practically every seat filled, Erene James headed to the front to open in pray for the couples and marriage grand event.

"Bless the Lord, O my soul. Oh Lord my God thou are very great; thou art clothed with honor and majesty. Who covereth thyself with light as with a garment: who stretched out the heavens like a curtain: Who layeth the beams of his chambers in the waters: who maketh the clouds his chariot: who walked upon the wings of the wind: Who maketh his angels spirits, his ministers a flaming fire: Who laid the foundations of the earth, that it shall not be removed forever," Erene prayed earnestly, lifting all the couples and marriages to God. He was moved by the spirit and the spirit was moving in through the event, causing the saints of God to stand and clap and praise the Lord mightily for all his benefits!

Doris had made her mind after discussing it with Finley and her husband, Russell, who wanted her to go but do be careful. She and Tetra wasted no time in getting a car and headed down to Oregon once Doris arrived at her home the day before. Doris had armed herself with maps and direction to help her locate the first place she had planned to stop.

"Miss Tetra, please turn at the next corner and 5138 is the address we want," she said, now feeling a bit nervous after arriving at the home. The grass had not been mowed in sometime and the placed looked disheveled but was not a surprise to Doris, she was expecting that, she stated to Tetra who walked up with a frown on her face. ON CLOSER INSPECTION

On closer inspection, the address was 5140 and the address they were looking for was next door and it appeared to have a lot of fire damage to the property. Doris looked at Tetra and sighed. "Well, I guess we will go back and try something else," she shared, a bit disappointed at the outcome.

"Let's not give up, you have got a week to look, and I'm trusting we will get some kind of answer," Tetra concluded, walking back to the car.

"Hey! Hey, yall looking fa Judy?" someone yelled loudly from across the street. A lady looking to be in her late sixties had her head out of the front window watching them walk away from the house and to the car.

"We are," Doris said loudly, she thought.

"What? Huh? What you say?" she yelled back.

Tetra caught Doris's hand and both walked over to the fence.

"Yes, dear, we are looking for Judy," Tetra shared. "Do you know her?"

"Yeah, hold on, I be right out, goin' put on my dress," she shared before coming out five minutes later as they stood on the curb. "Sorry bout that, yeah I know Judy, but she moved bout two or three years ago. Yeah 'cause Man man was just born, yeah bout two years ago when the house burnt down," she said, clearing her thoughts with surety.

"Oh my, was anyone hurt?" Doris asked sadly.

"Hu brother got burnt real bad he went to the hawspita.

Momma don't talk bout him much," she added.

"Do you know where Judy lives now?" Tetra asked, curious and for sure they had the right place.

"I don't know, hu and Momma is friends, you kin to hu?" she asked, looking at Tetra and then Doris.

"No, Judy was best friends with my mother, Faye."

"Faye? Faye is yo mother?"

"Yes, Faye Wright was my mother," Doris replied.

She had this look on her face and she stared at Doris from head to toe. "You shol is pretty, is you Dois Weeums?"

"Yes, I was Doris Williams before I married," Doris shared, smiling at the woman's strange behavior looking at her.

"You don't memba me?"

"I'm sorry, I can't say I do," Doris replied. Tetra was now backing up to go across the street to the car.

She laughed real loud before saying, "I'm Penny you know li'l Penny, Squeaky's sister. We had ours birthdays together," she confessed, laughing hard.

Doris was in shock and dismayed that this was that cute little girl she knew as Penny. She had put on the miles. She looked hard, but there was not a trace of Li'l Penny from her yesteryears. This woman was only in her late forties and she looked like life had given up on her sixty years ago.

"Way you live, you look so pretty?" she kept asking.

"I live in California, but I'm here visiting," Doris explained.

"Whoa, I memba when yo rich li'l sister came and you went to be a movie star. Is you a movie star?" she questioned, smiling with maybe four teeth across the front of her smile.

"Oh no, that didn't work out." Tetra stood listening to the conversation that she could tell was very healing for Doris as she stood remembering the childhood she wanted to forget.

"Where's yo sister, she still rich? She used to buy us lots of candy, you memba?" She was reliving again and moving around like Li'l Penny, jumping up and down like a little kid in the street as she told story after story.

"So is it possible I could speak with your mother?" Doris asked, enjoying the stories but not so much standing in the street.

"Mama at work, I'ma go call hu, yall wanta come sat down?" she asked, showing them in. "Sorry bout the house yall came while I was g'tting' ready to clean up," she said, moving things from the couch for them to sit properly. The house was a mess and one afternoon was not going to do the job one bit, Tetra thought, looking around trying hard not to judge. "Okay, Dois," she giggled, "Mama say Judy live ova on Main and Monroe and I can show you 'cause that's near the Liquor Mart."

Doris and Tetra hurried up from the couch and out the door. Soon Li'l Penny was coming behind them after putting on her flip-flops and jumped in the backseat of the car, yelling out the window for "hu neighba to watch hu house til she git back."

Hilary talked nonstop at break time about the young professional group both had attended at the Christ Deliverance Center. "Hilary, breathe, Hilly, so you met someone really?" Adele said, laughing at her. Hilary had been so excited since meeting this cute guy that night.

"But, Adele, didn't you find he was in to me, he kept wanting to partner with me, didn't you notice?" she asked over and over again.

"I guess he seemed nice, I guess a bit shy, I thought," Adele added.

"But that's good because you know I'm not, so opposites attract, right?" she said as she sat drinking her Coke and expressed herself. "Adele, how about you, did you enjoy yourself, I mean you seemed preoccupied by something. Maybe the cute Mr. James, he is fine!" she teased.

"Shut up, Hilary. I'm good, so are you going again? I'm not sure if I want to," Adele asked, looking across the small break room table.

"Are you kidding? I think I've made a connection, and I'd like to see where it goes, he called me already this morning when I got to the office," she confessed smiling, getting up to continue their workday.

"Well, only because I don't want to spoil your love connection, we'll go this Wednesday," Adele promised, embracing her friend heading back to their office space on the second floor.

"I thought Walter was kinda cute?" she said, looking at Adele.

"Hilly, you need to stop playing cupid, but I agree he has potential for a young guy." She laughed.

"Young?" Hilary said, looking curiously at Adele.

Erene hurried from the Deliverance Center's harvest celebration after another pep talk from Billy Parker that it was a great idea to go and meet his wife in New York. He had booked his flight after going back home changing his clothes, packing a light suitcase, and headed to the airport. He listened to the sweet message she had left him at home, he guessed when she returned back to her room for the evening.

"Thank you, God," he expressed over and over, "for getting me out of that temptation," he thought many times sitting in the airport now waiting for his flight. "I almost lost my love," he said quietly in his mind as he waited. Her voice sounded so sweet, he thought. *I must get to her and we're going to make this work,* he vowed to himself, now hearing them announce boarding calls. Because he was riding in first class, he had more time and decided to call her to see what plans she had for the evening.

"Hi, honey."

"Hello, sweetheart, I'm glad you called. I miss you," she said, greeting him. "How are things going at the fest?" she asked, seeing he was calling from his cell and probably not at home yet.

"Great, though I only wish you were here," he shared deeply.

"Honey I know, but I promise, I'm going to make it up to you," she repeated again.

"So how was the meeting?"

"Usual, but I'm in tonight, tomorrow is the big meeting I snubbed you for," she confessed.

"Oh, so you admit you snubbed me?"

"Honey, I'm sorry, but we have a lot of time to be together after this, your wife is a big asset to this company, we are going places," she shared as always when she talked about her career.

"Well okay, so you're in cramming all the numbers, getting all your ducks in a row tonight," he joked, smiling. "So you'll be up late anyway, mind if I give you a call when I get home?" he asked lovingly.

"Something like that, but sure I'll be waiting," she affirmed and disconnected the line as Erene boarded his flight, took his seat adjusting it, pulled out his magazine, locked his seatbelt, and waited after hearing the instruction for takeoff to surprise the woman he loves.

Going about ten or fifteen miles from where Penny lived, she instructed Doris to "turn right they-a," Penny said, pointing after about a block on Monroe. Doris saw the Liquor Mart on the corner. The neighborhood was better and certainly a lot cleaner, Tetra thought as Doris pulled the car to the curve in front of the home where a vacant lot sit between it and the Liquor Mart. Penny had been talking and asking questions the whole ride, which Doris didn't mind answering if she could, with Penny saying, "Yep, yep," each time Doris answered correctly to her questions. Tetra said very little. Doris just knew she was praying for their safety.

"Let down yo window, let down yo window," Penny yelled from the backseat. "Daz's Squeak. SQUEAK!" she yelled, sticking her head from the window. "SQUEAKY! Squeaky! You not goin believe who dis is?" she said, getting out of the car running over, leaving the ladies in the car wondering which house was Judy's, both thought. This woman who was only forty-nine very soon to be fifty looked so old and used from life it was hard to imagine what in the world did she do to get to this point! "Squeaky," she said loudly, grabbing him by his hand and pulling this man with his wild gray hair toward the car.

"Let the window up," Tetra said, seeing him coming.

"We will be all right," Doris found herself saying with a smile, looking at the terror on Tetra's face. Doris had grown up to be a teenager with these people, but looking at them today, she thanked God for deliverance as both came to the front window looking in.

"Guess, fool, who dis is?" she said, slapping his head.

"I don't know, Penny, who you dun found now." He smiled, still looking. "She pretty," he said smiling, looking at Penny.

"Das Dois, Faye daught.a"

"Say what?" he replied.

"Dois Weeums, who used to run wit you."

"Naw, k-ain't be, who said?"

"Hello, Harold," Doris greeted him.

He laughed, a bit shy he had heard his real name. "You is Dois, nobody know that's my name but you. Ha you doing?" he asked, putting his hand in the window for a shake. He was younger than Li'l Penny. "Judy lia right da," he said, pointing to a nice little house right in front of where they were parked.

Tetra smiled getting out and Doris followed suit as she noticed a woman standing in the doorway behind a screen door. Squeaky opened the gate and, with manners, allowed the ladies to walk in. Penny wanted to stay outside with Squeaky and his li'l brown bag, Doris figured.

"Hello," the woman yelled to Penny and Squeaky. "Are you all coming in as well?" she asked.

"No, ma'am, we's waitin out he-a til theys finished," Penny yelled back, heading to sit over on the stoop of the liquor store with others.

"I think I'm going to get away pretty soon," Katia stated, coming in from her bedroom for breakfast.

"Oh and when did you decide this and where are you going?" Dillard asked, pouring the coffee in the cups and bringing them to the table.

"I'm going to go and see the place where I was before you came and rescued me," she confessed.

"Oh now you're feeling the need to search out your roots, huh?" Dillard teased. "Really, would you like me to come along with you?" he asked, being protective of his Katia now.

"Umm, maybe, you owe me a golf outing with Tiger you do remember?"

"How can I forget that, you bring it up every time I'm watching a golf tournament with him in it?"

"Dillard, so do you know if Doris left on her trip?" Katia asked, sitting with him drinking their morning coffee.

"Yes, as a matter of fact, she has. She called me from the plane."

"What do you think she will do with all this newfound information?" she questioned, taking a bite from her buttered English muffin.

"What would you like her to do with it, tuck it away?" he returned with a question.

"You know I'm not really sure, maybe write a book." Katia smiled.

"Now that's a great idea," Dillard agreed, "a great idea!"

Doris and Tetra walked up to the door seeing a warming smile on the face of the woman standing holding the screen door wide open.

"Welcome, God bless you do come in," she greeted them with a hug as each entered her very neat and tidy little house.

"Myrtle said you were here," she said, turning to Doris. "My, you look so much like your mother," she said, smiling.

"I have to take your word for that, Mrs" Doris waited for an introduction.

"I'm sorry, I'm Judy Mcnesse and your mother's best friend," she shared with a tear. "Boy, I sure wanted you, but that grandmother of yours was a piece of work, though I'm looking at you now and you turned out all right, thank you, Jesus," she said, looking up.

"This is my friend Tetra Parker and I'm Doris Williams-Woods," Doris shared. "So you knew my grandmother?"

"Edith, yes, and she knew me. When your mother went to the hospital to have your sister, she left you with me, until her mother, Edith, came and took you away, boy did I cry for days," she admitted. "Can I get you ladies some coffee, tea?" She smiled. "I know you are children of the king," she shared, smiling. "I reach out to all the people around here," she said, getting up to fix a fresh pot of coffee and a cup of tea for her and the ladies.

After getting everyone settled with their coffees, Judy, a short and stocky woman, excusing herself, went into her bedroom of her modest small home and came out with an old album. It was tattered from years gone by but still probably as neat as the day she first put it together. "Can I tell you something?" she asked, smiling at Doris. "I haven't looked at this thing in years, my Coke-bottle figure is gone, I'm now more of a two-liter," she teased, laughing sitting down and spreading out some papers on her polished coffee table. "See this," she said, handing Doris a Polaroid picture hard to see but it she said was a picture of Faye when she left for Europe with her new boyfriend Richard. "You musta been about two years old then, I figure." She smiled. "Now this is me and Faye at the county fair, we went every year like clockwork." She laughed. "Boy, we always had fun, yes, we was fast too! My mama, God rests her soul, stayed on us. I know I'm living on my mama's prayers today," she acknowledged. "Been saved now for over thirty some years, try my best to help others 'cause I was a mess!" Judy shared, laughing, shaking her head.

Judy had lots of stories to tell and share but she never got around to what Doris needed to hear from her. "Mrs. McNeese, didn't you have a brother?" Doris asked. Tetra stood stretching her legs, she said, and walked out the front door looking out on the street. She just wanted them to have some privacy really.

"I did, I had two brothers, Marcus, my older brother, and Dornelton Hawkins," she acknowledged.

"Are they still around?" Doris asked, seeing she had to be about seventy.

"One is still here on this earth," she answered, "but the other one, Lord have mercy," she cringed. "I told him about you, and Faye told him too," she began. "So where have you been, I mean, where did Edith take you after Faye died. Oh my, how that hurt me so," she shared, wiping tears. "She was so beautiful and full of life, I think Edith was jealous, treated your mama so bad, 'cause her old man ran off and left her. That's why Faye and I were always together. If you saw Faye, you saw me." She gave a sincere smile. "You know I loved my brother, but we hadn't seen him since he left for Nam. He wrote me though, and I wrote him. But I was so glad when Faye got with that white man, treated her nice, took us to nice places, paid for clothes, a new car, everything. She deserved it all. God was taking care of her even then, I didn't understand at first, but I see now with different eyes," Judy said. "Dornelton came back home handsome as can be with his air force uniform on looking good and Faye fell for him, thinking he was her way out of here.

But Marcus, that mean old good-for-nothing cuss, tried to confuse things and lied to Dornelton about Faye and he left and I didn't think would ever come back. Faye liked Marcus first, he was always messing with us, and like I said, we was fast, but Faye was afraid of her mama, so she made sure whatever she did was going to secure her way outta here. Marcus was with all the ladies, child, he's got babies all over the place and nothing to show for it," she confessed. "Marcus tried to get Faye one night and she ran to Dornelton while he was home on leave knowing he was the better alternative, but then he left her. So when she and I went to that club, lied to get in, we wasn't even eighteen yet. She met that white man and she stayed with him waiting for Dornelton to come back 'cause that night she was with Dornelton, she finally had lost her virginity, she told me. And she told me it hurt, it was nothing romantic about it, we both had to laugh about it. I didn't know until later how Marcus had lied and bragged about what he had did to Faye, that's why Dornelton hadn't come back, then when Faye got pregnant with your sister, I thought she would marry that white man, but he was already married. He still took care of her, he was a good man, and he loved Faye. I wrote my brother about Faye's death, and he asked bout you. I told him Edith had taken you off and I guess he just didn't even look in our direction anymore is what I thought."

"So you're saying that your brother is my father," she said, looking at Judy, questioning it. "Because that's the name Faye has on my birth certificate," Doris smiled.

"That's true." And Judy began to cry.

Doris sat next to her and embraced her. "So you're my aunt Judy," she whispered, smiling and holding her tight. She let her cry because somehow Doris sensed she needed it. Tetra came back into the house after a time and prayed with them before refreshing the coffee she and Judy had and tea for Doris.

"Dois, Dois! I gotta go," Penny said, standing outside the screen door.

"Penny, come in," Judy said kindly as she always did.

"Naw, that's all right 'cause you goin' try and save me and stuff," she said, running off the small porch.

Doris went out to see where she was gone to because she had brought her there and she really wasn't ready to leave.

"I kin take hu home, Dois," Squeaky, her brother, said. "You go head on and talk to Judy," he added, standing by his 225 Buick, while Penny sat on the passenger side grinning.

"Okay, thanks, and I will come by again before I leave, Penny, okay?" she said, hugging her through the window.

"Good seeing you, you look good." Squeaky smiled, getting in his car and off they went.

Doris walked back into Judy's home to hear the rest of the story.

Erene was reading his Bible on the plane and had fallen asleep when he heard the announcement of putting the seat in the upright position. Not having a lot of luggage, he grabbed his overnight suitcase from the overhead and hurried from the plane. He looked at his watch and noticed it was 10:00 p.m. when he was hailing a cab to take him to his wife's hotel the Crowne Plaza in New York. He had gone there before, that's the one she stayed at most of the time for her business trips, so he felt very comfortable as he sat in the cab heading there. He wanted this to be a wonderful time spent together and let her know he understood she would be there if she could. He couldn't believe the jitters he felt in his stomach as he thought about surprising Nora at her hotel. The cabbie made his way through the thick traffic that at times actually stopped altogether. "Thank you, Jesus," Erene said, thinking of his blessings he was realizing.

Dillard hurried home anxious to tell Katia he just closed out a major case and had purchased tickets to attend a golf tournament featuring Tiger Woods at Pebble Beach. He knew she'd go through the roof from excitement after waiting for a while now to attend.

He ran in putting his jacket over his shoulder and up the wide winding staircase of his gorgeous home. Going into her bedroom, no Katia.

"Katia," he called out, looking on the spacious veranda where she loved sitting sipping champagne. The parlor was empty as well. He knew she wasn't in the kitchen. Why? She didn't cook. They ate out or a chef came in for the evening. But he went into the kitchen on his way to his study and saw the note Katia had left for him.

"Good you found it, I know this is the last place you would look. I am laughing, darling. Anyway I'm going to go and try to clear my head of a few thoughts. I should be in touch in a few days. Me, Katia."

Without a thought, Dillard was on his cell dialing her on the phone!

After a few rings, Katia answered. "Hello, Dillard, I'm not sure why I took the time to write a note I knew you would call anyway." She laughed across the airways.

"Katia, stop laughing, you know I wouldn't like you going off on your own," he stated to her.

"Okay, okay, you're right, but I wanted to do this, and if I would have shared it with you, you wouldn't have let me go by myself," she replied.

"I came home today with the tickets for our golf outing, Tiger Woods is playing right up the street at Pebble and I have a few free days," he shared sadly. "So where are you going, and for how long?" he asked.

"See, my timing is always off, that's the story of my life. I won't be long, I don't think, I'll call you in a couple of days, Dillard. Please, it's important that I do this, I will call," she insisted, trying to get him to understand before hanging up the line.

Dillard thought of getting an investigator and having a trace put on the cell phone to see where she had gone but he knew her and didn't want to push her away. "She will call," he said over and over to himself after the call. He in his own way had fallen for the beautiful Katia. Everyone thought they were an item, but she was a friend that needed his help and it had grown into love for him though he wasn't sure about Katia's real feelings for him. She played along, as they wine and dined together, all around Hollywood celebs, and A-list friends who knew Dillard as an attorney to the stars had come to know Katia as well. "She will call," he kept saying over and over, sitting in the dimmed lights of his exquisite home by himself sipping cognac and thinking of his beautiful Katia.

Judy had calmed quite a bit and was showing Doris and Tetra some Polaroid photos she had kept through the years.

"So where is Dornelton, is he still alive?" Doris asked since they hadn't got around to it.

"You want to know him?"

"Sure, I've come this far," Doris voiced, smiling.

"You do?" she asked, smiling, looking up.

"He's all I got left."

She began moving around the house like a bee, closing windows and shutting the blinds. "We can go see him if you like," she kept asking, putting things away neatly again. "My mother and father passed a while ago and that stupid Marcus got himself killed messing with another man's wife, and when God gave me back Dornelton, I had lost everything trying to keep Marcus out of trouble. Dornelton is not the man he used to be, but we have each other," she said sadly, getting her shawl and purse while showing them out the door and locking it securely. "I'll drive my car, you can follow me if you want to see him. I was there earlier. I go every day," she said, pausing for Doris to answer.

"Let's go, I'd love to see him."

Judy walked out getting into her big Oldsmobile and backing from her driveway next to her home. Closing the gate back behind her, she was gone with Tetra and Doris following close behind.

By the time Erene arrived at the Crowne Hotel, it was late. He walked up to the desk flashing a warm smile at the lovely lady behind the counter. He had visited Nora before on her business trips for a day most of the time, but it just was something he really didn't like to do, traveling on planes was not his thing. He was very familiar with the hotel layout, having been there several times before with Nora.

"Hello, I'm here to see Nora James, please." He smiled. The clerk looked questioning, "Oh, I'm her husband, I'm surprising her and I got caught in traffic so I'm a bit late getting here," he said, looking at his watch.

"I can call her room," the clerk said, picking up the phone.

"It's so late, do you have to wake her? I'd like to surprise her," he said, showing off the bouquet of flowers he was carrying from the florist on the corner when he got out of his cab.

Hesitantly, she asked, "May I see your ID?" smiling across the counter.

Erene understood the concern and pulled out his badge as well to let her know he was a good guy.

"Okay, Mr. James, I'll take you up, the elevator is over there—"pointing"—and we will go up to the seventh floor and room 736." Smiling, she secured her drawer to leave when up walked another not-so-patient guest at the desk checking in. He wasn't willing to wait until the clerk returned, she tried to explain.

Erene stood smiling patiently for her to finish. After about five minutes, she just waved to him to go on up as she continued serving her customer and trying to please him with the reservations he was not pleased with after having his secretary make them for him.

Doris parked in the lot at the Oregon Veterans Home next to Judy. Judy hurried out of her car and through the doors and up to the front desk.

"Hello, Mrs. McNeese, is everything all right, did someone call?" the staff asked, knowing her brother's condition, a call could go out to her at any time. She was there earlier and the staff who was now on shift were surprised she came back so soon after leaving. It was quite a distance for her to drive at her age.

"No, how's he doing? There is someone special here to see him," she stated, now prepared to go to his room. "Please wait here if you don't mind, while I go in first," she said, pointing at Doris and Tetra to the waiting area, which was very nice. The waiting area had many of the medals and accolades of veterans displayed all over the walls.

The staff worker and Judy walked down the hall and through a door to Dornelton's room. It was so neat and tidy. His awards and accommodations were on the wall.

"Hello, Dornelton, hello, you're not gonna believe who's here?" she said, looking at what was left of this man lying in bed. "Get his uniform from the closet," she said, sitting him up in bed holding his back to keep him up. The worker was very accommodating to Judy knowing her very well. She came every day to see her brother.

"Thank you, now where is his hat?" she asked, putting what was left of a man in his air force dress uniform. Dornelton had one arm and no legs left after gangrene, a serious and potentially life-threatening condition arose when a considerable mass of body tissue died. It occurred after an injury that caused infection to the aged veteran. His Purple Heart was displayed over his bed where his sister Judy had placed it in a beautiful shadowbox style displayed with photos of the very handsome him during that time. He had spent a lifetime in the service of his country. Dornelton had served eleven years when by honorary appointment he was promoted by the board after review of his record to captain. His total service was thirty-five years. "Okay, please would you go and get the ladies that came in with me, I'll stay here with him," she asked, smiling.

"Sure, Mrs. McNeese." And off the worker went.

Dornelton communicated with her by blinking his eyes or squeezing her hand and his mind was as clear as a bell. Judy had him sitting up in his wheelchair when Tetra and Doris walked through the door. As Doris walked through the door, he began blinking wildly with his eyes before tears begun running down his cheeks. Tetra moved to a chair over to the side and prayed thanking God she shared with Judy who was crying as well.

"Hello, I'm Doris," she said, very tenderly holding his hand.

He looked, blinking with his eyes and squeezing her hand tight moving it up and down.

"Oh thank God, he knows, he's happy," Judy interrupted from his actions. Then he kept looking at Judy, moving his head slightly. "Okay, okay, I'll get you a pencil and paper," she said, going over to get it from his bed's nightstand. Judy positioned it on his chair and put the pencil in his hand. "You, know what? He had to learn to write with his left hand," she shared, smiling.

"I knew I'd see you before I die," he wrote, smiling.

Doris held her hand aside of his face and smiled.

"You look like Faye, so beautiful," he wrote. "I'm so sorry I wasn't there for you, my daughter."

Doris was in tears, letting him know she understood and he was forgiven. Judy said her heart was overjoyed as Doris patiently answered all his questions, and he answered the questions she asked as best he could, writing the answers out in the hours they were all together. The bars on the shoulder and medals pinned on the chest of his uniform, which Judy kept polished, were shining bright. He explained his pay grade to captain as well, because Doris asked. So many tears of joy were shed as prayer led by Tetra was ushered into the room.

"Will I see you again?" he wrote again, giving a squeeze to her hand before Doris left his side.

"I will be back soon," she said, seeing his condition and his age, he was seventy-four years old. "I love you, Daddy," she said, kissing his forehead before leaving the room. Doris was very pleased she had met her aunt Judy, pieced together her life, met her father, and she just knew Dana would be pleased with her bravery of not giving up.

CHAPTER 24

BILLY AND NADA HAD JUST returned home from filing the paperwork for Riley's adoption. Since Annie had left instructions in place regarding her daughter, it was a relatively easy matter that Billy had Oren, one of his attorneys at his firm, to handle.

"Thanks, guy. Nada and I are going home to celebrate with the girls, I will see you all tomorrow," he said, leaving the courthouse with Nada, very pleased it was not a messy matter with lots of fighting. Billy hurried to call Mrs. Mater to see how she was and to share with her about the matter of Riley.

"Take good care of her, and if she ever asks about me, tell her I love her, good-bye, Mr. Parker, and thank you for everything." And she hung up the phone.

William shook his head and walked into the room where Nada was playing dollhouse with the girls.

"Hi, Daddy," Peyton said, running to him for a hug. "Come on, Ri-ee." Peyton was learning her name. It had been two months since that awful day and Nada and Billy wanted to make sure Riley was okay, praying nightly to God on her behalf.

Riley looked at Nada who smiled and with a pit she'd have to pray through said, "Go to your daddy too, Riley."

Riley smiled and ran getting up on Billy's lap. Nada had been telling her each night about her mom and dad went to heaven and she was going to stay with them and be their little girl now.

"Mommy, you have to come and get a hug too!" Riley said, "Come, come, come."

Nada came over and wrapped her arms around everyone and the girls giggled loudly about all the playfulness.

"Okay, time for cake!" Billy announced and off they went to the kitchen calling Mil-ly as they ran.

Billy put his arm around Nada and walked behind them.

Erene hit the button and got on the elevator with another gentleman going up.

"Good evening," he said, smiling, holding his bouquet and showing his anxiousness to see Nora.

"Wow, either you're apologizing or you're a nice guy, which?" the man asked, smiling.

Erene could smell he had probably had a drink and was a little tipsy. "Oh, I'm the good guy."

"I used to be," the gentleman said.

"Oh, what floor?" Erene asked, standing by the buttons of the elevator's control.

"Seven," he replied, "got someone waiting for me, but I had to put the old lady down first." He smiled. "Know what I mean," he added, nudging Erene with his elbow.

Erene couldn't pass judgment on the man, but he said, "Don't you love your wife?"

"Sure, but it's not about love, it's the excitement of the chase," he responded. "Besides she will never find out. Furthermore, this little hot thing is too good to pass up, been after this for three months now," he bragged.

The man was in his sixties, no doubt, well groomed, and was wearing an expensive watch on his wrist, and shoes were top-notch, Erene noticed being so close to him on the elevator. He also mentioned he had been married over thirty-some years. As the elevator came to the seventh floor, the man straightened up his tie and brushed back his hair, sharpening his appearance. He wasn't a bad-looking guy, but clearly he was headed in the wrong direction, and Erene knew all the signs, because he had been there himself a few months ago, he thought to himself.

"Have a good evening," he voiced to Erene, heading in the same direction.

Erene smiled and slowed to let him pass, seeing he was in a hurry. Erene's learned scripture was going through his head. "Can a man take fire in his bosom and his clothes not be burned? [Proverbs

6:27]." Not that far behind him, he saw the man stop at #736. His first instinct was to stop him, but he was an investigator at heart, so he stood back pretending to go to another room. Soon the door opened and Erene saw with his own two eyes Nora's arms welcoming him in.

Erene threw the bouquet to the floor. "Lord, help me. Lord, have mercy," he pleaded, pacing the hall about three or four times up and back. "Okay, Erene, don't be stupid, think, Erene, think!" he was reasoning with himself. "You've got to confront this, and move on. But I love her!" His conscience was screaming loud. Erene looked and saw a couple coming from the elevator pointing at the flowers spilled on the floor. Erene hunched his shoulders pretending not to know about the bouquet scattered on the floor. He took a deep breath after the couple went into their room and went to the door. Erene figured someone would be up soon if the couple called for cleanup, so he had to move quickly. He immediately went to the door, knocking.

"Room service," he said from the pit down in his stomach. After a few more knocks, the gentleman opened the door with his shirt off and bare chest showing. Erene James held back tears wanting to flow as he made eye contact with Nora, his wife, lying in the bed in his favorite teddy. He stood there frozen he'd guess for about three minutes with the guy saying, "Get out, fellow, you're in the wrong room," is what he said first. Then looking a bit closer, he said, "Oh my, you're the guy from the elevator," quickly grabbing his shirt and shoes while heading out the door.

Erene conjured up everything he knew good before turning his back to walk out the door as Nora called to him from the room. "I'm sorry, Erene, I'm so sorry!" Without looking back, he left the hotel room and, within hours, New York City for his home in Maine.

Doris had a wonderful time, she told her aunt Judy, who was beaming from the visit to see her brother. "You ladies have warmed my heart, and one is my niece, oh, God is so good!" she acknowledged, inviting them back to her home for dinner and Bible study after prayer that night at her little church she shared gladly.

"We would love to, Mrs. McNeese," Tetra replied.

"Aw, call me Judy, but you"—pointing to Doris—"you call me Aunt Judy, 'cause I sure like the sound of that." She smiled, getting in her Olds and heading home.

"Aunt Judy, while you and Mrs. Parker are sharing recipes, I'm going to go and see Penny, I promised her I would stop by before I left, and since I'll be back to see Daddy earlier than planned, I'll go by now, if you don't mind," she asked, looking at both ladies for a response.

"Well, it won't be long before the meal, maybe an hour at the most," Judy explained, picking greens in the sink.

"Plenty of time," Doris said, "and you, my friend?"

"I'm so happy, God is good, and I love to see him work!" Tetra voiced, smiling and rejoicing to some of that good ole gospel music Judy had been playing as they cooked.

Doris drove about thirty minutes back to Penny's home and there she was sitting on the porch with friends, she'd guess. As the car pulled up, everyone scattered except Li'l Penny.

"Dois, what you do-in back he-a?" Penny asked.

"I told you I would be by before I left and I wanted to thank you for all your help in finding my aunt Judy," Doris said, smiling.

"Oh, she yo an-tee, 'cause I saw you in there with Judy and yall was doing that praying stuff," she voiced, fearing they were after her.

"Penny, prayer will never hurt you, and I do pray, a lot," Doris confessed, coming closer to sit in her expensive suit on the porch steps next to Penny. "I'd like to help you and Harold and a lot of people because that's what I do," she explained.

"You want to help us, why? What do you do, Dois?" she asked, looking directly at her.

"I own lots of businesses, you know, have you heard of the Salvation Army, Goodwill, Purple Heart, and other stores like that?" Doris asked.

"I used to work for the Goodwill at Fifty-fifth, but it closed now," Penny said. "You own all the Goodwill stores and stuff and you goin' help us git jobs, how?" she again asked, standing up waving some others that had been watching to come closer. "My ole man works at the carwash, been dar fa ova ten years, thank you kin hep him too?"

"Sure, very good." Doris stood up. "That is a small part of the things I own," she explained. "I will be back and I'm going to put you all to work." There were some grumbling. "Those who want to work," she clarified. "I'm going to put some businesses here in your neighborhoods and we all can help one another."

Penny and some of the others were smiling. "Dois, you really geow come beck and let us work?"

"I promise," Doris said, wiping tears. "I'm going to start working on it as soon as I get back to Los Angeles."

"She's a movie star friend of Li'l Penny!" someone kept yelling.

Penny had called Squeaky from her cell phone and he and some of his buddies pulled up four deep in his Buick Electra 225 known in the hood as "deuce and a quarter." There was a small crowd by now around the front of Penny's house.

"See, I told you, Squeak, she ain't no joke. I'll be he-a, Dois, I promise you I'ma be he-a," she said, reaching to hug her.

"Okay, see you all soon," she said as everyone scattered but still talking about the movie star from Hollywood.

Doris gave Li'l Penny an envelope for her and her six children is what she told her as she leaned in the car to say good-bye.

"Next time, Judy wannta pray, I'll let hu." She smiled waving, watching the car pull away.

Dinner was delicious. Home-cooked greens and rice, cornbread with ham hocks, apple pie made from scratch, and red Kool-Aid. Doris hadn't eaten like that in a long time. Tetra was bursting for joy as it brought back childhood memories for her as the three enjoyed stories each shared and revisiting the visit to Captain Dornelton Hawkins in the vet hospital, to a powerful prayer meeting and delightful sharing of the Word to feast from until Sunday.

Judy stood in her door waving. "Good night, until next time," she said, sharing a big smile.

Erene caught the first flight leaving heading back to Maine. When he got on the plane, he was furious, shaking from anger as he called a friend to meet him at his home and he would explain. He was just running off of adrenalin at this point and so glad he was now off the ground. Something was saying go back to the hotel but he knew that wasn't a good idea, and he thanked God over and over for getting him on the plane and far away from Nora at this point. He sat in his seat and thought to himself about what he would have done before his affair. He knows his affair with Adele is what saved him from strangling or coming very close to hurting his wife, Nora. His feelings were confusing his being, as he went from sad to hurting, and then anger to sorrowful for the whole thing. He was ready to renew his relationship with Nora, try and understand her side, and she was having an affair on him! He shook his head knowing he had a while before getting back on the ground in Maine and explaining about this whole thing. Maybe it's a bad dream, he thought reclining in his seat on his way back home shedding tears from the deceit.

Doris's plans were to spend time with Tetra after they got back to Washington State, but Tetra understood she wanted to return again to Oregon sooner than expected and Doris had caught a flight out that evening to Los Angeles.

"Mrs. Parker, thank you for being there with me and for me, your prayers strengthened me," she shared, driving home from Oregon.

"I'm glad you allowed me to share that moment with you, dear, it was priceless," Tetra shared, patting her hand as the two drove down the highway listening to "I Don't Mind Waiting on the Lord" on the car's CD player.

Katia had gotten a hotel room in downtown with plans to go out during the day seeing the place she once lived. It hadn't changed too much in three years since she was there. She had gone through a lot in the last months here and the successful career she had made for herself she had to lose to save her life. She had spent time locked behind bars before clearing herself with help from her friend and attorney Dillard Patterson. He had the difficult task of keeping the secret that she still existed but wanted no one to know, especially her son and family. Katia knew Marge had to be cleared of murder though she did serve the time for the brutal beating she had inflected on her before getting released. Dillard, her attorney, had made a monetary deal with Marge, the woman who had supposedly killed her with time served for the shooting, and leaving the area for good, Katia was now a free woman again.

Katia stood thinking over her past standing over by her window view. It was payback for what she had done to Nada François, Billy's then fiancée, she reasoned. Dillard was there through it all he had come to her rescue when she was left for dead after being shot. Thank God for her training, she tied a tourniquet around the wound and slowed down the bleeding. And after a few hours filled with panic of being found by authorities and hiding along a familiar riding trail for a whole day and night, she was finally picked up by Dillard after she contacted him on her cell phone. He brought her back to his home in an elaborate disguise, thousand plus miles away from the place she once called home. She knew she was out of danger but still had to hide if she wanted a normal life again. Now with all the legalities behind her, she still couldn't let anyone know her real story. Dillard had been there through it all. Thrown from a car, she had her cell phone in her jacket pocket. The screen was shattered, but it worked, and she called the only person she knew who wouldn't question her at the time as she fought for her life. Dillard agreed to fly out and get her. She hid away for two days waiting for her savior and dear friend who showed up and whisked her away. He was shocked at her condition but amazed at her stamina to live. Putting his own life on the line to help her, he gave her a new life. Katia gave a sigh as she looked out of the high-rise window view onto the city she once called home.

C H A P T E R 25

BILLY WAS SO THANKFUL TO God after being woken in the middle of the night and finding his household all safe and tucked in as he walked into the girls' room before heading to check on Trevor in the nursery. He smiled knowing how blessed he had been growing up without his father in the home and a praying mother who kept him grounded in the love of Christ even before he knew Him.

He walked into his study of his large estate of his home reflecting on him when he was a child of five and the small little church in Washington State where his mother came to live after leaving his father in Maine where he was born. He recalled sitting on the benches of the little church bundled in scarves and mittens as the preacher talked a long time about a lot of things he didn't understand. But today he understood how God was grooming him for this moment in time. Though growing up without his father in the household, God had given him a friend who lived next door whose father was a minister in the city. And he taught him along with his son about the love of God. He remembers how Pastor Reed, his best friend's father, had comforted him through the loss of his mentor, Mr. Parson, and it enabled him to return the comfort when Pastor Reed went home to be with the Lord. He stood and gave encouragement and comfort to his best friend and the family, which, they shared with Billy, meant the world to them. He couldn't believe the God who so many times spared his life as he stood by Glenn's bed and prayed for God to save his life after the accident, and he struggled to understand why God chose to allow Glenn to be in a wheelchair even today. But his understanding had grown so much from that little church and reading and studying God's word had been instilled in him not only by his mother, but God had placed the Pastor Cornelius Hathaway to guide him and over shepherd his path.

Billy sat at his desk and opened his Bible. So many times he remembered learned scriptures and verse from Sunday school and Mrs. Ann's Bible quizzes, he smiled contently. How the God he has come to love, respect, and adore knew him and what he would need even before he did.

"Hallelujah!" he shouted quietly from within. God had let him raise his son and he didn't even know until it was time that his heart was so broken from losing his fiancée to the September 11 tragedy that the only thing that would heal it was a Son's love, that's the kind of God he serves.

"Thank you, Jesus," he again said, thanking God for sending Nada, his wife, how he chose to trust God one day in a cabin in Kansas, and God declared, if you first seek the kingdom of God and his righteousness, everything else shall be added. "Through the loss of my grandparents, you kept me with a constant friend of Glenn Reed to keep me smiling. Oh God, thank you for it all, thank you for my mother, thank you for my father who repented after hearing your word and you made him a man after your own heart and brought my parents back together again as intended. Praise your name. God, I know I'm not worthy of all you have for me, but I trust you, and I know you are controlling it all."

He stood looking at his accomplishments, awards, and degrees of law framed on his wall, and now he had come to the end of seminary, which could lead into full-time minister. "God, the path for me as I look back today was written, and I'm so glad you allowed me to see with new eyes and a heart that hungers for you daily. And today, God, I surely thank you for my wife, my companion, help mate, and friend. My daughters and my son who I pray daily that I am an example for them to know you as their Savior, I know I am nothing without you, Lord. Comfort the families whose lives I encounter daily. My prayer is that they come to know you as their personal Savior and they allow you to lead and guide their footsteps in the path of righteousness. Thank you." As he closed the

Bible after reading and praying, he had left a note for Nada on the nightstand. He was about his father's business!

Erene couldn't believe the timing of his friend. He was praying it turned out this way but he had no idea that it would. He wanted someone to talk to and to share his burden as he pulled the car in his Maine driveway early that morning at four. William pulled alongside the curb.

"Thank you, Jesus," Erene expressed, getting out of the car.

William could tell he was visibly shaken and Nora was nowhere in sight.

"First, thank you for coming. I'm so sorry to bother you at this hour, but I honestly didn't know what else to do," he shared heavy-hearted, putting his key into the door of his home.

"Okay, Erene, please calm down. I'll make coffee and we can talk," William in his minister friend role said going into the kitchen.

Looking from cabinet to cabinet, he was able to get the coffee to the pot and before long into cups and the two sat at the kitchen table.

"William, you know when I spoke with you earlier last night at the church and you advised me on going to meet Nora."

"Yes, I thought that would be a great idea, since she wasn't able to be with you," Billy replied.

"Yes, well that was not true!" Erene shared. "I rode up in the elevator with the guy who I later met in her room half undressed together," he said, hurt from the recall.

"What? Erene, tell me, please, you didn't do anything stupid," he asked, standing now looking at the withdrawn body of a man slumped over the table.

"No, I was so hurt, I guess," Erene responded sadly.

"Thank God, and where is Nora, is she all right?"

"I walked out and left her there and made my way to a plane because who knows what may have happened had I not got out of there," Erene stated.

"Let's pray." Giving a sigh, William began to pray. As he prayed, he thought about the time he saw his girlfriend Jillian having lunch with a guy when she was supposed to be shopping, or the time he caught his best friend's wife with another man. "Oh God, have mercy, mend his heart," William prayed. He embraced Erene with brotherly love, and as William asked God's help for him, Erene could only shed tears and sobs. "Erene, pack a small luggage of necessities you'll need from your home," Billy suggested. "And just to clear your head, you can stay at my home in the pool house," he added. William was overjoyed he agreed knowing his brother in Christ needed comforting right now. And Billy didn't want to go through another scene like the one of Annie and Keith ever again. Erene was broken, hurt, and had found comfort from his brother who would pray with him and for him allowing God to do his work in his life.

Fletcher had spent some memorable days with his brother Hanson who was on leave from the navy and was soon going back to Iraq. The two had just finished helping their brother Malcolm and his girlfriend move into a bigger place.

"Guys, thanks I will have Sasha fix you guys dinner" he said smiling.

"No, Fletcher said, shaking his head. "I love Sasha you know I do bro, but her cooking? can't do it" he said patting his brother's shoulder.

Hanson looked at Malcolm. "It's true, but she's trying," Malcolm shared, agreeing by shaking his head yes.

"Let's do pizza at Rico's, Riggins is going to meet us, brother bonding," Fletcher said. "And this is going to shock you all, I will pay." He laughed with the brothers heading out the door laughing for fun and bonding.

Nada woke to the note from Billy saying he was meeting Erene at his home and that he would call her as soon as he could with what was going on.

"Honey, is everything all right?" she asked after getting his call.

"Honey, Erene is going to spend some time with us," he said.

"Okay, honey, what am I missing? William, where is Nora?" she asked, knowing the couple very well from church.

"Sweetheart, Nora is fine, I will explain it all to you when we get there. Please have the staff get the guesthouse ready. Thanks, honey."

Nada hung up the phone and it was soon ringing again, shocked when she heard, "Nada, this is Nora."

Nada thought for a minute before responding. "Yes. Hi, girl, what's up?" she teased her as she always did.

"Have you seen, Erene?" she asked.

"No, was I supposed to?" she asked.

"No, I know he and William are very close from their brotherhood meetings, so I thought he'd come to him."

"Nora, I'm not sure what you're talking about. I haven't seen or talked with your husband, what's going on?" Nada stated, questioning.

"Well," she said, smacking her lips. "He came to New York unannounced, and he saw something I didn't intend for him to see," she confessed.

"Is he all right?" Nada asked.

"He left here and I haven't spoken with him, but I hope he's all right," she shared callously, Nada thought.

"Nora, what did you do?" she asked as sister to sister, they knew each other for four years and had helped Nora with her wedding to Erene two years ago now.

"He saw me with my GM," she started.

"What's wrong with that, were you two having dinner, dancing, what happened that you wouldn't know where he is, or that he left and you're worried?"

"Nada, I messed up in his eyes. Erene is a good man, we were in my room ready to discuss the meeting he was chairing today," she said.

"Umm, so why did that upset him, Nora? You're not telling me something."

"I just hope he is all right," Nora shared again. "I should be back home today as soon as I can secure a flight."

"Okay, you don't have to tell me what happened. I think I can figure it out if he's that upset," Nada stated.

"I'm really sorry, he should have just stayed home and he'd be a happier man for it," Nora alleged, not taking responsibility of her infidelity.

Nada knew Nora, but she was having a hard time understanding the stance she was taking in this matter. "Nora, when are you going to be back here in Maine, if at all?" Nada asked.

"Well, I would have been there next weekend, but in light of what has happened and my general manager insisting I take care of this matter immediately, I'm coming sooner to see if I have anything left in the house or get my things," she stated.

"Sounds like whatever happened is causing you to write off your marriage?" Nada asked, a bit puzzled.

"What I'm doing now is what I'm planning to continue to do, which involves traveling because I love my career. I'm sorry I hurt Erene, and if you see him, please let him know I'd love to talk."

"Nora, I'm praying for you," she said before hearing the phone buzz loudly in her ear. Nada got up and got down on her knees and prayed for her friends.

Katia had a good night's sleep but was up late writing in her diary she was keeping now. She had plans today to drive around town and see some of the sights she remembered. She knew Dillard was probably worrying, but he shouldn't be, she thought. She has every intention of returning to her new life with him. She just needed closure. She sat having tea and buttered muffin in her hotel room and thinking about what she expected after this visit. She knew her life could never be the same anymore. But she was fine with living in plain sight as long as she could be around those she loved and Dillard was there for that, he had promised.

"I'd better call him. I don't want him worrying to death," she said, dialing his office to talk. She had been gone two days.

"Katia! Oh, it's good to hear your voice, are you okay?"

"Dillard, I'm fine. I'm enjoying myself and getting done what I need to live a restful life," she replied with a smile. "Do you realize how glad I am to hear from you?" "Dillard, you worry too much, I'm a big girl." "Okay, Katia, when are you coming home?"

"I love the sound of that, coming home," Katia responded. "I should be satisfied with my stay here by the week's end and I'll call you from the airport when I'm headed back."

"Katia, you flew from Los Angeles, where are you?"

"Dillard, I'll call, please stop worrying." And she hung up the line. Dillard, though sad she had hung up, was smiling she had called him.

Erene asked if he could just be quiet tonight and not eat with the Parker family. Billy understood he needed time alone and had the staff deliver his meal to the guesthouse. Erene sat reading his Bible trying to reason what he would do when he confronted Nora. Every time he felt hurt, he'd somehow remember Adele. Would Nora be hurt from his wrong if she had found out about it? He was angry, but why? Was he angry because he couldn't point fingers when he himself had done the same thing?

"Oh, my God, your word is so true," he cried out. "Help me to forgive her! Please help me do the right thing, make the right decisions, and say the right things if it's what you have for me," he cried out alone sitting by a dimmed light of the guesthouse on the Parkers' estate. Erene was saved and questioned about why this happened. He had repented. "Why, God, is this a test? God, help me to not fail. I'm so sorry it hurts so much, I didn't mean to cheat on her and hurt her, and now I know how that feels. God, help me to forgive her, she is my wife. Oh, my God!" Lying prostrate now on the floor, Erene cried out asking for mercy!

Billy had spent an hour talking and praying with his friend who was spending a few days with him. He and Nada had joined in the concern for what was going on. Nada had shared with her husband about the conversation she had with Nora.

"William, I'm not sure if Nora is willing to fight for the marriage. What feelings do you get from Erene?" she asked as they left tucking their children into bed and going into their bedroom for the evening.

"Honestly, Nada, he's not there right now. Erene is really hurt and I'm not sure what Nora shared but he walked in the room on her and the gentleman."

"What! Are you kidding? She didn't go into details but I certainly had no idea that's what had happened," she said sadly. "But, William, she did say she wanted to talk," Nada added.

"That's good, that has got to happen before anything can get resolved."

"Maybe they're willing to go to a marriage counselor if they chose to save the relationship," Nada shared.

"Well," Billy said after a moment at his bedside for prayer, kissing Nada, and lying on his pillow, "I'm praying he gets his broken heart mended and he's healed of hurt and able to forgive. My prayer is that he is allowing Jesus to lead and guide him in whatever direction this situation has caused."

"I know Nora and we are going to really have to pray," Nada confessed. "Billy, she's a real piece of work," she added, turning off her bedside lamp and lying on her pillow. "Good night, sweetheart."

Adele and Hilary had gone out to dinner with two of the guys they met from the church group. Adele was going because Hilary had asked her. She wasn't really interested in the guy she was double-dating with. The group of four had decided to go to Chili's restaurant and it really was a great time of conversation and lots of laughs and sharing. Hilary was really into her guy and he liked her. So all night it was obvious their relationship had grown in the month they had met. Adele was having a good time, but she was just out for fun. She wasn't looking for a relationship she was in love with Erene James, and even though he had broken off the extramarital affair, her heart had not stopped longing for him. "Was he still thinking about me?" she thought as Walter, her date, tried getting close to her all evening.

Everyone got through the night with no one really getting on one another's nerves, and each one respecting the other one's space. Hilary's date had drove them to the restaurant, so as everyone got in the car to leave, Adele asked to be dropped off first at her home. Sharing with Walter she had a wonderful time but making it clear to him there were no sparks, she said good night to him after he walked her to the door looking for at least a kiss. She went in and locked her door behind her. She looked around downstairs before heading up the stairs, peeping into Fletcher's room. He was home. Smiling, she turned and went into her room and turned on her VandrossCD, pajamas on, hopping into bed, and went to sleep.

CHAPTER 26

DORIS AND HER HUSBAND, RUSSELL, were sitting down to lunch in Beverly Hills near her boutique. He had left a meeting with some of their partners for the rehabilitation stores they had already opened around the Los Angeles area.

"Hi, honey, so glad you had time to meet and have lunch with me. I have the information you asked for regarding expanding our centers to Oregon." Russell smiled, pulling out the chair for his beautiful wife to sit.

"That's wonderful, dear, I never underestimated your ability to do the job I requested, you are a God-sent," she replied, pleased he was a great partner, not only as a husband, but Russell was business savvy. He nodded at the waiter to bring a bottle of his favorite wine before laying out the plans and what it was going to take to expand their already-growing rehabilitation centers and Goodwill stores. Doris had owned her boutique on Rodeo Drive long before meeting Russell Woods, but this venture was one they both shared in and was very passionate about.

"Honey, I think that's a wonderful idea to have some of the personnel go down to Oregon and train at the stores. It will allow them to have a paid vacation if they chose and for some a chance to see another part of the world, volunteer basis only, that way no one is obligated," Doris reasoned, now taking the menu to order lunch at McCormick and Schmick's on N. Rodeo Drive. "Russ, I didn't share this, but Sonjee has agreed to go with me to Oregon next week."

"Good, I'm glad you're not going alone, I'd worry too much." He smiled, giving the menu back to the waiter after ordering the meal.

"Yes, I called Aunt Judy today and she is bursting at the seams about me coming back so soon and I haven't even shared with her about Sonjee. She did mention Dornelton was still holding on and he remembered the visit," Doris explained with a heavy heart that the meeting had taken so long in coming. Doris would have liked more time with him, she thought.

"Now Judy is who?" Russell asked, taking a bite from his meal.

"Judy is his sister and a beautiful Christian, she has a testimony, Russell, that just warmed my heart. God allowed me to meet her. I had written all those folk off, I remembered nothing good from my childhood, and along comes Aunt Judy. God has such a sense of humor," Doris concluded, smiling.

"You go and enjoy your visit and spend the time you need with your dad, and I will make sure things here stay on track and things there are getting started. I've looked in the demographic area that you specified for the centers, and when all the papers are in order, you and I can go out and make the final assessment to start the project before opening the stores."

"Thank you, honey, I love you!"

"Dillard Patterson!" he heard is name yelled across the garage. It was Milburn.

"Larvy, how are things?" he replied back, now a lot closer so he didn't have to yell and wake up all Los Angeles.

"Haven't seen you out in the city much these past few weeks, things all right with Miss Norfen?"

"Katia and I are fine," he said, having spoken with her a week ago now. *She needs to come back from wherever she's gone to think. I really miss her,* Dillard thought to himself standing, waiting for Milburn's next statement as they walked in.

"Had Howard out on my yacht last weekend, he's a very nice man and knowledgeable retired lawyer," Larvy admitted. "Roslyn's mom sure took to him, he's a charmer," Larvy added.

"Yes, that's Mr. Stuns, he is a character, but as nice a guy as you'd find, so glad you guys hit it off," Dillard responded, now stopping in the terrarium to head in the direction of his office.

"Hey, look, Roslyn and I have been selected this year to give a Christmas gala and I'd love to put you and the lovely Katia on our guest list," Milburn asked, smiling.

Dillard wanted so much to say yes. But where is Katia? And what was she up to, and more than that, when is she coming back? "You know, let me speak with Katia, and I'll get back to you," Dillard said, bidding Milburn a good day turning and walking away.

Erene had spent a soul-searching weekend with the Parkers in their guesthouse trying to decide what to do next. Sitting down with William for breakfast before heading out to the precinct, he had decided after prayer that work was a good solution. "Good morning," William greeted him smiling.

"Thank you for your hospitality. I'm sorry if I inconvenienced you, but I'm so glad you were here," he shared thankfully.

"I'm glad you thought enough about me to ask, how are you doing?" Billy asked, pouring a cup of coffee to join him at the table.

Dante came in with both breakfast meals sitting them on the table, and with a good morning, he walked away.

"William, I called Nora this morning, she said she came in late Sunday night, so I'm going to meet with her are my plans," Erene said, taking a drink from the hot coffee in front of him.

"Are you sure? I'm not trying to discourage a meeting. I just want you to be in total control of you," Billy shared with his friend. "Hey, I know what you're saying. I have been praying for the past forty-eight hours about this. I've gone back and forth on the issue. I have reasoned and I just can't make sense why God would allow this, William. Nora says she's willing to talk. I don't know why or how I'm going to get through seeing her this soon, but I have to try. The longer we let it go on, the worse for me it will be," Erene confessed, then made a joke about coming over every morning for hash browns, pan sausage, and eggs after taking a bite of his delicious meal to hide the hurt.

"Erene, my calendar is not that heavy this morning if you need me."

Erene held up his hand. "Thanks, man, you have done more than enough already," he said as both men sat enjoying the breakfast meal. "Well, at least promise me you will call when the meeting is over," Billy asked prayerfully.

"Now that I can do," Erene responded, "great meal, thumbs-up to the chef." He smiled before getting his small bag from the guesthouse and leaving heading home.

Adele was sitting at her desk logging into her computer when Hilary walked into the office.

"Good morning A-dele," cheerful and bright was her greeting.

"Don't tell me, you really like him?"

"How did you guess? He's so thoughtful and kind and you saw for yourself what a gentleman he is," she shared, prancing around by her desk that was just across the hall in a cubicle near Adele.

"Don't you think you're moving pretty fast with this one?" Adele asked at her over-the-top persona.

"Adele, we met at church, duh, and I'm meeting his family next weekend."

"No!" Adele responded.

"No, what do you mean no?"

"No, I do not wish to join you in meeting his family," she stated.

"Adele, I can't believe you, not that I was going to ask you to come with me to Augusta to meet his folks, but I would think a real friend would," Hilary said, sitting now to start her day.

"Too fast, Hilary, way too fast!" Adele voiced, turning to give attention to her work displayed in front of her.

"So, Mother, this is where you grew up, huh?" Sonjee asked as the plane was landing at the airport in Oregon.

"Yes, Sonjee, this is what I had to come back to face in order for me to go forward."

"You know I grew up several miles from here, about forty miles on the north side."

"Oh really, Mrs. Reeves said she lived in Crystal Heights, a very posh neighborhood," Doris shared. "I met her not far from here, but that place is long gone. And the WASH building has relocated to the north side as well," Doris added. She was the lady who raised Sonjee. Doris had given her up for adoption at birth. "Your Aunt Dana had did most of the digging, but I was never opened to seeing any of these people again," Doris replied, embracing her daughter.

"So Dana knows about this place as well?"

"Yes, but she was on the other side. She had been adopted by a Caucasian family after Faye passed away in childbirth, and Edith, our grandmother, would bring her to see me about once a month when the Dematos came to visit their parents. Though Edith had taken me to live with someone on the east side of town."

"Wow, David Michael shared some of what Dana had shared with him about her childhood though I don't remember Oregon being mentioned."

"You know what, when we get home in Los Angeles, I'll share with you about our childhood if you want to know. That way you won't feel a need to return digging through the past to find the future."

Coming slowly to a stop, the plane was disembarking on the runway. Doris looked forward to seeing her Aunt Judy and sharing Sonjee, her daughter, with her. After a few frantic minutes of dealing with the overhead luggage, the two laughed seeing Aunt Judy standing in the area where the passengers were unloading holding a sign over her head with her own name on it. "Aunt Judy." She was turning around and around as the hurrying passengers made their way through the airport and passed her.

"Aunt Judy," Doris said, gently walking up to her.

"Oh my, thank God, you saw me 'cause I would be lost in this place, did you see my sign?"

"I did, I certainly did and thank you," she said, embracing her elderly aunt. "And, Aunt Judy," holding her around her shoulders firm but gentle, she said, "this is my daughter, Sonjee."

Judy stood with her mouth opened for minutes before the air Doris guess came back into her. "No, Doris, you didn't tell me, oh my god, she's as beautiful as a picture, she is," Aunt Judy shared. "Look at you, my God is good, he not only has a daughter but a granddaughter too." Judy by this time had others sharing her excitement of meeting her great-niece and niece again just from hearing her. She caught them both by the hand after she had turned Sonjee loose from her embrace. "Doris, I've cooked a lot so I hope you're hungry, and you, you're so thin, do you eat?" she asked, laughing as the three walked out the airport door after the bellhop put and fit the entire luggage brought in the trunk of Judy's vintage Oldsmobile.

Erene took a deep breath and walked up to his door at home. He could see Nora left the garage up a little, so he knew she was home. He walked in and noticed she was sitting on the sofa reading her Bible.

"Erene, I'm so sorry, please forgive me. I love you," she voiced, starting to cry.

Erene had thought over and over about what he would say and God only knows what he would do when he saw her. She looked so helpless and so vulnerable sitting there as he approached her on the sofa. He dropped his small carrying case in front of her. Her eyes were showing fear as he reached down and picked her small 110 pounds with all her clothes on frame and embraced her gently.

He looked at her with a broken heart and sad eyes, joining her with a passionate kiss while walking her to their bedroom to make unbelievable love.

Katia had been gone about two weeks and had only called Dillard one time. She was getting past a lot of baggage she had stored up in her mind. She visited so many places she had seen before, but they seemed different, it was a different time. The once-famed amusement park had closed and relocated, billboards were weathered from storms past, and the trees were so tall they appeared to reach the sky, Katia thought gazing over the land she once knew like the back of her hand. She took a drive along a long dusty road, the places she remembered seemed so long gone. All she saw there now was a huge dilapidated barn and broken-down fences with lots of tumbleweeds and brush blowing by.

"Hee-haw to the Okay Corral," Katia said, throwing a dry twig in the air letting it fall to the ground. The pavement had cracks and grass growing up through so many places it was in disrepair. "And I thought this was good times," she said to herself, getting back in her car to drive away.

Aunt Judy drove very slowly across the highway back to her home. "So, dear, you think you're going to like your visit?" she asked, looking back over her shoulder at Sonjee from the front seat.

"I think so, Aunt Judy. Mother has told me a lot about Oregon. I went to school at Gonzaga, not far from here, for a while before moving to Los Angeles with Mother."

"Oh you did, so seeing all these trees around here doesn't bother you." She smiled.

Sonjee didn't want to get into her growing up in Oregon with her adoptive parents because that would open up another door, she reasoned, and she didn't want to go there.

"Well, I'm so glad your mom brought you to see me. I thought my brother was all the family I had left in this world," she shared sadly, "and you see, God gave me Doris and now you." She smiled then laughed, pulling into the driveway of her quaint little home.

Judy had a wonderful dinner prepared for the ladies, too much food for any one of them to consume it all. "Well, well, you can eat, but where you putting it?" She laughed as the love was shared around the room.

Sonjee teared a bit because she reminded her of Beulah Reeves, the woman who had raised her all her life. Dinner was filling and delightful as Judy shared story after story, and Sonjee and Doris answered questions she had concerning family. Judy had taken out pictures and Doris had brought pictures to share as well. Sonjee was delighted hearing the stories about her childhood told by her real mother, Doris, who no doubt was told the stories by her dear beloved adoptive mother, Beulah Reeves.

Sonjee laughed seeing the Polaroid snapshots and hearing about the camera. As a matter of fact, Judy had an old Polaroid camera she kept. It didn't work, but fun nonetheless. She had purchased it from the money her brother had sent her from Vietnam for her sixteenth birthday. Judy's guest room was all dolled up in lace trim on the curtains and stiff starched dollies on her dresser.

"Now just wait," she said as both walked into the room seeing one tall huge bed. They didn't have a problem sleeping together. It was expected. They could have gotten a hotel room if they wanted to go that route, but they wanted to spend time with their aunt Judy.

"Oh I've got my pajamas and Mother has hers, we will be fine," they shared, laughing, embracing Judy and enjoying their surroundings of her warm, cozy home.

"Now, baby, if Doris kicks you, there is a roll-away bed in the closet, you can pull out," she teased.

Everyone commented, sharing a laugh together. Doris thought about the roll-away, she wasn't sure Sonjee even knew what it was, but on second thought, she probably did.

"Thanks, Aunt Judy, good night."

Erene must have been traumatized. He didn't even think about what he was going to do, it just happened, and now both lay in bed surprised and dazed after it was over. Feeling guilty, he guessed, Erene got up and went into the shower while Nora sat on the bed wondering what was going to happen next because that was amazing!

After about fifteen minutes, Erene came from the bathroom dressed in his sweats. He had taken a day off from the office to talk with Nora.

"Nora, I'm sorry, I didn't mean for that to happen," he said, apologizing for his action.

"Don't apologize, Erene, that was amazing, you're amazing. I'm so sorry I hurt you," she confessed, getting up to put her hands around his waist.

"Nora, let's go to the family room, please," he suggested.

"You go. I'll be out in a bit," she replied.

Erene walked out and Nora headed to the bathroom hearing her cell phone ring. She answered it and took care of whatever the question was hanging up and running in to the shower. Erene had made coffee when Nora came out with a beautiful housedress, which Erene didn't recognize.

"It's beautiful."

"Thank you. I went shopping the weekend and bought some new things," Nora replied.

"Sit down, Nora, let's talk," Erene started, handing her a cup of hot coffee with saucer.

"I was ready to move, I didn't think you would ever be able to forgive me," Nora shared.

"I didn't either, my heart hurts so much you wouldn't believe, but I guess I love you," Erene confessed, wiping a tear.

"Oh, Erene, I'm not sure what happened. I love you. I don't know what got into me. You're the best thing that as happened to me, and I don't want to lose you," she admitted, pouring her heart out to him.

Erene was hurt but he had done the same thing. He just didn't get caught. Would she be forgiving if it was the other way around? Had is love for her diminished or hers for him? That romp sure didn't feel like it had, he thought sitting looking at her defenseless side.

"Nora, are we saying that this marriage can be saved? Can we find trust again?"

"Erene, I promise you that was a mistake that I will not repeat," she confessed.

Should he tell her about the conversation in the elevator? Apparently the gentleman hadn't. She's confessing to being caught this one time but he knows it's been going on before she got caught, but again, he was guilty too!

"Nora, we need to get counseling, are you willing?" he asked.

"Erene, no, I know we can get through this. It would be harder if we start letting other people into our business," she argued.

"But what will happen if you continue traveling? How will I know that you're not going to do this again?"

"Erene, I promise, I want this marriage to work. I don't ever want to see that look of hurt in your eyes again," Nora pleaded her case, and after an hour or so, Erene had given in to her suggestion, calling to let his friend Billy know he was going to continue to fight for his marriage.

Nora had made promises of less travel and she'd be more involved in things he liked and more committed to family life. As a matter of fact, this Friday she was going to her in-laws' home for dinner. She hadn't been to Erene parents' home since his younger sister's high school graduation a year ago now. She never had the time. Did Erene give in because he had an affair too? She would never know because he promised himself that he would never cheat on Nora again with anyone.

"I'm praying for you, Erene, and I'll see you Tuesday at the meeting." Billy laughed, knowing his brother in Christ needed encouragement. "Aha, you got me, now I have to make a call to one of the other brothers," Erene shared, laughing through what Billy knew was clearly hurt.

The next day, the ladies enjoyed a hearty breakfast prepared by Judy who enjoyed cooking for her newfound family.

"Are you sure you two don't want to come back home, Oregon?" Judy asked as they got their jackets to head to the veterans' home to see her brother.

"Judy, we are certainly enjoying ourselves and you are making us feel right at home especially with those home-cooked meals prepared with love," Doris shared, embracing her.

"And I am going to end up spending at least a week every day in the gym and I've only had dinner and breakfast so far," Sonjee teased about the size portions Aunt Judy served.

With her comment, the ladies all shared a laugh including Sonjee. As they drove the hour and a half to the Veterans Center in Oregon, Sonjee was actively asking all kinds of questions.

"So, Aunt Judy, did Grandma Faye like dancing?"

"Hahaha," she laughed. "Your grandmother Faye love dancing, however, she had two left feet it seemed, but that didn't stop her from dancing to any beat. But she was a lousy dancer, though she was so beautiful men didn't mind they would always make excuses for her missteps and asked her over and over."

"I love to dance, you must come and see me sometime," Sonjee said.

"You know, thank you. I would love to, dear, you're all the family I have left. I pray we stay in touch," she said sadly but from her heart.

"Aunt Judy, there is no way you're going to get rid of me now," Doris teased, lightening the mood, "I've got to learn those recipes," she added.

"Aunt Judy, do you have children?" Sonjee asked because it really hadn't come up in all the time she had been there.

"God never blessed me with any of my own, but I've raised lots of children. That's why I always had your mother when Faye went out. Faye had left her with me when she went to Europe on vacation a year before she got pregnant with her sister. I hadn't seen her around for a while until she showed up on her way to the hospital to have your sister and that mean ole Edith came and took you," she responded. "I searched and searched for you after asking her over and over about you. She said you were with family and stopped me from coming around. When we heard Faye had passed, I insisted on raising you but she had taken you off and I never saw you again," she explained teary-eyed. "Anyway"—wiping her face—"the church I attend is filled with single-parent families. The mothers are the breadwinners and most times the children are left to their own devices and most lend itself to mischief. I've made myself available for them all. Some I've cared for in some capacity since they were babies. Kermin, Penny's oldest son, will be my first to graduate high school this June. I'm so proud of him. He's very smart."

"Oh that's wonderful, Aunt Judy, so does he have plans after high school?" Sonjee asked.

"He does, he could be the next president of the United States," she said with a giggle, certainly proud of that young man she had mentored.

"Aunt Judy, I'd love to meet him before we leave."

"Oh sure, I'd love for him to meet you as well, he comes to church with his grandmother," Judy replied, now pulling into the parking lot. So excited for Donelton's visitors, she hurried from the car into the double doors and signing in at the desk.

"Hello, Mrs. McNeese, he's been waiting for you today, he says he's tired."

Judy wanted to go in alone to get him presentable to see his guest. She could tell he wasn't at his best but he squeezed her hand that he understood and knew she was there. Dornelton's weak-looking eyes got really big when he saw Doris.

"He recognizes you," Judy voiced, smiling, and he forced the best smile he could on his face.

He reached for Doris to come and hold his hand. She obliged and kissed his forehead and rubbed his face saying hello. Judy grabbed his tablet and pencil and wrote, "This is your granddaughter," and put her arm around Sonjee as she put the tablet in from of him. He was squeezing Doris's hand so tight and tears were running down his cheek.

"Hello, Grandpa Captain Hawkins," Sonjee voiced, smiling.

Doris held him up on the pillow and allowed his hand to be free as he reached to hug his granddaughter, then nodded for his tablet to write. Judy helped sit him up in bed comfortably, and Doris took a chair by his side. Sonjee sat on the bed near his writing table and tablet. He started off by introducing himself and Sonjee did the same.

"Oh thank God," you could hear over and over from Aunt Judy and Doris. "He had held on long enough to see another blessing God had saved for him," Judy whispered.

He and Sonjee bonded immediately. She thought about her training in Africa and all the people she had helped. Now she's meeting her grandfather who had given so much of himself as a commander serving a company-size unit in his military service. He would need another tablet by the end of the visit, because he had so much he wanted to say to Doris and Sonjee, and they certainly wanted to know all things about him. Judy was shouting for joy as this scene comes to an end. God is good and His mercy endures through all generations.

Katia entered the huge hospital entrance and looked around at the changes that had taken place. They had gone through a major renovation and had added a new hospital and another wing to the existing building structures she once remembered. She looked at the director on the marquees wall plaque, and it was clear things had certainly changed from the last time she was there. She quietly walked around from floor to floor ending up in the place her office used to be.

"May I help you?" She turned to see this woman standing behind her looking at her trying to turn the knob of the door.

Thinking quickly, Katia explained, "I'm turned around. I'm lost, can you direct me out of here?" she asked, looking at her best friend Molly who certainly didn't recognize her with the blond hair.

"This way, ma'am," she said, showing her out to the corridor. Katia wanted to ask more questions but she was afraid to blow her cover and end up giving somebody a heart attack. She gave a thankful wave and left.

Fletcher, Riggins, Malcolm, Ariel, and Adele stood waving good-bye to Hanson who had spent three wonderful and memorable weeks with his family. He was on his way back to Iraq to fight for his country and they were certainly proud. He had introduced them to a buddy, Vincent Charles, at the airport who was on his way back too after visiting his family. The guys looked so handsome in their Midshipman Third Class single-fouled anchor on the right collar point of their dress uniforms, Adele thought, wiping tears saying, "Good-bye and see you soon."

"Now you have the Skyping instructions, right, 'cause I surely can't trust Malcolm to Skype with me." Hanson laughed, sharing love.

"Bro, I will miss you, stay safe." And they watched the four guys in his unit board the plane to leave.

What a week! Like clockwork, every day the ladies made their way to the Veterans Center for their visit. Judy had held on to the faith that Dornelton was getting better and maybe he could come home for a visit. Sonjee even braved the drive down on Wednesday in her aunt Judy's Oldsmobile. She wrote on her granddad's tablet that she also had driven a tank! He responded, "Haha. Judy is still driving that old Olds, huh, that is a tank!" It was one of the many precious moments captured from the visit. By Friday, Judy rolled Dornelton out to the dayroom where he sat and wrote on his tablet with others like him, wounded veterans. Nobody knew how many days Dornelton had left to serve, but he was pleased he got the chance to see the daughter he knew he had and the cherry on top, his granddaughter.

CHAPTER 27

BILLY SAT IN HIS OFFICE reading over some briefs when Oren, an attorney on his staff, tapped at his door. He nodded and Oren came in giving him the final papers for Riley Poultons legal adoption and name change.

"It was really quite easy since Annie had all the legal papers in order. She had requested that you and Nada Parker become Riley's legal guardians if something ever happen to her anyway, you were her godparents, so it was just a matter of changing the child's name," he informed Billy.

"Oren, thank you, I appreciate you getting this done so timely. We are trying to bring as little friction in Riley's life as possible."

"How is she doing?" Oren asked.

"She's doing well, she has those moments when she misses them both, but we just try to be there, and she's only five, so we keep her involved with loving time, hoping that works to help her get pass it and heal her little broken heart," Billy said, heavy-hearted this had happened.

"Well, sir, good luck. I applaud you and Nada, she's a good woman taking in another woman's child."

"Yes, she is, and she's doing her best not to make her feel like an outsider. Nada's a wonderful mom to Riley and a God-sent wife for me," Billy boasted to his fellow attorney.

As Oren was leaving, Billy looked up seeing Erene coming through the door.

"Hello, it's good seeing you, what's happening?" he said, getting up to greet his friend.

"Just coming by, I missed you the past few Sundays after service. Nora and I are trying this thing where we are trading off the visit. I go to her two weekends where she is and she's home two weekends out of the month, so for now it's working, how about you adding another?" Erene asked.

"Funny you would ask, my attorney on this case just brought me in the final adoption papers and I can't wait to share with Nada. Speaking of Nada, she wanted to know when you and Nora were coming out to the house for dinner?" Billy asked, looking at him smiling.

"You know what, soon, I really want to get out there again. Your chef impressed me with just breakfast," he teased. "No, I'd loved for Nora to see how the other side lives, you know, a family and children, your estate isn't bad either," Erene acknowledged.

"Erene, I'm just glad you guys recovered from that incident and things are back to normal, right?"

"We are certainly working on it. I forgave her now, I have to put it behind me. I can't keep bringing it up if I want it to get better. But I'd be lying if I said the trust we had was still there," Erene shared.

"Did you guys seek counseling, you know the church has a great staff on our board."

"Bill, we decided to do this without counseling from an outside source. It's just a matter of me forgiving her."

Looking at his body language, Billy could tell he didn't want to go there, what was done he wanted to forget, and Billy prayed that it was truly forgiven.

"I'm leaving, let's walk out together," Billy suggested, getting his coat and briefcase, logging off the computer, and waving to Abby at the front desk to ride down the elevator with Erene on his way home.

Russell and Doris were very busy getting all the policies and affidavits and supporting documents to do business in Oregon. Doris was making trips back to Oregon twice a week, sometimes with Sonjee when she was able or not busy pursuing her dancing career. Russell had concerns for her health though she assured him she was fine and in close connection with her physician.

Dornelton was the same it appeared, and she enjoyed the stories he wanted her to know about his life. There were years of active-duty pictures he had kept in albums, thanks to his sister's caring hands, his travels from base to base and country to country. Doris was very proud of his service to this country and only wished he could enjoy life after the war for all he gave. She and her aunt Judy bonded more and more. Judy was so happy to introduce her niece Doris to her church friends, and Doris was overwhelmed to see her smiling and happy, some of the burdens of life were lifted for the both of them.

Six months had passed and Russell had finalized the business expansion, working tirelessly and long hours. He knew how important this venture was for Doris, and he wanted not to waste time getting it done.

"Good evening, Aunt Judy, how are you today?" Doris asked, calling her as she did every day at 6:00 p.m. since she met her.

"I'm blessed, dear, how are you?" she'd ask.

"I'm well, and your visit?"

"Oh he's fine, he's still talking about Sonjee and, of course, you. We have delightful conversations now. He reminded me about a letter he had wrote me some years ago, and you'll never guess." She giggled. "I've been sitting here since I got back bout an hour ago going through his letters, 'cause I kept every one of um, and tomorrow when I go back, I'm going to read it to him, 'cause he was right. Every time I'd write him, I'd say now don't you get killed, and come home safe, and he would say he would never die until he saw his daughter 'cause he knew you were somewhere and he just believed he'd see you, ain't that something," Judy expressed across the line.

"Yes, Aunt Judy, he's a remarkable man with a remarkable story. I only regret that I didn't come looking for you sooner," Doris shared. "Well now, dear, don't go beat yourself up bout that. God controls and who knows what that outcome would be like. We know this one was beautiful. God always knows what He's doing, always," Judy said.

Then there was an interruption. "Hold on, dear, this phone is ringing, I tell you, what happened to the day when you could talk without somebody else coming in on the same line. I'll be right back, dear," she said, clicking over her caller ID. It was the veterans' hospital and the news she thought she'd hear long ago. "Thank you, you all did a wonderful job. I'll see you all tomorrow," she said.

"Yes, Ms. McNeese."

"Oh, would you please call that other number on his file for me, it's long distance and I'm not sure if I could dial right now," she requested to the staff on the line.

"Sure, Ms. McNeese."

"Good night!" Judy hung up the phone and sat reading letters to soothe her heart. Maybe five minutes after Judy hung up the receiver, Doris called back to check on her because she had gotten the staff call to her. "I'm fine. I have a lot to do tomorrow, so I'm turning in, dear."

"Aunt Judy," Doris shared, letting tears for her run down her cheek, certainly felt though unseen through the phone. "I love you."

"I love you too, good night."

Katia was shaking as she turned off the highway and down a dusty road about two miles. She could see a ranch in the distant was still intact. It looks like life had stood still. The huge gate was wide open, but she had no intention of going in. Katia only wanted closer and to put all the nightmares she had experienced from her trauma there to rest. She had turned her car around heading out when she saw a truck coming toward the ranch.

"There is no way I'm going to talk," she thought, looking at this huge truck coming directly toward her. It stopped a few inches in front of her and Katia could see it was a blond woman. Not giving any thought to what might happen, she turned the wheels of the car and swirled out, kicking up dust and rocks getting out of there. She looked back to see the woman throwing her hands in the air, showing disapproval for that action. Breathing hard, she slowed down and made another turn heading to the shores of the Atlantic River.

Nora and Erene seemed to have dodged a bullet in their relationship and all was right with their world. She drove her own car to and from the airport these days.

"Honey, I'm home, but I'm going to stop by our cell service provider and have them check my phone, it's been messing up all week and I've lost all my contacts," she said, very frustrated with the matter.

"Okay, darling, sorry to hear that. I know how annoying that is, so I'll start dinner," he said, smiling.

"Thanks, hun, sounds good." Nora pulled into the lot, and before long, she was at the counter explaining her problem. She had turned her device over to the rep at the counter. He stood, checking it out, pushing buttons, and asking the same questions again and again. "May I have a readout of my calls while you're checking things out anyway,?" Nora requested, flirting a bit to get things done.

"No problem, let me get that for you." And he left going into the back. Coming out again after ten minutes, he informed her she probably needed a new device and he'd be glad to order one for her and then handed her a thick stack of papers for three months of backlog, he explained. "Wasn't sure how far you wanted." He smiled.

"No problem, this is fine." Nora had very important numbers that she did not want to lose. She sat down again in the waiting area as they continue to diagnose her device to see what was causing the problem.

At closer look, she saw they had also given her Erene's cell phone numbers as well. She looked seeing numbers she recognized as the precinct, his mother's, church, and others. He's so predictable, she thought smiling. Then another number kept repeating itself over and over. "Umm, I'll check it out when I get home, whatever he was working on required a lot of talk time," she reasoned, looking at the length of each call.

"Mrs. James, we have ordered you a new device, should be here in a couple of days, and hopefully, this one will work okay until we can change it out. It seems to be working fine right now?" he said.

"Okay, so I'll pick up the new device in about two days?" Nora asked, clarifying what she heard.

"Oh did you want me to shred those for you," he said, reaching for the stack of papers.

"Oh, these, ah absolutely not, I'm going to keep all my numbers until I get my new device." She smiled and walked out the store.

Adele had agreed to meet with Walter at the park near where she worked downtown. He was a financial advisor for a major bank and, like Adele, bubbly personality.

"I can't believe you finally said yes," he voiced, walking up to the bench where she was sitting.

"Why, hello to you too," Adele responded, smiling.

"So is this always here, I've never noticed it, and I pass this park all the time," he asked about the craft fair.

"It's here once a week during the warm weather and sometimes it brings in a good crowd," she said. "Let's try the burgers from Jake's, they're pretty tasty," Adele suggested, getting up seeing he had not been here before.

"Sounds good, how about this table?" Walter asked while Adele was getting napkins for the burgers.

Adele laughed and talked and enjoyed the hour spent with Walter. She found out that the guy Hilary was dating was his cousin and they grew up together. He wasn't pushy and seemed to have settled on the fact that all she wanted was a friendship. He thanked her for the lunch and hurried off as not to be late getting back. She walked back around the corner to her office to bring another day to an end.

When Aunt Judy got to the Veterans Center the next day, she was met by Doris, her niece. Doris had gotten a flight out that night after getting the call that her father had passed away. She wanted to be there for her aunt Judy and she could tell it was a great idea.

"Oh, Doris, I'm so glad you're here," she said, coming over to embrace her. "So how did you get here so fast?" she asked in Judy fashion.

"Aunt Judy, I got a flight out after the staff here called me last night," Doris explained, holding her aunt's hand.

"So you're here by yourself?" she asked, looking around for no doubt Sonjee.

"I came with—" Then Finley stepped from another room where he had been talking with one of the ladies on staff about the center.

"Why, hello, Aunt Judy," he said with his British accent, surprising her.

"Doris, your husband talks funny." She giggled.

Doris laughed and Finley certainly laughed as Judy looked at them puzzled with her statement and the reaction.

"He does talk funny, doesn't he," Doris teased to get her aunt smiling.

"I'm sorry but he sounds like that little green lizard from television," she said, hunching up her shoulders and lifting her hands upward.

Finley was laughing so hard he turned to hide his face and Judy moved over and whispered to Doris, "You got an old one, huh? He's handsome though, sharp dresser," nudging her gently.

Doris thought, *What will she really think when she sees Russell, my husband, he's Caucasian!*

But the laughing was good for everyone right now. Doris soon introduced Finley, her butler, to her aunt Judy.

"A butler, well, sir."

As they sat at the funeral director's office getting all the plans laid out for the Captain Dornelton Hawkins's home-going, Aunt Judy had shed her tears, but realized he went home peacefully and happy his life had meaning. They put him away quickly but certainly not quietly for the hometown boy. His service was beautiful and the neighborhood watched in awe as Captain Dornelton Hawkins, the hometown hero, was carried in his coffin by six of his fellow soldiers, an unbelievable dance by his granddaughter Sonjee, songs sang heavenly from Aunt Judy's choir members, a flag presented to Doris, his only daughter, his accomplishments of service presented to all over a big screen. It was a home-going the small town would remember for a while, which included an amazing twenty-one-gun salute. Larvy had showed up again in Dillard's office since he had not gotten back to him with an answer on his invitation.

"Dillard, my man, how are you?" he said, entering into his office.

Dillard held up his hand. He was on the phone. "See you then."

"Milburn, why are you in my office? Let me see, you want me to say I accept your invite."

Larvy just gave an "okay" look on his face.

"Okay, I'll be there."

"Good, now see how easy that was. Not sure what gown Roslyn's wearing, but is Katia coming?" Is what he really wanted to know. Dillard turned Milburn toward the door and slowly pushed him out.

"I will be there, Larvy!"

"Seven o'clock, Patterson, seven o'clock," he echoed as Dillard pushed him out, locking the office door behind him.

Nora sat in her hotel room the next week looking over the readout of numbers from Erene's phone. She called a number that showed up about five or six times.

"You have reached the County of Maine," was a recording, call back during business hours. Nora thought nothing about it because in Erene's work, they worked a lot with the county. She called some other numbers and was satisfied they were business too. Further down the list, she saw a number that repeated itself a lot, but it was always after five, so she called the number.

"Hi, Adele, hello, hello."

Nora hung up the line. Then she took out a highlighter and went down the list highlighting the number and the minutes used for each call. *What was that name? I'd better write it down,* she dialed again.

"Hello, hello," then Adele hung up the line. She didn't recognize the number. She shunned it off and continued watching her television program.

"Nora, you're crazy," she said to herself. "Erene has forgiven you, now you're trying to find something on him, you know you won't find anything, the guy worships the ground you walk on, be thankful," her conscience was saying. "But what if he forgave me and made me out to be the bad guy and he's having an affair on me, maybe that's why he forgave me without a fight?" she reasoned in her head, playing the devil's advocate. "Auuuug, I hate that I got caught, I mean I really didn't want to hurt him, but now I know he's watching every move I make and my GM won't even talk to me anymore!"

Ring. Ring.

"Hi, Erene, I was just sitting here thinking about you. Yes, all good stuff," she said. "I will see you on Friday, my flight is already booked and comes in about noon." Erene informed he was going her way this week and letting her know to expect him because neither wanted any more surprises. "My phone, yes, it's working well, I picked up the new one, so I'm back in business. You work a lot with the county, don't you?"

Erene was surprised by that question but thought nothing of it other than conversation. "All the time, why?"

"Just asking. I was looking at *CSI* and Eames and Goren were interfacing with the county on the show," she lied.

"Yes, that's one of the entities we work with a lot," Erene restated. "Well, sweetheart, tell me about your day?" he asked, settling in to talk to his wife and lover.

Riley was easily becoming comfortable with her new family surroundings. She loved being a big sister to Peyton and Trevor, and Nada and Billy strived hard to assure her she was a member of the family. Billy had just got off of a phone conversation. He had been speaking with Keith Poulton's mother who had called regarding Riley. Mrs. Poulton's concern for her granddaughter was if they could make up for her missing her parents. She thought it was only right that Riley stay with her family. Billy really didn't want to go into it with her being she was only doing what was expected of her. Her husband was still fighting pancreatic cancer and both were passed retirement age. Could they even care for a young child? Billy thought.

"Mrs. Poulton, Annie left a legal document will giving myself and my wife sole custody of Riley. We are really all the family here she has ever known," he explained. "She is doing fine thus far and we will never let her forget her parents," he shared.

"Well, that's very kind of you, Mr. Parker, though Riley should be with her own kind. I know that's what Keith would want." She paused.

"Mrs. Poulton, I hate to be rude, but your son is the one responsible for her not having a mother and himself and he is the reason Riley is a child alone, don't you want to honor Annie's wishes for her?"

"I'll have my lawyer call you and kiss my granddaughter for me," she requested, disconnecting the line.

Billy knew she really had no case. Annie's prepared documents were legally binding and custody had already been settled and now she calls months later. He really didn't want a court fight, but bottom line, Riley was his daughter, not Keith's.

Katia drove down by the edge and parked the rental car. A steel railing had been put near the edge of the landing where her car had been put in gear and pushed over the cliff. The steel railing had only been put up in recent years. She looked seeing the pink wild roses that David Michael and Billy had planted for remembering the last place Dana Williams was alive.

Oh, Billy, he was her love and would always have a place in her heart, but she had moved on and found a devoted love in Dillard Patterson, her longtime attorney and friend. She kept a close watch on her son, David Michael, visiting him from a distance at the university through the lens of her camera. Katia got very emotional when she thought about the night her son led her to Christ.

"Thank you, Lord," she murmured. Then quickly her thoughts went to the brutal beating she received before faking her death by pushing a large boulder over the ledge and causing her pursuer to think she had fell to her death into the chilly Atlantic River. Her attacker turned around allowing her precious moments to conjure a plan to save her life. With a well-devised plan and help from a true friend, Katia now has a chance at a new life. She wiped the tears from her eyes and got back into her car to drive away. Looking up, she saw the big two-ton Ford truck coming toward her again with the same driver. The truck must have followed her, she thought, because she was still on the property, Katia reasoned. She hit the accelerator hard, and with wheels spinning on her rental car, Katia turned the steering wheel getting off the property, leaving the driver of the truck to wonder who the heck that was. The truck was eating the dust of the Mustang Katia drove like Andretti getting away from the scene. The truck followed her to the entrance of the property before stopping and turning around.

Nora and Erene spent some beautiful days in the Big Apple. Strolling together down Broadway to take in shows on Times Square was always fun for the both of them. Nora loved sharing the restaurants and other sights she encountered day to day during her work week.

"Sweetheart, do you think we can be here for New Year's, it is something I've always wanted to experience," Nora asked, walking hand in hand bundled in a warm scarf and fashionable jeans.

"Honey, what are we talking about four weeks from now, if that's what you want, let's start making plans. I know this place goes mad around here for the New Year's celebration, so you've got to get in early," he responded, excited their future looked bright.

CHAPTER 28

D ORIS WAS PLEASED SHE HAD met her father, but more pleased was she that she had met her aunt Judy. She liked Finley and named him Mr. Gecko, because of the way he talks, she explained laughing. Finley enjoyed his time there and laughed remembering his walk down the street in South Central Los Angeles and thought the neighborhood Judy lived in was indicative of LA's south central.

Doris was shocked when he volunteered to go over to the liquor store for a bottle of hot sauce to eat with Aunt Judy's mustard greens and cornbread.

"Finley, are you sure you don't want me to tag along?" she asked, questioning his decision.

"I'm good, just let somebody try and roll up on me," he said, cocking his small brim to the side of his head. If you think that didn't sound funny with Finley's accent, the person bothering him would probably laughed themselves to death, Judy and Doris thought, watching him put on his hard look going out the door.

"He will be fine, he doesn't have far to run," Judy teased, going back to preparing the meal.

"So, Aunt Judy, when are you coming to Los Angeles?"

"Ooo, you mean with all the movie stars like Ed Sullivan and Marilyn Monroe. I don't know how I'd fit in there, dear," she replied, stirring her yams in the pan so they wouldn't stick.

"Aunt Judy, I think the two you named are long gone, but that's not all that's there."

"Oh yeah, that cute Will Smith." She giggled.

"True, he comes through there, but we have a wonderful church?" Doris shared, "And you will like how the pastor presents the Word, he can really preach."

"Yeah, you have a big church, I'd bet, not like our hundred folks on a good Sunday," she chuckled. "It's a little bigger than that, Aunt Judy, but the spirit is certainly present in your small church though I'd love for you to come and visit with us and me in my home so I can introduce you to my church family," Doris shared, embracing her.

"Ahh, I'll think about it."

"Okay." She laughed.

"Now where is Mr. Gecko?" she asked, looking at the clock. Finley had been gone longer now than both expected and the store was just next door with an empty lot in between it and Judy's home.

Doris called his cell and got no answer. "Aunt Judy, I'd better go check, the heaviest thing Finley picks up during the week these days is probably a spoon," Doris teased, but she was concerned he had been gone twenty minutes now.

Doris walked quickly down the sidewalk, hearing loud laughing and someone shouted, "The dude is crazy! Hahaha." She could see a small crowd gathered by the door getting bigger as others came from around back where they stood all day by a barrel warming from the cold.

Doris picked up the pace when she heard, "He is hilarious yo, the brother is from the Motherland!" Doris was almost running across the small rocks and pebbles that covered the ground in her Giuseppe Zanotti peep-toe pumps. "Ouch." There were only a couple of cars parked with folks sitting on the hood and hanging out the windows. She pushed her way around two big guys standing looking down.

"Finley!" she said loudly before seeing that Finley had everyone's attention and they were intrigued by this "African" brother they thought with the funny sound but very cool voice.

"Hey, the man is funny!" one laughed, looking back, saying, "I think he's from Africa."

Finley was enjoying himself as he told the story of Jonah and the whale as only Finley could with his British accent!

Katia had satisfied her longings and had accepted another chance in life as she boarded her flight back to Los Angeles to be with the man who had helped her become the person she always wanted to be. Meanwhile at home, Dillard was reluctantly getting ready for this grand event Larvy Milburn invited him to at the private club of the L' Eritage in Beverly Hills.

"Katia would love this," he thought, adjusting the tie of his fashionable tuxedo for the evening. He had thought it out and rehearsed it over and over to himself the excuse he was going to tell the Milburns as to why Katia wasn't with him. He looked again at his caller ID and checked his cell phone, making sure it was on. He called her cell over and over but got only her sweet voice on her recorded message, "Please leave a message, I'll get back."

"I love you, Katia," she heard before hanging up the phone. He had a few more minutes before he would battle his way through the almost holiday seasonal traffic, as if LA needed a reason for the traffic jams on their freeways. Katia wanted to surprise him, and after landing, she hurried in hailing a taxi big enough to fit all the luggage she had taken and, of course, purchased in the month she was gone. Giving the cabbie her address, she settled back in the cab for the long ride to Brentwood.

Dillard was now in his Maybach and on the freeway when he discovered he had forgotten the invite the Milburns had sent. He knew if he goes back home for it, he'd be late, so he called his friend.

"Larvy," he said, finally getting him on the phone.

"Now they said this was important, no excuse as to why you're not coming," he aired.

"No, no, quite the contrary, I left home without the invite, and if I turn around, you might not see me," Dillard explained.

Dillard and Milburn didn't always see eye to eye, but Dillard had a stellar reputation amongst his fellow attorneys of honesty and integrity and he wasn't going to blow it on one night he knew would soon pass.

"Oh, shoot, don't worry about that, you and Katia just come right on, I'll look for you pressonally," Larvy responded smiling.

Dillard didn't bother explaining that Katia wasn't coming. He knew that would be the first thing he'd have to explain to Roslyn who probably only wanted to see the gown she was wearing anyway.

After a good solid hour, the cab was pulling away from and exiting through the huge gates of Dillard Patterson's elaborate

Brentwood home. The cabbie had helped Katia with the Louis Vuitton set of luggage, placing it in the middle of their room-size foyer, stacked neatly.

"Thank you," Katia said, giving him a very nice tip along with his fare. She wondered where Dillard was. She looked and sure he wasn't still at the office. His last call on her cell came from the home phone.

"Dillard! Dillard!" she called again, laying down her purse and jacket of the chair in the parlor. "D-i-l-l-a-r-d!" she called out again, running upstairs to his bedroom. "Where is that man?" she thought, heading back down and going in the direction of the kitchen. No Dillard. She looked out on the mezzanine and paused a moment to take in the view from their balcony. "Okay, I guess I'll just have to spoil things and call him," she said, heading back in to the phone sitting on the counter in the kitchen.

There Katia discovered the invite Dillard had forgotten in his hurry to be on time.

If there was ever a time you needed patience, it is certainly when driving on a Friday night in Los Angeles traffic during the holiday season. "Who in their right mind would accept an invite and drive to an event downtown Beverly Hills? I should have gotten a limo. They get more respect," he reasoned, sitting in the middle of bumper-to-bumper traffic looking at his Rolex. *Tick, tick, tick.*

"I'm sure I just set a record for myself," Katia thought, dressed in her gorgeous Gucci gown she had purchased on her trip. It was even more beautiful, she thought, adorning it with her Cartier diamonds Dillard had given her for a past birthday gift. She stood with her Silver Fox Mink draped across her arm waiting for the limo she had called to pick her up and take her to the event. Finally getting in, Katia felt a bit like Cinderella riding out to meet her prince who was not aware she was even coming.

"Please get me there safely but on time, hurry, hurry," she said, giving him the direction on the invite.

L'Eritage, he knew exactly where that was! There must be a secret manual for limo drivers when in a hurry and heavy traffic, Katia thought, because sitting in the back of her limo, she can't recall slowing too long or stopping. Did he take flight? She did say she would make it worth his while!

At six fifty, Dillard was pulling in looking for a valet to hand his keys to. The place was a zoo out front and the red carpet was in full effect. Dillard stood tall adjusting the collar of his jacket. This was some event the Milburns were putting on and he only wished Katia could share it with him. He stood in a line that moved slowly as lights and cameras flashed movie starlets and A-listers galore.

"Excuse me." Dillard looked to see a media guy with a microphone in his hand. "Dillard Patterson, correct?" he asked. Dillard was a bit surprised he tried to steer clear of the paparazzi and cameras; to his credit, he had some pretty big-name actors on his payroll! "So what do you think about this fund-raiser for awareness?" the reporter asked.

"It is for a very good cause and I'm here to support a friend," he said, quickly turning to get away from the questions and moving closer to the door going into the entrance of the magnificent gala thus far. As the line moved up slowly, Dillard saw limo after limo dropping off celebs. He looked again at his Rolex and thought about Larvy standing waiting near the door for him. Sure that's not going to happen? Then he heard a bit of a commotion as someone was getting from a limo. He just thought with that applause it had to be someone like Angelina or Halle and he wanted at that time to just be rude and cut the line and get out of the way. Whoever it was was being escorted up front like he could have been had he not forgotten his invite. He was stuck going in with those other folks, reporters, media, and B-movie celebrities. He looked from side to side with his peripheral vision seeing this beautiful blonde. It was rude to stare, he knew. But then she spoke, "Excuse me,' he heard her say to someone as she passed going in. The voice, the voice, his thoughts screamed out.

"KATIA?" came out loud before he was even sure. He had been thinking about her all day and every day since she left. Hearing her name, she turned back and saw Dillard and he saw her.

He pushed his way tactful as he could getting to her. "Excuse me, sorry, sorry, excuse me, please let me through, excuse me," he said, running into her arms. "Oh my Katia," he said, giving her a passionate kiss for the very first time!

Nora allowed Erene to believe the drama was over and he had let down his guard and moved on. He prayed daily thanking God for helping him to forgive Nora and worked on putting his marriage back on track. Nora was still calling numbers from the readout she had gotten from their cell phone provider and getting nowhere that satisfied her until she got an idea. Erene was mowing the lawn Saturday morning and left his cell phone on the table in the den. Nora had called a number earlier that week and she wanted to check it out. She was going shopping with her sister-in-law and formed a plan. She took Erene's phone and texted the number asking to meet at Montello's downtown. All she needed was a glimpse at the person on the other end of the phone to see if he was up to something, she reasoned.

"Erene, I'm leaving. I'm meeting your sister at the mall," she said, waiting for him to come to the back door for a kiss and off she went. Nora drove downtown with mischief ruling her thoughts. She had said in her text to meet about an hour after she had sent the text, so she parked across the street and waited. "Who's investigating now?" she thought to herself sitting waiting to see this Adele she had called. Then like clockwork, she looked up to see a young woman standing near the front looking around and looking at her watch. Nora got out of the car in a very fashion-forward outfit for shopping.

"Excuse me, are you waiting for someone?" she asked very politely.

"Yes, I am?" Adele responded, knowing she was not who she was waiting for and she didn't recognize this woman.

"I'm Mattie and I'm waiting for Patricia," Nora lied.

"No." Adele sighed a relief. "Adele is my name," she said, moving away as Nora went back to her car and waited a bit before pulling away.

"No worries with that one, she's just a naive child," Nora reasoned, heading to the mall to shop. She was having a wonderful day with her sister-in-law shopping for the upcoming season. "I'm just not sure what I will buy Erene this year, he's not into a lot of things?" she questioned, speaking as they walked. Then looking over, she saw Nada coming from the Louis Vuitton store holding on to Peyton's hand.

"Why hello, ladies," Nada expressed, knowing the ladies from the church they were all members.

"Hello, Mrs. Parker," Nora said with everyone embracing each other. Nada caught Riley's hand. "You have your hands full."

"Yes, I do these days, these are my girls and we are out to see Santa, he just came in today," she explained.

Nora could see the girls were dressed very festive in their beautiful red-patterned dresses and black patent leather shoes.

"They are so cute," Nora voiced.

"Oh, ladies, as you know, I was coming out of that store, they have gorgeous designer bags for the holidays," Nada shared, pointing to her purchase along with others. "I didn't come to shop, but I just couldn't pass up a deal," she added.

"So you have three now, Nada?" Nora asked, looking around.

"Yes, three precious little ones, and a college student," Nada affirmed, smiling from her growing family. "Millicent is changing Trevor, oh, here they come now," she said, looking up to see Millicent coming pushing the stroller toward them. He was dressed as well with a cute little bow tie to match his big sisters'.

"My hands to you, girl, 'cause three, Erene would be happy with one," she said, shaking her head.

"So are you thinking about having a child, Nora?" Her sister-in-law excused herself from the conversation. I'm sure she had heard this before. "Not in the plans anytime soon, but you know, if Erene had his way . . ."

"Speaking of Erene, how are things?" Nada asked.

"He's good, he is a forgiving man, I don't think I could be as forgiving," she admitted, giving her neck a jerk.

"What do you mean?"

"If Erene cheated on me, I don't think I'd be so ready to understand, that's all I'm saying."

"Nora, Erene is a good man and so kind, opposites attract, I guess," Nada whispered. "Millicent, take the girls right over there to the play area and let them run a bit, they'll be fine."

"If I thought Erene forgave me because he was just getting by on something he did, I would dump him like it was the thing to do," she confessed.

"Do you love this man? You're a mess, girl." Nada laughed, but it really wasn't a laughing matter. "I called a number I took from Erene's cell phone of someone named Adele? Ha, she turned out to be a teenybopper, not sure what that was all about?"

"Adele? She is a teenybopper, well, young, twenty-four years old, I believe, but if you were into your husband and his work, you would know he helped her find her mother?"

"Find her mother? That was long ago?" she questioned. "So why is he still calling her?" Nora thought.

"Hey, that you will have to ask your husband, but like everything else, I'm sure there is a good explanation. She is a really nice young lady, as a matter of fact, I invited her to the young professionals on Wednesday at our church, take care, gotta go," she said, leaving and leaving Nora with a lot of questions as she continued on her holiday shopping.

"So tell me all about you and Finley's stay with Aunt Judy. How is she doing?" Russell asked, sitting across the breakfast table with his wife.

"Finley's left his stamp on the town for sure, they loved him, he was himself, and believe it or not, he even taught a lesson."

"Finley? At Judy's church?"

"That would be a no, in front of the liquor store, babe."

"Doris, I don't want-a know," he teased, smiling, shaking his head.

"Russell, it was great, Finley kept her laughing and me as well and I think that helped get her through."

"So is she planning on coming for a visit to Hollywood?" he joked because somehow everyone seems to mention Hollywood when speaking of Los Angeles.

"She is, she is still getting a lot of things settled that Dornelton left her. She wanted me to have it, but I shared with her she was a devoted sister and deserved his pension and other benefits he had coming to him. She will be fine. I also had Dillard recommend a good face-to-face lawyer near her to explain things to her in terms she can understand and to set up a college fund in Captain Hawkins's name for the children she wants to help."

"That's my wife," Russell said, "but speaking of Dillard, I ran into him last week coming out of a corporate meeting and he seemed a bit down, did mention his lady friend was on some kind of getaway."

"Oh funny you would say that, you're right, when I called him regarding Aunt Judy, he was all business and hurried off the phone, so unlike him of late. I'll give him a call soon," she said, allowing Russell to reach over to kiss her while handing her a folder.

"So are you ready for our next task. I spoke with Herb and they got the lot cleared to start building."

"Really, that's wonderful, dear," she said, taking a bite of her toast smiling. "I'm really glad I got this opportunity to share with the people which I grew up around, God is good!"

"Katia, you will never know how glad I was to see you," Dillard shared, riding home from the elaborate gala at the Milburns'.

"I think I do, because you've only said it, what twenty-four, twenty-five times," she teased, touching his nose smiling.

"Well, when Milburn invited us, I didn't exactly say you were not coming," Dillard confessed, "so I had added pressure of explaining why you were not there. Anyway it was fabulous and even more so because you were there," he toyed back, glad they were together and headed home. "Did your trip do what you needed it to? I sure missed you," he questioned, driving along down the highway to Brentwood.

Katia had her head resting on his shoulder and had nodded off to sleep. She had explained about the long flight home and how she was looking forward to a long hot bubble bath and putting her feet up under a warm throw and going quickly to sleep, but after she discovered the invite with their names on it, she set out to find him. So all the dancing and conversation and mingling had worn her out and she fell quickly to sleep still trying to answer his questions.

Nora was content for now. Traveling for the company had halted until the first of the year. It was a time when all employees stayed close to corporate headquarters in Maine and enjoyed the year come to an end.

"Honey, what dressing do you want on your salad, ranch or vinaigrette?" Nora asked, bringing their servings to the table for dinner. She put both dressings on the table and waited for Erene to wash his hands and come to the table. Sitting down, she started right in after the grace. "I saw Nada Saturday at the mall?"

"Oh you did?"

"Yes, she and the children, she's got three, now that's a handful," Nora added.

"What I wouldn't give for just one."

"That's exactly what I said to Nada." She laughed. "We also talked about Adele?"

"Adele?" Now this could have been done and over, but men are so transparent. "What about Adele?" he asked, getting up getting water from the refrigerator.

"Is your food too hot, Erene?" she asked, noticing how fidgety he had become.

"No, but what did Nada say about Adele?" he wanted to know.

"So you know her?"

"Yes, and you met her too, she's the young lady I helped find her mother," he said, taking a large bite from his plate.

"Oh, so she did find her mother?"

"Yes, it was sad, she was homeless and on the street, but I had found her and reunited them, case closed," he was thinking, looking at Nora smiling.

"So when was that, just recently that this happened?" she questioned.

Erene was starting to sweat but couldn't show it at least, he sure didn't want to, but what was she fishing for? "Nora, that case was over long ago, why are you bringing it up now?" he asked, exhaling.

"Nada said she had invited her to the young professionals at the church and I was just wondering how old she was, I really can't remember when we met?" Nora naively stated.

"Honestly not sure if it came up, but she is one of six children, so she has to be about, ummm, twenty-four, twenty-five, I'm not sure," he said, hurrying through his plate and getting up to put it in the sink.

"Boy, you were certainly hungry," she joked, knowing he wanted to get out of the room and away from her questions. "So do you do follow-up on your clients to see how things are going?" she asked loud as he walked out the door of their dining area to the television area.

"Follow up, not really," he said, turning on the television to watch Monday night football. He should have answered truthfully and maybe just maybe this would be over.

"But if you had a client you helped last year and according to you case closed, why are you still calling her a little less than three months ago?" Nora asked, feeling Erene was hiding something now and vowed to herself to keep looking.

Adele and Fletcher left out heading to morning service as both did often. It was what the family was indebted to, and it most certainly kept them together through the years. Malcolm and his girlfriend, Ariel and her husband and their son Gabriel, walked in together seeing Adele and Fletcher already sitting.

An older gentleman sitting at the back in a wheelchair caught Malcolm's arm as he passed. "Where's the soldier?" he asked, having seen him for the past two Sundays with them.

"That was our brother Hanson Hodges, sir, he has returned back to active duty, sir."

And the gentleman gave a smile and a salute to Malcolm, letting him know he had served as well, as he went down the aisle and the row his family sat on.

The family again was blessed this day as again Riggins, their brother, was asked to share during prayer time over the congregation. Adele looked over at Hilary's mom, but she didn't see Hilary. She had said she may not be there. She was going to service at the Deliverance Center with Semaj, her date. The plans were to go to Ariel's home after service, which everyone looked forward to with gladness!

Doris was so excited about her family and the holidays and her aunt Judy who had said she would come for the Christmas season. The project in Oregon was now off the ground and she and Russell had planned a trip in two or three weeks to see the progress of their new project. She stayed in touch with her aunt, speaking with her practically every day.

"Sonjee, are we shopping this Saturday?" she asked, taking a break to call her daughter whose life was busy, busy, busy, auditions, and callbacks, were always the reasons of late because she was trying to get a dance career off the ground.

"Mom, I'd love to say yes, but then if I call you Saturday morning and cancel, you'll be mad," she replied.

"Oh, Sonjee, let's just leave it tentative and I'll be here just come or call and we will meet."

"Oh, Mom, I talked to Aunt Judy this morning. She remembered me."

"Sonj, we just left yesterday," Doris joked with her laughing at her statement. "Aunt Judy has a very clear memory, Sonjee, she probably will never forget you," Doris shared, loving.

"Yeah, she is sweet, I like her a lot."

"She's coming for the Christmas holidays, so please, please, put that on your calendar, and if you talk to David Michael, remind him too."

"Sounds good, Mom, love you, and Jace says hello, bye."

"That child, let me call Dillard and maybe if Katia's not back, I'll invite him to dinner to cheer him up," Doris expressed, dialing his office. His secretary said he was in a meeting, she'd give him the message.

Dillard had thought long and hard about his Katia Norfen. He had fallen in love with her but did she have feelings for him. That kiss the other night said she did and he didn't want to scare her off and thought hard all week about asking her to marry him. "If I ask her and she leaves, I'll be devastated," he thought driving home. They slept in the same house but different rooms and she's been back two weeks and nothing's changed. "What should I do?" he pondered, hitting the button to answer his cell phone.

"Good evening, Patterson," Doris greeted after he answered.

"Hello, how's your venture going?" he asked curiously.

"Dillard, I only wish I would have done this years ago, when Dana was alive, it could have helped us both," she confessed.

"Oh really, so you were able to uncover your roots?"

"Yes, and I met the most wonderful woman, my aunt Judy. I only wish Dana could have met her too, she was our mother's best friend."

Dillard coughed. "Well, that's good. I know it was very therapeutic, you sound regenerated," he admitted, smiling across the line.

"Anyway, did you get your message, I called?"

"You called, when, today?"

"Yes."

"Oh, I see it, sorry, she had Ms. Woods, yes, yes. I know it's you. I have to work on seeing you that way. Was it important, or can I call you tomorrow from the office?"

"Oh, Dillard, how is Katia? Russell said she was traveling right now?"

"Yes, when I saw him, oh, I remember seeing him coming from the courthouse, oh yes, I did share that with him," he talked nervously and didn't know what Doris wanted now.

"I was calling to invite you out to my home for dinner, since you're going solo these days," she joked to get a smile, she hoped.

"You know let me check my calendar and I'll get back to you tomorrow."

"Sounds good. I'll anticipate your call, good night," she said, getting off the phone as Dillard pulled in the driveway of his Brentwood home. He had stopped in the foyer looking at the gorgeous flowers he had sent to Katia earlier today.

"Katia, I'm home," he said loudly, going in and down the hall to his study, quickly putting down his briefcase and placing the jacket across the soft leather executive chair in front of his oak wood desk. His nervous stomach flipped thinking she wasn't there or she had left when after a few calls she still had not answered. He looked on the terrace out back before going up to her bedroom on the second floor.

"Katia, I'm home," he said again before entering her room from the hallway. Peeping into her room, he saw clothes lying on the bed, her shoes were out of the boxes, and then he realized the mess, things were moved all over. Panic had set in the suave attorney to think his Katia was moving out and leaving him. What had he done? he thought standing there now in his massive main hallway. Then he heard a sound coming from his bedroom at the end of the hall. His bedroom was the size of most single family's whole house.

"Katia," he called. Was someone breaking into his home and had kidnapped Katia? He ran into her room and picked up the poker from the fireplace mantle and headed down the hall slowly to his room. He stopped and looked at his emergency button switch in the hallway, but opted to wait until he researched a bit more. Dillard tiptoed slowly in his room. It was also turned upside down, he thought looking at some of his things had been taken out of his very neat closet. Just as he was about to turn around after hearing something drop in the closet to go and push his 911 button, out walks Katia with his shirt on her head, flailing her arms in frustration.

"KATIA!" He sighed.

"Oh, Dillard, how long have you been here?" she asked, looking at him standing with the poker in his hand.

"What happened? These rooms are a mess," he stated, still puzzled with what he was seeing.

"Oh, Dillard, come here," she said, giving him a hug and kiss, "I got your card and flowers."

"I saw them, did you like them?" he asked, raising his brow.

"I do," she said smiling.

Dillard was still puzzled as to why she had the rooms in disarray. "I wanted to surprise you, I wanted to have this all done before you came home, but it was a bigger job than I figured. I have a lot of shoes," she rambled.

"Oh, honey, the housekeeper will be in tomorrow and we will get both rooms straightened out again," he shared, embracing her for the thought.

"So you did send the flowers?" Katia asked because he still hadn't responded like she expected.

"Yes, Katia, I did. I was thinking about you a lot today and I went by my favorite florist and sent you flowers and a card."

"And you sent the card?"

"Yes, Katia, I sent the card that accompanied the flowers, why are you acting so strange?" he then asked.

"Because I said I do and you are just acting like it's no big deal," she replied.

"Okay wait, we are talking about flowers, right?" Dillard asked, moving over toward the door. "I'll be back." He went down the hall and ran quickly down the stairs to start over again. He stopped and looked at the flowers and then his card sent. The card had somehow got mixed up and the one he thought he had sent was, "I love you, have a beautiful day." Instead the card he sent was him asking her to marry him. He had written that on the card but it was only a thought that had now been conveyed.

"I DO, I DO, I DO," he was saying as he ran back swiftly up to his bedroom.

"Yes, sweetheart, I wanted to be all moved into your room since you had asked me to marry you and I said I do."

"Oh, how the universe knows what we don't always expressed to each other. I love you, Katia, will you marry me?" he asked again, down on one knee!

"I will, Mr. Patterson, I will!"

C H A P T E R **29**

AUNT JUDY WAS FEELING THE joy of the Lord when she walked into the grocery store to buy groceries for the week. She saw some children laughing and looking at the pictures picking out their favorite breakfast cereal.

"Hi there," she said, looking at a four- or five-year-old big bright eyes looking back before running away.

Soon around the aisle came Penny. "Hi, Miss Judy," she said, walking up pushing her grocery buggy with two young ones hanging on the sides.

"Why, good afternoon, Penny, and these are your darlings?" she said, smiling warmly and greeting her.

"Yes, ma'am, dis my kids," she replied and added, "be still," swatting at them both with her hand. "I saw dat bil-din Dois puttin' up, wow, it looks real big," she stated.

"Yes, she's a God-sent to this neighborhood," Judy said. "She's going to do a lot of good to help us as well."

"I still kain't bleve dat's Dois, she looked good."

"God takes care of all his people, Penny," Judy said.

Penny just shook her head. *'Cause Miss Judy will fine a way to talk bout God's goodness in the nightclub,* she thought standing there. "Well, I been watching and I hope I git a job there when it opens, Dois said I could."

"Penny, I'm sure if Doris said that, she will make it happen," Judy encouraged, looking at the single mother who really needed to be taught how.

"Nice seeing you, Miss Judy, and ah, pray fo me," she said, hurrying off with the children giggling and making noise as they went.

Judy stood right there near the oatmeal and did just that.

Dillard called and accepted Doris's invite to her home but wasn't taking Katia with him. Yes, it was Katia's idea not to go. Dillard understood Doris Woods wanted to share her findings with him since he had been the one who not only helped her sister, Dana Demato-Williams, with all her issues but also encouraged her to do what she had done in going back to face her past, discovering her dad and her aunt Judy.

Dillard had made reservations at a very swank restaurant in Los Angeles called Boulevard 16, which is located in the Kimpton Hotel in the Westwood neighborhood. She had said she wanted to do something different for the evening and he wanted a romantic candlelit dinner in which to present her with the elegant diamond engagement ring he had picked out for her. Putting all the thoughts of what Doris could bring up on Friday night, his only aim was to please his gorgeous Katia Norfen. She was now in his room and had hired a decorator to design both bedrooms to her liking. Katia didn't want a big wedding; as a matter of fact, they were going to have a private ceremony with only a justice and the witness there at their home, ending with a big party of friends to celebrate another court victory. (Hollywood can always find a reason for a party.) It wasn't what she envisioned for her end, but if she wanted any kind of life that was not a media circus, this is what she'd have to do hide in plain sight. She had been up close and personal with those who should have known her on the spot. Her blue eyes and luxuriously long locks of blond hair was so different from what she had before that often she even fooled herself with the disguise. Her beautiful skin tone always kept her in the game of envy of all other women. She had the plans all laid out, and Dillard continued to be her savior, friend, and soon to be her husband.

Nora had went into the mobile phone account and pulled up data further back than what she had received initially. She was curious now about this twenty-four-year-old woman that ran so quickly to meet Erene at the restaurant.

"Good evening, sweetheart." Coming in finding her home was a dream for him. Nora was being the wife he had married and he was the happiest man alive.

"Some day today," he shared, "how about yours?" he asked, seeing her busy with her laptop in front of her.

"It was good, dear, this is really our downtime when there's no traveling, just walked in about ten minutes ago." She smiled, lifting her head to kiss him.

"I wish you were here all the time when I get home," Erene said, going to put away his briefcase and jacket. "Are you going to the church tonight? If so, we could have dinner at Carmelito's on the way."

"Sure, sweetheart, that sounds good, let me finish this e-mail." And Erene walked into the bedroom leaving Nora to her laptop. Nora had to check out the store where Erene had used their phone account to pay for purchases. She had stored everything into her files and tomorrow she was going to go and check it out. "Erene, darling, would you like a glass of wine before we go?"

"No, Nora, and you shouldn't either." He smiled, grabbing her face and kissing her before walking away. He loved her and knew she had things she needed to repent of, but it wasn't for him to judge.

Billy and Nada were headed out as well with the children to service this evening.

"Honey, I have Trevor in his car seat, come on, we are getting impatient," he shared, yelling from the garage.

"Mommy, can we take our doll?" Riley asked, coming toward Nada who was putting Peyton's sweater on.

"I want," Peyton said.

"I'll get it, Mommy, she wants Daisy," Riley shared, running upstairs to their room to get it.

With every child satisfied, Nada buckled Peyton in her seat and Riley had her big sister seat in the back as well. They were adjusting to it all and doing a wonderful job of it.

"I spoke with Mrs. Bookens today, she called my office just wanting to know about Riley," he explained, driving along. The children couldn't hear the conversation they were sitting in their seats watching a cartoon on the SUV'S video screen.

"Oh, that's nice, how is she doing?"

"All right, I guess. She did say some of her neighbors moved out. Oh I don't know if it had anything to do with what happened across the street, it's only been about six or seven months now, she just wished us well and love to Riley."

"Thank God there are a lot of people who wants what's best for her like we do," Nada shared.

"I spoke with the Poultons' lawyer today as well and I'm still not sure if Mrs. Poulton really understands. Her lawyer seems like a pretty sharp attorney and wants only what's best for his client. I gave him copies of the documents to look over last time we spoke and he's satisfied. I only wish there was something I could say to Keith's mother to make her understand. Well, we will pray about that fervently to God, who understands all things."

"Oh, did you talk with Erene about Adele?"

"Adele? You mean Adele Hodges. No, he hasn't mentioned her in a while, he did tell me at the beginning of the year that her mother passed away but not of late. Why?"

"Nora was asking me about her, if I knew her? I did invite her to join young professionals at the church and I helped her with some style advice but that's it."

"Seems Nora's trying to find something to do with herself since she's not traveling," Billy voiced, pulling into the parking lot.

"Speak of the devil," Nada said, seeing Nora and Erene just walking up to the huge sanctuary for Bible study and prayer.

Dillard was looking sharp in his stylish Italian suit and Prada penny loafers as he stood waiting for Katia to come down the stairs going out for the evening of fun, and a surprise for her. She wasn't aware Dillard had purchased her a ten-carat diamond ring by Cartier and he could hardly wait to get to the Kimpton in Westwood. Looking up, he saw what he voiced a vision of loveliness. Katia was dressed in a gorgeous little black dress by Vera Wang, a sophisticated lady, and it was hugging her curves perfectly.

"Wow, I didn't think it was possible for you to be lovelier," he stated, seeing her come toward him. Katia walked right into his arms and shared a passionate kiss. "Are we ready?" he asked, smiling.

He surprised her by having a limo waiting to whisk the two of them out to a very romantic evening. Katia had made up her mind that this was what she always wanted to be someone's princess, from the first time she laid eyes on the guy she thought to be her prince charming, but another stole his heart and left her wanting, and this happened more than once, causing her so much hatred and pain.

Now she had an older man who wanted only her and she had over the years put back together the broken puzzled pieces of her life and was determined to make him happy forever after.

Dillard never saw himself with a gorgeous woman like Katia, oh, he knew her in and out. He knew her past and was willing to take a chance of a lifetime to be with this woman of mystery. She had brought him to life and made him the man that every woman longed for, but he only had eyes for Katia. The two had finally got together and agreed this just feels right.

From the first sip of wine and before finding themselves in each other's arms dancing the night away, the ardent sound felt through the slow jazz music playing was so pleasing to their ears. The soft laughter united from a remembered story, to the shared bite of caviar fed to Dillard with Katia's delicate hands touching his lips was a night neither would forget, especially when it ended with a yes as Dillard again asked Katia, "Will you marry me?" A passionate kiss across the small candle-lit table caused a very bright sparkle as he put the fabulous ring on her finger followed by soft applauds by the surrounding tables watching!

Nora was off to the office. Kissing Erene good-day, both headed out together. She again had pulled her trick when Erene was in the shower and had made plans to meet Adele at the park near where she worked.

"Some investigator," she said, patting herself for finding out where the place was that Erene had made his purchase. It wasn't easy. She had worked on it for two weeks because it was a craft market in a park and the purchase was only forty bucks but it was a necklace, probably for his mom, she liked that kind of stuff. She just had to check it out. Crazy he forgave her, and she just wanted to make sure he had not done anything she needed to forgive! "Yeah, right? Just forgive, Nora, you got caught! But no, I'm too close," she thought. And at lunch, she was going to see what this chick was all about.

Dillard was a bit nervous because tonight he was having dinner at Doris's home in Beverly Hills and he wasn't sure really what her motive was for the invite. Sure she had said to thank him for all the help with putting her life back together and all the help he had provided to her sister, Dana. He was just finishing up with a client when in walked Milburn into his office.

"Hello, Patterson, just stopping in to say hello, haven't seen you much since the gala," he stated.

"Larvy, that was wonderful, Katia and I had the best time. I even saw some old friends," Dillard shared.

"Sooo you and Katia seem to be making a go at this, so she's a keeper, ah?" he teased in his Milburn kinda way.

Dillard was on top of the world these days and nothing Milburn could say was going to upset him.

"Yes, I think I will, especially if it bugs the heck out of you," Dillard joked back, smiling.

"No, no, I'm glad to know she's more than eye candy, Patterson, you deserve it."

"Yeah, yes, I see where this is going," Dillard voiced, "thanks for stopping by," he added as he logged off his computer and click off his desk light, looking for Milburn to take the hint and leave.

"Hey, do you think you and Katia would like to go out on the yacht?" he then asked, seeing Dillard put on his jacket ignoring much of what his sarcastic colleague says most of the time.

"Larvy, have a good evening," he said, walking toward his door to leave while Milburn backed out still jabbering about how his expensive yacht performs on the water.

Dillard called Katia and reminded her about his early evening plans at Doris Woods's home. She was still okay with not going and shared with him to enjoy himself but she couldn't wait for him to come home. Before long, Dillard was stopping at the front gate of the Woods's home. After getting cleared, he was soon knocking at her front door.

This wasn't Dillard's first time at the home. After all, he was her attorney and handled all of the legal matters for the family.

"Good evening, Patterson," Doris said, greeting him as he came to the door with a bottle of vintage wine in hand. "Thank you very much," she said, passing the bottle of wine to Finley who had opened the door for the guest. "So are you still solo, or has

Katia come back?" she asked, noticing he seemed in a jovial mood entering.

"I'm here alone," Dillard replied, making the words ring true. "Come in," she said, inviting Dillard into the parlor where Russell, her husband, was.

"Good evening, sir."

"Yes, good evening, so glad you could make it, my wife would have worried me to death about you being lonely over the Thanksgiving holiday," Russell stated, smiling.

"Oh, I'm fine, Katia will be home soon and we've planned a big celebration," he replied, telling a little white one, but thought it's okay.

Finley came in with delicious hors d'oeuvres and drinks. After making small talk for about twenty minutes, Russell excused himself to check on Finley in the kitchen with the staff, at least that's what he said, but he knew Doris wanted to share with Dillard and he gave her space.

"So you and Katia are really making a go of things," she started.

Dillard looked at her after the remark out of left field. "How did we get on Katia?" he asked.

"Milburn called, he said you two were the talk of the gala, she is such an attractive woman," Doris shared.

"You know you're right, but I think the thing with most people, especially Larvy, is that I'm with her, how did I get such a gorgeous woman, who's not just eye candy as he refers to women," Dillard stated, a bit teed Doris could tell.

"Do you know, Patterson, that narrow-minded people have never bothered me? I got so much flack when I married Russell because he was not in my league, they would say, but years have proven me right and them wrong. Russell is the best thing that has happened to me, excepted only by reuniting with my birth daughter Sonjee," Doris expressed with her heart.

"Yes, but that man seems out to get me for something, but you're right, people will talk, and if you satisfy one, the other will whine. Anyway, you know I remember when I was first introduced to you, you thought I was just another white man trying to get over, you were death on a brother," Dillard said with a chuckle, "after you found out I was on your team, a black man made to look white, you did cut me a little slack," teasing Doris mercifully.

"Okay, you're right, but I have found out many of our forefathers went through that same thing, some were splitting images of their masters," she added, slapping five with her friend as they took a walk into her home office.

"Speaking of that, when I first started practicing law here, I didn't disclose my race, wouldn't have gotten a single client, because Hollywood was Caucasian and there were very few blacks accepted in the business. There were a few Sidneys or Lenas when I graduated law school, so if I was going to make this work, I just kept my mouth closed and my hand opened," he joked, but true, lifting his hand in the "swear to tell the truth" position. "The blacks who needed a lawyer or could afford one saw me as an asset, with me telling them to keep their mouth shut, and when the Caucasian clients discovered I was just another black man, I had proven myself to them by getting them out of a whole lot of mess they seem to get themselves into," Dillard explained with a shared laugh, "and they wouldn't let me go! I have taken my knocks in this career but wouldn't trade it after meeting people like you and your family," Dillard shared, embracing Doris. "And I'm good on Katia and I think she's even coming around to liking me." He smiled.

"Good, you have allowed me to put my family back together including Dana, my sister, and for that, I will always be grateful," Doris said, a bit teary-eyed. "Look at this," she said, getting up to show him the albums of her daughter someone had given her and kept for her. Doris was crying and wiping tears by the time she got to the awards, plaques, and ribbons for her dad she had gotten to meet before he left this earth. "It all started when you shared about your brother, the artist, who painted our mother, who knew how connected we were?" Doris added.

"It is a small world, and that's exactly what I told your sister when she approached me for the first time. I wouldn't have taken it in further had she not been adamant and very persuasive," Dillard shared, taking another sip from his Grey Goose calming his jitters, he was enjoying with the smoked oyster appetizers before dinner.

Before Erene could get into the door at the precinct, his cell phone was ringing. He looked at the caller ID to see it was from Adele and quickly disconnected the call. He went through the briefing for the day and his phone rang again, looking only to disconnect. "It had only been a half hour since the last call and why is she calling me?" he asked himself, getting busy for the day when he heard, "James, you have a call on line 2," someone yelled across the room.

He hurried to the phone. "James," he announced after getting on the line.

"Please don't hang up," he heard and knew it was Adele's voice.

"Is something wrong, why are you calling?" he asked. "I asked you not to call me here or at all, what's going on?" he again iterated.

"You texted me to meet you at the park," Adele said.

"What? I haven't texted you, I'm sorry this is effecting you, but, Adele, I didn't text you," he said sadly over the line, feeling bad this had happened.

"Erene, what's going on? About two weeks ago, you texted me to meet you at Montello's and you don't show and now I get a text from you today and you say you didn't text, what's going on?" she asked, just as puzzled as he was.

"What happened at Montello's? Did you see someone?" he asked.

"No, you never came, did you?"

"No, Adele, but did you see anyone there?" he clarified.

"No, I was standing out front and some woman came up and asked for . . . I can't remember the name, but that was it."

He took his cell phone from his side, and after looking through about ten texts, he found the text to Adele and knew he hadn't sent it. "Adele, I'm so sorry, I'm not doing this. I'm so sorry you're involved in something I thought was over."

"So you're not meeting me today at the park on J Street downtown?"

"No, Adele, and please don't go there, I'll try and figure this out and call you back, I promise," Erene affirmed, getting off the line, hurt and a bit angry, but finally realizing all those futile questions Nora had been asking was her up to something and his quenched hate for being deceitful had rose to the top, saddened, but he found himself there this day!

Nada was all smiles as she watched Billy's parents interacting and playing with the girls after spending Thanksgiving together in their home. Trevor was the cutest little boy his grandmother Tetra had ever seen. His big bright eyes and curly black hair was to be envied by all photographers when he flashed a big smile as she talked to him lying in her arms. She'd sat and played with Trevor and the girls for hours during her visits, and this time was no exception.

"I tell you, Nada, you and William have done a great job with the children. Riley loves being a big sister to Peyton and Trevor and all three are so adorable," she shared, coming out back where Nada were with the girls after she had laid Trevor down for his nap.

"Priscilla, please put his blanket over him," Tetra said, coming out to sit with Nada.

"They love this playground you and Dad purchased for them. I can't get them to come inside most days, they absolutely love it, look at them," Nada said. "I could be out here all day and they'd play from the sandbox to the slide and everything in between, I probably won't find them this summer when we come to visit?" she then added warmly, sharing conversation now that Tetra had joined her in the spacious backyard of their home.

"Wow, times flies, he's six months old already. Soon Trevor will be out here jumping all over things," she added.

"Oh and a grandmother's delight, those pictures you all took with Santa I'm having framed as we speak, I took them to the framer yesterday." She laughed. "I could never get William to be still that long on Santa's lap," Tetra again laughed, sharing a warm moment with her daughter-in-law.

"It wasn't an easy task, but it wasn't Trevor that wouldn't be still, it was Peyton Jr.," Nada voiced, laughing.

"Well, David and I have certainly enjoyed ourselves this week and thank you for allowing us to spoil them rotten, you and Billy can straighten them back out after you leave."

"Yes, you're right, Mom, you're always right."

Adele decided to have lunch with Hilary and some coworkers since her original plans were squashed.

"Hilary, where are you guys going?" she asked, leaning out of her cubicle with loud office voice.

"Subway, Adele, are you going? I want to tell you about meeting Semaj's parents."

"Sure, sounds good, just find me when it's time. If I'm not in the cube, I'm very busy today running all over."

Erene normally drove cars that where undetected in his work as an investigator. But this day he had signed out a black-and-white patrol car to drive around by the park. He knew Nora wouldn't suspect anything because that's not the kind of car she would be looking for. As lunchtime approached, he pulled into a nearby lot and sat watching cars on a busy intersection, and for the most part, it looked normal for a black and white to do. He had gotten there early, and before long, he saw Nora's car drive around the park before pulling to the curb side to park. The crafts fair wasn't going on because it was winter and there were only a few people walking through the park or stopping to allow their pets to relieve themselves. Erene watched as Nora got out walking around looking aimlessly for Adele, he suspected. She walked from one end to the other of the small but very popular community shared park downtown. She stopped and sat looking, taking off the stylist pumps she was wearing with her heels getting stuck in the dirt as it pushed through the grass.

Erene moved his car closer as she seemed to be getting frustrated after walking up to a woman sitting on a bench reading and then turning away mad. After forty minutes or so, she got back in her car and left. Erene knew then for certain that Nora was surely up to something and she was not going to rest until she found out. How could he confront this woman? He had caught her and, for the most part, forgiven her, and now she's playing huntsman on him! Unbelievable, he thought, heading back to the precinct. When Erene got back to his desk, he called her.

"Hi, honey?" she greeted sweetly.

"Hey, just saying hello, how was lunch?" he asked.

"Not bad, just went out with Megan and Floyd to Montello's," she lied quickly.

"Oh well, I guess dinner is out there tonight," he teased back. "That would be a yes." She laughed as if telling the truth.

This lady can lie with not conviction, Erene thought to himself over the phone. "Okay, hon, I'll see you at home," he confirmed, hanging up. *What would be the first question I should ask to get this started? Does Nora even love me? I can't believe she's doing this!* Erene went on about his day, but his thoughts were going hundred miles an hour as to what would and could happen tonight when he gets home.

"So she didn't show, maybe I'm imagining things? Do I really want him to have done something? I got caught and now I'm trying to find something to pin on him so I won't feel bad, trifling, Nora, and you know it," she thought to herself. "Umm, so maybe there's nothing to it. I will let it go. Mr. Westagill, my GM, still won't look at me, and I'm ashamed too, I guess being a married woman, but I'm sure not the only one out there, I just happened to be married to a saint. Yes, and okay, got caught!" Nora thought to herself, heading into another meeting with her coworkers wondering who else knew.

Dillard had been to Doris's home close to an hour when Russell returned back now to her home office where she and Dillard had concluded looking at all the memorabilia she had collected along her journey. She had the flag she received from her father's funeral that was presented to her in her hand as Russ walked in to say dinner was served.

"Dillard, you're family to me, and again, thank you," she expressed, linking her arms between the two gents and heading to the large dining room.

"You just missed Hanson, I was just Skyping with him, he's back on active duty, says he'll call again soon," Fletcher said to Adele coming through the front door.

"Did Erene call?" she asked without commenting on her brother's call from overseas.

"Not since I've been here, haven't seen him lately either at the park, hear lady dragon's been in town lately," he shared, joking about Nora.

"Why, you look like you've lost your best friend," Fletch joked.

"No, busy day, got a headache, gonna go up and rest a bit. If he calls, wake me if I don't hear the phone," she requested, heading up the stairs.

"Yeah, okay, but I'm going to study hall at six o'clock, Adele," Fletcher yelled from his sofa seat watching television.

"That's fine, let me know when you leave." And she shut her door to the world!

CHAPTER 30

KATIA SPENT WEEKS GETTING EVERYTHING ready for the fabulous party they were catering to celebrate their marriage but disguised as just another victory party for Dillard, the attorney. She didn't want to call it a reception, but that's what it was, and it was like everything Katia did, over the top. The gourmet desserts, five-star entrées, and expensive champagne and cheeses were only a small part of the night's menu. Candelabras, flowers, and lacey decorations were being brought in from Dina, a wedding planner she had hired to make it all a success.

"Dillard, did you get the band we talked about?" she asked, looking over the plans for the table arrangements and for seating.

"I did, calm down, I've hired the jazz band we heard at that trendy club on Wilshire, and yes, the neo-soul singer as well," he replied, getting out of the way of things going on.

"Thanks, Dil, and you did drop all the invites for our party off, yes?"

"Yes, Katia, I'll be in my office," he said, running now away from all the questions she asked.

"Oh, Dillard, Doris Woods called," she finally said.

"Doris, what now, this woman is kind to a fault, but I'm just not sure what she wants. I'll call her from my office."

"Hello, Doris Woods, please?" he asked, calling her home and not hearing her voice.

"Doris Woods," she finally greeted after coming to the phone.

"Yes, Doris, you called again."

"Dillard, did I tell you I found another one of your brother's portraits, and I'm having it shipped," she shared.

"You did, where?"

"It was an online French auction and I saw the name Patterson, paid a great price for it, but I'd like to make it a thank-you gift, so I'm having it shipped to your home and wanted you to know."

"It isn't necessary, Doris, that you do this, but thank you so much, it will mean a lot," Dillard replied.

"It's the least I could do since you were so gracious in letting me have the one Dana received from the Demato estate sale," Doris said and added, "and please let Katia know I just received my winter shipment, and I'll give her a private showing so that she doesn't have to run into Roslyn Milburn. Good evening," Doris expressed, hanging up the receiver and the call.

Erene went home from work wondering what he'd meet when he arrived. Nora had dinner already cooked and she was sitting having a glass of wine before dinner. She had made Erene's favorite Italian meal and the house smelled very good as all the aromas moved through the air when he walked in.

"Hello," was his greeting, but the cheerfulness of it was gone.

"Surprise!" she said, coming over to kiss him. "I'm sorry about having lunch at Montello's today, so I made your favorite, spaghetti." She smiled, flirting up close and personal.

Erene honestly didn't know what to make of her mood. Was it really over? Did that really fix the problem? he was asking in his mind.

"Hon, go and put away your case and get relaxed. I've made you some tea to help you relax before dinner."

"Nora, where is Nora and what have you done with my wife?" he teased because she was being so sweet. He laid his cell phone and keys on the end table and went into the room to unwind and put on some relaxing clothes. Nora quickly grabbed up his phone and went through his call log. Nothing. Erene had deleted his recent calls from Adele this morning, but he had also deleted the text Nora had sent.

"Umm, so he saw it," she thought, "maybe he warned her or she warned him?" She put his phone back on the table and filled her glass again of the Chardonnay she was drinking.

Erene came out smiling, feeling good about the evening. "Are you ready to eat?" After sharing their day and finishing the drinks, both got up and went into the dining room. Nora had set the table so beautifully and had fresh flowers on it as well.

"I will not go to Montello's any day if you promise to cook me a meal like this," the conversation started.

"Oh, Erene, you are sweet."

Dinner went well and plans were discussed about Times Square for New Year's Eve. With dinner filled with good food, flirtatious laughter, and warm compliments, the two cleared the table and headed into the den with plans to sit by a cozy fire and watch a movie. Nora opted to hear some soft music and cuddle with her man. Everything was going great it seemed and not sure what was on Erene's mind when Nora asked standing modeling her new sleepwear after disrobing her housedress she had purchased from Miss Knowles's lingerie line and just knew she looked good!

"Who do I remind you of?" And he answered, "Adele."

"What? Who? Did you say Adele? I know you're not talking about the singer?" she asked, miffed at what she heard.

"What are you talking about?" Erene asked, but it was too late to recant. The cat had come out of the bag!

"Erene, I heard you plainly, have you been with her? So is that why you're so willing to forgive me because you're doing the same thing! Talk to me, Erene! Did she call you today and tell you I was on to you? Ah, Erene, oh, you can't talk now, church boy!"

Erene sat there quietly with Nora calling him everything but a child of God. "I can't believe you chose a mindless child over all this," she said, showing off her curves in front of him. "Oh, just wait you haven't seen fury! So when were you going to tell me? So how long have you been sleeping with the heifer? Just wait, I have her number and you had better not get in my way? You will be sorry, Erene. I promise you, you'll be sorry!"

Erene couldn't believe how fast his evening had unraveled. How could he be so stupid as to bring up Adele's name? Especially when he knew Nora had sent that text from his phone. Adele's name had slipped out!

"Nora, look, I'm not sure what you are talking about," he said, lying but guilt got the best of him and he began his confession. "Nora, please sit down, let's talk, please," he asked, reaching for her hand.

She had gotten the chair from the dining table and sat it across from him staring in his face and yelling obscenities. "Erene, you hurt me," she cried, "I never expected you to do this to me," she shared tearfully to him.

He got up and reached for her hand and she sat next to him on the sofa. He put his arm around her as she cried hurtful on his chest. She was angry and so very hurt and now vulnerable to Erene. He couldn't believe this was the same woman from a few weeks ago.

"I'm so sorry, Nora, please forgive me, I'm human and I messed up," he started out saying. "You're always away from home traveling in your work and I got lonely and I sinned," Erene confessed.

"But why, you say you love me, Erene, why?" She cried and cried.

"Honey, you know how things happen. I didn't mean for it to, I didn't plan for it to happen. It just did and I'm sorry. Will you forgive me?" he asked, embracing her lifeless body in his arms. There was silence for about ten minutes as each cried out the hurt and anger regarding adultery.

"Erene, I need time, please give me time. I was so blindsided by this confession, I would have bet my life on you not doing this. I'm crushed to think you were with someone after marrying me," Nora shared. "I know, you forgave me, was that why?" she asked, now looking at him sitting there ashamed.

"No, that was something I had to do for myself. I had repented for what had happened before I saw you in that hotel room."

"So you honestly forgave me and you're not trying to hold it over my head and doing this to get back at me?" she asked.

"Nora, no, I'm sorry. I messed up and I have asked God to forgive me, and I pray now that everything is in the open, you will forgive me because I really love you, Nora, I do."

"Did you tell her you loved her?"

"Nora, please, we have got to let this go if we are going to make a go of this marriage," Erene voiced, getting up from the couch.

"Erene, I love you, I do, but I need time," she said, getting up, the wind was clearly out of her sails as she headed to the bedroom for the evening.

"Doris, hello, dear, this is Aunt Judy," she announced, calling.

"Well, surprise, surprise, I was just thinking about you, so glad you called," Doris said, smiling over the line.

"You are, well, that makes me feel good," she replied, "you remember me."

"Aww, Aunt Judy, no one would ever forget you once they meet you."

"Well, thank you, dear. I was wondering about some papers I got about an, an nu . . .," she kept repeating.

"Oh, annuity," Doris clarified.

"Yes, it's spelled A-N-N-U-I-T-Y, and I think it's from Dornelton, something they say he left for me?"

"Sure, what's going on?" Doris asked.

"'I'm not sure, it's a lot of words in here I don't understand, and I was wondering if I could go or call that lawyer you let me speak with about his retirement fund?"

"Ahh, Aunt Judy, you most certainly can, he's your lawyer and any questions you have at any time, just call and he will answer or set you up with an appointment to come to his office," Doris explained.

"Really, you mean I can call him myself?"

"Yes, ma'am, you can at any time."

"And he knows I'm calling?" she questioned.

"Yes, he's there for you," Doris reiterated with a smile.

"Okay, I need to call him and he will explain this in a language I can understand and I'll call you and let you know how it goes," she kindly volunteered.

"That sounds wonderful, Aunt Judy. Have a good evening."

"You too, dear, good night," she said, hanging up the line.

Billy and Nada were getting ready for the holiday season and it looked to be a wonderful year filled with lots of joy and laughter. The children were running around the house and the staff was so happy to have the house filled again after David Michael and his friends. The house was buzzing with laughter as the staff took out all the holiday décor filled with silver and gold. Nada wanted this year to be filled with reds and greens and all the colors of the season, the kind of Christmas she grew up with, and the staff buzzed around like bees to make it happen.

"Look, sissy, Treber is coming," Peyton said, sitting in her high chair at the table in the kitchen where she and Riley were eating breakfast and both were ready for school.

"Oh, Trevor, look at Trevor is going to be big soon," Riley said.

"He's not walkin," Peyton added.

"Not yet, but soon, sissy, soon."

Nada wasn't far behind him after kissing Billy good day and she was smiling. Trevor was crawling so fast down the long hallway.

"Mommy, he's not walkin like me."

"No, he'll get there just like his big sisters," she shared, smiling at his crawling antics.

"Mommy, is Trevor going with us in the car?" Riley asked, getting down on the floor with him to play.

"No, he's going to stay with Milly."

"Aww, bye, bye, Trevor, love you," Riley said, getting up to put on her jacket and head to the study to kiss their dad good day with Peyton close behind. "Wait, sissy!" The girls had stopped to see the staff putting bulbs on one of the trees in the parlor.

"Come on, girls, we will decorate the tree in the great room today when you get home and we will have so much fun," she said, "now run along and kiss Daddy so we won't be late."

"Daddy, are you going to decorate the tree with us?" Riley asked as both sat on his lap sharing a kiss to his cheeks.

"I wouldn't miss it for the world!" he replied.

"YEAH!" both yelled loudly, running off to meet their mother. Katia was so nervous when she went into the boutique a few weeks before her wedding day. She wanted to wear a dress from Doris's boutique collection and needed to make sure it was a perfect fit. She wouldn't have time for alterations and time was upon her.

Katia walked in looking around when a clerk came from the back. "Miss Norfen, hello," she greeted very friendly.

Katia exhaled, glad it wasn't Doris. She quickly explained the gown she wanted and the designer to hurry things along.

After a while, the clerk came out with the requested gown but asked, "Are you sure I can't get you something to drink?" It was a courtesy of the shop for their patrons—tea, latte, wine.

"No, I'm in a bit of a hurry," she said as she kept looking at her watch on her wrist.

"Right this way," the clerk said, escorting her into a dressing room with the gown she had across her back.

"Are there any others I can get for you, Miss Norfen?"

"I know this will work, just let me try this and I'll call you to zip me," Katia requested, sending the clerk out. The gown was gorgeous. It wasn't a wedding gown, but it was the gown she wanted and it was handpicked by the owner of the boutique she knew as she slipped into it. It was a silk mermaid-style gown by Taylor and sophistically simple. Dillard will love this, she thought. "You can come in now," she said to the clerk who stood outside the door, but when it opened, it was Doris Woods.

"Why, you are lovely, and that gown wears you well," she said, reaching to zip the back of it. "You know I chose this one myself," she said, sharing.

"I read that on your site, it is gorgeous for my party." Katia smiled nervously seeing Doris Woods, the boutique's owner, standing admiring her in the handpicked gown.

"You know if I didn't know better, I'd say this gown was designed especially for you, it fits perfectly," Doris complimented, looking at the beautiful Katia from head to toe.

Katia was so filled with emotion she started to cry.

"Are you okay?"

"I'm fine, I can't believe I found my gown already. Dillard's throwing a big party and I wanted to wear white and this is perfect," she shared, looking in the full-length mirror. She stepped out on the pedestal outside of the dressing rooms and turned around admiring herself as well as Doris and the clerk. "I'll take this exquisite gown," she voiced, smiling, "and thank you so much," she said as Doris walked away.

Katia hurried in to take it off, and while she was getting dressed, the clerk was getting everything ready.

"Miss Norfen, you want it delivered to the same address on your account?" she asked after finalizing her purchase with delivery in two days.

"Oh no, I'll take it with me," she stated.

"But this is the floor model. I don't think Mrs. Woods will sell that one to you, please let me ask her?" she said, quickly heading to Doris's office to explain the question.

Katia waited nervously for an answer. She was fretful and tensed she'd have to go somewhere else. The clerk came back without Doris. "This can't be good. She's not going to even speak to me about it."

"Miss Norfen, let me put this in a box for you, it will be just a few minutes," she said, hurrying the dress to the back to have it boxed so she could leave with it out of the store.

"Thank you and please give my regards to Mrs. Woods," Katia shared, walking out smiling with her gorgeous purchased gown.

Nora was clearly shaken by Erene's confession of infidelity. She would never think he would do this. He was a good man, and he loved her dearly. What went wrong? she thought, driving along to the office. Erene had shared how he had made a mistake, he had said he was sorry and asked for forgiveness, why did she still feel victimized?

She realized she was in the same situation a few weeks ago, but that didn't make it any easier. My, oh my, who else knows about this? What an awful feeling, she thought all day as she went about her tasks at the workplace.

"Hi, Nora," a coworker came in to the break room, seeing her sitting there reading a magazine, "so have you finished your shopping?" she asked, smiling.

"For the most part, but I don't know what to get Fred. He's been a bad boy this year," she teased with her longtime friend and coworker.

"Not Fred, what could Fred have done to be in the doghouse?" Nora asked, curiously thinking maybe men are just dogs and can't help themselves and Fred is in his fifties.

"I caught him the other night." She laughed, sharing a soda and a tease. But before she could finish, Nora was so bent on bashing men by this point. "I know with a skank," she voiced boastfully.

"No, Fred, my Fred, no, his doctor has taken him off foods with high cholesterols, and the other night, he had a night light in the kitchen cleaning out the fridge, it was the funniest thing I had ever seen." She laughed across the table.

Nora managed a smirk, disappointed there was no bashing involved.

"So what are you getting that handsome man of yours this holiday season, has he been naughty?"

"AH." Nora got up and stormed away from the break room with the coworker wondering what she said to upset her.

All day Nora walked around under a dark cloud and it seemed everyone was talking about giving, duh, it is the season after all.

Erene was also experiencing the coldest moods as well, but he kind of expected it. Tic for tat he knew was not right and somehow it seemed like that is what happened only in reverse. He walked in to no dinner and Nora sitting in her pajamas leaned over her laptop with very little to say all evening. This went on for three days straight before he decided to say something again.

"Nora," he said, sitting beside her on the couch. "Are you going to church with me tonight?" he asked.

"Why?" she blurted out. "So that everyone can laugh at me?"

"Nora, what are you talking about, this is between us," he explained.

"So you didn't tell your brotherhood about us?"

"No, we share a lot of scenarios and some share what they feel about things going on and there is even what-if's, but I haven't specifically brought up our situation," he again shared hurtfully.

"Erene, I can't believe you didn't say anything to anyone?"

"Not necessarily the brotherhood, I did speak with William as a minister," he confirmed.

"So Nada knows you were unfaithful to me?"

"I'm not sure what Nada knows. I didn't speak with her, I stayed two days in their home when I left New York to get away from the house and you. I'm sure she knows something was wrong but I never spoke with her, only in confidence to my brother in Christ," Erene shared.

Nora jumped up from the couch. "I can't believe I've been walking all around this town and you've been babbling to everyone about us!"

"Nora, really, you are taking this way too far. I told my pastor because I needed to vent the anger and not take it out on you, that's it, I'm going in to get dressed for prayer service. I'd like you to come," he said and walked out the room, leaving her standing in the middle of the floor.

What Erene had said was eating her insides that Nada may know about her. "She will judge me. I just know she thinks I'm not good enough for him. I wonder if he told them what he did? I hate what he's done, he had no right to tell them about me! Maybe I should just tell everyone about his cheating, oh my, what are people thinking?" Nora was hung up on what everyone was thinking and really no one except the couple themselves knew they were struggling. "No, I'll just stay home." And Nora slammed the door behind him.

"Hello, Doris, this is Aunt Judy," she shared, calling Doris at her office. "Your building is really going up fast, I was by earlier today and it's starting to look like a very big building," Judy added. "Well, that's good to hear, it is a thrift store and a rehabilitation center to help the community," Doris explained, "the ones I have here are doing quite well, so I am excited to see how this one does and maybe later one or two more around the area," Doris expounded.

"I'm excited and I know they probably won't hire me for nothing," Judy expressed.

"Now, Aunt Judy, you don't need to work with your hands, your work is with your heart, caring for sinners' souls," Doris shared lovingly over the phone.

"Well, God bless you for saying that. Oh yes, remember I said I was going to talk to my lawyer?" She giggled. "My lawyer, ain't that something, anyway, Dornelton left a lot to me. I can pay off my home he had bought on his GI bill, and it's more than I can use for just me. He left everything to me, but it's only because he had not seen you or his granddaughter, so if you need anything, you let me know," Judy shared, heart filled.

"Why, thank you, Aunt Judy. I will, but I want you to give yourself the best of everything, you deserve every dime your brother left for you."

"Oh, Doris, you're more like your mother than you know, you're so kind, and caring, and I'm so glad God allowed me to know you before I left here," Judy said.

"No, Aunt Judy, I'm sure you are my blessing," she said with a smile so warm it was felt across the phone. "Now, Aunt Judy, I have purchased your ticket for you to fly to Los Angeles to visit for the Christmas holiday, you do remember?" Doris asked with a smile.

"I did, but you didn't have to buy the ticket."

"I know, Aunt Judy, I wanted to. I love you and enjoy your service tonight."

"Oh you remembered, God bless you, dear, bye."

Katia was very excited as the days drew closer for her nuptials. After this, there was no looking back to the past at all. She could love her family and live the life she always wanted to, very posh, elegant, and exciting. She couldn't believe that she had pulled off the big one. All her life she had managed to hide out from something or someone, now she had figured a way to hide in plain sight and share the best of both worlds.

Nora made it through another day at work and decided to get a pick-me-up with a new 'do. Her coworkers had started to notice a difference in her attitude these days. She walked into her favorite hair salon after work and, wouldn't you know it, met Adele Hodges standing at the counter checking in for her appointment. Neither one recognized or even knew for that matter that either went there, but when Adele's stylist called her name Nora James, ears perked up. She jumped from her chair and stopped Adele in the middle of the salon.

"Erene is a married man, keep your distance," she said viciously, and those close enough to hear and watch knew it wasn't a friendly encounter.

"Adele, girl, did Nora say that to you!"

"Who, I don't even know that woman," Adele replied, which was true. She had seen her with Erene a while ago but didn't remember her.

"Look, she ain't nothing nice, and she been talking about her man with some skank, so I hope for your sake it ain't you!" her stylist said, putting her at the bowl for a wash.

Adele had met Nora, the real Nora for the first time, and all she wanted was to leave the very busy salon. Adele said nothing to anyone as she moved around getting her weekly 'do. Walking out after paying for the service and Nora she guessed was under the dryer, her stylist yelled out, "See you next week."

Adele was trembling as she walked very fast to her car. She could feel Nora's eyes on her the whole time sitting in the salon. She had got caught in the middle of a mess.

"God, have mercy," she said after reaching her car and pulling away.

Ring, ring, ring.

"Please answer, please?"

"Hello," she heard Erene's voice. She had pulled over to the curb around the corner after leaving the front of the salon.

"Erene, I'm sorry to call you, but I just saw your wife."

"What? What happened?"

"Nothing, she was at the salon. I didn't realize she went there. I don't remember ever seeing her there before," Adele believed.

"She and my assistant pastor's wife go together often to the International Hair Unique on Sixteenth."

"Oh, you mean Mrs. Parker?"

"Yes, so what happened?"

"She didn't know who I was until my stylist called me to the station, but she stopped and announced to the whole salon that I had better not be sleeping with her man! You said this was over. What happened? We have not slept together in three months, Erene."

"Adele, I'm sorry you're in the middle of this mess, but she's going through it. I told her last week about it."

"And you told her about me?"

"No, Adele, she figured that out after you showed up to Montello's."

"Darn, so that's why you weren't there."

"No, Adele, I didn't send the text, Nora did. So for me, please change your number and change your appointment days or salon if it's not asking too much," Erene requested. "And, Adele, please unless you need emergency help, please don't call again," he stated. "I know this will pass soon and it will be behind us. And thanks for the call," he said, disconnecting and getting ready to deal with Nora when he gets home.

Abby had taken over the lead role in the office and the desk as well. Really she always wanted the position but not at the expense of a life. The office had expanded at the beginning of the year when Keith and Annie were still there, and it not only housed the four attorneys William has on staff, which Abigail supports as legal secretary, but paralegals and two clerks that assist over in that department.

This past week, she has been training a new hire to help her in her department after the extensive hiring process William's firm goes through with each applicant. Abby was still as proficient as ever and loved her added responsibilities as lead legal secretary in the prestigious firm. She had also secured a date for the holiday parties to ensue and life was moving on.

"Abby, how are things going?" William asked one morning coming from his office, "Good, William, the new hire seems to catch on fairly quickly, and so far so good," she replied. "Oh, while I have you here," she said, going to her desk to retrieve a file, "the Baconette case all finished, I had time yesterday, so I just stayed after and finished it up." She smiled, handing him the very thick file he wasn't expecting at all this week.

"Oh thank you, you certainly didn't have to, but I appreciate your dedication this year, this firm took a big hit in losing Keith and Annie, and you have certainly done your part to keep it going," William shared, extending his hand to her.

"I thank you, sir, for the opportunity. How's Riley?"

"Oh wonderful and thanks for asking, our oldest son was down and we had so much fun trimming the tree and making new memories for her to share, she's adjusting just fine," William voiced, thankful Abigail had asked about her because she knew how much Annie loved her daughter.

"Thank you, sir," she responded, heading back down the hall as William went back into his office. She walked into the ladies' room to express how she felt about the comment closing her eyes and smiling, shaking her head jumping around, glad Mr. Parker had let her into his world. Before heading back to the floor, she composed herself, the consistent professional.

It was strange as Erene walked into his home. "Guess who's home," he yelled with a smile coming in, not knowing what to expect.

"Oh, Erene, I'm in the kitchen," he heard Nora's happy response. Her hair was beautiful but he wasn't going there as he walked over, giving her kisses to the lips.

"Something sure smells good," he said, smiling.

"Down, boy, we still have about an hour before dinner, so I recommend you just relax," she said again, sweetly touching him gently to push him out of her kitchen space.

Erene was shocked. "She looks like Nora, and sounds like Nora, but I'd better watch this one closely," he thought, going in to change and relax by the television while looking over some papers from his office. The night went off without a hitch, the couple even made love and talked about their New Year's plans in Time Square. And though Erene was relieved, he was very puzzled by the new Nora. The one that never brought up a single word about seeing Adele at the salon or anything negative the whole night. Sunday morning, she got up and beat him getting ready to leave for service.

"Wow, is it true, can she really be back?" he asked himself after a miserable two weeks of hell. He'd take it with "Thank you, Lord," and the happy couple were on their way.

When they arrived, Erene went about his duties, leaving Nora to do what she normally does unless she's involved in a planned activity.

"Hi, Nora," someone yelled. She had missed a few Sundays of late.

"Good to see you," she heard from another.

Nora flashed a forced smile and service began. It was wonderful, praise was high and the spirit was moving all over except in Nora's heart. She was just going through the motions of trying to satisfy her husband and forgive him of his infidelity. She knew she didn't love her GM, something she did for her career, but Erene had a lovely young professional girl, who he probably told her he loved her.

"Ugg, I hate her," she thought, sitting there among the saints through the entire service. She looked at Nada who she hadn't seen since Erene's reveal of his infidelity to her and got angrier that Nada knew or probably knew. After service, Erene came to her and stood shaking hands and greeting those leaving out. Nora did the same forcing a smile until Nada walked up. She ignored her, turned, and walked out.

"Nora, Nora," Nada called to her. Others tried to get her attention but Nora walked out and never looked back, getting in the car and driving away, with Erene having to get a ride from one of his fellow brothers to get home.

She was done pretending, she was hurt, and just couldn't forgive Erene. She was ashamed thinking everyone knew her dilemma. Nora later called Nada and explained her quick departure.

Needless to say, despite Erene's prayer and pleading and the couple split heard down at the salon, they were no longer together. Heartbroken, she relocated to the office in New York, away from Maine and near Times Square.

Katia was beaming as the big day had arrived, December had arrived, and she was beaming with joy. The private ceremony was taking place in less than two hours, and Dillard had sweaty palms and a fluttering heart. He was down the street awaiting the call to come home to see his bride all dressed up for their wedding nuptials. Katia had gotten the call that the justice of the peace and their witness, his friend Howard Stuns, were on the way.

Immediately a call came in from the gate for a delivery. She looked at her watch and opened the gate to let them in. It was the delivery of the large portrait Doris Woods had sent Dillard. She quickly signed for it. "Just put it over there," she instructed, seeing the two men standing holding the heavy seeming package. Suddenly she heard one of the staff calling her for instructions on where to put something. "Just leave it in that room aside the wall," she said quickly, heading to another part of the massive home as the two men walked in, and when she returned, she saw the package aside the wall and watched the van pull away, leaving the property.

Katia was back to business, the house was magnificent, she thought, Dina did a fabulous job. She had the hired staff check and recheck the camera for recording her beautiful day. Looking around, her only regrets were she would have no family there but felt close as she slipped on her dress purchased from Doris Woods's boutique for her vows. With Dillard now in place, Katia made her big entrance, her gown with all its exquisite detailing did not go unnoticed by her handsome groom in white tuxedo standing, waiting for her at the front of the stunningly decorated room. With soft music playing to enhance the moment and the words written by both to express their love for each other, Katia Norfen and Dillard Patterson exchanged their hearts with tears streaming from Katia's face.

As both turned after hearing, "I now pronounce you husband and wife," Katia couldn't believe her eyes, standing in an adjoining room watching the whole ceremony being officiated was Doris Woods and Finley, her butler.

"Oh my god!" Katia yelled, shocked to see anyone standing in her home. "How did you get in here?" she asked with Dillard embracing her to calm her.

Doris walked up to the couple. "I came in with your delivered package, and congratulations, Dana," she said, holding her by the wrist. "Your secret is secure with me, I've known for a while now! But I wouldn't have missed this for the world," she said with her heart.

And the two embraced with tears flowing while the surprised but relieved Dillard looked on.

ACKNOWLEDGMENTS

TO GOD BE THE GLORY for all the things that He has done. I paused to thank the staff at Integrity Publishing for helping me to keep my dream alive. To Dr. Ronn Elmore for his encouragement to never stop writing and also being an example to follow. My darling husband of now 45 years of marriage and loving and encouraging me unconditionally. Last and most important God's Word instilled in my heart. Thank God for His knowledge and learned ability in Him to write. And being able to read and discern for myself from the Holy Bible. All Glory to God.

ABOUT THE AUTHOR

TRESSA OLDEN HAS HAD A passion for reading books at a very young age. At elementary school she looked forward to going to the library to check out a book each week. She loved the stories especially those which drew you in and took you along as one of the characters. The stories that gave vivid descriptions of the clothes worn the scenery or place where the story unfolds. She loved how the characters were portrayed and how you're made to feel the part in your imagination. Her first job was helping the younger students to read, she was now in Junior high school. She remembers those days fondly and of course that very large projector that had to be rewound after use. Very quiet personality she read a lot of books growing up. In high school she worked in the school's large library with hopes of one day having a book there it was 1970. Life went on and her dream she thought had as well. She worked at a hospital caring for the elderly and loved sitting to hear their stories that few folks would take time to do. She loved them and they loved her. Life went on children, husband and a day to day simple but productive life. She is a Christian and loves God but went through trials just like everyone else. For years she worked and enjoy life with her family, grandchildren. In 1999 an untimely surgery stopped her from working for a while and reading had taken center stage again. Life threw her a curve and she plummeted into writing to uplift herself from depression she guesses. Beautiful cries for help poured out of her daily. Poem after poem God was speaking to her, uplifting her and reshaping her path. She soon realized she had been given a gift. Before her home stay was over, she had picked up a pen and began writing poetry to pass the days. Long poems had turned into stories and writing had begun it was now 2004. She published a poetry book later that same year and now has 4 novels to her credit. With God all things are possible.